BLURB

When Ava Thompson met the cerulean eyed rock god, Jasper White, her whole world was tipped on its axis, and nothing has been the same ever since.

Thankfully, life for Ava has settled, and that includes being in a healthy, stable relationship with Jasper at long last.

Their turbulent love has withstood many obstacles, but when not one, but two bombshells are dropped at Ava's doorstep, will she and Jasper be able to survive? Will the cunning ex and bothersome mother rock the stable foundation they have built together?

Will Ava get her happy ending? And will that happy ending be with the man everyone desires?

SURRENDERED

International Bestselling Author

MONICA JAMES

SURRENDERED

OTHER BOOKS BY MONICA JAMES

THE I SURRENDER SERIES

I Surrender

Surrender to Me

Surrendered

White

SOMETHING LIKE NORMAL SERIES

Something like Normal

Something like Redemption

Something like Love

A HARD LOVE ROMANCE

Dirty Dix

Wicked Dix

The Hunt

MEMORIES FROM YESTERDAY

Forgetting You, Forgetting Me

Forgetting You, Remembering Me

SINS OF THE HEART

Absinthe of the Heart

Defiance of the Heart

ALL THE PRETTY THINGS TRILOGY

Bad Saint

Fallen Saint

Forever My Saint

The Devil's Crown-Part One (Spin-Off)

The Devil's Crown-Part Two (Spin-Off)

THE MONSTERS WITHIN DUET

Bullseye

Blowback

DELIVER US FROM EVIL TRILOGY

Thy Kingdom Come

Into Temptation

Deliver Us From Evil

IN LOVE AND WAR

North of the Stars

Fall of the Stars

REVENGE IS SWEET SERIES

Crybaby

HEART MEMORY TRANSFER DUET

Heart Sick

Love Sick

KISS OR KILL DUET

Bad For You

Kill For You

LOVE HARD

Love Hard

Love Harder

STANDALONE

Mr. Write

Chase the Butterflies

Beyond the Roses

Someone Else's Shadow

Like a Boss

CHAPTER ONE
Child's Play

"Ouch," I mutter, slapping my hands over my face with playful animation.

As I hear the creepy voice of a serial killer, who, just for fun, is possessing a child's doll, I realize I need another set of hands to cover my ears.

"You're such a baby," says a husky voice to my left.

But there's no way I'm going to open my eyes to present the owner of that deep, profound voice, the evil I'm currently bestowing him in my mind.

Why my boyfriend, Jasper White, had to choose a movie starring a crazed doll, whose favorite article to carry around is not a cute, cuddly teddy bear, but instead a big, pointy knife, is beyond me.

Ugh, give me romance any day. At least when I watch a romantic movie, my dreams usually involve hunky hotties, as opposed to foul-mouthed, homicidal dolls.

Bravely parting my fingers an inch, I peek through the gap, as I don't hear anyone dying, at the moment. But of course as soon as I do, Chucky gets all stabby.

"Eww, this movie is seriously disturbing. My teddies are so facing the wall tonight," I murmur from behind my hand.

Jasper laughs in response with that deep, throaty chuckle that makes my insides dance, and my hormones demand I do something productive with the sound.

Jasper and I have been through hell and back. Well, okay, a bit of an over exaggeration, but we have been to Singapore and back.

If I am to revisit that memory for too long, I seriously need to take a valium after I'm done reminiscing because our journey has been far from easy, and sometimes, I don't know how I survived it without ending up with a lobotomy.

And I say that in all sincerity.

It all started the night Jasper and I met. The crazy stars were obviously aligned that evening, as everything that has happened from that day forward has changed me, and most definitely challenged me. Jasper pushed me when I didn't want to be pushed, because he knew what he wanted, and I say proudly, he wanted me.

And I wanted him, too.

One would only have to look at him and they would be putty in his hands, but none of that mattered to Jasper. He never exploited his out of this world looks, because Jasper was looking for someone to love him for him, and that someone was little ole' me.

We fought incessantly and it definitely wasn't smooth sailing, but Jasper and I, we work. I put it down to him being the most amazing person I've ever met. Correction, most amazing male person I've ever met, as my best friend, V, takes that title for most amazing female.

My dream in life is to become a renowned chef, and

I'm almost seeing my dream become a reality. Jasper has supported my aspirations from the very beginning, and he understood why I had to pursue my dreams, even when those dreams led me to Singapore.

I was lucky enough to be offered a scholarship to study over at the Culinary Institute of America—Singapore Campus. I accepted because it was an opportunity of a lifetime, even if it meant I had to leave Jasper behind. But he understood, and he supported me the whole way.

Well, that was until I fucked up—big time.

But I survived, and that's all because of the man sitting beside me.

My reason to breathe.

As hard as it is to believe, over five weeks ago, I was engaged to be married to a man—correction, I was engaged to be married to an A grade jackass. And that jackass is my psychopathic ex-boyfriend, Harper Holden. Yes, I know what they say, a cheater never changes its spots, but Harper was that good, he convinced me he was the exception. I accepted his marriage proposal when I shouldn't have, but I was at the lowest point of my life, because Harper did the unspeakable. He lied to me, but not your average lie. No.

He made me believe that Jasper no longer loved me, and he did so with a smile.

He managed to do this after Jasper and I had an argument over me keeping something from him which I shouldn't have. I never told him that Harper and I had re-established a friendship when I moved back to Singapore. And he never told me his ex-girlfriend Indie (the tramp), had kissed him. Harper used our argument to his advantage, and used me as a pawn in his scheme to play happy family so he continued getting his inheritance.

All sound a little like a soap opera? Well, try living it.

But out of every single thing that has happened throughout the course of my life, something I found out a day ago takes the cake.

Yup, just because my life wasn't interesting enough, I think I may quite possibly have a little Chucky, bar the homicidal tendencies, growing inside of me.

Okay, probably not the best way to describe my, 'Maybe Baby,' but I'm still trying to get my head around it.

I was a little preoccupied dealing with my dramas, and the one and only time Jasper and I had unprotected sex, I totally forgot to get the morning after pill. I guess I should have re-prioritized my priorities.

The idea of me being a mom is one I really can't get my head around. At age twenty-three and three quarters, being a mother is not how I envisioned my life playing out.

But life is full of surprises.

"Baby, we can turn it off if you're scared."

"Huh?" I question, turning to face the potential daddy-to-be because I'm totally lost in thought.

"You're shaking. I didn't realize you were *that* much of a chicken," he says, tickling my sides.

"Stop!" I choke out, batting his hands away.

Little does he know, I'm shaking for another reason.

"Surrender?" he smirks as he leans over me, pushing me into the couch cushions.

"I surrender," I whisper, running both my hands through his messy, bedroom hair.

He pulls in his bottom lip, toying with his scar. A scar that shows the world what a survivor he is.

"Say it again," he says, leaning forward, running his nose slowly down my neck and over my collarbone.

No doubt he can feel my heart beating like a bass drum, but I don't care. Even if I willed myself to calm my nerves, my traitorous body wouldn't listen.

He kisses my neck and I shiver under his warm soft mouth, surrendering to him. As he twirls his tongue in the hollow of my neck, I arch my head back, exposing my throat. He continues kissing down my chest, which is revealed by my low slung tank, and I mewl under his skillful mouth, gripping onto the sofa beneath me to stop myself from launching off the cushions.

"You smell so good," he murmurs, which comes out muffled as his head is buried between my breasts.

Unable to construct a sentence when his hand snakes down my thigh, slipping lower over my center, I raise my hips in encouragement, wanting more.

Yanking him up by his cheeks, I smash my lips to his, needing to devour him this second. He returns the kiss with as much vigor, running his tongue over my lower lip and biting the corner of my mouth. I open up to him as he slips in his sinful tongue, wanting more.

We are totally making out like high school kids, on a sofa while watching a bad movie. I think this was his plan all along. And when he runs his pointer finger along the elastic waistband of my PJ bottoms, I know I'm right.

His lips feel amazing and I fist both hands in his hair,

positioning him so I have better access to his wicked mouth. He smells so good, I can't help myself as I deepen the kiss, melting into him. He groans in the back of his throat when I suck on his bottom lip, then bite it softly, rolling it between my teeth.

To pay me back, he slips his hand into my bottoms and begins tormenting me with his skilled fingers. I say torment because Jasper is the master of teasing. I try and shuffle under his fingers, but as usual, he dances around the spot I want him to be.

"You are such a tease," I gasp while gnawing on my bottom lip.

He lets out a cavernous, throaty chuckle while releasing my lip with his thumb seductively.

"Can't have you getting bored," he murmurs, leaning forward and kissing behind my ear lightly.

No chance of that happening when his clever fingers are inching their way closer and closer to my—

Holy shit!

Freezing suddenly, I have an image of him poking the 'Maybe Baby' in the eye or face. I don't even think that's possible, because I'm pretty sure it's just a bundle of goo at the moment. But it still provides me with images that give Chucky a run for his money.

"Are you okay?" Jasper asks breathlessly.

His hands have thankfully stalled as he awaits my response

He looks at me expectantly, wetting his perfect bow lips, which are plump and swollen from all the making out. I nod, but I need to come up with an excuse and fast, because I'm so turned on, he knows it's not because of lack of enthusiasm as to why I stopped.

"Are you sure?" he asks a second time.

I nod again, quicker this time to wipe the concerned look off his face.

"I'm fine," I reply, brushing my hand over his stubbled, strong jaw.

"I just, um, feel weird doing this on V's couch."

Jasper arches a disbelieving eyebrow, but being the gentleman that he is, he removes his hand from my pants.

He leans up on his elbows and looks down at me with a dimpled smile.

"You didn't feel weird "doing this" up against the hallway wall, or in the kitchen against the fridge. And I know you certainly didn't feel weird "doing this" in the shower three days ago by the way you threatened to tear out my hair if I stopped," he says, making air quotations marks every time he drops the phrase, 'doing this,' with a playful smile.

I smack him playfully on the arm. He lets out a chuckle as he sits up, placing my legs across his lap.

Looking over at him guiltily, I want nothing more than to allow Jasper to have his way with me, but I can't, because of what might be potentially growing inside of me.

"I'm sorry," I say, pulling a sad face.

Jasper smiles while reaching for his beer. "Don't worry about it," he replies, tipping the top of the bottle my way. "You can make it up to me some other time." He winks before taking a swig.

Normally I would be all over that invite like yesterday. But now because of my situation, I only nod and count down the hours until my best friend returns.

I need her to hold my hand when I find out if my 'Maybe Baby' is to be, or not to be.

CHAPTER TWO
Confessions

Waking up early, I roll over to find Jasper sound asleep.

He is the most beautiful thing I have ever set my eyes upon. His bow lips are slightly parted, inhaling and exhaling softly and peacefully with each breath he takes. He hasn't shaved in a few days, and the dark growth shadowing his perfect jaw line complements his strong, angular face. His scruffy hair sits in disheveled peaks, but this just adds to his rugged look. He looks dangerous, or should I say, he looks dangerously *hot*.

I mentally slap myself and stop with the drooling before he wakes up and finds me checking him out like a total creeper.

I sneak downstairs to make Jasper breakfast, as going back to sleep is simply impossible. I have tossed and turned all night thinking about my predicament, and my brain can't take a second more.

Parting the kitchen curtains, I take a moment to appreciate the view. I love dawn. It's such a beautiful time of day. Everything is fresh and new, and the troubles from the previous day can be forgotten.

Well, almost.

Jasper thankfully hasn't pushed to know why I freaked out on the sofa yesterday, and after everything that has happened between us, I can't lie to him. That's what got me into trouble in the first place. I thought I was doing the right thing, but it had the opposite effect, and I'll never make that same mistake ever again.

Standing up on my tippy toes to reach the flour, I feel Jasper's t-shirt I snatched off the floor ride up, exposing my butt.

I'm all alone, so I'm not self-conscious that I'm totally flashing right now. I repeat my peepshow for a couple more minutes while reaching around V's kitchen cupboards, searching for the ingredients to make Jasper's favorite breakfast—pancakes.

Having everything I need, I turn around to start on my breakfast.

"Aw, is that it? I was just starting to get comfy."

Letting out a startled yelp, I hold onto the counter to stop myself from face planting onto the linoleum.

My boyfriend is sitting at the kitchen table, straddling a chair, shirtless. I can't help myself as my eyes go to town on the tall, dark and perfect in front of me.

His cerulean eyes are so bright, just like they usually are when he first wakes up, and as usual, they take my breath away. His upper body is a sight of pure perfection, with muscles that are so well defined and sculptured, I want to run my tongue over each hardened bump. My eyes travel down his chest, lingering on his ripped six pack, and then descend to the snail trail which is peeking out of his black CK boxers, which I can partially see, thanks to his low riding blue jeans.

"Enjoying the show? I should start charging you," Jasper says, chuckling softly.

That snaps me out of my gawking, and I give him a small smile, embarrassed he caught me visually molesting him.

As he gives me a cocky smile, I roll my eyes, pretending I'm not about to melt into a puddle of Jasper goo.

"Ha! You're one to talk. How long were you sitting there ogling my butt?" I ask, smiling broadly while reaching into the bottom draw to find a wooden spoon.

"I'm not sure. I lost track of time when I saw you strutting around the kitchen half nude," Jasper replies, a hint of humor in his voice.

I look at his smug face and throw a dishcloth at him.

"You perv." I chuckle.

"Hey, I'm not complaining. Shit, that's going to give me great images to fall asleep to tonight when I'm all by my lonesome."

Lonesome?

I feel myself falling to pieces in a nanosecond, as I have slept beside Jasper every day for the past five weeks. The thought of sleeping without him sends me into an uber panic.

Jasper senses my terror and leaps up from his seat quickly. He's in front of me in three long strides, pulling me into his arms, and burying my head into the crook of his neck.

"What's wrong, baby?" Jasper asks, his deep voice resonating in his chest.

I tighten my arms around his back, crushing his chest to mine.

"I can't sleep without you," I confess in a small voice.

Jasper tightens his hold on me. "Then you won't."

Pulling back to peer into his deep blue eyes, I ask hopefully, "You'll stay at my parents' with me?"

V and Lucas are back from their honeymoon today, and Jasper, being the thoughtful, courteous person that he is, hasn't presumed we'll be spending the night together. We've been house sitting while V and Lucas have been on their honeymoon, but now that they're back, there's no need for us to be here.

"I'll stay wherever you want me to stay," he replies, kissing the tip of my nose. "Although, I think staying at my place would be a little more practical, as I don't want your dad knowing what I'm doing to his little girl," he says with a dimpled smile.

Rolling my eyes playfully, I give him a small smile as I reply, "Thank you."

He rests his chin on my head as he sighs, "Any bed is way too cold without you in it. And even with you being a spider monkey, I still can't sleep without you."

I let out a small giggle, as I have awoken perched on Jasper's back on many occasions.

"What time do V and Lucas get in?" he asks.

"Um, like midday," I reply as I step out of his embrace regretfully and start our breakfast.

I can feel Jasper's eyes on me as I begin whisking the ingredients together.

My cheeks heat when I turn around and bend over to grab a frying pan, because I know he's checking me out. Within five seconds, his front is plastered to my back. I relish in the thought that my boyfriend can't keep his hands to himself.

He begins rubbing his hands over my bare skin and cheekily slaps me lightly on the butt.

"Ouch!" I giggle, wriggling out of his grip because I know where this is headed if I don't end it now.

And I can't because of my situation. That thought is one I don't want to have over my Sunday breakfast.

"Sit." I smile, pointing my knife over to his chair.

He pouts, which makes him all the more adorable.

"If you want your breakfast anytime soon, you'll go sit," I say when he doesn't move.

He pulls me into him, his bare chest heating my body from head to toe. "You'll always be my most favorite thing to eat," he murmurs seductively.

I nearly gag on my tongue, and he laughs at my reaction before begrudgingly letting me go.

"You're bossy when you're in the kitchen." He smiles, popping a strawberry into his mouth as he leans against the kitchen counter.

"Well, you're bossy in the bedroom," I retort; it's out before I can stop myself.

I really have sex on the brain. And that's because I have been denied something I usually have more than once a day, and sometimes, even without asking.

"I didn't hear you complaining last week," he says, giving me a heated look, the strawberry painting his lips a deep red.

Blushing at the memory, I wish I hadn't said anything, because now, all I can think of is sex!

"I wasn't complaining. I was just making an observation," I reply, feeling a heat creep up over my neck.

"Well, if you're not complaining," he says, taking a step towards me.

I have to stop this before I succumb to those eyes and that insinuating voice.

Placing my palm on his chest to prevent him from proceeding further, I say with a grin, "What part of sit don't you get?"

Jasper taps his chin. "All of it."

Letting out a chuckle, I step out of his embrace and turn on the stove, trying very hard to dismiss his advances.

He sighs over dramatically. "Okay, but these pancakes better be amazing," he teases as he walks over to the table and thankfully sits.

Turning my back, I begin stirring the batter, counting down the hours till my best friend sets foot on home soil.

I need her here to help me.

She'll know what to do.

She always does.

I can't help but feel bittersweet whenever I enter LAX. The feelings I experienced when last here are ones I never want to feel again. Airports and I have not had a happy relationship, so as my palms begin sweating, and my heart threatens to burst out of my chest, I clam up.

Jasper senses my emotional shift. "What's up, baby?" he asks, squeezing my hand in his.

The word baby coming out of his mouth sends me into a tailspin, and a term I usually adore has now taken on a whole different meaning.

"Nothing, I'm okay," I reply with a smile that barely reaches my lips.

Jasper being Jasper, who is totally in sync with my feelings, of course doesn't buy into my speech.

"Don't do that. Don't pretend everything is okay when I know it's not."

I know he's right, and I've learned the hard way that relationships are built on trust. And if you don't have trust, then you've got nothing.

I stop dead in my tracks because we're in this together and he has every right to know.

He too stops and turns to look at me. All I can see in his big, blue eyes is apprehension. I hate myself for making him feel this way.

This was certainly not how I envisioned telling him I may quite possibly be pregnant, but I can't stand to have him looking at me this way.

Reaching for both his hands, I squeeze them lightly.

This is it.

I look into the face of the man I love with all my heart and notice he gulps.

"Jasper, I think I'm—"

"Ava!"

Stopping mid-sentence, I snap my head to the left, because I swear I just heard my name being called.

The ghosts of this airport will not let up!

"Ava!"

Before I have time to process another thought, my best friend has her arms around my neck and won't let go.

"I've missed you!" she exclaims, squeezing me tighter.

I don't know if my best friend has the worst, or best timing. Either way, I'm so happy she's here.

Peering over her shoulder, I notice Jasper looking slightly disappointed for the interruption. I unwrap her hands from around my neck so I can greet her, and breathe.

"Wow! Look at you, you bronzed goodness," I say, commenting on the sun-kissed skin peeking out of her short denim shorts and red halter.

She spins in a showy circle with her arms out to the side. "I know, right? It was so beautiful I couldn't help but want to be outdoors all the time."

Lucas approaches us and lets out a small chuckle. "Yeah, you also couldn't help but want to take your clothes off, while outdoors—all the time."

I look at her, eyes wide.

My friend, the exhibitionist—why doesn't that surprise me?

She scoffs at Lucas. "Only when no one was around," she says, waving off his comment with her hand.

He shakes his head playfully. "You gave the pool boy his first erection."

Snorting, I cover my mouth while trying to contain my laughter.

"Oh whatever. I didn't see you complaining."

Lucas smirks. "What's there to complain about? My beautiful wife, naked, is a sight I will never get sick of." He pulls her in for a passionate kiss.

Oh God—vomit!

Jasper looks at me with a smirk on his handsome face as I shuffle uncomfortably.

"C'mon, lovebirds, the honeymoon is over. Enough of that," I say, prying them apart.

Yanking on V's arm, I force her to walk a few steps away from the boys, who are sharing a manly hug.

"What's up with you, grumpy pants?" she asks. "I thought you'd be all sexed out after having the house to yourselves. Judging by your mood, you're the one who should have been walking around nude."

I turn my eyes upward and smirk. Good to see my friend is in fine form.

V leans in to whisper softly, not to be overheard. "I'm serious though, what's up?"

How the hell does she know? Am I that obvious?

"I've known you my whole life, Ava. I can read you like a book. A highly dramatized, frustrating book," she says, huffing.

I let out a small laugh. "I need to talk to you, but not here," I reply quickly, motioning with my head to where Lucas and Jasper are.

Her eyes widen in understanding. "Okay. But I swear

to fuck if you dare tell me you're engaged, leaving for another country, or single, I will lock you in my attic and throw away the key. I will make the grandma from *Flowers in the Attic* look like Mary fucking Poppins," she whispers from the corner of her mouth, as the boys have caught up to us.

I just give her a pained look as Jasper comes up behind me, putting his arm around my middle.

If only it was that simple.

The car ride is nothing short of awkward.

With Jasper and V both aware of something being up, I'm surprised I have yet to run us off the road. Catching a glimpse of V looking at me curiously in the rear view mirror, I decide I will use my side mirrors from now on.

If the uncomfortable atmosphere isn't enough, the radio is taunting me, playing "Hey Baby" by No Doubt. I quickly reach down to change the station to something less baby-orientated.

When Jasper places his palm on my leg, I jump, slightly startled because I'm beyond edgy. Biting my lip, I know he's trying to decipher why I'm acting like a nut job. And I feel like an ass because I owe him an explanation, but I just can't do it now. Especially in a car filled with our best friends, and I don't want to do it until I'm sure.

His hand tightens on my thigh and he begins stroking it lightly with his thumb. I sneak a peek at him from the corner of my eye, and can see he's deep in thought. I know he's racking his brain why I'm behaving like a crazy person.

I need to do this pregnancy test like now.

Finally, I pull into V's driveway and all but leap out the door to go inside.

I'm climbing the porch stairs when I realize Jasper isn't behind me. Turning around, I notice him slapping Lucas on the back, shaking his hand.

Wait, what? He's leaving?

Racing down the stairs, I approach him and ask softly, "Are you leaving?"

Jasper nods, giving me a small smile.

"Oh," I reply, disappointed.

He steps forward, brushing a lose piece of hair that has slipped from my ponytail behind my ear.

"Yeah. I gotta work at the shelter later on, anyway."

It's now only two o'clock, and I know he doesn't have to start till ten.

"Okay," I say, trying my hardest not to pout.

He raises my chin with the pad of this thumb. "You're still going to stay the night, right?"

His comment calms me somewhat and I give him a big smile.

"Try and keep me away," I reply.

I'm rewarded with a big, dimpled smile which takes my breath away.

Lucas is pulling out the luggage from my tiny trunk, watching our exchange. "Catch ya later, J," he says as V gives me a worried look over her shoulder, before following Lucas inside.

When I hear the front door close, I place my hand on Jasper's taunt chest.

"I promise to finish what we started talking about today."

"Okay," he says, looking at me expectantly.

Looking around the neighborhood, I decide telling him that he may be a father while the neighbors are mowing their lawns, and a group of kids are screaming, pumped up on way too much sugar, is probably not the best timing.

"But not now, or here. There is something I have to do first. And I promise once I get it done, I will tell you everything."

Jasper gives me a troubled look. "I don't like you keeping secrets from me, Ava."

"I know, but it's not a secret. I just want to make sure before I tell you."

I *have* to be sure before I tell him something so big, something that will ultimately change his life, our life.

Jasper sighs, running a hand through his long hair. "Is that some kind of chick code? Because I have no idea what you're talking about."

I let out a small giggle at his adorability. "Trust me?" I ask, placing a palm on his cheek.

I know this is asking a lot, and I wouldn't blame him if he threw everything that has happened between us in my face.

But he doesn't.

He leans into my embrace. "With my life," he replies with conviction, staring deeply into my eyes.

His statement warms my heart because I have finally regained Jasper's trust.

"I love you." I smile, placing my forehead against his.

"And I you," he replies, dipping his head to meet my eager lips. He kisses me with such passion and love, it takes my breath away.

I pout when he pulls away all too quickly.

"See you later tonight."

"Okay," I whisper, watching as he hops into his truck, leaving me to my impending doom.

I trudge up the stairs as I am about to face the scariest thing I have ever had to face before.

Finding out if I'm pregnant.

As I enter the house, I see V waiting by the front window, totally spying on me and Jasper.

"Okay, spill it," she says, grabbing my hand and plonking me onto the sofa.

Oh dear God, how do I tell her this?

I begin fiddling with my charm bracelet; the one Jasper gave me for Christmas.

Taking a deep breath, I push down my nausea.

"V," I whisper, unsure where Lucas is. "I think I'm pre—"Before I can get it out, I gag on the word. It is literally catching in my throat and won't come out.

V scrunches up her face. "You're what? Pretty? The president? A pretzel? What?" she asks, trying to decode what the hell is going on.

Letting out a hysterical nervous giggle, I slap my hand over my mouth to stop myself from bursting into inappropriate fits of laughter. But sadly, it's out before I can stop myself.

I begin laughing like a homicidal lunatic, and then suddenly, as the situation I'm faced with dawns on me, my laughter turns to tears. I start sobbing uncontrollably, burying my head into my hands to avoid looking at my friend.

"Ava? Babe?" V asks, and the sincerity in her voice makes me sob harder.

She pulls me into her arms and rubs my back, letting me cry my eyes out. After a few minutes of blubbering all over her, I feel slightly better.

Pulling back, I wipe my eyes with the back of my hand. I'm so embarrassed about my meltdown, and I wonder if this is my hormones going haywire because of the... baby.

I blanch.

V searches my face, rubbing my arm supportively when she notices my reaction. "You okay?"

I shrug because I don't know how I'm feeling at the moment.

"Talk to me. Whatever it is, you *need* to tell me," V says.

Looking at her seriously, I nod because she's right. I take a deep breath before I spill my guts. "V, I think I'm... pregnant."

V's mouth pops open, almost hitting the ground.

O-kay, probably not the best reaction.

"V?" I ask, after a minute of her staring at me, stunned.

I need her to make me feel better, and tell me it's going to be okay.

"Are you sure?"

Hallelujah, she speaks!

Shaking my head, I lower my eyes.

"You haven't done a test?"

I shake my head again.

She stands up abruptly, shoving her hand in my face, and I gingerly take it.

"Where are we going?" I ask as she hauls me to the door, my feet all but dragging on the carpet.

She stops and turns to look at me. "To find out if I'm going to be an aunt."

CHAPTER THREE
Ignorance is Bliss

V and I are patrolling the aisles of the local supermarket, on a mission to get to the bottom of my situation A-sap.

I have my hood on, attempting to disguise myself because V is placing every available pregnancy test into our shopping cart, while happily humming "Baby Love" by The Supremes.

"One is more than enough," I mutter under my breath, my face cast downwards. "And can you quit it with the singing?"

Thankfully she ceases with the singing. "Pssh, no, it's not. Better safe than sorry. Hmm, I guess you're past that stage, though," she says, laughing at her inapt joke while tossing another test into the cart.

"Can we leave?" I whisper loudly, darting my eyes up and down the aisle, afraid someone I know will stroll down the walkway at any moment.

V shrugs, looking at the cart. "Yeah sure, we have enough for now."

She pushes the cart towards the registers while I drag behind, sinking further into my hood by pulling the sides over my face, afraid the bright lights will highlight my blushing red cheeks.

"Ava, c'mon!" V yells over her shoulder while waiting in line, looking directly at me.

The people in front of her look over their shoulders to see who the loud, tattooed lunatic is yelling at.

Well, so much for anonymity!

As I catch up to her, my eyes widen when I witness the cart is filled with pregnancy tests and nothing else. I lunge for the shopping cart, which jars V to a sudden standstill, as she was proceeding forward.

"What the hell?" she asks, looking at me like I've lost my mind.

"Put a few other items in there," I whisper, looking at the cart like it might detonate.

"What for? We're not here for a shopping expedition."

Pinching the bridge of my nose, I reply, "I know, but it's embarrassing. The checkout clerk will know I might be pregnant."

V rolls her eyes. "Seriously?"

I nod quickly, mortified and beyond embarrassed this is happening right now.

"Fine." V sighs, throwing her hands in the air.

She looks over her left shoulder, and because we're next in line, our options of covering the evidence is very limited. So she reaches for a pack of gum and throws it alongside the other goods.

"Happy?" she asks, rolling her eyes.

Looking at the tiny packet, which looks ridiculous sitting alongside all the pregnancy tests, I feel anything but happy. But it'll have to do because we're next to be served.

I blush profusely while V is totally oblivious, humming along to some tacky song playing over the speakers.

However, the sixteen year old cocky checkout boy is anything but oblivious. He looks at me with a sleazy stare as he scans my products, and then has the cheek to let out a small chuckle when he scans the pack of gum.

Finally after he bags my five pregnancy tests and one pack of spearmint gum, he brings up the total. Paying with cash, I tell him to keep the change as I grab my bag and bolt out the door.

V is trailing behind, chuckling as I throw myself into her car when she unlocks it with the remote. I sink into my seat, waiting edgily for her to get into the car.

After a minute, she leisurely opens the door and hops in without a care in the world.

"For someone who was track champion in high school, you sure know how to dawdle," I say, looking at her smiling face.

V laughs, pulling down the sun visor to check her reflection. "Ava, please, you've waited this long to find out, I'm sure a few more minutes won't hurt."

But that's where she's wrong. I have been on edge this whole time, and the only thing getting me through was the fact I was seeing V in a couple of days.

Now that she's here, I'm barely hanging on.

I heave a sigh, thankful when she starts the car and reverses out.

V notices my apprehension as she peers over at me.

"When do you think it happened?" she asks, trying not to sound too nosey.

Blushing, I confess, "It happened the night of your rehearsal dinner. Up against the boathouse wall."

V turns her head quickly, looking at me, her mouth agape.

"I know, V. Don't look at me like that. I feel like enough of a tramp without you giving me that look," I say, covering my face with my hands.

V lets out a loud laugh. "You whore! Looks like I'm not the only one parading around naked outdoors," she jokes, laughing hysterically.

I groan. "I know, right?"

After V stops laughing at my expense, she asks, "Do you regret it?"

Thinking back to the feeling of having Jasper inside me after so long, I shake my head. "No way. I could never regret being with Jasper that way."

V pulls into her driveway and turns off the car, turning to face me. I'm staring straight ahead, afraid of what I am about to do.

"It'll be okay, babe, I promise."

I just wish I believed her.

I'm standing in V's kitchen, forcing down my third glass of water.

"Do you need to pee yet?" V asks, sitting on her kitchen counter, hopeful I will say yes.

I have been procrastinating for the past twenty minutes, but as I push on my jelly belly, I know it's time.

"Yes," I reply nervously, placing my empty glass in the sink.

"Finally!" V exclaims, jumping off the counter and yanking me upstairs before I back out.

We both squeeze into the tiny bathroom and she pulls out all the pregnancy tests, lining them up on the floor. As soon as I see them side by side, I feel my knees go weak. I plonk onto the toilet seat before I faint.

"I can't do this," I mumble, rubbing my forehead.

"Yes, you can," V encourages, but I can hear the slight hitch in her throat. She's just as apprehensive as I am.

Shaking my head and squeezing my eyes shut, I reply, "No, I can't. I feel like I'm going to be sick."

V crouches down in front of me, rubbing my shoulder.

"Yes, you can," she reiterates confidently.

I bite my lip and open my eyes, looking down at my best friend, who's on her knees before me. What would I do without her?

V gives my knee a reassuring squeeze while unwrapping the first pregnancy test.

"Okay, this one will show up with two lines if you're pregnant. How cute," she says, reading the directions and laughing at the yellow smiley face on the box.

I scoff. "Cute? They should have a picture of a gavel, seeing as if it's positive, it's a life sentence."

V stops reading and looks up at me. "So I take it you don't want it to be positive?"

Groaning, I clutch my queasy stomach. "I don't know. I've been living in denial, hoping this is all just a bad dream. The thought of being a mom at age twenty-three is not how I envisioned my life."

V nods, letting me vent because we haven't spoken about the possibility of me being pregnant.

"But the thought that I could have something growing inside me that is part Jasper, part me, is just surreal. I can't not want something that is his," I confess. Saying it out loud scares me, as the reality of my situation sinks in, and hard. "But on the other hand, I'm not ready to be a mom. Oh V, I'm so confused."

"I don't think anyone is really ready, Ava," V answers, chewing on her lip ring.

"I know." I nod because she's right.

"C'mon, let's get this over with." V thrusts the test stick into my trembling palm, giving me a reassuring smile.

I look down at it, and then back up at her.

"I'm not peeing with you in here," I say, horrified.

V laughs. "It's not like I haven't seen you pee before."

"I know, but this is different. I'm scared. And nervous," I admit softly.

V smiles and I instantly feel slightly better.

Reaching for a pregnancy test, she begins unwrapping it and says with a grin, "Here, I'll do one with you. I can be your pee buddy."

Rolling my eyes playfully and laughing at her, I reply happily, "Okay," because the thought of her taking the test gives me a false sense of comfort.

While looking at the back of the box, V smiles when she sees the little pink stalk picture. "These are all so cute," she says, totally oblivious of my reaction.

Clearing my throat in rebuttal, V quickly recovers with, "Okay, I get it, so not cute. Let me go pee on this in the other bathroom and give you some privacy."

"Thanks," I reply, rubbing my sweaty palms on my jeans.

She squeezes my shoulder. "It'll be okay. Whatever the result, we'll deal."

"Thanks, V," I whisper, on the verge of tears.

She gives me one last supportive look and closes the door quietly, leaving me to face the music. I look at the stick and wonder how a tiny device can be the decider of one's future. Whatever the result, I can't change it now. I just have to get this over with.

I follow the directions and once it's done, I flush the toilet and wait for the results. I have never anticipated any result as much as I have these.

"Ava, can I come in?" V asks softly from outside the door.

Washing my hands, I open the door with my stick in hand. "Sure."

V holds up her stick proudly. "I peed. Did you?"

"Yes," I reply, looking at her pregnancy test. "That's so gross," I say with a chuckle.

V waves off my embarrassment. "The directions say we have to wait five minutes."

Being stuck in this tiny bathroom, awaiting my impending doom sounds like a horrible idea. I need to get the hell out of here before I suffocate.

"Let's go downstairs and wait it out down there. I can't stay in here."

V nods, her high ponytail bobbing up and down. "Okay, babe, whatever you want."

Ripping off a piece of toilet paper, I rest my stick on it, while V does the same.

Linking my arm through hers as we ascend the stairs, I say, "I need a drink."

"Lead the way," she replies, squeezing my arm.

What a gal!

V looks up at the clock as I'm casually sipping my second glass of red. "It's been longer than five minutes."

"I know, but the results won't change. So, I'm going to finish off the bottle," I reply, downing the wine.

"You shouldn't be drinking. You might have a baby inside of you," V says softly.

Holy shit, she's right!

Very ungracefully, I spit out the wine and groan. What kind of mother drowns her Maybe Baby in Merlot?

V leans her hip against the counter, folding her arms over her chest as she witnesses my face drop, because it's time to face the inevitable.

"You really don't want it to be positive, do you?" she asks sincerely.

Fiddling with the wine label, I shrug.

"Not really, V. But if it is, I'll just have to figure it out," I reply, my eyes downcast.

"Ava, even if it is positive, you're pregnant with Jasper's baby, not an alien. It'll be okay. It'll be hard at first, but you'll make it work. You, Jasper, and the baby will be fine."

I know she's trying to make me feel better, but every time she uses the word baby, I cringe.

"Please stop saying baby," I mumble.

V comes up behind me, pushing me out of the chair. "Go," she says, pointing upstairs.

"Fine," I sulk, wobbling slightly as I take a step.

"Are you okay?" V asks, steadying me.

"Yup. I guess I shouldn't have had that second glass. See, I already suck at being a mom," I say unhappily.

"Don't say that." V huffs, bracing both my arms and looking me straight in the eyes. "You'll be a fantastic mom. Whether that's now, or in the next five years, you're going to be the best. Okay?" she says, giving me the slap in the face I needed.

I nod, letting out a deep breath.

"You want me to come with?" she asks.

I shake my head, because as much as I appreciate her support, this is something I need to do alone.

"No, I'll be okay. I need to do this on my own."

V nods. "I understand, but if you're not back in five minutes, I'm coming up."

Giving her a quick kiss on the cheek, I march my way

upstairs and lock the bathroom door behind me. Leaning up against the door, I peer over at my future, almost afraid to look.

My heart is about to burst from my chest as I walk to the sink, taking tiny steps, trying to prolong my journey. I stop a step away and close my eyes.

I can do this. Whatever the result, I can do this.

Taking a deep, calming breath, I slowly open my eyes, and my stomach drops when I see the results.

Holding up the pregnancy test, I cover my mouth with a trembling hand. As I stare at my future, a single tear rolls down my cheek, burning my flesh in its path.

I slump onto the floor, the cold tiles biting into my bare legs. As I look at the stick once again, I throw it across the room in rage. It hits the wall and skittles under the basin.

"Ava?" I hear V outside the door.

I know she has her ear pressed up against the door, listening for any sounds that might give her some indication of the results.

But I can't talk. My voice has closed over.

"Ava, open the door," V says, a little louder this time, while turning the doorknob.

Thankfully I locked it, as I need two minutes to process everything.

"Ava, if you don't open the door, I will find a way to get in there." I hear the determination in my friend's voice and I know she isn't joking.

"Just give me a minute," I say, clearing my throat, afraid if I don't answer her, she'll hack into the door with a chainsaw.

I blindly reach for the stick, and once I find it under the sink, I toss it into the trash. I slowly get to my feet and do the same with V's, discarding both tests.

While washing my hands, I splash some cold water onto my cheeks and stare at my reflection in the mirror. I look better than expected, which gives me some hope that maybe I won't break apart at the seams.

V is knocking incessantly, and I can tell by the frantic sound she's about to break down the door in about two seconds. I take a calming breath and open it, and V falls forward with her hand poised in the air, mid-knock. I latch onto her arm to stop her from falling and timidly look up at her.

"Well?" she asks, cocking an eyebrow at me.

Once I say it, it'll mean it's true and this is really happening. But this is a fate I can't change, and I need to accept it for what it is.

Looking into my best friend's bright green eyes, I whisper the two words that will change my life forever.

"I'm pregnant."

CHAPTER FOUR

Maybe Baby

"You're pregnant?" V asks, shocked.

I nod, staring at her, but not really seeing her.

Wow, I'm pregnant.

Totally thought I'd be carted off in a straightjacket once I announced those words.

But I'm quite calm.

"Are you okay? You look…" V stops, looking at me while making a face. "I don't know… calm? Why aren't you crying or cursing or something?"

I shrug, because I don't know how I feel.

An interesting choice of words V has selected to describe my reaction, because I have a niggling feeling that this is the calm before the storm.

Reality sets in and I gasp, "I've gotta tell Jasper."

Thinking about how I'm going to break the news to him sends me into a panic.

"Are you going to go to the doctor first, you know, to make sure you're 100%…" V says uncomfortably, not wanting to say the words I fear aloud.

Burying my face into my hands, I try to come to terms with the fact that I'm going to be a mom.

"We haven't spoken about kids. I don't even know if he wants them. I don't even know if I want them."

"Are you going to keep it?" V asks softly, afraid of how I'm going to react to her question.

Shit, I hadn't even thought about that being an option.

The big A.

Something I never really thought about, because I never thought I'd need to.

"I don't know what I'm going to do. All I know is that I need to tell Jasper and hope he doesn't hate me," I reply sadly, my hands slipping to my sides.

V looks at me with a confident look in her eyes. "He won't hate you. I promise he won't."

I'm crossing my fingers and toes that she's right.

This car ride over to Jasper's has been one of the hardest things I've ever had to do, and believe me, I've had to do some tough things.

How does one break the news to their beloved that they are going to be parents? Is there a protocol I am to follow, because right about now, I'll take any help I can get.

I'm so afraid of Jasper's reaction, because I honestly have no idea how he's going to react.

Pulling into his driveway, I notice he has left the porch light on for me. He's so thoughtful and would make a fantastic parent, unlike I, who thirty minutes ago, was downing a glass of red like it was going out of fashion.

I take a deep breath and look at my reflection in the rear view mirror. My eyes look flighty and my lips are red from gnawing on them the whole trip over here.

Looking out the window, I shake my head at the predicament I find myself in. How the hell am I going to do this? How the hell am I going to tell Jasper that he's going to be a dad?

I raise my eyes and meet my reflection in the mirror once again. I won't make the same mistake with Jasper twice. I lied to him once, and it nearly destroyed us. I'll be damned if I do it again.

Giving myself a reassuring nod, I exit the car and begin my walk of shame. As I climb the three steps, my tongue feels as if it's stuck to the roof of my mouth.

Taking yet another calming breath, I will my heart to stop beating so rapidly, in fear I am about to have a heart attack.

My hand is poised, ready to knock, when the door opens and Jasper's breathtaking face greets mine. Right about now, I would usually be throwing myself into his arms and kissing him madly, but now, I am reserved and lower my eyes. My insides are trembling in fear.

I can't lose him, I just can't.

"What are you doing standing out here?" Jasper asks softly.

Bravely peering up at him, I see his head is cocked to one side, no doubt taking in my fearful posture, knowing something is up.

"I was about to knock, but you beat me to it," I reply quietly.

My voice doesn't sound like mine.

Jasper braces his hand against the doorframe, which stretches his black t-shirt across his chest, highlighting all that yumminess underneath.

"You don't have to knock, you know. That's why you've got a key." He smiles, leaning forward, brushing the back of two fingers across my cheek. "What's the matter? You're shaking," he says.

Am I?

Shit, not a good start.

"We need to talk," I whisper, looking at him from under my lashes.

He lets out a small sigh and steps out of the doorway so I can enter.

Walking over to the sofa, I plonk down onto it, folding my legs underneath me. Jasper takes a seat near me, and I turn to face him. His shoulders are hunched and his breathing is deep, revealing just how apprehensive he is.

With both legs parted, and his hands interlocked between them, he turns his head after a moment of staring straight ahead. His eyes are searching mine as he asks, "Are you going to break up with me?"

The air whooshes out of my lungs. "What? Of course not!" I reply, horrified he would even think that.

"Then what? Why are you acting so weird? Tell me," he begs, fisting his hair into a mohawk.

I know this is a trait of his when he's frustrated or nervous.

But I can't vocalize it as the words are stuck in my throat, just like they were at V's.

My heart begins beating wildly, and a light sheen of

sweat coats my skin. I feel faint and I latch onto Jasper's forearm for support.

"Ava, please don't shut me out. I can't take it. Not again."

I bite my lip, and the memory of what he's referring to comes rushing back. I begin thinking about my life without Jasper, and how that life was not one worth living. What if I tell him and he leaves me? What if he gives me my marching orders and refuses to forgive me this time?

But then another though hits me. What if I'm not pregnant?

The car ride over here had me thinking about V's comment. These tests are not 100% accurate, and there is a still chance, no matter how small, that I may not be pregnant. It's slim, but it's possible. And until I am 100% certain, I can't be sharing this life changing news with Jasper. Because that's what this is—life changing.

So instead I settle for another pressing issue I've been meaning to talk to him about.

"It's about your birthday next weekend."

Jasper frowns. "What about it?" he asks, clearly puzzled with where I'm going with this.

"What are we going to do for it?" I ask quickly, hoping he will buy into the derailment.

Jasper doesn't answer straight away as he seems to be thinking. "This is what you wanted to talk to me about?"

I shrug. "Yeah." Not.

He looks at me unbelieving, but he humors me anyway. "I'm not sure. I haven't even thought about it."

"Is your mom coming?" I ask in a little voice.

Jasper's mom hates me.

I know it.

Jasper knows it.

Everyone in a fifty mile radius of us knows it.

She has hated me from the moment she met me. Jasper has tried to tell me otherwise, but I have eyes, and I know she loathes me. She does, however, love Jasper's ex-squeeze, Indie, as Indie can do no wrong in her book. Well, her book can go to hell, as Indie is the most manipulative, devious person I've ever met. The fact that she and Jasper's mom are BFFs really has me questioning Jasper's mom's credibility.

Jasper swears he and his mom have stopped talking to Indie, but I'm inclined to believe his mom is taking her son for a ride.

Plain and simple—I don't trust her.

And I sure as shit do not trust Indie.

Jasper lets out a large puff of air. "So this is what has been upsetting you? You don't want to see my mom?"

Well... er, kinda.

But I reply quickly, "Yes."

Jasper wraps his arms around me, pulling me into his lap. "Don't ever scare me like that. Holy shit, I thought you were going to break up with me," he murmurs into my hair.

"Don't be silly. I'm here to stay," I reply against his chest.

Little does he know, I will always be a part of his life if the results are positive.

"Good. Don't worry about my mom, okay? I'll tell her

no birthday celebrations this year. They kinda get lame after ten, anyway," he jokes, kissing the tip of my nose.

"No, you should do something. I was just worried that your mom wouldn't come because she hates me," I say quietly.

I hate discussing this with Jasper because he's either in denial about it, or totally blind.

Jasper lets out a tiny chuckle. "She does not."

So, looks like he's totally blind.

"Ah, yes she does," I correct as I pull back to look at him.

He nuzzles into my neck, inhaling deeply. "She loves you because I do."

I reply with an unconvincing, "A-ha."

But I don't want to discuss his mom, as I have other important matters to deal with, like what a chicken shit I am for not telling him what I originally came here for.

Looking into his big cerulean eyes, I remember his comment from earlier.

"How could you think I'd ever break up with you?"

Jasper shrugs, and brushes a loose piece of hair behind my ear. "Because sometimes I have to pinch myself just to make sure I'm not dreaming. We've come so far, and I'm afraid you'll get sick of me and move on," he confesses.

Did I just hear him right? This amazing, awe-inspiring man before me thinks little ole' me will get sick of him?

I grab onto his cheeks, my eyes searching his beautiful face. "Don't you dare think that. I will never leave you. I'm in this for the long haul," I declare, meaning every word of it.

I just hope he is, too.

He leans forward, licking his lips, and plants a light impassioned kiss on my willing mouth. I bow into him, and happily return his affection.

Falling backward, Jasper pulls me down with him so I'm lying on his hard chest. The feel of him underneath me is amazing, and I can't help myself as I begin shaping my body around his. His sharp contours are caressing me in the right way, leaving me needy and wanting more.

Jasper lets out a groan in his throat, which vibrates throughout my entire body. It's been too long since I've felt his skin up against mine and I need it.

I crave it.

But I can't. Not until I do some research to determine whether having sex is okay if or when pregnant, as I'm totally out of my field here.

I need to stop this, and I need to stop this now.

However, judging by the solid, thick length pressing into my side, stopping is going to be an issue.

Jasper kisses my cheeks, nipping my jaw as he works his way down to my neck. His lips are scorching my skin and I fold, feeling him press up against me so deeply. I will want Jasper with my last breath, and saying no to him is killing me.

His clever mouth is kissing my breasts through my thin t-shirt, and I close my eyes because watching him worship me is just too much. His hands slide down my body and slip under my denim skirt, and he begins rubbing me in a way that should be illegal in every state.

When he passes his hand over my center, I arch into his touch, on fire.

I want more, and Jasper senses my needs as he slips his index finger inside the waistband of my underwear, stroking over my wetness.

He hisses a breath through his teeth. "I need to be inside you," he says passionately.

Throwing my head back, I whimper loudly, because his words, combined with the feel of his fingers, are about to tip me over the edge.

I would like nothing more than to get lost in Jasper, but God dammit, I can't.

Gathering what little willpower I have left, I reach for Jasper's belt, unbuckling it with unsteady fingers. Finally getting the thing undone, I snap open his top button and glide my hand into his pants, feeling him ready for me. He's so hot under my hands and I mewl, enthusiastic to continue.

I begin stroking him, his hand stills in my pants, which is what I wanted.

"Holy shit, Ava," he says huskily, arching into my grip. "You keep that up, and I'll be useless to you."

Leaning down, I bite his lip softly. "That's impossible."

Jasper will never be useless. He's all that matters to me.

I begin stroking him faster, from root to tip, and Jasper shudders with the contact. The look on his face is enough to set me off, and he's not even touching me.

He closes his eyes and tilts his head back, exposing a vulnerability that sets my heart alight. His lips are parted, and the tiny exhalations coming out of his upturned mouth give me an indication he's about to come undone. He's rolling his bottom lip between his top teeth, and every so often, his tongue darts out to moisten his lips.

The sight of him about to explode because of me is one of the most erotic sights I have ever seen.

His eyes snap open when I rub over his sensitive tip, and he looks up at me with stormy eyes. "What about you?"

Smirking at him, I reply, "Don't worry about me, I owe you."

And with that, I take my lover to a place he has taken me time and time again.

CHAPTER FIVE
This is Where it Begins

The next morning, I wake to two of the most delicious scents known to mankind.

Jasper and coffee.

I crack open an eye but close it quickly, as the sun is peeking through a sliver in the curtain, blinding me. Turning my head into the pillow, I inhale deeply and sigh at my lover's signature fragrance.

Reopening my eyes, I realize I'm hogging the whole bed, as usual, as I'm sprawled out practically horizontal on it, with my head resting on Jasper's pillow.

Gosh, I love waking up to him. Well, at least I love waking up to the smell of him.

Lifting my head, I turn to listen to the noise downstairs.

I know Jasper is down there making me breakfast, and my heart skips a beat. How did I get so lucky? After everything we've been through, he has stuck by me and our love has prevailed.

Placing my hand on my stomach, I sigh.

"I hope when he finds out about you that won't change," I whisper to myself.

When is the right time to tell him? And when will I be ready to tell him this life altering news? I know the right time will be when I get my ass to the doctor and confirm once and for all if I am actually pregnant.

When that day comes, I better be ready, as I don't know how long I can keep him out of my underwear without him getting suspicious.

Throwing my arm over my face, I'm so frustrated at my inability to open up. This is just... so hard. How do people do this every day? Tell their partner they're pregnant without clamming up and having a heart attack.

My phone vibrates in my bag, thankfully interrupting my thoughts, and I reach over to see who it is.

It's Jasper.

I made you waffles.

How does he know I'm awake? I know how. Jasper has always had an uncanny sense of reading me—even when we first met. And this fact will sooner or later bite me in the ass if I don't tell him I'm pregnant. Or pretty sure I am.

He'll figure it out, and I'd rather tell him myself than have him play twenty questions.

Snapping me out of my funk, my phone beeps again.

Hurry up, they're getting cold

I can't stop the huge smile spreading from cheek to cheek as I throw the covers off the bed, excited to see my boy.

The Ramones t-shirt Jasper slept in is thrown on the floor, and I slip it over my head, seeing as I'm naked.

Bringing the collar up to my nose, I inhale his fragrance and my mouth waters. Waffles be damned, I just want to eat Jasper for breakfast.

I bounce down the stairs and as I turn the corner, I stop dead in my tracks, because what I'm faced with deserves my full attention and appreciation.

Jasper, standing in his kitchen... topless.

He has his back turned to me, and by the way his faded blue jeans sit low on his hips, I know he's wearing nothing underneath.

Oh God, that image has my heart galloping violently.

His arms are braced against the counter, and he is leaning forward, watching his coffee spin circles in the microwave because he likes it scolding hot. His pose is doing amazing things to his back muscles, and I wish I could trace my finger over every hard, unyielding, well-defined bump.

My eyes travel of their own accord, focusing on his perfect ass. His butt will always remain a mystery to me. How it can appear hard and firm, but soft and supple under his smooth skin, always blows my mind.

Enough with the looking, I need to get my hands on the piece of perfection in front of me.

Skipping over to my man, I throw my hands around his waist, snuggling into his back.

His deep throaty chuckle vibrates against my cheek, which is pressed up against his spine.

"Mornin'," he says, rubbing my hand with his.

"Good morning," I reply, kissing between his shoulder blades.

I reluctantly let him go when the microwave dings, missing the connection instantly.

He turns around to face me, and his eyes scan down my body. Of course I do the same to him.

Wow, and I thought the back of him was impressive.

"Nice shirt." He smirks, dimples on parade.

"Oh, this old thing," I joke, picking at the hem.

Jasper shakes his head, grinning at my stupidity.

Peering over at his breakfast table, I suddenly get all giddy.

"Aw, Jasper... did you do all this for me?" I ask, nodding towards the breakfast table filled with waffles, eggs, bacon, spreads, juice and coffee.

And if that isn't enough, a daisy sits in a tall glass in the center of the table.

I look up at him, eyes wide. No one has ever been this nice to me before. And I feel a pang of guilt for not telling Jasper my news yet.

Well, our news.

I am so conflicted. Should I just tell him or wait? What if the results are negative and I've worried him for no reason at all?

He runs his thumb between my brow, smoothing out my frown lines. "One of these days I will be able to figure out what's going on behind these beautiful brown eyes of yours."

I hope that isn't anytime soon, I internally mumble.

"Where's the fun in that?" I playfully reply, placing a chaste peck on his lips and strolling over to the table.

Everything looks amazing and smells even better. I didn't even realize how hungry I was until I sat down to all this food. Jasper has gone all out, and I can't wait to dig in.

Placing a bit of everything onto my plate, I burn my fingers when I pick up a piece of bacon and shove it into my mouth hungrily.

"That's hot," I say, fanning my mouth with my hand.

Jasper smirks, pouring me a glass of juice as he sits down near me. Taking a big sip, I feel his eyes on me, watching me closely. I nervously wipe my mouth, just in case I'm caked with juice and/or bacon.

Peering over at him, his broad chest is taunting me with all its silky perfection and I nearly choke on my juice.

Jasper arches a cocky eyebrow at me, knowing all too well the effect he has over me.

"What?" I ask, finally giving up.

"I've been thinking," he simply replies.

I gulp. "About what?"

"What you said about my mom hating you."

I let out a relieved breath. Although, I guess that's something I shouldn't be relieved about.

"Yeah, what about it?" I ask, wondering where he's going with this.

"Well, I think it'd be a good idea if we have dinner, just the three of us, so you can see how much she loves you." He picks up his coffee cup and takes a sip, while I feel my bacon rising in my throat. "What do you think?" Jasper asks, grabbing my palm in both of his hands and kissing the back of my knuckles.

My mouth pops open—he's serious!

I don't know how to respond, because spending an

evening being judged and sneered at is not my idea of a good time. But as I look up at him, into his warm affectionate eyes, how can I say no to him?

"I love you, Ava. You're my forever and a day."

His kind words cement what I have to do.

"This is important to me," he says quietly.

Even though every part of me is saying no, I go against my better judgment.

"Okay."

"Yeah?" he asks, his eyes widening in excitement.

"Yeah," I confirm.

"Thank you, baby," he says, placing another kiss on my knuckles. "I love you, and you'll see that my mom loves you, too."

The hopeful gleam in his eyes warms my heart, and I'm happy I said yes.

But in regards to his mom loving me?

I won't hold my breath.

CHAPTER SIX

I Don't Think We're in Chicago Anymore, Toto

"Ava, tell me what you have done here," asks Sally Spencer, looking at my chocolaty dessert, suitable for any woman PMSing.

"It is a Chocolate Coconut Banoffee pie, but I've added a thicker bourbon biscuit base and two caramel layers. I have the usual creamy coconut topping and banana toffee for the filling," I reply, proud of my creation.

Sally nods happily. "Very good, Ava. Looks like my own personal piece of heaven." That earns a chuckle from the class.

The bell chimes, indicating class is over for the day.

I have been back at CIA for two weeks, and it seriously feels like I never left. I have slipped back into my classes easily enough, but the workload is pretty intense, as I have to play catch up with courses I missed while my transfer was taking place.

Grabbing my iPhone out of my backpack, I'm relieved that V has replied to my text about coming shopping with me this afternoon, because I really need her help in buying a gift. I have an idea with what I want to get Jasper for his birthday, which is five days away. It's the gift I want to purchase for his mom, for this stupid dinner I agreed to go to tomorrow night, which has left me reeling.

Quickly stuffing my books into my bag, I look up at the clock and curse, because V said she would pick me up at the front gates five minutes ago. I make a mad dash to tidy up my desk and am done in record time.

Just as I reach the door, Sally asks, "Ava, can I have a word?"

I spin back on my heels. "Sure."

I'm already late. What's another couple more minutes?

"What's up?" I ask Sally, who is wrist deep in soapy water, cleaning up.

She wipes her hands on her apron, and walks over to her desk.

Sally is a kind-hearted soul, and I am forever in her debt. If it wasn't for Sally and her string pulling, I'm not sure where I would be. She's the reason I'm back here and not in Singapore.

She pulls out a piece of paper from her top drawer and hands it to me.

"What's this?" I ask, skimming it over.

"Read the bottom part," she answers with a big smile on her round, delighted face.

As I proofread it quickly, I snap my head back up at her.

She gives me a warm smile. "I am to recommend a pupil who I believe would be best suited to work at

Metropolis. It'll be a full time position, starting once you've graduated."

"Why are you giving me this?" I inquire, but I know why.

"Because I'm going to recommend you."

My mouth drops open because this is my dream come true.

Metropolis is where people like me, people who treat food like art, only dream about working at. It is modern, hip, and stylish. Think the most classy, fashionable restaurant you've ever eaten at, bar the pretentious suits and snooty attitudes, and that is Metropolis.

"Thank you, Sally!" I only just stop myself from throwing my arms around her and tackling her into a bear hug.

"It's okay, Ava. You've worked hard for it. There's only one position available, and they are only interviewing five applicants from our school, so your chances are good. Once they make their decision, the lucky person will be head chef in New York," she says animatedly, clapping her hands together happily.

Whoa! What? New York!

I quickly reread the fine print, and it indeed is for a position at a new Metropolis restaurant opening in New York.

My heart sinks.

I can't uproot my life to N.Y., because it's not just me this affects now.

After I stomach that thought without breaking into tears, I give Sally a weak smile as I say, "Thank you, Sally, but I can't accept this."

Sally looks stunned. "Oh, okay," she says, clearly in shock at my refusal at this life altering opportunity. "May I ask why?"

I can't tell her the reason why. I can't tell her that my Maybe Baby is my first and foremost responsibility from now on.

So I settle with, "I just can't leave L.A. It's not a good time. I just got back, and I don't plan on leaving."

Sally nods, but looks surprised that I would turn down such an offer. "Okay. This is entirely your choice, and I won't push it. But please, will you at least give it some more thought? I don't need to submit this for another two weeks."

Looking down at the piece of paper in front of me, I'm holding my dreams in my hand. And as I stare at the word New York, I know that dream is something I'll never see come true.

My future is my baby.

But I humor Sally, not wanting to disappoint her after she has done so much for me. "Sure."

Folding up the piece of paper, I unzip my front pocket and stow it away in my backpack.

"Thank you again, Sally," I say, giving her a quick hug.

And then I'm out the door before she witnesses my avalanche of tears.

"Ava, what the hell happened now? Seriously, your life has more drama than an episode of *Days of our Lives!*" jokes V, as I'm sitting in her car trying, but obviously failing, at putting on a happy face.

I have to tell someone as I feel like my life has turned to shit in the span of two days.

"I got offered a job at Metropolis," I mumble, looking out the window, watching L.A. flash before me.

"Oh my God! Ava, that's great," V squeals.

She stops at a red light, and when I haven't replied, she looks over at me curiously.

As she takes one look at my somber expression, she presses, "Isn't it?"

Nodding, I adjust my seatbelt as it suddenly feels like it's choking the life out of me.

"It's a once in a lifetime opportunity, one that every chef dreams of."

"But...?" V prompts.

"But..." I sigh. "I can't accept it. I'm going to be having a baby, one I haven't even told Jasper about," I reply, sinking into my seat.

Even though I haven't been to the doctor yet, I know the probability of me being pregnant, as opposed to not being pregnant, is pretty much a done deal.

V knows I have yet to tell Jasper my news. She understands I'm not ready, and that I also want to wait until I know for certain. And surprisingly, she hasn't yelled at me.

"So what, Ava? Just because you might be pregnant, it doesn't mean you have to stop living. I understand it's a big life changer, but women have kids and a career all the time," V says, looking over at me quickly while attempting to keep her eyes on the road.

"The job is in New York," I mumble.

Suddenly I'm tossed into the passenger door, deafened by the car horns blaring at us. Thankfully, V is back on the right side of the road, after she swerved into oncoming traffic when she heard my news.

She turns to look at me as she adjusts her red bandana, which is wrapped around her head like a headband.

"Ohh," she says, biting her lip ring. "Now I get your dilemma."

"There's nothing to get. I'm not going, and that's that," I reply, totally aware I sound like a sulking five-year-old.

V touches my knee while mercifully keeping her eyes on the road. "I'm really sorry, babe."

"It's fine. This is my life now; I just have to deal," I reply unconvincingly.

"Enough of this depressing talk," V claps, taking both hands off the steering wheel.

I quickly take hold of the grab handle above my head because this woman is a menace on the roads.

"What are you going to buy Jasper for his birthday?" she asks.

Just the mention of his name brings a big smile to my cheeks.

"I have a few ideas, but there is one particular thing I really like. I wanna show it to you, though, and hopefully you won't think it's totally lame."

V nods, popping her gum. "You know me, as blunt as a three-legged dog"

I let out a small laugh. "That doesn't even make any sense."

V laughs. "I know, but I got you to smile, didn't I?"

Man, I love her.

"So, what are you getting the wicked witch of the East?" V smirks.

"V!" I reprimand with a smile because I totally agree with her.

"What? Three-legged dog, remember?"

I laugh loudly, because in the span of two minutes, I've almost forgotten my troubles thanks to my bestie.

"I have no idea. Any suggestions?" I question as we pull into the mall's parking lot.

She zips into a parking space, totally cutting someone off and laughs when they give her the finger.

"I don't know. Maybe a heart," she answers honestly, unbuckling her seatbelt.

Shaking my head, I bite back a smile. "That doesn't help, but I can see your point."

My reply earns a loud cackle from V.

Glad someone finds this funny.

As we make our way towards the entrance, I sigh, "Let's start with Jasper's mom's present, as I know what I want to get Jasper. I need more time to find her something, so this could take me all night."

"Oh, I know," smirks V as the double doors open and we enter the chaotic mall. "What about a pair of ruby slippers, so she can click her heels three times and go the fuck back to Kansas."

"I think you mean Chicago." I laugh hysterically.

"Kansas, Chicago, who cares, same thing."

Linking my arm through my best friend's, I bless the day she came into my world.

"**S**eriously, Ava, you're buying for Jasper's mom, not the Queen! Buy her a candle and let's go eat already. I'm starving, and we've been here for like three hours," complains V, who has her hands on her stomach.

I roll my eyes playfully at her, as we've been in the aromatherapy shop for twenty minutes, not three hours.

Speaking of queens—Gee, what a drama queen!

"A candle? Really?" I ask, making a face when I come across one that smells like patchouli.

"That's not a lot. I'm trying to make a good impression, and giving her a tacky, smelly candle is not exactly good impression material," I say a little too loudly, as the shop assistant who walks past me gives me a snooty look, obviously overhearing my rant.

I give her an apologetic look while V's stomach grumbles loudly.

"Ava!" she says, giving me an over-the-top, pained look.

"Okay, okay. Fine, let's go eat." I cave as I can't stand to see her pull that face any longer.

Replacing the candle onto the shelf, I cringe when I smell my hands, which reek of hippy markets and weed.

"Yippee!" V says, clapping her hands and jumping up and down.

We head over to the food court and I order Chinese, while V is in the mood for Mexican. We take a seat in the busy eatery, and when I notice her meal, I raise an eyebrow.

"Chili con Carne? Since when do you eat chili?" I question, because if anything remotely hot touches her tongue, she's screaming that her mouth is on fire.

As V gulps down the majority of her meal and groans, "Yum," I look at her like she has grown a second head.

"Who are you?" I joke, shaking my head while pushing around my food unenthusiastically.

V shrugs. "I dunno, I felt like chili. And this isn't that hot. Not like the one you made. Holy Jesus, that nearly blew my head off."

Chuckling at the memory, I tease, "Maybe married life has toughened you up."

V smiles happily at my comment, and it goes without saying she's over the moon being Lucas' wife. While she happily chews on her chili, my thoughts wander back to Jasper's mom's gift.

"What am I going to get her, V? I want her to like me, and I know buying her a gift is kinda like a bribe, but I don't know how to break the ice."

"Well, that's because she's the ice queen," V says around a mouthful of food.

"Not helping," I chuckle, giving her a small smile.

V takes a sip of water and shrugs. "What about perfume?"

I ponder on her suggestion. "Yeah, that could work. But what kind does she like? It's so personal. And I don't know her like that. Or at all," I mumble.

This was a bad idea.

To drown my sorrows I steal a bit of V's chili, but as soon as it hits my tongue, my eyes instantly water.

"What the hell! That's freakin' hot," I pant, fanning my mouth.

Stealing her water bottle, I take a big long sip, which barely takes the edge off.

"How the hell can you be eating that?" I ask, as my mouth feels like a forest fire has spread from the tip of my tongue down to my esophagus.

V looks down at her meal, and then back at me. "I don't think it's hot."

She looks concerned as she questions, "Do you think it's because of the baby?"

She whispers the word baby, and looks around to make sure no one is listening. I have to laugh because she is so damn cute.

"Maybe your taste buds are more sensitive?"

Sitting back, I wipe my mouth with my napkin, wondering if that's possible.

"You're probably right. I can't have sex, so this doesn't surprise me. Oh, the joys of motherhood," I say, sarcastically.

V purses her lips, looking horrified. "You can't have sex? Who told you that?"

Shrugging, I answer honestly. "No one. I just guessed it would be unwise. I mean, what if it gets brain damage?"

V snorts so loudly an elderly couple a few seats over turn to look at her, unimpressed by the loud, pierced tattooed hooligan cackling away.

"Ava, you are such a dweeb sometimes," she says, wiping her wet eyes on her sleeve.

"Oh okay, so it won't get brain damage?" I ask hopefully, as I have been clawing at the walls to get down and dirty with Jasper.

"I don't think so. I mean, that's just gross if it's true," V says, scrunching up her brow. "However, the best person to ask would be a doctor. Speaking of which... when are you going to see Dr. Hemming? You can't keep putting it off."

"I know, I know," I reply, putting my hands up in surrender before she grills me further. "I will go, soon."

"How soon?" V inquires, throwing her napkin into her empty bowl.

I lower my eyes guiltily. "I don't know. Soon."

V raises an eyebrow. "You better."

Her tummy grumbles, interrupting her lecture.

She looks at my untouched Cashew Chicken, and I swear she begins salivating. "You going to eat that?"

Peering down at my plate, I push it towards her. "Knock yourself out."

She snatches up my fork and shovels down the food like she didn't just polish off a huge bowl of chili.

Gee, with an appetite like hers, anyone would think she's the pregnant one.

I've given up on finding an appropriate gift for Jasper's mom. I'd rather get her flowers or chocolates, instead of something she will hate, causing her to hate me more than she already does.

Fortunately I have more luck with Jasper's gift, as V agreed it was a winner. I'm slightly nervous to give it to him, but it's personalized, so he can't take it back.

"Thank God that's over. My feet hurt and I need ice cream."

I let out a small chuckle. "Are you serious? You've eaten enough to feed a small starving nation," I say, looking at a pair of Jimmy Choo sandals I so can't afford.

"Well, you've dragged me around for like five hours. A woman needs to eat."

I don't know where she puts it. If I ate like her, my ass would remind me of my indulgence for a week afterwards.

We're on our way to get Ben and Jerry's, when just by chance, I walk past a store I have never noticed before.

"Stop!" I yelp, lunging for V and latching onto her arm.

"That's it!" I exclaim excitedly while peering into the shop window.

V joins me, and when she sees what I'm looking at, she smiles.

"Bingo."

CHAPTER SEVEN

Atomic Bomb Love

My room looks like an atomic bomb has gone off inside.

I have every single garment I own strewn everywhere. And I mean everywhere.

On my bedside lamp, my rocking chair, my unmade bed, my messy floor, my ceiling fan—you name it, it's covered in clothes.

Tonight is the dinner I have been dreading since Jasper suggested it. But I have to do this because I know how important it is to him, and I have to at least try, for his sake, to get along with his mom.

After my shopping spree, I snuck into Jasper's house while he was at work to complete his mom's gift. I just hope she likes it.

I have a good feeling about it, and I'm pretty sure she'll love it. But I'm not going to count my chickens before they hatch.

One thing I'm not so confident about is my outfit. I don't know what to wear, and it doesn't help that I hate everything I own!

I have been getting ready since 3p.m., which was two and a half hours ago. Jasper will be here any minute and

I'm still not ready. You'd think that fact alone would help me choose something quickly—sadly, it doesn't.

My iPhone beeps, and of course it's lost amongst my mess. Only when it beeps again do I find it tucked under a mound of clothes on the floor.

It's from Jasper:

> I'll give you twenty more minutes. I know you're still half dressed.

I let out a tiny chuckle, and within a second of opening it, I receive another.

> I just reread my last MSG. I'll be there in 5 😊

Covering my mouth, laughing, I mumble to myself, "Perv."

"Okay, enough with the stalling, get dressed already," I say out loud like a crazy person.

It's way too hot for jeans and I know anything too constricting will suffocate me. I have an inkling I'll be suffocating enough under the ice queen's death stares all evening, therefore I don't need anything to add to the constraint.

My eyes land on the only thing I don't hate.

My yellow baby doll dress.

Slipping it on, I happily finger the short, loose-fitting garment. The ruffled hemline sits just above my knees, and I adjust the thicker straps to sit snugly on my shoulders. The empire waist hugs into my middle, and the square neckline is just right, as it doesn't expose too much cleavage.

It's perfect.

Quickly touching up my minimal makeup, I reapply a thin coat of lip gloss to complement the hint of foundation and mascara I applied earlier.

The heat is stifling, and I can feel sweat beginning to collect at the back of my neck, which of course means my long hair is sticking to the dampness. I quickly twirl it up into a messy bun, and push in the stick to hold it into place with my barrette.

Slipping on my white flip-flops, I grab my bag, placing my lip gloss and perfume inside the inner pocket. Just as I'm zipping around looking for my cardigan, the doorbell rings.

A big smile spreads across my face.

Great timing.

Placing Jasper's mom's gift in my bag, I collect my white cardigan on the way out of my room and bounce down the stairs to answer the door.

Giving myself one last look in the hallway mirror, I think I look okay, maybe a little nervous, but no one can blame me for being a tad apprehensive.

As I open the door, my heart skips a beat.

"Wow," Jasper says, mimicking my thoughts when I give him a quick once over.

"Do I look okay?" I ask, fidgeting with my hemline.

"Okay? You look more than okay," he replies, suddenly making me blush with his not so discreet examination of me.

He steps towards me, thumbing my lower lip. "Fuck, you look good enough to eat. I'm thinking we skip the dinner, and head straight for dessert."

He picks me up playfully while ascending two steps.

"Put me down!" I giggle, slapping his arm lightly.

He complies begrudgingly, setting me on my feet when he descends the stairs.

"How am I meant to keep my hands to myself with you looking the way you do?" he says, running the back of his fingers down my face.

I instantly blush deeper.

"You can't blame me for wanting you. It's been way too long since I've been lost in you."

The heat in his blue eyes punches me in the guts, and I clench my thighs together, totally turned on by this conversation.

I know he's referring to our lack of sex over the past couple of days, which reminds me. I really need to make Google my best friend and find out the Dos and Don'ts of being pregnant.

I'm hoping the Dos are literal, because I want Jasper to be at the top of my To Do list.

Man, that thought has put really inappropriate visuals into my oversexed brain. And it doesn't help when Jasper is staring at me with his heated, bedroom eyes.

"Whatever you're thinking, I like it." He smirks as he pulls me into his chest, kissing me lightly.

I can't help myself as I open up to him, deepening the kiss, because the taste of him is mouth watering. Groaning in the back of my throat when he slips in his wicked tongue, I tug on the long strands of hair which are sitting messily atop his head.

As Jasper begins trailing hot, wet kisses down my

throat, I know now is the time to pull away, otherwise we won't be going anywhere.

I half-heartedly drag my neck away, and when I do, I'm confronted by a pouting Jasper.

His expression makes me laugh.

"I know, I know," he says, puffing out a big huff. "Now I'm really going to struggle to keep my hands to myself."

"Gives you something to look forward to," I reply cheekily.

Jasper tips his head back and groans. "You don't play fair."

I giggle, loving the fact he has no restraint when it comes to me. "I never said I did."

CHAPTER EIGHT
Table Manners

"C'mon, baby, it'll be fine," Jasper coos, unbuckling his seatbelt and looking at me encouragingly.

Gazing out the window, I peer at the house where his mom is currently cooking us dinner and gulp, as fine is not a word I would associate with tonight's proceedings.

Huffing out a breath, I nod. "You're right. Everything is going to be totally fine."

Even when I say it out loud, it still sounds as unconvincing as it did it my head.

Wiping my sweaty palms on my dress, I look over at Jasper.

"I'm nervous."

Jasper chuckles. "Really? I couldn't tell."

Slapping him lightly on the arm, I smile. "This isn't funny."

Jasper latches onto my hand, bringing it up to his mouth and placing a gentle kiss on my knuckles.

"It kinda is," he replies with a dimpled smile.

He is so enjoying watching me squirm—jerk.

"Let's get this over with," I say with a sigh.

"I love you," Jasper says softly, giving me a heart-stopping smirk.

That smirk makes me feel remotely better, but knowing I have Jasper's affections is what gives me strength to soldier on.

"I love you, too," I reply, leaning over and giving him a chaste kiss on the cheek.

As I'm about to pull away, he holds my face in his palm, resting our foreheads together. "Thank you for doing this."

I nod unhurriedly. "Anything for you. I love you."

Jasper closes his eyes and breaths a deep lungful of air. "Say it again."

My face hurts from smiling so hard.

"I love you," I whisper softly.

This moment of stillness between us is simply beautiful, and I don't want it to ever end. To be this comfortable with another individual without saying a word, is just... epic.

However, all too soon Jasper pulls away, kissing the tip of my nose.

"Ready?" he asks, searching my face.

"Ready." I nod in vain.

Opening my door, Jasper is out before my feet hit the sidewalk, extending his hand for me. I place my clammy hand in his warm one and take my first step towards my nightmare.

As we walk up the short driveway to the American Foursquare house, the four wide steps before me suddenly feel like four hundred steps. It's a pretty home, with multi-color flowers hanging in baskets from the porch ceiling swaying lightly in the hot breeze.

As Jasper all but drags me to the front door, he

presses the doorbell, and the heavy sound resonates in my belly and I begin to feel uneasy.

Loosening my hand out of Jasper's hold, I rub my sweaty brow with the back of my hand.

"Relax, baby," he says, looking over at me with a small smile.

That's easy for him to say, however. Before I can think another thought, the door opens and we're greeted by the smiling assassin.

"Oh, Jasper, you don't have to ring the doorbell. This is your house as much as it is mine," his mom says, stepping forward and capturing Jasper into a tight embrace.

She looks laid back in a loose flowing brown skirt, and a black t-shirt, which hangs off her small frame.

As I stand off to the side awkwardly, I notice his mom narrow her eyes at me over Jasper's shoulder. It's only for a nanosecond, and then it's gone as she pulls out of his embrace, looking at me with a big smile.

"Hello, Ava. You look lovely." She beams and opens her arms for me to hug her.

I am stunned. She is so not pulling this, 'I'm happy to see you' stint, is she?

As her arms open wider, I know she is. With no other choice, I step into her embrace and give her a small, distant hug. In a circumstance where I should feel warm and fuzzy, I feel the complete opposite.

I feel cold and distant.

Pulling out quickly, I give her a forced smile.

"Hi, Danielle, thanks for having me."

"It's not a bother, please come in." She steps inside, holding the door open for us to enter.

Jasper latches onto my hand, giving it a small squeeze as we enter the dragon's lair.

As we step inside, I smell a subtle woody fragrance. She's burning some scented candles. I all but kick myself for not going with V's gift suggestion.

Her home is lovely. The walls are a bright white, which contrast beautifully with the dark furniture she has scattered throughout the living room. The trinkets she has strategically placed around the room give her home a warm, welcoming feel.

"Can I get you anything to drink?" she asks, her cerulean eyes looking at Jasper and I.

I still can't get over how her eyes can differ so vastly from Jasper's. Her son's eyes only reflect love, but hers, they only reflect hate, especially when they look my way.

Jasper shakes his head, his messy hair slipping over his brow.

"I know where the fridge is. You and Ava catch up." He takes off, leaving me alone with the ice queen.

Clearing my throat, I feel awkward standing, so I take a seat on the itchy, chocolate colored sofa. I tuck my dress underneath me, and try to be as ladylike as possible.

Danielle follows suit and sits near me, looking just as uncomfortable as I feel.

She's a short, slender woman. Not as short as me, but very small framed and petite. Her long brown hair reaches mid-back, and I notice she tucks a stray lock of hair behind her ear inadvertently. Looks like I know where Jasper gets his nervous habit from.

Her face is hard and lined, and her mouth is pulled into a small frown. Her looks are so sharp and harsh, not soft and caring like her son's. I can't help but wonder how is he a creation of this person sitting near me?

The silence stretches out between us, and I smooth out invisible wrinkles from my dress, attempting to suppress my nerves.

So, this definitely is not a good start. I need an ice breaker, and thankfully, I remember my gift.

"I got you something," I mumble, looking through my bag for her present.

"Oh?" she replies, slightly surprised.

"Yes, to thank you for having me over," I answer as I finally find the wrapped present stashed under the junk in my bag. I hand it to her shyly, and hope to God she likes it.

Looking at it, she accepts it cautiously, like it might detonate. "Thank you," she says. Finally she undoes the silk silver bow, and removes the white tissue paper.

Once she has uncovered the gift, she stares at it for a long while, her long brown hair covering most of her face. I can't read the expression behind her blue eyes, as she has the perfect poker face.

Only when I shuffle uncomfortably does she meet my eyes.

"Thank you, Ava, this is very... thoughtful."

Okay, is 'thoughtful' code for I hate it?

"What's thoughtful?" Jasper asks as he strolls into the living room with a beer and a tall glass of ice tea.

I'm hoping the beer is for me because I need it.

Danielle holds up her gift. "Ava's gift."

Jasper looks slightly stunned, taking in the picture of

him and his mom I stole out of his bedroom. It sits in a heavy mahogany frame, with a gold rimmed border.

He places the drinks down in front of me, and takes the frame from his mom's outstretched hands. I eye the beer like it's my salvation.

"You didn't tell me you were doing this." He smiles, looking at the picture affectionately.

Breaking my transfixed gaze from the beer, I look up at him.

"I'm full of surprises," I joke.

"Did you break into my house again?" he questions, cocking an amused eyebrow at me.

Letting out a small giggle, I recall the last time I 'broke' into his house. I did have a key, so technically I didn't break in.

Jasper hands the picture back to his mom, and gives me a quick kiss on the forehead before sitting near me.

"You're the best." He smirks, his bright eyes sparkling affectionately at me.

Returning his look, I give him a big smile.

At least someone likes my gift. Too bad it isn't the person it was intended for.

"So, I better check on the chicken."

Jasper and I break our love stare and I quickly stand, as Danielle is headed towards the kitchen.

"Let me help you."

I slowly follow her. I would rather steer clear of the kitchen, as there are way too many pointy implements she can poke me with.

"No, please, Ava, you're my guest. Sit down and relax," she says over her shoulder.

I look back at Jasper, who shrugs and pats the couch cushion near him.

I'm torn.

As much as I want to stay with him, I feel obliged to help Danielle out.

When she senses my dilemma, she smiles. "I insist."

"As long as you're sure," I reply, secretly breathing a deep sigh of relief.

"Of course."

Danielle is headed towards the kitchen, but then stops and turns back around. She walks past me, heading over to the mantel. She places my gift on it, and adjusts it until she's happy with the positioning.

I smile, touched that my frame is important enough to sit beside the other family portraits on display. However, that feeling is short lived when I see what sits alongside it.

Danielle takes a step back and looks at the picture, her hands clasped in front of her.

"Perfect." She beams, and it's the first genuine smile I've seen all evening. She gazes at the picture one last time, then excuses herself as she makes her way into the kitchen, humming happily.

Suddenly, I feel hot and claustrophobic.

My gaze is still fixated on the mantel. I storm over to it, just in case my eyes have deceived me.

Sadly, they haven't.

I see red. Well, actually, I see Indie.

My beautiful frame is shadowed alongside a photo of Indie and Jasper. What the fuck?

"What's wrong?" Jasper asks, picking up on my bad mood instantly.

But I can't respond.

I am silenced by a teenage Jasper and Indie, sitting on Santa's knee. I do a quick calculation from the date on the picture, and realize this was taken when Jasper was sixteen years old. He looks grungy in a faded Nirvana T-shirt, with long shaggy hair which falls into his eyes. And Indie. Well, even as a teenager Indie looks like a whore.

"Ava?" he asks, walking over to where I remain frozen.

He looks at what has caused me to freeze up like the Arctic and sighs. I try to appear calm, but Jasper knows me too well. He reaches for my hand, which I didn't even realize is clenched into a tight fist.

"I'm sorry about that," he says, jutting out his chin towards the picture.

"Don't worry about it. It's fine," I reply, trying my best to sound nonchalant, but failing.

"No, it's not fine. I would be pissed if I went to your parents' house and they had a picture of Harper on their mantel."

I can hear his teeth grinding at the mere mention of Harper.

The combination of seeing Indie and hearing Harper's name within the span of two minutes makes me want to puke, and I put my hands on my tummy, afraid I might throw up my lunch.

Is it nerves, or anxiety, or anger, or is it the... baby? The baby I have yet to tell Jasper about.

This is all too much and I need to take a seat before I pass out. Sitting down onto the sofa, I hug a beige throw cushion to my chest, staring off into the distance. I am a stone's throw away from rocking backwards and forwards when Jasper sighs, standing in front of me.

"Baby, I'm—"

Shaking my head, I wave him off. "It's fine, really. I'm just not feeling well." Which is technically the truth, as this whole situation is making me feel sick.

Jasper's head snaps up. "What's the matter? Are you sick? Do you want to leave?"

As much as I would like nothing more, I can't do that to him. "No, we'll stay. I just feel a bit lightheaded because I had a small lunch," which is true.

Jasper takes a step towards me and then stops. He spins around quickly, and grabs the photo of Indie and himself.

Looking up at him, curious as to what he's going to do, he surprises me by opening up a cabinet drawer, and not so gently placing the frame inside. He then slams the drawer shut and dusts off his hands.

"The power of Jasper compels you," he says, using the classic line out of *The Exorcist*.

I let out a tiny giggle and he rewards me with a big dimpled smile as he picks up my ice tea, handing it to me.

Damn, looks like the beer isn't for me.

"Drink. There's enough sugar in there to send you into a syrupy coma," he says, sitting near me.

Taking a sip, he's right, and I make an 'I just sucked on a lemon' face, putting the glass down on the stained coffee table.

"It's not *that* bad," I lie, as I feel my teeth disintegrating in my mouth.

"It so is." Jasper lets out a deep throaty chuckle,

which punches me straight below the belt. "I should really tell," he says.

He then lowers his voice into a conspiratorial tone as he whispers into my ear. "My mom can't cook to save her life. And I will apologize in advance if you choke on her Rubber Chicken, sorry, I meant Butter Chicken."

I am so not listening to a word he is saying, as all I can smell is his unique scent, and feel his soft breath tickling my neck.

Jasper senses my desire and leans forward, kissing the side of my throat, just under my ear. I can't stop myself as a barely audible whimper escapes me. But Jasper heeds it loud and clear as he nuzzles further into my neck.

"I was serious," he breathes in between kisses.

"About... what?" I reply breathlessly, as his kisses are warming me from head to toe.

"About skipping dinner and heading straight for dessert." He moves up to my chin, which he nips softly.

My eyes roll into the back of my head, as the feel of his wet mouth and rough stubble is driving me crazy.

"We... can't," I answer, only just getting the words out.

"Why not?" he questions, sucking on my earlobe.

"Be-because," I stammer. But for the life of me, I can't come up with a valid reason.

Suddenly I hear plates banging in the kitchen, and that is all the reminder I need.

"Because your mom has gone to a lot of trouble and I feel—"

Holy shit, he just totally tongued my ear.

"You feel what, baby?" he whispers.

At the moment I feel like I'm about to explode. "Bad," I finally reply after finding my breath.

"After I'm done with you, you will feel anything but bad."

He kisses the corner of my mouth, and I'm ready to blow this place and have my way with him in the backseat of his truck.

Sadly, he interrupts my plans of ravishing him. "You're right."

I almost pout. I don't want to be right. I want to be sexually satisfied!

As I open my eyes, I witness his pupils are dilated with desire as he leans forward, his face inches from mine.

"But the only thing I'm hungry for... is you," he says, wetting his bottom lip. "Dinner be damned."

My breath catches in my throat and I claw into the edge of the sofa before I tear his shirt off.

I'm just about to reply when I hear a throat cleared quite loudly. I pull back quickly, slightly embarrassed to be caught almost riding Jasper's lap.

Shyly sneaking a peek at him, Jasper looks anything but embarrassed. He looks mighty proud of himself, with a big mischievous smirk plastered across his rosy cheeks. He crosses his leg over his knee and leans back into the couch, pulling me with him, so I am snug into his side.

"What's up, Mom?" he asks cheekily.

She looks at us, and I could swear she glances at the mantel for a fraction of a second. When she turns back, a deep scowl forms on her harsh face, and I shiver at the coldness behind her look. But it could be my imagination because Jasper doesn't seem to notice it.

"Well, if I can interrupt you two lovebirds, dinner is ready," she says. The scowl is readily replaced by a sickly sweet smile.

Jasper kisses my forehead quickly and stands up, pulling me up with him.

"Smells good." He smiles walking past her, tightly holding onto my hand.

I, however, lower my eyes, totally embarrassed she caught us all but making out in her living room. As I pass her, I bravely peer up at her and am given serious stink eye.

What the?

It's gone before I can analyze it any further, and again I question if I'm seeing things.

"I won't be a minute. Jasper, show Ava into the dining room while I bring out dinner."

Jasper nods and gives her a heartbreaking smile.

"Yes, Mom." He happily leads me into the dining room.

I have never seen Jasper so content and relaxed, and I know the reason behind that is his mom. No matter what weird vibes I'm picking up from her, I have to try harder.

I have to do so for him.

However, as soon I look at the table settings, my resolve for trying harder plummets into a fiery ball of doggy doo.

Jasper's mom has set the table quite oddly, and I know she has done so with intent.

There's a setting at the head of the table with a beautiful goblet of Red, which I'm presuming is where Danielle will be sitting, judging by the lipstick stain on the rim of the glass. To the left of her china, is another setting which has a beer set in front of it—Jasper's seat.

Now the oddity of this is where I am meant to sit.

No guessing where.

She has set my place at the other end of the table, facing her. Yes, I am at the head of the table. But I am at the other end of the table where I am far, far away from her and Jasper.

Me, against them. Well her. Okay, not at all awkward.

Jasper looks at the table arrangement and scoffs.

"What the hell? She's probably had one too many wines," he says, eying the table arrangements distastefully.

I chuckle uncomfortably because I know she did this deliberately. But I don't say anything, as I'm contemplating escaping this train wreck of a scenario, like pronto.

He walks over to my setting and picks up my plate and cutlery, placing it down next to his. Giving him a sheepish smile, I take a seat, silently praying this will be over soon. He sits near me and rests his hand on my knee, giving it a light, reassuring squeeze.

Danielle comes out, hands full, and halts when her eyes fall to where I'm sitting. It's only for a split second, but she quickly composes herself before Jasper notices anything is off.

Am I totally going crazy and imagining these looks, because Jasper looks none the wiser to her defiant stares.

"I hope you guys are hungry," she says in a singsong voice which sends goose bumps down my arms.

She places the rice and chicken down in front of us, and then rushes back into the kitchen, claiming there's more to come.

My eyes drift over what is sitting in front of me and I scrunch up my face.

It looks... interesting.

Jasper leans into me. "Told ya," he whispers, referring to our conversation earlier.

Looking at the rice, I can see it's stuck together in one big lump, and the butter chicken which is bright red in color, is sitting in no sauce, and looks like it could be used as a doorstop.

In this circumstance I have to agree with him, although I'll give her points for trying.

"I bet it tastes amazing," I whisper back.

Laughing lightly, Jasper reaches for his beer, taking a long sip. "I think I'll stick to a liquid diet for this evening," he teases, licking the beer from his wet lips.

Kicking him lightly, I reply, "You will not. She obviously went to a lot of trouble."

Jasper smirks, his left dimple taunting me with its perfection. "Okay, but only because you said so."

Raising my eyebrow, I ask, "Since when do you listen to me?"

A slow grin spreads from cheek to cheek. "The quicker I eat, the quicker I get you home and out of that dress."

Seriously, he needs to stop this before I liquefy into a gooey mess.

"What are you two whispering about?" Danielle asks while setting more food down in front of us.

I quickly lower my eyes and Jasper chuckles at my guilty expression.

"Nothing, Mom. Just telling Ava how much I'm looking forward to dessert."

I blush at the hidden innuendo, but Jasper's mom beams. "Oh, I've made your favorite. You used to love it when you were a little boy."

Favorite? How does she know what his favorite is? She was too busy paying more attention to her pills than she was her kids.

Brushing aside that nasty thought, I force a smile when Danielle gestures for my plate. Handing it to her, I try not to blanch when she cuts, (yes, cuts) the rice to separate the grains from the gluey ball it's rolled into.

Once she hacks into it and is able to divide it apart, she spoons up way too much and it makes a loud thud once it hits the plate. She then dumps in three spoons of the non-fragrant chicken. Keeping this down is going to be a miracle.

She hands me my plate, and my hand nearly drops with the weight of all the dense, drab food sitting unappetizingly before me.

She reaches over to the bamboo bread dish and extends it my way.

"Oh, no bread, thanks," I say quickly, my hands wielding her off.

"Don't be silly. How are you going to wipe up all those delicious juices?"

Her hand is still waving the bread dish in my face, so

with no other choice, I reach for a bread roll, placing it on the small dish to my left. Looking at the mountain of food before me, my stomach gurgles in protest.

Jeepers, I'll be eating into next week.

Jasper covers his mouth to hide his smile and I have an urge to kick him in the shin.

"Okay, Jasper, your turn," she says, looking at him fondly.

Jasper reaches forward, handing her his plate. "Not too much, Mom, I'm watching my figure," he says, patting his stomach. "Anyway, I bet Ava will eat what I don't."

Giving into my urge, I kick him subtly under the table. He lets out a grunt on impact.

Danielle glances at us with a puzzled look, and I try to cover up my violence with a small smile.

She looks down at my plate and frowns. "Ava, please don't wait for us. Start eating."

Crap.

I was hoping to fake my way through dinner, using the over stimulating conversation as an excuse to not eat. But sadly, now I have no ploy to hide behind.

Picking up my spoon, I decide to do what I used to as a child when eating broccoli. I will just swallow it, so this way, I won't taste a thing. Scooping up a small spoonful, I gulp it down quickly, trying not to gag.

"Hmm," I smile. "It's good."

Jasper covers up a chuckle, and I have a right mind to stomp on his foot.

Thankfully Danielle is serving herself up a plate and I can stop force feeding myself.

"So, Ava, what do you think?" she asks as she takes her place near Jasper.

"Yeah, Ava, what do you think?" Jasper smirks, teasing me.

He is so going down for this.

"It's great, Danielle," I reply, lying through my teeth.

She gives me a genuine smile and I don't feel too guilty lying to her, because I just earned my first legit smile for the evening.

"Jasper, have you decided what you want to do for your birthday?" she asks while chewing around her meal.

Jasper shrugs, poking his chicken, which doesn't move an inch. "Nothing much. Staying in bed all day sounds like a great birthday to me."

He squeezes my knee which sends a shiver down my spine.

"Oh okay," Danielle says with a small frown.

Jasper looks at her, and I can read his expression instantly. He feels bad.

"Why? Was there something you wanted to do?" he asks, his hand still resting lightly on my knee.

Her face lights up and I feel a wave of annoyance pass over me, as I don't like the control she has over him.

"Well, I was thinking," she says, smiling. "How about we go to a karaoke bar?"

This time I nearly gag because of her suggestion, not the food. Karaoke bars hold bad memories for me. Not to mention, it's a fucking lame place to have a birthday.

Jasper hesitates, and says uncomfortably, "Ah, Mom, really?"

He looks over at me, knowing Harper broke my heart

in a karaoke bar, and that I would rather eat glass than go to another one ever again.

"Yes, really. I never get to see you sing. I thought this way I could," she replies huffily.

Is she *serious*? He'd be performing other artists' songs, not his own, while singing into cheap equipment which will do his voice no justice at all. And if that isn't deterrent enough, the tacky animation bouncing around on the screens should be. If she really wants to see him perform, she should come to one of his shows.

"Come see one of my shows then," Jasper says as if reading my thoughts.

"Oh Jasper, you know I don't like that loud music. When you were younger, all you did was play on that blasted guitar. I couldn't bear a whole hour of that."

I have to bite my tongue because I'm about to give her an earful.

Only when Jasper rubs the back of his neck, giving me a 'help me' look, do I intervene. I can tell he's torn, as he doesn't want to disappoint his mom. But he also doesn't want me to get weirded out by being at a karaoke bar.

He toys with his bottom lip, and I decide to make the decision for him. "Sounds like a great idea, Danielle." I smile.

Jasper turns to look at me, narrowing his brow.

"Really?"

Both he and his mom question me at the same time.

The look on both their faces is quite comical, or maybe I'm just losing it.

"Yeah, it'll be fun," I say, looking at Jasper, nodding my head, hoping to appear more convincing.

Jasper moves his luscious lips from side to side in contemplation.

"Okay?" he says looking my way.

"Okay," I confirm.

He squeezes my hand, which is sitting in my lap.

"Okay, karaoke it is, then," he says, looking slightly confused by this whole situation.

Danielle claps enthusiastically, her entire face lighting up. "I can't wait."

Smiling happily, I can feel the ice around her heart melt a fraction. Who would have thought some good could come out of karaoke?

"Oh Ava, you didn't eat very much," Danielle says, looking at my plate.

Shuffling in my seat, Jasper senses my discomfort, but I just can't eat it. It's tasteless and I can't punish my taste buds, which have been so good to me in the past. But I also can't offend his mom.

Giving her a small smile, I pick up my spoon, but before I have a chance to ladle any up, Jasper reaches over and steals my plate, pushing his empty one aside.

"Jasper, don't be rude," his mom says, smirking, secretly enjoying him wanting seconds.

He scoops up a big mouthful and stuffs it into his mouth, swallowing it quickly.

Looking over at him, I give him a big 'thank you' smile as he smirks, and takes a big swig of beer to wash down his toxic waste.

We both just took a bullet for the other, although I have a feeling that the decision I just made is going to bite me in the ass.

CHAPTER NINE

My Life Without Jasper

After some idle chitchat, Danielle clears the table, insisting I stay seated. I feel a tad bad as I've been raised with the mentality, you eat, you clean. But she's pretty adamant, and I don't want to argue with her.

She's preparing coffee to serve up with her infamous peach cobbler, which I hope is better than her dinner.

The evening hasn't been too bad, but I'll be glad once it's over.

Jasper leans over, nuzzling my neck. "I promise dessert will be better than dinner."

"I thought I was your dessert," I say innocently with big eyes.

Jasper smirks. "You're my midnight snack."

"I think you've eaten enough," I tease, referring to him finishing off his dinner as well as mine.

Jasper wraps his arm around my waist, yanking me over to his seat, and I let out a tiny yelp as he slides me onto his lap. My legs are dangling off to the side, and I can't help but giggle at how ridiculous this whole night has been.

"I'll never have my fill of you," he says deeply.

My heart begins beating steadily, and all I want to do is smash my lips against his.

"Yeah?" I ask, fascinated by his luscious mouth.

"Yeah," he confirms, giving me a small smirk.

Wriggling on his lap cheekily, Jasper groans, while I inch my lips closer to his, more than ready to seal the deal. But the doorbell chimes unexpectedly, sadly interrupting a moment that was about to turn pornographic.

"Jasper," his mom calls from the kitchen. "Can you get the door?"

Jasper lets out an exaggerated sigh, and I know he too is saddened by the disruption. He gives me a quick peck on the lips, and I pout involuntarily. Rewarding me with a crooked smile, he thumbs my lower lip, and I can't help myself as I slowly wrap my lips around his finger, sucking it into my eager mouth. He shakes his head at me and cheekily pushes his thumb further into my mouth, and I happily embark on sucking it harder.

"You're a bad, bad girl, Ms. Thompson," he says breathlessly, fixated on my mouth.

The doorbell sounds again, and I begrudgingly let go out of his thumb, which makes a 'pop' sound as he removes it from my mouth.

Jasper's eyes darken in desire and I give him a sassy grin.

He gets up, shaking his head at my cheekiness and disappears to answer the door. I stand up and peer out the window, thinking about the evening.

Everything, bar the Indie picture, has been bearable thus far. How is it that that troublemaking bitch can make my skin crawl without even being in the same room as me? Thankfully, I never have to be in the same room as her ever again.

"Hi, Ava."

My breath catches in my throat and I choke on it, coughing loudly and letting out a small gasp.

My name has never sounded so dirty as it does right now, passing through her lips.

Seriously?

You've got to be *fucking* kidding me!

I spin around so quickly my bun loosens slightly with the momentum.

Closing my eyes for a heartbeat, I curse the irony of this situation. Taking a calming breath, I reopen my eyes so I can look upon the vixen that is Indie.

Every time I look at her, something inside of me snaps, and I'm holding onto the last tether of patience I possess when it comes to this troublesome bitch.

I know she and Jasper are looking at me, but I can't move or speak, because all I can hear on repeat is Danielle saying 'perfect' when looking at the picture earlier. She's up to no good. I just know it.

"Ava?" The voice of my beloved snaps me out of my rage.

Meeting his eyes, I see his expression matches my mood. His luscious mouth dips into a slight frown, and his eyes are attempting to read my blank expression.

"It's been way too long, Ava," Indie says sarcastically.

My eyes narrow as I see Indie's amused, smug face, and I claw the inside of my palm to stop myself from slapping that smug smile off her face.

She looks a little more respectable than usual, and I guess I should be calling the *Sunday Times* that I can't see her lady parts!

Her tight blue jeans sit so low on her slender hips they expose her ghastly hipbones. Her dangling belly ring is catching in the light, and I have a satisfying image of me ripping out that piercing and stabbing her in the eye with it.

I work my way up to her cream boob tube, which reveals way too much cleavage and midriff, and I can tell she's not wearing a bra as she's blinding me with her headlights.

Her makeup rivals that of a clown, as it's so thick and caked on. And her long blonde hair sits straightened and perfect, not a wisp out of place.

I want to change that however by pulling out her lush locks, strand by strand. Sadly, my vision of hair pulling like a four year old is interrupted by an excited squeal.

"Oh Indiana, you made it! What great timing. I'm just about to serve up dessert."

Ugh, Indiana. Sounds even lamer than Indie.

Danielle brushes past me like I don't exist, and wraps Indie in a warm, tender embrace. I can't help but compare my hug to Indie's. Wow, I totally got shafted. I peer over at Jasper who is standing behind the two BFF's, rubbing the back of his neck uncomfortably.

He meets my gaze over their shoulders and mouths, "I'm sorry."

Shaking my head, I attempt to give him a reassuring smile, but I know I must look like I have just eaten glass.

"Jasper, where are your manners? Give Indiana a hug." Danielle steps away from Indie and gives Jasper a pointed look.

Jasper rubs his brow and I can actually see him cringe. But he does as his mom asks and gives Indie a light, loose, awkward hug.

She, however, pole vaults onto his body, wrapping her arms around him while rubbing her boobs into his chest. I quickly look away before I pry them apart with a crowbar.

Danielle is overjoyed, as she stares at the couple lovingly with her hands clasped over her heart.

My heart sinks when I witness her happiness. Why do I have a feeling this is the start of something sinister?

Jasper slips out of Indie's claws and subtly removes her hand from his forearm when she doesn't let him go.

He looks... pissed.

I silently celebrate the fact he's as unhappy as me, because when it comes to Indie, she always stirs up feelings of insecurity in me.

"Come now, the cobbler is getting cold." Danielle smiles, linking her arm through Indie's, heading into the kitchen.

Jasper shakes his head angrily. "No Mom, we're leaving."

Everyone's mouths pops open, especially mine.

Scrunching up my brow, I look at him, attempting to gauge what's going on behind those deep cerulean eyes.

Danielle's face drops, and I almost feel sorry for her. Almost.

"What? Why, son?" she asks.

Indie is alongside her pouting. I bite my lip to stop myself from laughing.

Jasper collects his jacket off the back of his chair and shrugs into it. When he reaches for my bag and cardigan, I stand, stunned. We're really going?

In that case, no need to ask me twice. He walks over to me and hands me my bag with a small smile.

I gingerly take it, but am suddenly hit with the guilts when I hear Danielle sniffle.

Jasper holds the arms of my cardigan out for me, and I slip into one sleeve, but halt when I hear Danielle let out a muffed sob.

Jasper freezes when he hears her whimper.

Slowly slipping into the other sleeve, I sneak a quick look at Danielle, who looks to be on the verge of tears.

Even though she totally set up Indie coming here, I still feel a pang of sympathy for her. I look up at Jasper, who has a torn expression on his face, and as much as I'm going to hate myself for my next comment, I do it anyway.

"Ah, c'mon, party-pooper, we can stay for dessert. You're only young once, and considering you're turning a year older next week, you need to live large before it's all about early nights and laxatives."

It's a lame joke, but I need him to know that it's okay. That I'm okay.

I know he's leaving because of me, as he can sense my discomfort, but I won't force him to choose between me and his mom.

He looks at me with a puzzled look on his beautiful face, and I give him a reassuring nod, as I can sit through this because I know how much it means to him.

"Are you sure?" he asks, searching my face.

"You betcha," I reply standing up on tippy toes, kissing his stubbled cheek.

As I pull away, he gives me a look filled with love and compassion, and I happily return his gaze of affection with one of my own.

"Okay then, the coffee is getting cold."

I turn to meets Danielle's eyes, and the look in them isn't pretty.

Indie flicks her hair over her shoulder and plonks down into my seat like a spoiled brat.

Dear God, what have I done to deserve this?

Jasper senses my discomfort instantly, so grasping my hand in his, he leads me over to the other side of the table, pulling out the chair for me. I swear he's doing this to tick Indie off, and I couldn't be happier.

I bite back my smile when I witness Indie's sour expression.

Jasper sits near me, holding my hand tightly in his under the table. I look over at him and smile. I can feel Indie spearing daggers my way.

"I hope you like peach cobbler, Ava," says Danielle with a forced smile as she places the dessert in the middle of the table.

"Yes, I love it. I love anything that's bad for you." I

blanch as soon as the words are out of my mouth. "Not that your food is bad," I correct quickly. "I just meant, you know, desserts are usually bad for you, but I'm sure yours is great. Full of nutrients."

I need to shut up, as I'm totally blabbering, but my brain isn't connected to my mouth right now.

Jasper rubs his thumb over the back of my knuckles, and it instantly calms me down. I quickly bite down on my lip to stop my verbal diarrhea.

Jasper reaches for the coffee pot with his right hand, as my right hand is still enclosed in his left. He pours himself a cup and raises the pot my way, indicating if I wanted a cup.

As I give him a small nod, I can feel Indie glaring at his simple, kind gesture. I know his mother is also.

"Jasper, don't be rude. Pour Indiana one, too."

Jasper sighs, slightly annoyed, but he doesn't make a scene and pours her one. He slides it over to her without an acknowledgment, and I know she's all but seething, because he does all this with our hands still linked under the table.

After Danielle has dished up the cobbler, we all dig in, and thankfully her dessert is better than her dinner.

We're all dead quiet and the air is so thick I could cut it with a knife.

After a few moments of polite chewing and sipping our coffee quietly, Danielle decides now is a good time to play Remember When.

"Indiana, do you remember when you were younger, and you'd sneak over to our place for dessert? You cheeky little rascal, sneaking in two desserts."

Indie lets out a high pitch laugh. "Oh, how could I forget? Your desserts were a million times better than my mom's."

Jasper shuffles uncomfortably next to me, but continues eating. I try and catch his attention, but his eyes are cast downward.

"Oh Danielle, do you remember the time you caught Jasper and I sneaking home, blind drunk when we were fifteen?" Indie asks, letting out a small chuckle.

"Of course I do." She laughs loudly as if reliving the memory.

She looks over at Jasper. "You two were always up to no good. Remember, Jasper?"

Indie turns to look at him, waiting for a reply.

Jasper shrugs, pushing his cobbler around with his fork. "I don't know, I can't remember," he replies on a sigh.

"Oh come on, of course you can," insists Danielle. "It was the weekend your father was away in Fresno and he brought back that red guitar you loved so much."

Jasper stiffens at the mention of his father, and as I peer over at him, my heart breaks when I see his chest expand on his heavy exhales, obviously uncomfortable with this conversation.

What the hell is wrong with his mom? Why is she pretending that his childhood was anything but horrible?

This time I'm the one who offers him comfort by running my thumb lightly across his knuckles, as our hands are still intertwined under the table. He looks over at me, and I offer him a small smile, which he thankfully returns.

"I think I might have a picture somewhere. I'll have to dig it up," Danielle says, sipping on her coffee casually.

Jasper tightens his grip on his coffee cup, and I wish his mom would shut her mouth. How can she be so insensitive?

"I also have a photo of your high school prom floating around. Oh Indiana, do you remember your dress 'malfunction'? I secretly believe Jasper was behind that," she says, winking at her.

Knowing Indie, that 'malfunction' was deliberately done by her, and would probably involve a big hole cut out of her crotch.

Sinking low into my seat, I'm hoping to slip away from this tortuous conversation. As Jasper looks over at me, I sink even further as Danielle continues her reminiscing.

"Jasper, you were always such a little terror. Your father may have had a firm hand with you, but..."

I'm about to leap out of my seat, ready to defend Jasper's honor, but he beats me to it.

"We're leaving," he says, pushing his chair backwards and standing abruptly.

Danielle looks over at Indie, who is mirroring her stunned expression. What did they expect? How could Danielle make excuses for Jasper's dad? Jasper was abused by the man who should have protected him against harm, and Danielle is lucky he's even talking to her right now, because she failed him as a mother by turning a blind eye to the abuse.

"You haven't finished," she says, looking down at his dessert, her voice faltering.

"Oh yes, I have," he replies quickly, and I'm quite certain he's not referring to his meal.

Placing my napkin on the table, I quickly stand, because I can see Jasper shaking in fury.

"Jasper," Danielle says, standing up.

The worry lines clearly etch over her forehead, but I don't care because she deserves everything he throws at her.

"No, Mom, don't. We can see ourselves out. You and Indie can play catch up and pretend that my childhood was a happy one, and I didn't get beaten daily by a spineless asshole!"

Both Danielle and Indie's mouths pop open, and before she can say another word, Jasper latches onto my hand and we're out the door.

As soon as we descend the last step, he lets go of my hand and fists his hair in frustration. I don't know what to do, as the pain and fury is clearly reflected in his haunted eyes.

He stalks ahead of me and I try to keep up, but I have to run to keep in step with his huge strides. As he reaches his truck, he begins kicking the front tire repeatedly. I flinch when I hear the loud sound echoing in the quiet neighborhood. Istare at him, my mouth agape, and my heart breaks into a million pieces when I witness his pain.

When he's not satisfied kicking the living hell out of his tire, he begins punching the front panel, creating a huge crater.

As he lifts his fist to punch it again, I quickly intervene. "Jasper, stop it. Enough."I approach him cautiously, as I can see he's blinded by anger, I place my hand on his upper shoulder firmly and plead once again. "Jasper. Enough."

He stops. His truck definitely looks worse for wear, and I know he'll regret this in the morning.

His head hangs low as he takes wild, rapid breaths, which echo deep within his chest. My heart goes out to him, and I can't help the tear that rolls down my cheek. I wipe it away quickly, because now it's my turn to be strong for him.

"Jasper?" I whisper. "Look at me."

After a moment of ragged breathing, he slowly turns to face me. His expression is plagued with such raw emotion it rips me into two. He raises his head to the heavens and interlaces his fingers behind his neck.

"I'm sorry," he finally says, looking up into the cloudless sky.

His apology surprises me.

"Sorry? What are you sorry for?" I ask.

He meets my eyes with a haunted look in his." For everything. For me losing my shit back there. For me suggesting this stupid dinner. For you having to listen to my mom and Indie play catch up. I can't imagine how uncomfortable that must have made you feel... I'm sorry," he says, lowering his eyes.

The look on his face is killing me. I need to make that look go away.

"Hey, don't," I say, reaching forward quickly and grasping his chin, pulling his face to meet my gaze.

When he meets my eyes, his usual vivid blue eyes are plagued with anger, fear, and frustration.

"This isn't your fault. You've got nothing to apologize for. You hear me?"

"Yes, I do. I made you come here. I was convinced that I could play happy family. I should have known better," he says softly, shaking his head.

"You didn't make me do anything. I wanted to be here, for you. I know how important this is to you, Jasper," I reply, stroking my palm against his cheek.

Jasper toys with the scar on his bottom lip."It was important. But my mom obviously can't see the significance of getting to know someone who means more to me than life itself."

I give him a small smile.

"Maybe Indie invited herself over," I suggest, knowing all too well that's not the case.

Jasper reaches forward, brushing a loose tendril of hair that is catching in the wind behind my ear. "Always the optimist, even when you know nothing about tonight was coincidental."

I bite my lip because I know he's right. "I'm sorry, Jasper." I don't know what else to say. All I want to do is take him in my arms and comfort him like he has done for me so many times before.

"Let's just go home," he says, crushed, resting his forehead against mine.

I give him a small nod. It saddens me to think his mom's place, a place he should be able to call home, is anything but.

CHAPTER TEN
Girl Interrupted

We arrive at Jasper's, both physically and emotionally drained after sitting through a dinner from hell. We both crash, twirled around one another's bodies, with Jasper holding onto me tighter than usual.

I awake with his arm wrapped around my middle, hugging me to his chest. His cheek rests on the edge of my pillow, and his gentle exhalations tickle my neck.

Craning my neck, I peer over at the bedside clock, which reads 9a.m.

I'm glad Jasper is sound asleep, because after last night, he deserves a peaceful slumber. And also because today is the day I tell him that I'm pregnant. Yes, I wanted to wait until I was 100% certain, but he needs to know that no matter what, I... well, we, will never let him down. We will always be his family and never treat him the way his mom did last night.

I just hope he embraces the news and doesn't flip out. Gulping at that thought, I feel my stomach roll with nausea.

"What's wrong?" a raspy voice asks.

I shiver when I hear the roughness of Jasper's morning voice.

It shouldn't surprise me that he can read me with his eyes closed, but it still does.

Brushing my hand down his stubbled cheek, I reply, "I was just thinking."

"About?" Jasper prompts.

About our baby, I silently answer.

When I remain quiet, he opens his eyes and the color rivals the bluest, cloudless sky.

"Your eyes blow my mind," I confess, running my fingertips over his full eyebrow.

He is the most beautiful thing I have ever seen, and I doubt I'll ever see anything that will measure up to his beauty.

"You blow my mind," he replies, his dimple dipping low in his left cheek. "You know what else blows my mind?" he asks.

"What's that?" I reply, snuggling closer into him.

"When you tell me what's on your mind."

I bite back my smile.

"You know, Ava, sometimes you just need to not think before you speak. Just tell me what's going on without overanalyzing it. I bet my reaction won't be half as bad as you think. You work yourself up over nothing most of the time," he says wisely.

In any other circumstance, I would absolutely agree with him and be all for the overshare. I would happily divulge all my secrets, every single one of them. But this isn't a secret, this is something he has to know. I just don't know how to tell him.

Jasper secures his hands around my waist and rolls me onto him playfully.

Giggling loudly, I sit up on his waist, looking down at him and admiring the view. He reaches up and brushes a loose strand of hair off my forehead, giving me one of his coma-inducing smiles.

"C'mon, spill it. Otherwise I'll kiss it out of you," he says mischievously.

Arching my eyebrow, I smile. "That's not much of a threat."

That sounds like heaven.

He shrugs, which does amazing things to his bare chest. "I was going to do that anyway, but I thought if I said it in a stern voice, you'd listen."

Laughing softly, I rub my hands across the hard planes of his upper body. "You're a dork."

He massages my exposed thighs. My skin instantly prickles with the contact of his hands on my exposed flesh.

"So, you going to tell me?" he questions, licking his lower lip quickly.

"Hmm," I smile, tapping my chin in contemplation. "I'd rather you kiss it out of me," I answer truthfully.

Jasper smirks. "I think I can manage that."

He leans up and I eagerly meet him halfway. Our lips are mere inches apart, when suddenly the doorbell rings, and we both groan at the lousy timing.

He glances over at the clock. "This better be good," he says, slumping back down onto the pillow.

I begrudgingly slide off him and gape at his naked butt as he slips out of bed. He grabs the blue jeans that are thrown over the back of his chair and steps into them quickly.

Wow, when I get a glimpse of his perfect ass wriggling its way into those lucky jeans, I am so thinking the person at the door can wait.

As he buckles up his belt, he leans over the bed and kisses me quickly.

"Whoever it is, I'll get rid of them. Promise," he says, grinning.

As he bounces down the stairs, I collapse into the pillows and spread my arms out wide. Jasper's words from earlier comfort me because he's right, I do work myself up. I'll just spit it out and we'll deal, just like we always have done in the past.

I listen, hoping to catch wind of whom Jasper is speaking to, but I really have to strain my hearing as their voices are low and muffled. However, as soon as I hear the other person, I instantly recognize the voice.

It's his mom.

I don't know what to do. Should I go down there? After seeing Jasper react the way he did last night, I think it's best that I do.

Quickly slipping on my jeans and a t-shirt, I tie my hair up into a high ponytail and quietly creep out the door.

I'm at the top of the stairs when I overhear them talking.

"I'm sorry about last night, Jasper. I was just trying so hard, I wanted everything to be perfect."

"Well, it was going fine until you invited Indie over,

Mom. What were you thinking? Do you realize how awkward that made Ava feel?"

"I know. I wasn't thinking."

"Bull fucking shit," I whisper.

"It's just that Indiana is still your friend. If Ava has a problem with her, she'll just have to get over it. You've made it quite clear who you want to be with."

I see red.

"No offense, Mom, but you've kinda got the blinkers on when it comes to Indie," Jasper retorts.

"No, Jasper, I think you do when it comes to Ava."

Excuse me?

Grabbing onto the banister, I'm about to charge down the stairs and take everyone's blinkers off so they can see the real me kick Danielle's ass.

I'm not sure of Jasper's reaction to her comment, but I don't think it's a good one, as I hear Danielle apologize quickly.

"I'm sorry. That was wrong of me. I'm just overprotective, Jasper. After everything she put you through, I don't want her hurting you again. Surely you can understand that."

What horseshit!

"I appreciate your concern, but you have nothing to worry about. I love Ava and she loves me. She's the best thing that has ever happened to me, Mom, and she's here to stay. I suggest you get over whatever issues you have with her and learn to get along, because I know she's trying with you."

My heart inflates with his kind words.

"Okay, I'll try. But don't shut Indiana out."

Closing my eyes in frustration, I decide to creep back up to his bedroom, not wanting to hear another word.

After ten minutes, Jasper comes back upstairs looking beat. By the way his hair is sticking up into an angry mohawk, I know the conversation didn't go well.

"Everything okay?" I ask, propping up on an elbow to look at him as he closes the door behind him.

"Yeah, fine," he says quickly, and totally unconvincingly.

"Who was at the door?" I ask in hopes of not sounding suspicious.

Jasper looks at me and frowns slightly. "My mom."

Before I have an opportunity to question him, he walks over to his closet and begins searching for clothes.

"What's wrong? I know you're not telling me something. I also know that you're mad," I say, as he has interlaced his hands through his hair, yanking on it painfully.

He turns at the waist with a small smirk. "You can't see my face. How do you know I'm mad?"

"Because I know you," I reply quickly.

Him fisting his hair—dead giveaway.

"Well, I know *you're* not telling me something," he says defiantly, turning to face me.

I gulp.

This is it, Ava.

The hard resolve in his eyes suggests he's not going to let this slide. And a part of me still thinks I should wait, but I can't keep this from him. Whether I'm pregnant or not, we'll deal.

"You're right, Jasper," I reply, sitting up slowly. "I think I'm—"

My heart begins slamming against my ribcage, as I am one word away from changing his life forever.

However, before I can continue, I hear "Highway to Hell."

And I mean that literally.

Jasper looks at his iPhone, and then he looks at me.

"It's fine, answer it." I sigh with a small smile, waving at the phone.

I really don't want to read into the significance of that song and my situation.

Jasper reaches for it, cocking an eyebrow. "It's Lucas," he says, looking at screen. "Sup, man? Yeah, its fine, we're up."

I watch Jasper's face transform from miserable to ecstatic in a matter of seconds.

"You're fucking kidding me! Holy shit."

Jasper pauses, and I can hear Lucas' deep voice speaking quickly to Jasper from where I sit.

Jasper lets out a stunned breath and looks at me, eyes wide. "Fuck yeah, I'm in! What dates? This is amazing. Okay, when... tonight? Yeah for sure, we'll be there."

He quickly ends the call, throwing his iPhone onto the desk and stalking towards the bed animatedly.

"What?" I ask apprehensively, almost afraid to ask.

"We got the gig at the Rip it Up festival in Seattle!"

"Oh my God, Jasper, that's great! Congratulations!" I yelp, jumping up on my knees and crawling over to him.

I know how much this means to him and I'm overjoyed at the news. It has been P.O.E's dream of playing this festival since it was first announced months and months ago. It's a three day festival showcasing the world's biggest musical acts, and P.O.E will be amongst them.

No freakin' way!

"I know! Can you believe it? It's huge. We've never played to a crowd that big before," he says excitedly.

I nod happily. "I just knew it. You guys have worked so hard to get where you are. No one deserves it more than you."

"But there's more good news," he says with a twinkle in his eye.

"More?" I question.

Jasper nods as he reaches for me, wrapping my hands around his neck.

"Yes. Lucas said we've been offered a six week tour supporting Flames around the States, and if that goes well, we might go to Europe. Fucking Europe! Can you believe this shit?"

My mouth pops open. Holy crap!

"That's great!"

I all but throw myself into his arms as I'm so happy for him, but then I stiffen.

This sounds like Jasper's dream come true.

A dream that doesn't involve a baby.

Fuck.

"What's wrong?" Jasper asks, pulling out of the embrace, searching my downcast eyes.

When I don't reply, he says in a rushed breath, "Of course you'll be coming with me. I already worked out the dates. You would have finished school by then, so you're free to come with. You and me on the road. No ties or commitments. It's perfect, baby."

My heart sinks further. The last few words are so ironic, I have to laugh.

It's perfect, baby.

It's anything but.

I try my best to fake a smile, because I can't ruin this moment for Jasper.

"I'm so proud of you, Jasper."

The look on Jasper's face is one of pure happiness.

How the hell can I tell him now?

"So what's going on tonight?" I ask, remembering his conversation with Lucas.

"Andy is throwing a party at Marian's beach house. It's gonna be huge," he replies, giving me a quick kiss on the cheek.

Jasper walks over to his phone and begins scrolling through his numbers. "I better get my shit organized. Get someone to cover my shift."

He turns in the direction of the bathroom and stops, spinning around to face me.

"Shit, Ava, we were totally having a conversation before Lucas called. What were you going to tell me?"

Looking at him, it takes all my willpower not to crumple into a heap of tears.

"Oh, nothing. It can wait," I reply, surprised I haven't choked on my words.

Whether Jasper is riding on cloud nine or he believes me, I will never know. But he gives me a big smile and heads into the bathroom, not pressing the issue.

As soon as I hear the water running, I slump back onto the pillow in defeat.

I'm certain my friend has a bottomless pit for a stomach.

As I'm watching her pile topping after topping onto her rye bread in her kitchen, I wish I had her appetite. I haven't eaten a thing all day, and I doubt I'll be able to stomach anything ever again.

"I agree, timing not cool. But Ava, seriously, you need to just do it," says V while squashing down a whole baby beet onto her leaning pile of condiments.

"I know, V, and I was going to do it today. Then your husband called and rained on my parade," I answer, playing with the coffee mug that sits in front of me.

V looks at her sandwich, which is about to collapse, and decides another piece of cheddar will balance it out.

"Oh, Ava, please. If it wasn't Lucas, you'd have used another excuse. Just do it already. Ha, well I guess you wouldn't be in this position if you didn't," she replies with a smirk.

I scrunch up my face, puzzled by her comment.

She looks over at me, using her knife as a gesturing tool. "You know, 'do it.'"She laughs at her inappropriate, lame joke.

I'm glad someone is finding this funny.

Rubbing my temples, I groan. "You are not helping."

V shrugs and completes her sandwich with an alfalfa sprout.

She looks at it proudly. "And you went to school for this shit. Look at that," she says, her lips all but smacking at the meal before her.

She picks up the monster of a sandwich with both hands and carefully places it onto a plate, which looks dwarfed by its colossal size.

She takes a seat across from me and I eye her lunch.

"Have fun eating that." I smirk when I notice the beetroot has bled through the bread.

V picks it up while giving me a smug look. It collapses just before it reaches her mouth.

I can't help but laugh. "Karma's a bitch, or in your case, a soggy sandwich."

She pouts and I laugh harder. Who would have thought a soggy sandwich in my best friend's kitchen would cheer me up?

V pushes away her plate and crosses her arms over her chest.

"What are you wearing tonight?" she asks, ignoring my chuckling.

That stops my laughing. I haven't given it much thought and I really should, seeing as I would like to wear something show stopping for Jasper.

"I'm not sure. I hate everything I own," I confess.

V cocks an eyebrow at me and a big smirk spreads across her heart shaped face.

"Shopping?" she asks, hopeful I will say yes.

I can't say no to that face. "Sure, why the hell not. I better make use of this body," I say, gesturing mockingly to my figure. "Before all I can fit into are baggy sweats and maternity bras."

V laughs hysterically, nodding. "Shit, you're going to be a mini Buddha!"

Gee, some best friend.

CHAPTER ELEVEN
Truths

Okay, I take it back.

My best friend is never short of good ideas. Her suggestion of shopping was a brilliant idea.

As I'm gazing at my reflection in the full length mirror on the back of V's wardrobe door, I like what I see.

I have opted for sexy, but casual, and chosen a royal blue A-line short crepe dress with a v-neck. And although it isn't indecently short, I'll have to ensure I don't drop anything, because there's no way I can bend down without flashing everyone in a five mile radius.

The skirt is pleated, and although it pinches my midriff, I love it. My hair is simply styled, opting for it to be half up, half down. And my makeup is the usual, nothing heavy, but I have placed emphasis on my lips with a light pink lip-gloss.

"You sexy bitch." V smiles at me over my shoulder in the mirror. "Jasper is not going to be able to keep his hands off of you." She witnesses the alarm in my face and laughs. "Google, Ava, make it your best friend. If we weren't running late, I'd be all over finding out if you can bump uglies."

"It's fine." I shrug her crass comment off because I don't want to think about it.

"Oh yeah, like you're not clawing at the walls," V jokes while slipping on her cardigan.

I laugh it off, but make a mental note to get onto Google as soon as possible.

Peering up at the glass mansion before me, a thousand memories of this place assault my memory bank.

The way I fit in Jasper's arms for the first time will always be my most treasured memory. That night I knew that nothing between us would be the same ever again. I may have stupidly denied it, but from that night forward I was his, and I always have been ever since.

"Stop with the reminiscing and let's go," V says, linking her arm through mine.

"You can see your man and make new memories the quicker we get inside," V jokes, slightly out of breath, as the walk up the hill is freakin' steep.

She's right. I know I'm procrastinating as I'm scared to see Jasper. The longer I leave not telling him, the harder it gets.

When we finally reach the front door and step into the extravagance, I take a deep breath for two reasons. One, I'm so outta shape and the windy driveway has given me a serious stitch, and two, I've just spotted Jasper talking to some blonde across the room.

The fact some tramp is pawing him hungrily doesn't bother me like it usually would.

Kudos to me.

But the fact I am impervious to her wandering hands is because of the way Jasper looks.

There is only word that can describe him.

Epic.

I scan down his body and then back up again, not believing the exceptional sight before me.

He has rolled the sleeves of a white button down shirt up past the elbows, exposing his taut forearms, and the shirt is tucked loosely into his tight fitting black jeans. And of course my eyes can't help but linger on the parts of his body that the snug jeans emphasize.

My gaze creeps further up his torso and I almost gag on my tongue when I see a thin black tie sitting slackly around his neck, giving him a casual, yet sophisticated look. And if that isn't mouth watering enough, the first two buttons of his shirt are undone, calling attention to his chiseled upper body.

Just when I thought he couldn't possibly get any hotter, I see that his hair sits in an untidy, but styled mess, just the way I like. Mental images of me fisting that hair swarm my senses. And I have to remind myself we're in the company of others, because in about five seconds, I'm going to push him into a closet and do unspeakable things to his face.

As I meet his eyes, Jasper is totally aware that I have been intentionally eye-fucking him. But as he rewards me with a big dimpled grin, I know he doesn't mind one bit. I dare say he relishes in the thought that I am all but drooling over myself.

Sadly, V's squeal interrupts my inappropriate thoughts of defiling my boyfriend in public.

"Hi, husband," V chirps while Lucas wraps his big arms around his wife, kissing the side of her neck.

I totally ignore them as my eyes are glued to Jasper, who's walking towards me like an apparition of a Sex God.

As soon as he's a few feet away, I am assaulted by his familiar, warm smell, and holy hell, my hormones are prepped and ready to give Jasper his own personal lap dance.

He wraps his long fingers around my waist, pulling me close so I'm flush against his hard body, and then he smashes his lips to mine. No words are needed as our actions speak louder than words.

He deepens the kiss by wrapping a hand in my hair, pulling me closer to his mouth. I'm breathless from the intensity of his embrace, but I don't care. Moaning when he slips in his tongue, my legs begin to tremble when he claims my mouth as his own.

A loud wolf whistle alerts me to where I am, so I pull my lips away just before Jasper can deepen the kiss. I'm panting in wanton need and if I don't break away now, I won't be able to stop.

Jasper half-heartedly lets me go, but still has a hold of my hair.

His big blue eyes soften as they search my face. "How

did I get so lucky? You are so fucking beautiful. Every time I see you, you take my breath away."

My mouth parts as I am touched by his words.

He asked how he got so lucky. But he's got it all wrong, because I'm the lucky one.

"Well, you look pretty good yourself," I smile looking down at his attire, toying with the end of his tie.

Jasper smirks. "Glad you approve."

"I approve of anything you wear *or* don't wear," I add cheekily.

Jasper's eyes instantly heat at my comment.

"Well, the latter part I can definitely manage. Speaking of which," he says, pulling me closer into him. He lays a single kiss on my neck, just under my right ear, and that single action is enough to leave me clawing at him like a cat in heat.

"You. Me. Tonight. Naked?"he says in a mere whisper.

The images swimming around in my head are spreading goose bumps all over my body, but those images are sadly interrupted by a malicious snicker.

"There you are," sneers the blonde girl I saw pawing Jasper earlier.

She looks at me challengingly, while crossing her arms over her bountiful chest, cocking a sculptured eyebrow.

Oh bitch, please. You're not even on a blimp on my radar. Compared to Indie, this girl looks like Mother Theresa.

I give Jasper a quick peck on the cheek. "I'm going to go find V, who no doubt is raiding the liquor cabinet."

Jasper nods, giving me a small smile.

I know he has to humor these girls, because at the end of the day they are his fans, and this, sadly, is one of the cons of being a rock star.

"I'm holding you to your promise," I say, full of assurance.

Jasper smirks. "Yeah?"

"You betcha," I reply quickly, returning his grin.

Random girl looks between us like conversational ping pong.

"What promise? What's she talking about, Jasper?" she asks, and I nearly reach forward to yank out her extensions when I hear Jasper's name pass through her pouty lips.

I take two steps away from her, before I toss over my shoulder, "The promise to fuck his brains out tonight."

And I take great satisfaction in seeing her mouth pop open and Jasper shaking his head with a dimpled smile.

"Bye, lover," I say, blowing him a kiss.

Walking off smugly, I make sure I leave him with a clear view of my ass wiggling away from him.

I chuckle to myself, thinking how much fun that was and how proud I am for not caving and running away. In the past, I would have let that girl get to me, but now, I find it all quite comical.

After searching for my troublemaker of a friend for about five minutes, I finally find her.

"Ava!" she screams, pulling the beer bong away from her ruby lips. "Come support me. I'm about to prove to the boys that I can drink more than them."

I chuckle as I approach.

"V—" but she doesn't let me finish.

"Hold this," she says, yanking off her bag and shoving it into my chest. She rolls up the sleeves of her cardigan and smirks. "Time to get serious."

After twenty minutes of watching V get absolutely sloshed, I decide to save my friend. "C'mon, Miss. I think you've had enough."

I walk over to where she stands in the kitchen, surrounded by random people. She has beer dripping down her chin, and that damn plastic pipe is still attached to her hand.

Lucas lets out a loud chuckle while wrapping his hands around her tiny waist. "Ava's right, babe."

V hiccups. "You're just jealous," she slurs, pointing her finger into his amused face.

Lucas and I humor her. "Yes, we're jealous. Now come outside and get some fresh air."

Lucas nods, his shaggy hair slipping into his eyes. "Come on, Bub, let me help you."

V shakes her head and sways. "I can walk out by myself you know. I have two left feet."

Lucas and I laugh at her drunkenness, and her position of beer bong queen is quickly challenged by some airhead who pries the hose from V's hands.

"Hey!" V yells, ready to play tug of war with this brunette bimbo.

"C'mon, V, I have something really important to tell you," I state, lying through my teeth. I know this will get her outside in an instant.

"Oh! Why didn't you say sooner?" she says, tossing the bong hose at the brunette and hurling her arm around my neck.

Grabbing onto her wrist, I look over at Lucas, who mouths, "Thank you."

I give him a reassuring smile and push through the crowd.

"You, young lady, need to come with a warning," I joke, thankful the swarm of people let V and I through.

V laughs hysterically. "You are my bestest friend, Ava Thompson, and I wuv you."

"You wuv me?" I ask, laughing at her pronunciation.

My laugh dies however when I see the throng of patrons blocking my exit. When did all these people arrive? I wonder as I look at the endless amount of bodies mingling around the house.

"Excuse me!" I yell to be heard over the music.

I'm still holding onto V's arm, which is around my neck, and I'm using my other hand to part the sea of unmoving people in front of us.

Finally, after shoving my way through two brick shit-houses, I look up and my heart plummets to the floor as the sight before me turns my stomach with nausea and pure fury.

Indie has her arms wrapped around Jasper's neck, her lips way too close to his mouth for my liking. Jasper is turning his head away, attempting to pry her fingers off the back of his neck, but she won't let up.

My face contorts in rage, and if I wasn't holding onto V, I would be storming over there, giving her the beat down she deserves once and for all.

V sees my fascination and follows my line of sight.

"You've got to be shitting me!" V yells. "I've had enough of this bitch!"She shrugs out of my hold, screaming at the top of her lungs.

"Keep your hands to yourself, you fucking home wrecker!"

Indie turns, her high ponytail flicking like a whip. She glares at V and then her daggers are directed at me. That's it! Game on!

I flick a glance to Jasper, who looks mortified, and as he meets my eyes, he knows it's on.

Happy patrons have turned to look at the commotion, and I swear the music has dimmed slightly, preparing for the approaching smack down.

Lucas is by V's side in an instant, trying to calm down his angry, drunk wife, but she swats his hands away. I'm by her side, and I feel my fists clench of their own accord.

Indie's hackles flare up as she takes a small step towards me and V. "Call me that again. I dare you," she sneers, lunging for V.

I see Jasper spring at Indie, his face absolutely livid, but Indie is stopped in her tracks as Lucas latches onto her arm, putting himself between V and Indie.

"If you so much as touch her... you and I will have a problem," he spits.

In that moment, I could hug the hell out of him.

"Walk away, Indie. Now," Lucas commands, pinning her with a look dipped in venom.

I have never seen this murderous side of Lucas, and Indie mustn't be as dumb as she looks, because she backs away, tail between her legs, storming outside.

Lucas looks at V, who is about to charge after her.

"C'mon, V, it's over. Let's go home," Lucas says, grabbing her arm lightly, but she rips out of his grip, eyes wild. Suddenly, I don't like that look one bit. Narrowing her eyes, she glares at Jasper, whose face is twisted in rage and frustration.

She points her finger at him, wielding it like a weapon. "How about you man the fuck up, Jasper, and tell that tramp once and for all to go to hell!"

Jasper looks taken aback, and even though I agree with her, now is not the right time to discuss this.

"V!" I reprimand, as I know what's about to happen, but I'm powerless to stop it. She ignores me like I haven't spoken.

"Be a man and stick up for Ava, for fuck's sake! You were man enough to get her pregnant, so how about you man up where it matters!"

In this moment, everything freezes, and my eyes are the only things that move, taking in the chaos before them.

V is looking at me, open mouthed, when the realization of what she's just said sinks in.

I watch as Lucas grabs V protectively, pushing her behind him, knowing that she's going to cop an ear bashing.

My eyes then move over to some random girl, who's looking between us with a Fight! Fight! Fight! expression plastered all over her drunken face.

Some couple to her left are eating each other's faces off, totally oblivious to the drama unfolding before them.

And then of course, there's Jasper.

He's standing utterly still, staring at me. If it wasn't for his chest rising in quick, successive breaths, I would say he has been frozen solid.

His eyes are wide, searching mine frantically, and he's asking me, without a word, if what V has said is true.

I lower my eyes, unable to hide the truth.

A small gasp escapes Jasper's lips, and then everything crashes before me with a loud thud.

I think I'm going to faint.

All of a sudden I feel hot and clammy, and my tight dress is suffocating me with each breath I take.

I need to get out of here.

And I do exactly that.

I turn around and run towards the exit like the wind.

CHAPTER TWELVE

Dance with Me

So, here I stand in the exact same spot, staring out into the ocean, watching a sea bird flap its wings against the full moon, crying once again.

This spot shares bittersweet memories, and as I think about them, as opposed to the new ones I have made tonight, which do I prefer?

I think about all those nights ago, crying over a stupid thing like a broken heart. What I feel here, now, is a million times worse.

"Ava."

I cringe as soon as I hear his voice, but instead of wiping away my betrayal like I did in the past, I allow my tears to run freely.

"Look at me."

I guess that makes sense. He wants to look at me when he tells me it's over.

Closing my eyes, I take a deep breath, wishing it gave me courage. But it doesn't.

Reopening my eyes, I turn towards him slowly.

The moonlight reflects off his pale, haunted face, and his usual milky white skin, appears ghostly.

Looking at him, standing before me, breaks my heart.

I can't lose him.

The sob I've been trying to hold onto escapes me and I choke on it. I bury my head in my hands and let the tears break free.

Luckily, the loud surf hitting the rocks below drowns out my anguished wails.

I don't know how long I've been crying, it may be five minutes or five seconds, either way, I don't feel any better.

I feel worse.

That is until my hands are gently removed from my face, and with shaky fingers, Jasper wipes away my avalanche of tears.

"Don't cry. I can't stand to see you cry," he says, brushing my tears away with his fingertips.

I try and snuffle up my tears, but fail.

"I'm s-sorry," I stutter as he quietly wipes away my continuous tears.

As I peer up at him, he appears blurred due to my watery eyes, but from what I can see, he looks broken and torn.

My heart drops and I begin shaking at the realization of what's about to happen. He's going to leave me.

If he's going to do it, then I will meet his eyes and respect his decision, even though I'm struggling to survive.

We stand, staring at one another. The silence is deafening. Why isn't he saying something? Anything? I need to know what he's thinking.

Jasper closes his eyes for a moment and takes a deep breath. As he reopens them, he places both his palms on my cheeks, resting our foreheads together. His warm breath caresses my face, and I hate to think this may be the last time I ever feel it.

That thought produces a fresh set of tears, and my body wracks with silent sobs.

"Ava, ssh... ssh. Don't cry," he whispers and pulls away, softly kissing away my tears.

The light flutter of his lips passing over my skin sends my already shaking body into a convulsion of shudders. Deciding to get lost in the moment, I close my eyes, drowning in his kisses, his lips never leaving my face.

After a few moments of stillness, Jasper whispers, "Dance with me."

Opening my eyes, I look at the man I love with my entire being.

"Dance with you? Here?" I question, sniffing.

He nods, his cerulean eyes sparkling in the moonlight.

"But there's no music," I whisper, hating to state the obvious.

Jasper shrugs, and the wind blows his soft tresses across his brow. "We'll make our own."

Before I have time to question him, he wraps his warm fingers around my waist, pulling me toward him. With no other place I'd rather be, I settle against him firmly.

I contentedly sag against him as I enfold my arms around his neck, snuggling into his solid chest.

Is this our last dance?

The thought is one I can't deal with, so I burrow my face into Jasper's woody, comforting scent.

He senses my anxiety and grips my hips tighter. "So it's true?" he simply asks.

There is no need for him to clarify what he is referring to, so I respond by giving him a small nod.

I feel his chest inhale, then exhale.

"How long have you known?" he asks, moving me slowly from side to side.

"Two days," I reply shamefully. "I was going to tell you. I just... I just didn't know how," I whisper.

Jasper stands rigid at my confession and panic overtakes me.

"I'm sorry, Jasper," I say on a sob.

"Ava, please don't apologize. You've got nothing to be sorry for," he says.

"But... but," I fumble over my words.

"But nothing. I understand, baby."

"You what?" I ask as I stop rocking in his arms, pulling back to look up at him.

"I understand," Jasper repeats.

"So, you're not mad at me? You're not going to break up with me?" As soon as the words leave my lips I feel like I might be sick.

Jasper looks as if I've snapped him. "Baby, no. You hear me? We're in this for the long haul. There is no me without you. Understand?"

Nodding, I feel tears prick my eyes yet again, and I bite my lip to stop them from falling.

He strokes my hip with his thumb and the movement calms me.

"I'll admit, this is a shock. A big shock. But we'll deal. We always do," he says, his eyes searching my face.

I can't help the relieved breath that whooshes out of my lungs.

"So you want to... keep it?"

I know it's not the right thing to ask, but I have to know if he really wants this. I don't want him to feel obligated to me, in any way, shape, or form.

Jasper stops caressing my hip and looks at me, stunned. "Of course I want to keep it. Don't you?" he questions, almost afraid of my reply.

I lower my eyes because I really don't know what I want.

"Hey, look at me," Jasper says, softly raising my chin.

Lifting my eyes, I take him in, and in this moment, Jasper White is my strength, he's my reason for existing. I know that on the inside he's just as scared as me, but on the outside, his actions don't betray his fear, and that's because he's being strong for me, for us.

Suddenly, all my fear and doubt carries away on the night's cool breeze.

Do I want this baby? Fuck yes.

"Yes, I want our baby," I answer with conviction, because I feel it, for the first time, I really want this.

The expression of absolute love shining on Jasper's face warms my heart, as he looks like a man who has just been given his purpose in life. He drops to his knees, surprising me as he wraps his arms around my middle, resting his cheek against my flat belly.

After a few moments of him gripping onto me like I'm his lifeline, he whispers, "I can't believe we made you."

I gasp, touched by his affection towards something he can't see or feel.

"I'm going to be the best dad. I'm going to give you everything I never had... I promise."

His sweet words touch something deep inside me, and as I look down, seeing him rest his cheek flat against my belly, talking to our baby, I can't stop the rush of tears.

He's going to give our child everything, and of course he's going to be the best dad, I never doubted that for a minute.

What a lucky baby.

Jasper presses a soft kiss against my belly, and rises to his feet with tears in his reflective eyes. He places his hand against my cheek, lowering his lips to mine and gives me the briefest of kisses before he pulls away, smiling.

"Ah, now I know why you were avoiding me in the bedroom."

I blush, as he knows me too well.

"Damn, I hope that's not true. Because I have no hope of keeping my hands to myself."

Wiping away my tears with my thumbs, I reply, "I need to talk to my doctor about that, and other stuff."

Jasper looks alarmed. "Oh, so you haven't been to the doc yet?"

I shake my head. "No. That's one of the reasons why I didn't tell you straight away. I wanted to make sure I was 100% pregnant, as those tests are not always accurate."

"One of the reasons?" Jasper questions, arching an eyebrow.

I bite my lip and nod. "Yeah. And the other is because I was too chicken shit to tell you. I'm sorry, I should have told you, but I just wanted to be sure. I mean this is… big. Really big," I reply.

Jasper nods. "I understand, Ava. I can imagine how hard it was. I'm an idiot for not guessing something was up. You could never resist my big blue eyes," he teases with a smile.

I smile, relieved he's making a joke instead of dumping my ass.

"So now that you know, I'll contact the doctor's office tomorrow to organize an appointment."

Jasper nods happily. "I'll come, too."

"You don't have to," I answer quickly, as my paranoia that this is too good to be true has taken over.

Jasper shakes his head stubbornly. "Like hell I don't. We're in this together."

I smile at his enthusiasm, grateful he has put my paranoia to rest.

"Okay."

"So, about this no sex stuff," he says, a big grin spreading from cheek to cheek.

That look gets me every time and I suddenly feel my insides heat.

"Is that really true?" he asks, brushing aside a lock of my hair and kissing just below my ear.

My skin prickles in awareness as he begins his descent down my neck and over my jaw, which he nips softly.

A low moan escapes my lips. "I'm not sure," I manage to get out. "But I will find out. Soon."

I gasp as he leads up to my ear, softly tugging on the lobe between his teeth.

"Good," he whispers into my ear.

He pulls back with a cocky smirk. My legs are about to turn into jelly.

"I love you, Ava. I love you so much. And now I have more of you to love."

Raising my eyebrow at him, I purse my lips. "You better not be referring to me growing into the size of a house," I half joke.

Jasper lets out a hearty laugh, but doesn't reply, leaving the comment hanging.

I slap him playfully on the chest, and he lets out a grunt on impact.

"I'm kiddin'." He grins. Latching onto my hand and holding it against his chest.

The steady beat of his heart drums lightly beneath my fingertips, and the feeling lulls me into a comfortable state.

He gives me a dimpled smile. "But even if you do get to the size of a house."

Raising both eyebrows this time, I give him a pointed look, daring him to continue.

He raises his hands in mock surrender as he continues, "Not that I'm saying you will. But even if you did, I would love you anyway. What I meant was, I have more of you to love, because we created a mini you."

"And you," I reply quickly.

Jasper nods, and I can see his brain ticking over the fact we have created something magical.

We have created a miracle.

He shakes his head, unbelieving. "A mini version of us. Our baby," he says. "Un-fucking-believable."

He looks at me like he's the happiest man in the world, and not for one second do I doubt that he just may be.

He surprises me by picking me up and lifting my feet off the ground, twirling me around until I am dizzy.

And even though the world is spinning around me, everything is the clearest it's been in days.

CHAPTER THIRTEEN
Doctor Love

"I'm sorry. Doctor Hemming won't be back till the twentieth of this month," the nasal voice barks at me from my iPhone.

"That's two weeks away," I say, annoyed, looking at the calendar hanging from a hook in the kitchen.

"Yes, Miss, I'm well aware of the date," she replies rudely. I can hear her clicking a pen incessantly while talking to me.

"Okay fine. I'll just wait till he returns," I respond, far from impressed with her so not helpful behavior.

I really don't want to wait, but what other choice do I have?

"Miss, you can see another doctor if it's urgent," she says casually. "I can book you in with…" she pauses, and I hear her tapping away at a keyboard. "Doctor Reger, today at four o'clock, if you like? And then you can discuss the results with Doctor Hemming when he returns, as the results usually take up to ten days to arrive."

Finally, the first lick of sense all day!

"That'll be perfect, thank you," I say on a quick breath.

After I hang up, I decide to sneak in some homework

before I have to face the reality of going to the doctor. All of this is so foreign to me, I need a handbook!

Hmm, I wonder if there is a handbook.

The doorbell chimes, which thankfully interrupts my thoughts.

Looking down at my bleach splotched yoga pants and baggy tank, I groan. I look like a total slob, as I was not expecting company. I really should change, but I don't have time. The doorbell chimes continuously, assaulting my eardrums.

I stalk through the living room, covering my hands over my ears to block out the racket.

"What?" I ask loudly, trying to be heard over the dinging as I pull the door open.

Before me, I see a humongous stuffed black cat, holding a love heart which reads, 'I'm Sorry.' He kinda looks like Oscar.

I raise my eyes higher to see a red, 'I'm Sorry' helium balloon attached to the cat's tail, catching in the wind. And if that isn't enough, my eyes fall to a huge bunch of mixed flowers with an, 'I'm Sorry' balloon, sitting in the center of the bouquet.

I peer up and see my best friend staring at me with red rimmed, raccoon smeared, anxious eyes. A tear slips down her colorless cheek, and I know there are more to follow. For once she's quiet, which is troubling, so I quickly put her out of her misery.

"So, I take it you're sorry," I say with a small smile, peering at the goods before me.

V drops everything she's holding onto the ground, wrapping her arms around my neck.

"Ava, I'm sorry! Oh, I'm such an idiot. I can't believe I told Jasper. It was out before I could stop myself. Please don't hate me. I'll do anything. I'll be your slave. I'll do your shopping. I'll be your personal masseuse. I'll even deliver your baby, just please forgive me," she says, finally out of breath.

I pull out of her embrace, smiling at her melodramatics. "Of course I don't hate you. This," I say, gesturing to her paraphernalia which is strewed on the floor, "wasn't necessary. But I'll take it anyway," I joke, grabbing the stuffed cat and flowers off the porch.

"This kinda looks like Oscar," I comment, holding up the stuffed animal.

V nods, her messy ponytail slipping out of its insecure clasp. "I know. That's why I got it. I knew you couldn't stay mad at me if I got you an Oscar lookalike."

I give her a challenging look, and her lower lip begins trembling uncontrollably.

"Come inside, you big crybaby." I smirk, holding the door open for her.

She wipes her eyes with the back of her sleeve, sniffing. "I can't believe you're not mad at me," she says as we walk towards the kitchen. She takes a seat on the barstool and I begin percolating some coffee, as this conversation requires a serious caffeine hit.

"It doesn't matter. In your own demented way you were sticking up for me. How can I be angry at you for voicing how I felt?" I question while watching the coffee filter.

"I know, but it wasn't my place to tell him, it was yours," she replies, tugging on her lip ring nervously.

I raise my hand to silence her, but decide to have some fun with her because she totally deserves it. "It doesn't matter. It's done now. I just have to accept that I'm going to be a single mom."

V's face is priceless. Her mouth drops open, and I can see the wheels churning, processing what I just said. She looks like she's about to have a mental breakdown.

"I'm joking," I quickly say, afraid she's going to collapse into the corner and begin rocking in the fetal position.

"Oh, that's a rotten joke, you bitch," she says, laughing. "But I guess I kinda deserved it."

"Damn straight you did," I reply, giggling.

"So, what happened?" she asks quietly, afraid of what I'm going to tell her.

What happened is that Jasper turned out to be the world's best boyfriend.

Feeling my cheeks tip up into a smile, V chuckles when she sees my glowing face. "No need to answer that."

Reaching for two mugs, I pour our much needed coffees, adding a splash of soy milk for me.

"He wants to have it, V. I've never seen him so happy before."

"And how do you feel about it?" she questions as I slide across her mug.

"Seeing his face light up when I told him he's going to be a dad," I pause. "It made my mind up for me. I want to have this baby."

V squeaks and claps excitedly. "I'm so happy for you two! Oh Ava, you're going to be a mommy." V's eyes begin to water and mine follow in quick succession.

"Oh, stop it," I chuckle, wiping my tears away with my fingers. "You're going to make me cry, and I won't know for certain until I go to the doctor."

V waves me off. "You know you have a little Jasper or Jaspette in there." She smirks, pointing at my belly.

I nod because this is the first time since I found out that it feels real, that I'm actually pregnant.

V smiles. "Okay, enough baby talk. Have you spoken to Jasper about New York?"

Okay, that's not at all random.

Her question throws me off and I begin stirring my coffee nervously. "No. There's nothing to discuss. I'm not going," I reply as I begin stirring my coffee more forcefully, making a scraping noise against the ceramic.

"I know you said that before. But now that Jasper knows about the baby, and is cool about it, you could work something out."

"There's nothing to work out," I reply, wishing she would just drop it already.

"That's not true, Ava. He has a right to know. You're in this together. A team. You have to tell Jasper."

"Tell me what?"

My stirring stops abruptly, and I look over V's shoulder to see Jasper standing in the doorway with a puzzled look on his face.

I close my eyes briefly and take a deep breath. As I reopen my eyes, I look at my friend, who has sunk guiltily into her seat.

"Sorry," she mouths when I glare at her.

"So, what do you have to tell me?" Jasper asks.

He casually walks over to the kitchen table, nabbing a green apple from the fruit bowl as he leans up against the counter. He takes a big bite and chews slowly, waiting for an answer.

"I, ah…" I stammer.

"I better go," V says, getting up faster than I have ever seen her move before.

She's halfway out the door when she sticks her head back in. "I got you Oscar in stuffed animal form. It means I'm forgiven, remember that."

Jasper cocks his eyebrow, totally lost, and I break out into half a smile before shooing her away with my hands.

"I will never understand you two." He smirks, shaking his head.

I give him a small smile, hoping he won't pursue what V and I were talking about.

Of course my hopes are shot when he asks, "So?"

Damn V and her mouth!

"It's no big deal," I utter nonchalantly, trying to shrug it off.

"Okay, well, in that case it shouldn't be a big deal to tell me."

He finishes off his apple and I shuffle out of his way so he can dispose of the core in the trash. He steps closer, waiting for me to continue.

I gulp.

"Sally was going to recommend me for a job at Metropolis," I blurt out quickly.

Jasper looks half relieved that the news is good. He

says in a quickened breath, "That's great, baby. I'm so proud of you!"

However, I wish it was good news, because it's not. "I can't accept it," I mumble, lowering my eyes.

"What? Why not? It's your dream come true."

I can hear the confusion echo in his voice and it crushes me.

To anyone but me this is a dream come true. But to me, it's just a dream that will never come true. I'll always be looking in on this dream with regret and disappointment.

Raising my eyes to his, I reply," It *was* my dream, but now, things are different."

Understanding glows in Jasper's big, blue eyes. "Just because we're having a baby doesn't mean you have to put your life on hold, Ava."

"It's in New York," I interrupt before I have to hear this speech a second time around.

Jasper's mouth parts. "Oh."

I nod. "Oh."

Jasper reaches forward and strokes the back of his fingers down my cheeks. "I'm sorry. I know how much this means to you."

I shake my head. "You mean more to me than anything in this world. Okay?" I say with sincerity, as every word of it is true.

Jasper nods, but I can see by the slight dip of his lips he doesn't believe me. I grasp his stubbled cheeks between my palms, needing him to believe me.

"Okay?" I ask again, searching his eyes.

"Okay." He smiles, but the gesture doesn't reach his eyes.

I give him a quick peck on the lips. "I love you, Jasper. Whatever sacrifices I have to make, I do for us."

And for once that '*Us*' doesn't scare me.

Jasper nods half-heartedly, but again his actions betray him.

He's silent for a moment and as his mouth droops into a frown, I know I'm not going to like what he has to say.

"Then I need to make sacrifices also."

"Like what? What would you have to sacrifice? Everything in your life can be juggled around having a baby," I reply quickly.

Jasper shakes his head. "Not everything," he answers sadly, meeting my eyes, and I know he means being in P.O.E. Traveling the world when you have a baby at home may be an issue.

Before I have time to question him, my home phone rings. Startled, I let out a small yelp. Looking at it angrily, not happy at the distraction, I answer it on the fifth ring.

"Hello."

It's the doctor's office.

"Aha. Oh okay, that should work," I reply, looking at the wall clock.

"Okay, thank you for the call. See you soon."

As soon as I place the phone back into the cradle, Jasper quickly questions, "Everything okay?"

I nod. "Yes, it was the doctor's office."

His face drops and I quickly add, "They said they can

fit me in today at two, instead of my original appointment at four, for my blood test."

Jasper's broad chest deflates as he exhales out a big breath.

He looks up at the clock. "Perfect. I'll drive."

I give him a big smile. "You still wanna come? It's only blood work, and it's not with my normal doctor."

Jasper returns my smile, and I see his dimple making a mischievous appearance. "Of course I'm coming."

He sets my skin on fire with a look that should be illegal. And I so should be used to that look, but I'm not.

He takes a step closer and licks his bow lips, toying with his sinful scar. "Anyway, I have a few questions."

No points for guessing what.

"**S**o, should she, or shouldn't she be lifting? And what about being on her feet all day?"

Okay, so when Jasper said he had a *few* questions, I didn't think he was going to ask every question known to mankind, sometimes twice. Who knew Jasper had so many questions? Subconsciously running my finger over the cotton wool taped over the crease in my elbow, I sorta feel like a bad mom for not having my own list.

"Well, she'll be fine as long as she doesn't over exert herself," she replies, looking at Jasper from her big oak desk, with a small smile on her wrinkled face.

"You might have a little morning sickness, lack of appetite, et cetera, but the symptoms vary for each individual," she explains, writing something down in my file. "Once Doctor Hemming is back from vacation, he'll be more than happy to address any other questions you may have, and also what comes next."

I nod, happy with the way she's answered all of Jasper's questions. And not judging me for my *lack* of questions.

"So what foods should she stay away from? I read she's unable to eat some things."

Whoa, what? Now that has my total attention for two reasons. Reason one, since when has Jasper been reading about pregnancies? And two, I can't eat certain foods? But I love eating!

"That's right Mr. Thompson. You have been busy reading, haven't you?" she says, giving him a small nod, her grey bun bopping vigorously.

I'm too busy worrying about the non-eating part to pay any attention to her addressing Jasper incorrectly.

"Oh, it's um, Mr. White," Jasper corrects awkwardly.

Doctor Reger frowns. "Oh sorry, my apologies. Back in my day, we didn't have much of a choice and had to change our maiden names," she explains, which actually confuses me further.

Maiden name?

Jasper shuffles uncomfortably beside me.

"We're not... married," Jasper replies. I can hear the embarrassment behind his words.

I, on the other hand, am still thinking about all the foods I have to sacrifice for the next... forever!

Doctor Reger clears her throat and turns a slight shade of red. She shuffles the paperwork in front of her, giving Jasper a strained smile.

"Oh, please excuse me for jumping to conclusions. Back in my day—"

"You were married before you had kids," Jasper finishes off quickly, rubbing his forehead.

I can tell he's uncomfortable talking about this, and I can't quite figure out why. I never took him for the traditional type, although marriage and kids has never really come up in conversation till well, now.

Marriage is the last thing on my mind, as I'm just getting used to the idea of becoming a mom. Being a wife, gee... that's a whole different kettle of fish.

I watch Jasper from the corner of my eye. He's fiddling with the pamphlet Doctor Reger gave him earlier, detailing the facts and myths about pregnancy. He looks deep in thought, with serious frown lines crinkling along his forehead.

I don't like how somber everyone is, so I do the only thing I can to lighten the mood. I ask my first and only question.

"So, Doctor Reger," I inquire.

Both she and Jasper focus their attention on me, grateful I've broken the silence.

"What's the rule with sex and being pregnant?"

My question seemed to loosen Jasper up slightly. Especially when we got the green light that sex and pregnancy is A-okay.

Woo hoo!

I thought Jasper would make good on that fact as soon as we left the doctor's office, but sadly, I was mistaken.

Jasper is preoccupied, chewing on his lower lip the whole drive home. He makes the automatic gestures when driving; indicating for lane changes, stopping at red lights, giving way, and so forth. But I know he isn't concentrating on anything other than what went down with Doctor Reger.

I don't want to interrupt him, as I too am going over all the things I discovered today. And some of those things just blow my mind.

I shuffle through the stack of brochures the doctor gave me, and draw back when I see a picture of someone giving birth. The pained expression on her face sends me into a tiny panic, as I haven't given much thought to that part, and I'm going to keep it that way until I *have* to think about it.

"Did you want me to drop you off at home?" Jasper asks, breaking the silence. When he sees me hesitate, he simply says, "I'm working tonight."

Oh yeah, of course. I forgot he had a shift at the shelter tonight.

"Sure," I nod, not liking the sudden distance between us.

I need to find out what he's thinking; otherwise it'll eat at me all night.

"What's wrong, Jasper?" I ask, placing my hand on his knee, which is poking through a hole in his blue jeans.

He's quiet for a moment. "Nothing is wrong. I'm just..."

He leaves the sentence unfinished, and pulls a right to turn onto the freeway.

"You're what?" I question uneasily, fiddling with the corner of a brochure.

Jasper shakes his head, his long rich locks spilling into his eyes.

"Nothing, baby, don't worry about it. Forget I said anything."

I don't press the issue, because judging by the hard resolve of his sharp jaw, I know he won't elaborate further.

I let out a small sigh and drop it... for now.

CHAPTER FOURTEEN
Sex on Fire

I'm lying on my bed, staring up at the ceiling with my hands interlaced over my tummy, deep in thought. Listening to my iPod usually helps me relax, but sadly tonight, it's just background noise, as all I can think about is Jasper's strange behavior after the doctor's today.

I guess listening to "Slipped Away" by Avril Lavigne is not really helping my mood.

Is he having second thoughts about the whole thing?

Being at the doctor's made everything so *real*, and maybe it has sunken in that this is really happening, and he's going to be a dad. God knows it has taken me forever to get used to the idea. Even now, I'm still trying to get my head around it.

A little voice inside of me whispers, "He's freaking out and will be on the next plane outta here."

I squash down that voice because I know Jasper would never do that. But that incessant voice keeps hounding me till I throw a pillow over my face, in attempts to block it out.

Ugh, I need to get out of this funk.

Throwing the pillow off my face, I look over at the clock which reads 11:24p.m. It's too late to do anything.

Or is it?

As "Sex on Fire" by Kings of Leon comes blaring through my headphones, I am struck with a brilliant idea.

I leap out of bed, shuffling around to the music while plotting out my ingenious plan.

I feel ridiculous. And I bet I look ridiculous.

My ingenious plan isn't so genius now that I'm actually acting it out. I'm a tad chilly and am getting a slight cramp, but I have no time to chicken out because the front door downstairs has just closed.

My plans of escape are long gone.

Rearranging myself, I shuffle up the bed quietly, listening intently.

I can hear bottles in the fridge rattle as Jasper opens the door, no doubt standing in front of it, the dim light inside bouncing off his perfect features as he grabs a beer.

I hope he's not hungry, as I can't remain in this position much longer without losing face.

Thankfully, I hear his heavy footsteps trudge up the stairs, and my insides do a tiny flip-flop in excitement, and trepidation.

This is it, Ava. You're a strong, powerful sexy woman. My goals are more important than my fear. I am the lioness of the jungle, ready to pounce.

Who the hell uses these positive affirmations, because they are so not helping right now!

Taking a deep, steady breath as Jasper opens his bedroom door, I can see he's taken aback when confronted with the millions of candles I have laid around the bedroom, trying to set a mood, and hopefully, not setting the house on fire in the process.

"What the..." he gasps, and then his eyes land on his bed.

Well, they land on me.

I am lying on his bed, in the most seductive pose I can muster, without looking like a total dweeb.

"Ava?" he asks as he steps into his bedroom, slightly stunned to see me sprawled on his bed like a Playboy Bunny.

"Happy birthday," I reply softly, giving him my best attempt at 'bedroom eyes.'

I practiced in the mirror for about twenty minutes, so it better come across as sexy, and not like I'm severely cross-eyed.

He strolls over to the end of the bed, looking down where I lay, propped up on one elbow with a knee bent, gazing up at him.

"Th-thanks," he stutters while eying my body not so discreetly.

Win for me! Jasper, who is usually so eloquent, is lost for words.

Smoothing out my black chiffon nightgown, which scarcely covers my bare skin, Jasper watches intently as my hands glide over my flesh. I demand the blush about to creep over my body to keep away, because now is not the time for modesty.

He licks his bow lips and runs a hand through his

hair, fisting it into a messy peak. He looks amazing. Even at 2a.m., after working all night, he looks as if he's stepped off a runway in his grey sleeveless hoodie and faded blue jeans, which are tucked into his loosely tied, scuffed combat boots.

"Are you my birthday present?" he asks, his eyes lingering on the sheer material at my breasts.

Before I have a chance to answer or blush he adds, "Because if you are, I want to unwrap you now."

As his gaze dips lower, I feel my face redden. But I need to get over my bashfulness because I'm here for a reason.

"Take off your shirt," I command. Wow, that sounded a little bossy. So I add, "Please."

Jasper raises a dark eyebrow and gives me a small smirk, but he happily complies. He lifts his arms and reaches behind, just below his neck, which in turn, flexes his upper arms very, very nicely. He yanks the top off over his head, and as the garment is lifted, it's like all my Christmases have come at once.

As he unceremoniously tugs the garment off over his head, he has messed up his hair further, and it sweeps across his face at different angles. I eye the dip between his collarbones and my tongue on its own accord, slips out, wetting my parted lips, desperate to lick the crevice repeatedly.

His chest is totally hairless, but as my eyes slowly descend to his glorious, hardened abs, I let out an involuntary gasp, as the candlelight illuminates the light dusting of hair on his stomach, which travels down into his hip hugging jeans. The flickers of candlelight have turned his soft, milky skin into golden, rigid planes.

Holy shit, he is fucking mind blowing!

"You're beautiful," I whisper aloud.

Slightly embarrassed by my choice of words, I gingerly meet his gaze.

"I think I should be the one telling you that, although beautiful doesn't even skim the surface of how incredible you look, sprawled out on my bed half naked."

Giving him a small smile, I watch hungrily as he steps out of his boots and crawls towards me from the end of the bed. I lie down slowly, welcoming the weight of his body on mine.

Our faces are mere inches apart, as his hands rest on the pillow beside my head, holding his full weight off me. I can't help myself as I tongue my lower lip, peering into his profound cerulean eyes.

"I love you, Jasper."

"I love you, Ava," he replies quickly, leaning down and capturing my mouth with his.

The kiss is fueled with emotion and urgency, and I embrace it with both hands as I reach up and fist his silken hair between my fingers. I know I'm pulling a little hard, but judging by his muffled moans, Jasper is enjoying the intensity.

With one hand still resting alongside my head holding up his weight, the other begins a slow, torturous journey of my body. His skilled fingers skim over my neck, running down across my breasts, and I know he can feel my pebbled nipples peaking through the sheer lace, as I am totally naked underneath.

I buck underneath him when his hand slips lower, brushing over the apex of my thighs, and I want him to be on me, in me, so I open my legs wider, showing him where I want him to be.

Thankfully he reads me loud and clear. He trails his fingertips up my bare thigh, finally touching my center.

"Holy fuck," he hisses when he feels how much I want him.

He knows what I'm craving, so he slips in his index finger and like a true musician, he plays me like an instrument made only for him.

Closing my eyes, I arch my back, wanting to take him in as deep as he will go. A low moan passes through my parted lips as he increases the speed, and then adds another punishing finger. I am all but riding his hand shamelessly, but I can't stop.

Jasper is panting quietly, and I know he's getting turned on, watching the way my body is responding to him.

I was made for him, and he knows all the right moves to have me mewling like a sex-crazed fiend in a matter of seconds.

But he surprises me as he suddenly removes his fingers.

My eyes snap open and I'm about to protest loudly, but he leans back on his heels and places his hand under my lower back. He raises my hips off the bed, so I'm high enough that he's able to slip off my nightgown by the hem, which he tosses over his shoulder.

Wow, now I am really, really naked.

Jasper's body then covers mine once again, and he

smashes his lips to my eager mouth, giving me the kiss of all kisses. I'm so lost in the feel of his mouth on mine, and I never want this feeling of rightness between us to ever fade.

Jasper tears his lips away from mine and I pout.

He rewards me with a grin. "Oh, don't worry, I'm not finished with you."

His promise sends a shiver down my body, and my skin breaks out into tiny goose bumps.

He kisses everywhere, leaving no part of me untouched. He pays extra attention to my heavy nipples, sucking on them for longer than I can handle. He knows my limits, because just as I'm about to beg for a release, he moves down my stomach and over to my hip, where he places a soft kiss.

"I've missed this between us," he says, looking up at me from between my legs, which is an erotic sight, as he is all tousled hair and swollen, pink lips.

I nod because it's all I am capable of.

"However, I have especially missed this," he whispers, dipping lower and kissing over my core.

I groan, and he takes that as my permission to continue.

And boy, does he continue.

The feeling of his wet tongue coiling deeply inside of me, slipping in and out of my body, sends me wild. I know I'm bucking crazily as Jasper has a firm grip on my upper thighs, attempting to hold me still. But his actions have the opposite effect and my head thrashes from side to side, as his clever mouth is working me over until there's nothing left for me but to explode.

However, just before I'm about to come undone, Jasper pulls away. I almost hold his head so he can't move.

He lets out a small laugh and licks his lips. "Don't worry, baby. I'll take care of you."

I know he's referring to something other than taking care of me sexually, but all thoughts are put on hold as he hastily unzips his jeans, tugs them off, and within seconds, he's poised at my entrance, looking down at me.

"Thank you." He smiles.

"For what?" I gasp as he eases the tip of himself inside of me.

"For the best present ever."

Raising a confused eyebrow, I'm about to ask what he means, but Jasper clarifies softly, "You."

He pushes into me steadily, allowing me to feel every hot inch of him.

I let out a small gasp as he fills me to the brim, but as he starts moving slowly, my body welcomes him home.

He quickens the pace as he feels me relaxing around him, and I encourage him to move faster as I rear up and bite him on the neck, sucking gently.

"Fuck," he curses, and obliges by driving deeply into me.

He pulls his throat away and crushes his lips to mine when he feels my body trembling in pleasure beneath him. We're all tongue and open mouth kisses, and even though he's inside me in a way that unites two people in the closest way possible, he isn't close enough. So I grind my hips against him, rotating my pelvis and the angle is... perfect.

Holy shit! I can feel myself beginning to come undone, but I know Jasper isn't close.

"Let me see your face when you come," Jasper says huskily, pulling his mouth away from mine to look into my eyes.

It takes all the willpower in the world to speak. "No."

I want to do this together.

I've waited so long for this to happen, I can wait a while longer until he's ready to come apart, too.

He drives his hips into me faster, and harder, and just at the right angle to brush over my core. A pleasured moan echoes in my chest, and I see a smug smile pass over his lips.

However, my plan tonight was to drive him crazy. I wanted him to focus on the moment of me and him becoming one, and forgetting all our worries, just for one night. I'll be damned if I don't achieve what I've come here to do.

I focus, and with what little resolve I have left, I turn and flip him over with my legs, so I'm straddling him. He looks up at me, surprised by my swift move, and that I was able to catch him off guard, as the whole movement was done while he was still inside me.

With me on top, I'm in control, and now I'm the one wearing the smug smile.

Placing my hands on his slippery chest for leverage, I begin rocking my hips against him. Jasper lets out a loud groan, throwing his head back, his tousled hair spilling over the pillow. I raise my hips and then slam back down onto him, taking him deeper into me.

"Oh, fuck! Holy fuck," Jasper pants, his eyes squeezed tight.

Not missing a thrust, I lean down and bite his strong, stubbled jaw, and he lets out a cry of ecstasy, enjoying the pain. I relish in his passion-filled whimpers, so craving more, I kiss my way down his smooth neck, sucking lightly. His steady pulse is pounding under my lips, and as I increase the pressure, the tempo increases, betraying just how turned on he is.

The feel of him in me, soaked into my every pore, is one that inspires artists to create works of art, because this feeling of complete fullness, with another, compares to nothing else.

His hips begin slamming into me and I welcome everything he gives.

He reaches down, rubbing his thumb over my core, and I throw my head back, unable to stop myself as I scream out my release, my hips pumping into him wildly, milking him. He follows a second later, crying out my name in winded breaths.

Holy fuck! Wow.

My heart is threatening to beat out of my chest and I collapse on top of him, very unceremoniously, with a loud thud. We are breathless, sticky, and totally satisfied.

After a few moments of catching our breaths, I feel Jasper lightly stroking my lower back.

"Happy birthday," I mumble as my face is pressed into his heated chest.

I hear the deep chuckle resonate within his body. "Thank you. Best birthday gift... ever."

Letting out a small chuckle, the minx in me whispers, "I'm not done giving you all of your gifts just yet."

Jasper groans. "Well, in that case, I'm more than happy to receive."

And for the next few hours, Jasper White receives gift, after gift, after gift.

After gift.

CHAPTER FIFTEEN
Harmonies Sucks

My body feels numb. Pleasurably numb, but numb all the same.

I crack open an eye as the smell of cinnamon wafts through the room, making my mouth water. Sitting on the bedside table is a bowl of cereal and a steaming mug of chai tea. But my breakfast can wait, because the sight before me demands my full attention—Jasper's naked back.

Taking in his glorious, stripped form, I can't take my eyes off him as he sits casually at his desk, sipping a cup of coffee while reading the paper. His hair is due for a cut, as the strands at the back of his neck curl up rebelliously.

He clears his throat, which interrupts my ogling. How does he know I am totally checking him out?

"Hi," I squeak when he spins around, seeing that his naked back matches his naked bottom.

My eyes linger between his legs, and obscene images plague my mind for about five seconds before I mentally slap myself to refocus.

"Why aren't you wearing pants?" I ask. My gaze falls to his crotch once again.

So much for focusing! The only thing I can focus on

is Jasper in all of his naked glory. A big grin spreads from cheek to cheek when he witnesses me almost swallow my tongue.

"What's the point? They're just going to come off as soon as I get into bed with you."

I can't help the giggle that escapes me. "Really?"

"Really," he confirms, nodding cheekily.

Folding up the paper, he stands tall, and just for show, he stretches his arms above his head, showing off his lean, taut body.

OH MY GOD!

"Get over here, you big show off."

I'm surprised I'm capable of speech right now, considering all the saliva collecting in my mouth at the sight of him being naked, very naked.

He gives me a crooked, dimpled grin. "Hey, it's my birthday, you gotta be nice to me," he says as he walks over to the bed, giving me a vision that has been scorched into my brain and eyeballs for an eternity.

With my eyes downcast, I reply, "Oh, I don't plan on being nice. I plan on being very, very *bad.*"

Jasper wasn't joking when he said he wanted to spend the whole day in bed for his birthday.

In between catching light naps and awakening to Jasper coaxing my body to come undone, time and time again, I'm absolutely spent.

Sadly, the day of lulled lovemaking has come to an end, as we're due at the karaoke bar in half an hour.

Even the word karaoke is freakin' lame.

Jasper is singing happily in the shower, and as tempted as I am to join him, I decide against it as we're already running late.

As I'm deciding what to wear, my phone chimes in my handbag, which I left sitting on Jasper's desk. I search for it in the clutter, and curse myself for not throwing out the unnecessary junk I've thrown in here.

When the phone stops ringing, my eyes pass over the newspaper Jasper was reading this morning. Cocking a confused eyebrow, I see there are big red circles in the employment section of the paper.

Reaching for it, as I want to get a closer look, I'm surprised to see the number of jobs Jasper has circled. He has highlighted almost every job available, and some are really, really shitty jobs.

Why is he looking for work? And why is he settling for just about anything, when he's more than capable to work at places which don't require him to be elbow deep in bacon grease?

Jasper is done in the shower, so I quickly replace the paper on the tabletop, not wanting to appear like I've been snooping.

But why do I have a sinking feeling that when I get down to the bottom of this, I'm really not going to like it?

Ugh, Ava, I scold myself. Snap out of it!

We're nearly at the karaoke bar and I'm trying my hardest not to frown, but I can't help it.

I can't stop thinking about that newspaper I found in Jasper's room.

I know this desperate search for work has got to do with some ancient belief of him having to support us. But he's got a job at the shelter, and if he's working all day, how can he practice with P.O.E?

I still have that sinking feeling, and it's only getting gloomier by the minute.

"You worried about tonight?" Jasper asks, snapping me out of my thoughts.

I look over at him, confused.

"You know, being at a karaoke bar and seeing my mom," he says, toying with his lip.

I hate he feels this way. And I especially hate he feels this way on his birthday.

"No, I'm not worried," I reply, turning to face him. "Everything about today is perfect. You're perfect."

Jasper's mouth turns up into a smile.

"Oh crap!" I yelp.

Well, it was perfect, until I forgot something vital.

"What's wrong?" Jasper asks quickly, his eyes meeting mine. "Are you okay? Is it the baby?"

Giving him a small smile, I reply, "Me and the baby are fine."

"Then what is it?" he asks as we pull into the parking lot.

I look at the big, flashing neon sign, which reads... Harmonies.

You've got to be shitting me!

Out of all the karaoke bars in Los Angeles, why did Jasper's mom have to pick this one? The one that has the same name as one of Jasper's admirers, who not that long ago told me they shared a 'special bond.'

I already feel nauseous.

Jasper can read my apprehension instantly, but remains silent.

Taking a breath, I try and forget the flashing sign taunting me with every flicker.

"I forgot to give you your birthday present," I say, answering his earlier question.

Jasper turns off the car and shifts to face me with a smug smirk.

"No, your real present," I explain, shaking my head at his cheek. "I was just a bonus," I add, giving him a small wink.

Jasper laughs. "I'm quite happy with what you've already given me. But if you want to give me more *presents*, I'll happily accept" he says, using the word 'present' as if it's a code word for sex.

He can't be serious. He surely can't have any stamina left. Can he?

Judging by the way he's looking at me, I think he has more than enough to last him a week.

"I can't help it." He smiles. "Look at yourself."

I look down at my torn blue jeans, chucks and navy top, which have three slits cut out of the short sleeves, confused. Yes, the top is tight and sits low because of the U shape neckline, but it's nothing special.

"You're just insatiable," I reply, shrugging off his comment.

He nods, his blue eyes shining. "When it comes to you, I am. And knowing that you're carrying my baby makes me want you all the more."

This is the first time we've really spoken about the baby since the doctor's. I know it's a conversation we'll have to have, and soon, but I thought it could wait till after his birthday.

I blush slightly, but joke, "You won't say that when I'm waddling down the street, devouring a family size pizza by myself."

Jasper gives me a crooked smile. "No matter what, I will always want you." He says it with such conviction; I can't help but believe him.

All this baby talk reminds me of something I've wanted to discuss with him since the doctor's.

"Jasper, would it be okay if we didn't tell your mom? Until we get the results."

I haven't even thought about telling my parents. Shit, that's a conversation I'll put off, until I can't hide my growing tummy.

Speaking of which.

My weight hasn't altered at all. Maybe I can get through this pregnancy without looking like a beached whale.

"Of course. Whatever you want. Just tell me what to do, and I'll do it," he replies, squeezing my hand.

I smile at his choice of words.

"We need to sit down and go through what we're going to do. What our plans are..." But I zip it because I am starting to sound like a party pooper.

But Jasper nods. "I know."

"But not right now." I smile. "Because right now, my best friend is about to charge toward the car, eager to live out her Madonna dreams."

Jasper looks over his shoulder, chuckling when he witnesses V blowing a raspberry on the window.

He laughs and shakes his head at her.

"C'mon, birthday boy. It's your turn to shine."

CHAPTER SIXTEEN

I'm a Rockstar

"This is so lame," V says, sipping her lemon margarita from a swirly straw.

Surprisingly, she has waited for Jasper and Lucas to go to the bar to voice her disgust at the lamest place on earth, which is Harmonies.

If you looked *lame* up in the dictionary, they would have a picture of this place beside it. The carpeted floors resemble the color of tricolored vomit, and maroon barstools and lounges are strategically placed around the makeshift stripper stage, pole included. The stage is circular, so everyone in the room can witness one making an absolute fool of oneself while belting out songs that are, yup, you guessed it.... lame. It's so dim in this place, and the only real lighting comes from the pink fluorescents hanging above the stage. The TVs that are placed around the venue have cheap animation dancing around on them while the lyrics being sung at the time pop up on the screen, encouraging others to sing along.

Goes without saying, it doesn't encourage me in the slightest.

The only thing going for this place is that the bar is well stocked, not that it matters to me. I sigh while sipping my bland mineral water.

V huffs as she rests her chin in her palm, drumming her fingers against her cheek, uninterested.

"Hopefully Jasper can bash out a song to shut his mom up, and then we can get the hell outta here," I say, but I know better.

V shrugs. "I'm just going to get drunk. Everything is more fun when you're drunk. Although, this place just sucks the fun right outta everything."

I let out a small giggle, but mope. "At least you *can* get drunk. I have to settle for boring." I pick up my glass and salute her, taking an unsatisfying sip.

V gives me a sympathetic smile. "This whole place is boring. Who the hell comes to these places by choice?"

I raise my eyebrow at her. "Hey, don't look at me."

V slurps up the entire contents of her margarita, and frowns when looking up at some random belting out Michael Jackson's "Thriller," dance moves and all.

"Nope, still no fun," she says, huffing out another breath.

I couldn't agree more, and my only idea of fun, being in the form of Jasper, is still MIA.

I glance around the venue, trying to catch a glimpse of him, but of course I can't see anything due to the crappy lighting. Thankfully, the Michael Jackson wannabe finishes his poor rendition of "Thriller" and the stage lights come up as he takes a bow. Yes, I am serious.

As soon as the lights shine, my heart drops into my stomach and I grab onto the table, in fear of slipping off my seat.

"Ava, what's wrong? Are you going to be sick?" V

asks, reaching for my stiff hand. I've got a death grip on the table.

I shake my head, unable to speak, as my eyes are still glued to the bar.

"What the hell?" she asks, following my line of sight, hoping to make sense of my transformation into a mute.

She turns back to me quickly, her pigtails whipping her in the face. "What. The. Fuck?" she demands, her voice raising an octave.

My mouth is agape and I shrug limply, because I have no freakin' clue why Indie and a horde of about fifteen Harpies are surrounding Jasper at the bar. Of course the leader of the pack is Danielle.

My heart sinks when I observe Indie giving Jasper an overly affectionate hug. But thankfully, Jasper doesn't return her embrace as he stands immobile, his hands dug deep in his pockets, leaning against the bar. However, he looks totally ill at ease when Indie attempts to give him an open mouthed kiss on the lips. He pushes her away lightly, shaking his head. She, of course, pouts, appearing surprised at his rejection.

I inadvertently tighten my grip on the table, which creaks in protest.

"Take a deep breath, Ava," V says, concerned.

I seriously doubt a deep breath will contain the flames of hell burning in my stomach right now.

"Why the hell is Indie here? And who are all the hoochies?" V questions me.

As I look at Danielle, who is standing off to the side, looking dotingly at Jasper and Indie, I know the answer lies with her. She'll stop at nothing until she gets Jasper and Indie together. Although, as I witness her push some random blonde girl with huge boobs and a pixie hair cut into Jasper's face, I know she'll settle for anyone, as long as she's not me.

Well, she has another thing coming. She wants to play dirty, then so can I.

"Ava, um, what are you doing?" V asks as she peers over at me.

I have bent down low and shoved my hands down my top, rearranging the girls to make them work for me in this low slung top.

"Showing those bitches that Jasper is mine," I reply as I stand up, quickly walking over to the DJ's booth before I lose my nerve.

I don't know what the hell is wrong with me, and I hate that I feel I need to prove a point. But it's either this, or I tell Danielle exactly how I feel about her, divulging it all. In the end, this is the better option. It'll embarrass the hell out of me, but the satisfaction will be well worth it.

Avoiding eye contact with anyone other than the DJ, I ask him if he has what I'm looking for.

He thankfully gives me a thumbs up and I linger off to the side. I'm nervously biting my black painted finger-nails, waiting for my turn to shine. Maybe this wasn't such a good idea. I reacted impulsively when I saw Jasper being pawed by a group of girls who would do anything to get into his pants.

And of course, a switch inside of me flipped to crazy, when I saw his mom glowing when anyone other than me was touching her son.

So, goes without saying the song I have chosen is directed at two people.

"Okay folks, we have a request for something a little edgier. She's pre-warned me that she can't sing to save her life." The crowd lets out a soft laugh, and I'm all but hyperventilating. "But she's going to be a good sport and give it a go. Ava Thompson, it's your turn to bring the house down!" the DJ says in a vivacious voice, attempting to rev up the crowd.

My heart starts beating madly and my feet stay cemented to the ground.

Holy shit, I really need to think before I act!

"C'mon girl, I can see you hiding back there. Get your ass up here." The DJ nods, giving me an encouraging smile.

I realize I have just drawn more attention to myself, so I step out from my hiding spot and receive a huge supportive wolf whistle from, you guessed it.

"Go, Ava, go!"V whistles loudly.

Ascending the three steps, I take my place behind the microphone stand, which is way too tall for me.

I attempt to adjust it, but the stand topples forward. Luckily I catch it in time before someone loses an eye. The feedback from the sudden movement is ear splitting, and I avoid covering my ears because as I attempt to correct the position, the microphone suddenly drops with a loud thud onto the stage, causing more feedback.

Great, like this wasn't awkward enough!

The DJ runs over to save me, and the silence in the room is deafening.

I seriously just heard the toilet flush!

The DJ looks at me, giving me a big smile while whispering, "You're going to be great. Show those bitches who's boss."

His words loosen me up somewhat and I stifle a chuckle behind my hand.

My eyes are lowered, as I'll chicken out if I meet anyone's gaze. Being up here actually shows me how brave Jasper is for doing this time and time again, and making it appear so effortless. That fact alone gives me the guts to lift my eyes and search the room for the people I'm singing to.

Indie and Danielle.

I am an incensed woman on a warpath when I see Indie standing near Jasper, making sure some part of her body is touching his. As I meet her venom-laced stare, she narrows her eyes, glaring at me something wicked.

My eyes wander on their own accord to Jasper, who is totally ignoring Indie, and looking up at the stage with a baffled, but intrigued look. When I catch his eye, I give him a quick wink, totally stealing his stage moves.

He returns my gesture with a small shake of his head, but I can't ignore the amused, dimpled smile spreading from cheek to cheek.

The drumsticks count in the intro, and as soon the music starts, something takes over and I get a surge of cool confidence. Suddenly, my inner rock goddess comes charging out of me... loudly.

I'm not much of a singer, and this is the reason why I've chosen "The Curse" by Devil Doll.

Taking nothing away from Devil Doll, who is one of my all time favorite singers, this song is one I can fake my way through. And instead of singing, I can half talk, half sing my way through it.

Every word I sing is directed at Indie, as the words are perfect. It was like this song was written for me, especially when I give her a look to complement the lyrics of staying away from my man.

As I get through the first verse without passing out, I get a little more poise and meet the eyes of the patrons around me. I notice most of the lady clientele are up from their chairs dancing, cheering me on, or saluting me with their drinks.

I know the reason behind their gusto. Every female has had an Indie in their life, so this song is for them all.

This song is for us.

I feel empowered, and as I begin the chorus, I open up my lungs and go nuts.

Unhooking the microphone from the stand, I begin stalking the small stage, not needing the TV with the lyric prompts, as I know this song word for word. I love being able to interact with my fellow comrades, high-fiving a couple of palms as their owners are en route to the bar.

By the second verse, I'm living out my rock star dreams, and adding little uncoordinated dance moves to accompany my singing.

I look ridiculous, but as I meet Jasper's eyes and witness him laughing hysterically, holding onto Lucas for support and hooting loudly for me, it's all so worth it.

But what makes this even more worthwhile is the look on Indie's face.

And also on Danielle's.

I have accomplished all I wanted by coming up here, but just to add salt to the wound, I stalk to the edge of the stage and direct my glare at Indie when the spoken word part of the song commences. I spit out the words, putting all my passion and frustration behind it. And when I snarl the words about chicks wanting your man, I point at Indie and wag my finger at her, making it clear I won't stand for her shit a moment longer, or I will totally stiletto her ass.

That earns me a ruckus of hoots, wolf whistles, and applause from all the women in the room. I belt out the last few lines with as much oomph as I can, and it feels good, because I know Indie and Danielle understand I mean business.

Once the song ends, I take a small curtsy and the room erupts into a round of applause. I even get a standing ovation. I give everyone a small wave and scurry over to the DJ to give him the microphone. During my Diva moment, I kicked over the microphone stand and I don't know where it ended up.

"You showed her, that skanky bitch," he says, giving me a quick kiss on the cheek.

Letting out a huge laugh, I thank him before running off, because without the microphone, I've lost my nerve.

On the way back to my table, I am high-fived, congratulated, and patted on the back by random women who have stopped me, wanting to tell me what a great performance it was. I give them all a shy smile, totally embarrassed that I just wailed like a wounded hyena in a roomful of complete strangers.

Oh well, everyone seemed to enjoy themselves, me included. So, fuck it.

After finally getting through the sea of vengeful women, I'm confronted by a pair of amused cerulean eyes.

The fact that I just attempted to sing and dance in front of a roomful of people hits home, and I can feel my skin turning a bright pink.

This just earns a bigger laugh from Jasper. "Gee, watch out, world. A star is born. You can totally duet with me any day." He chuckles and I slap him lightly on the arm.

"Shut up," I say, blushing further.

"Oh, come here." He smirks, his left dimple highlighting his amusement.

I walk into his outstretched arms and he pulls me close, whispering into my ear. "I kinda liked you going all *Basic Instinct* cross *Glee*. Real turn on," he adds while kissing my neck.

I smirk, feeling ecstatic that even though I made a right royal fool of myself, Jasper gets it. And so do Indie and Danielle, who are giving me the biggest stink eye known to mankind.

"C'mon, Diva." Jasper smirks, grabbing my hand and leading me over to the table. "Let's give them something to *really* be pissed over."

I raise my eyebrow, and just before we sit, Jasper pulls me towards him and lays one of the most delicious kisses on my stunned mouth. At first I'm taken aback, but that lasts for about two seconds, because when he slips in his tongue, I match his passion, kiss for kiss.

And just in case they haven't received the message loud and clear, Jasper dips me dramatically while our lips are still connected.

I let out a muffled laugh, and can hear disapproving grunts from our table at our scorching PDA.

But you know what?

They can all suck it.

CHAPTER SEVENTEEN
No Holding Back

"You said an hour," V whispers while drowning her curly fries in ketchup.

I speak out of the side of my mouth. "I'm enjoying this just as much as you are. So shut it."

We have been here for over an hour, and it has been the most painful hour of my life.

There are roughly twenty people sitting around our long table, and most are female. Some faces I know, like Jasper's band mates and their partners, but the others, I have no idea who they are. And I don't want to know, because the majority of them are glaring at me for breathing.

"So Jasper, when are you playing Rip It Up?" asks the pixie looking blonde with stars in her eyes.

She's the one who was all but shoved into Jasper's crotch by Danielle. I've seen her and Indie giggle and whisper to one another all night. It goes without saying I hate her already.

"Um, we're playing the 5th so, in a couple of weeks or so," he answers between sips of his beer.

She nods way too animatedly, waiting for him to elaborate, which he doesn't.

"So Jasper," pipes up a redhead, sitting across from

us. "Who are you guys playing with?" she asks, twirling a piece of hair around her finger suggestively.

No doubt, she's another of Jasper's stalkers, and I actually have to restrain myself from banging my head on the tabletop repeatedly.

The only good thing about tonight is that Danielle and Indie haven't said a word to me. It's still awkward, but thankfully I don't have to see Danielle, as Jasper is blocking her from my line of sight. Of course she insisted he sit near her, and then had the nerve to suggest Indie sit on the other side of him. Jasper put that suggestion quickly to rest as he placed me to his right, and his mom to the left.

"Jasper, darling, are you going to sing?" Danielle asks.

Jasper shrugs, peeling the label off his Budweiser.

"Yeah, maybe later," he replies casually, and I don't know if I'm reading into things, but he's been quite cold and dismissive towards her all evening.

In a circumstance where I would usually encourage him to be nicer to her, I don't. As I look around the table, of all the faces of the girls that are here, there's no doubt that some of them have seen more of Jasper than I care to think about. I know Danielle invited these girls with the intent to make me feel uncomfortable. And obviously, inviting Indie over for dinner wasn't enough punishment for me.

But funnily enough, her plan once again has back-fired, and has Jasper seeing her true colors. In a situation where she's attempted to drive a wedge between Jasper and I, she has inadvertently done that between him and herself. I have no sympathy for her in the slightest, and the only person I feel sorry for is Jasper.

Looking at him, I instantly feel for him, as he's trying his hardest to appear interested in some pointless conversation he's engaging in with some random brunette. I can see by the hard set of his jaw and the strain around his eyes that he's not having a good time. He's not one to make idle chitchat with the ghosts of his past. His mom doesn't know him at all. And sadly, I think Jasper is starting to see that.

"Jasper, do you remember the time we went to Blackout?" Indie asks with an edge to her voice.

I feel Jasper tense up and I don't like it. I suddenly wonder where she's going with this.

V mumbles under her breath, "Seriously, I am going to kill her."

I pass her a goblet of my untouched Red without a word.

"This is the only thing keeping me from going homicidal on her ass," she says before taking a big sip. She makes a pained face. "And it isn't even any good."

Lucas gives her a small kiss on the forehead and smiles. "I'm proud of you, babe. You're showing great restraint."

I let out a small laugh because I agree with him. However, as I hear Danielle speak, I wish I could show the same restraint as my friend.

"Jasper, Indiana asked you a question," she scolds like he's eight years old.

The hackles on the back of my neck instantly prickle in rage. And Jasper's hand, which is entwined in mine, squeezes gently. He can sense my irritation, but he's asking me to calm down.

Out of respect for him, I do.

"Yes, Indie, I remember. So?" he replies, annoyed.

I risk a glance at her and celebrate when I witness her looking a little offended at his curt response.

She purses her lips and flicks her blonde mane over her shoulder. "Do you remember what happened in the Pavilion? Or does your memory need refreshing?" she says, winking before shooting me a dirty look.

This time I give Jasper's hand a squeeze, but it is anything *but* gentle.

He exhales noisily and reaches for his beer like it's his savior. He takes a big sip and licks his wet lips when he's done. Every female at the table follows the movement, fantasizing about what that tongue is capable of.

Jasper interlaces his hands behind his head, looking extremely smug as he replies, "It mustn't have been that great, as I can't remember anything but the bands. However, what I *do* remember is you bitching and moaning about the mud, and how sore your feet were, due to the stripper heels you were wearing."

My mouth falls open, surprised at his tone, but what he says next drops my jaw to the ground.

"So, if that's what you're referring to, in regards to refreshing my memory, then no thanks. I'm reminded of it every time I see you."

I am so resembling a goldfish right now, my mouth opening and closing, incapable of speech. The table is suddenly silent, and everyone's eyes are on Indie and Jasper.

Well, everyone is silent except for V, of course, who snorts loudly, and then breaks into fits of laughter.

I really don't know what to do, so I bite my lip, hoping to stop my own bubbles of laughter, which are threatening to burst free at any moment.

Indie's mouth is hanging open and her eyes are bugging out of her head. I wish I could photograph this moment, as I would gladly frame the happy snap and give it to Danielle, seeing as she loves pictures of Indie so much.

After a few seconds of silence, Jasper leans down and kisses my cheek freely. He then tilts back into his seat to call out to Lucas, asking him what the basketball scores are, totally ignoring a fuming Indie.

Out of the corner of my eye, I see Indie and three of her minions storm off in a huff. The laugh I've been holding in comes cackling out of me loudly and I nearly choke on it.

V joins me and whispers around her chuckles, "I have a newfound respect for Jasper. His insult has outdone all of mine."

Nodding quickly, I wipe away the tears from my eyes, but I can't reply as I'm laughing uncontrollably, holding my stomach.

"It's about time," she says, raising her glass and saluting him.

"Jasper!"

My laughing sadly dies down when I hear the tone behind Danielle's words.

"What, Mom?" he says on an annoyed sigh.

She yanks him towards her and begins whispering

into his ear. The wailing up on stage blocks out the majority of their conversation, but I hear the words: apology, rude, and Ava, repeated heatedly.

I am all but leaning into Jasper, straining my hearing to catch wind of what Danielle is chewing Jasper's ear over, when the DJ announces, "Okay, folks, up next we have..."

But I ignore him, as I overhear Danielle say, "She is no good for you."

No guessing who she's speaking about.

"Holeeee crap," I hear V mumble.

Intrigued by what has her attention, I turn to face the stage and nearly fall off my seat, because standing up there is Indie. Well, it's Indie's back, but I know it's her, as those fake extensions are a dead giveaway.

The lights have dimmed, but I can clearly see the three bimbos, standing behind her, holding onto their microphones, heads bowed low.

What the hell are they doing? They look like they're backup singers for a wannabe Taylor Swift.

All my questions are answered when a bright spotlight shines down on Indie, and as soon as the music starts, she raises her fist in the air and begins tapping her foot in sync to the beat.

She spins around and begins singing, "Girlfriend" by Avril Lavigne. She points at Jasper, and curls her finger, beckoning him to come to her.

You've got to be *shitting* me!

Jasper groans and throws his head back in frustration, while I am about to commit first degree murder!

"That's it! She's going down," sneers V, standing up abruptly.

But Lucas grabs onto her hand and pulls her back down.

As Indie gets to the chorus, she and her entourage, who are her backup singers (vomit), begin scaling the stairs like they're performing on Broadway. Then, if that isn't bad enough, as Indie descends the last step, she stops and bends, and begins flicking her hair from side to side. Total stripper move.

This is ridiculous. If I wasn't seething, I would find this quite amusing.

She starts a shakedown of her entire body, shimmying and gyrating so inappropriately, that I witness a mother cover her son's eyes, mortified. She glides over to some poor chump, and places her stilettoed boot in between his legs. She then leans forward, and begins driving her hips into his face while looking at Jasper seductively, singing about how much she doesn't like his girlfriend.

The poor guy, whose face will need a scrub down, top to bottom, is looking at his female companion, with his hands raised and a, 'What the fuck,' look on his face. His friend looks like she's about to slam her fist into Indie's revolving pelvis.

I hear ya, sista!

After Indie has finished blinding the poor innocent bystander with her rotating crotch, she begins a preppy dance move while clicking her fingers down low, and sidestepping over to our table. She stands in front of Jasper and commences shaking her hips, Shakira style. I almost gag on how absurd she looks.

Jasper takes a big swig of beer, and I can tell by his body language he's had enough.

As she leans forward, hands braced on the edge of the table while singing how she should be Jasper's girlfriend, Jasper takes a hold of my hand and pulls me up hastily, kicking back his chair.

Danielle looks up at us and glares. "Where are you going?"

"Home," Jasper replies coldly.

Sadly, Indie and her threesome have other ideas.

They begin clapping over their heads so loudly, that it amplifies into the microphone, which squeals in protest. But that doesn't stop Indie, as she makes her intentions clear that she won't let Jasper leave by leaping towards him, attempting to clutch the scruff of his shirt.

He shrugs out of her grip and walks away from her, dragging me along behind him, but she only quickens her step and corners him so he can't move around her.

He backs up against the wall as she pushes herself up against him, singing inches away from his face.

That's it!

I'm about to grab the microphone and shove it down her throat, but Jasper pushes her away, yelling furiously, "Back off, Indie! Seriously, get a clue. I don't want you!"

Because the microphone is still on, Jasper's words echo loudly, and so does Indie's gasp.

Thankfully, the DJ switches off her microphone and puts on some pop song as a distraction, but everyone's eyes are still glued to the drama unfolding before them.

Indie throws down the mic, stomping her foot repeatedly.

"Jasper, how can you talk to me like that? I've known you since we were kids. I've loved you since then," she adds, her lower lip trembling.

"You don't love me," Jasper sneers. "You only want me because for once, you can't have me. And you never will, not ever again."

"Jasper, this isn't you talking," Danielle says from behind Indie.

As she glares at me over Indie's shoulder, my last tether of patience snaps.

"Who is, then, Danielle?" I ask, challenging her to answer.

She purses her lips, narrowing her cold blue eyes at me. "You damn well know who."

Well, well. I can see why she and Indie are BFF. They are both total bitches!

"Mom, you need to walk away before you say something you regret," Jasper sneers, putting his arm around my waist.

"No, Jasper, it's fine. Let her speak," I say calmly, because this is a discussion well over due, and I'm sick of pretending.

Let's do this.

"Oh believe me, you won't like what I have to say." Danielle snickers while pointing her bony finger my way.

"Mom, I mean it, quit it," Jasper implores, pulling me closer to his side.

"Look what she's done to you, Jasper! Turned you against your family," Danielle says while wrapping her arm around Indie, who is sniffling.

"No, Mom, *you* did that. With all this drama and

bullshit. Who the hell do you think you are? This person," he says, jolting me against him. "*She* is my family. She would never make me feel as uncomfortable as you have tonight."

Danielle's mouth pops open, but she quickly regains her composure. "But I am your mother. I'm your flesh and blood."

Jasper laughs bitterly. "Do you think you can just come into my life and pretend like everything is okay? I've forgiven you, but I haven't forgotten what a shitty mom you were. And when you pull shit like tonight, I really regret giving you a second chance."

"I'm trying to make amends," Danielle cries, tears pricking her icy eyes.

I have no doubt these tears are staged. She realizes she cannot win this battle with Jasper, so she's resorted to playing the sympathy card, hoping he'll fall for it.

But thankfully, he doesn't.

"I know you are, and that's why I've turned a blind eye to all the drama. But no more. You hear me? Ava has always been there for me. Not you, but her." Jasper is seething, and I can see the veins at his temple straining as he clenches his jaw.

Danielle is quiet and lowers her head into her hands.

"See what you've done!" Indie comforts a crying Danielle. "You're a little whore!" Indie snarls. "Jasper *will* get sick of you. You'll be a distant memory in six months' time, mark my words," she spits, walking closer and getting into my face.

I'm so ready for this. I lunge forward, ready to take her on, but Jasper steps between us.

"Enough! You take another step, Indie, and I *will* end you."

Both Indie and Danielle gasp, because Jasper is dead serious.

I see security approaching, so I pull Jasper back, as he has leaned forward, fists clenched. "C'mon, Jasper, let's go."

He stares from his mom to Indie and nods. "We're done here."

Jasper's mom sobs and yells at him, "So you're choosing her over me?"

Jasper's mouth turns up into a smile, which is dripping with malice. "There was never a choice to make. It'll always be her. It'll always be us."

My heart swells to the size of a mountain.

Danielle's face drops as she reaches for Jasper. "How could you? I'm your mother."

It's her final plea, but it's about to backfire on her, because I know what Jasper is about to say, and funnily enough, I don't stop him.

"Well, I'm about to be a father. And unlike *you*, I'm doing what's best for my child."

At that precise moment, the music stops and its official, everyone now knows that I'm pregnant.

I thought when this moment occurred I would be shy and withdrawn. But how things pan out in your mind are usually totally different to how they pan out in real life. This is one of those moments.

I raise my head proudly and meet the challenging stares of Indie and Danielle head on.

Indie looks as if she's just been told Botox and extensions have been deemed illegal. Her eyes are bulging out of her head, and if her mouth dropped any lower, I'd be able to see what she had for lunch.

But Indie's reaction isn't the one that has me hiding behind Jasper.

No, it's Danielle's.

She looks absolutely livid.

She also looks like she's going to strangle me. Her hands have formed into claws and I can see a tick pulsate under her right eye. This is not a normal reaction of a grandmother-to-be. This is the reaction of someone who would be tried in court and found guilty of infanticide!

"Jasper, let's go," I mumble, a little concerned for my safety.

Jasper nods, giving his mother one final look. "Okay."

And with that, we leave.

CHAPTER EIGHTEEN
Miracles

The car ride back to Jasper's house is just depressing.

Jasper has been silent since we left Harmonies, and I'm afraid he'll never speak again.

I don't know what to say to him, because there are simply no words to express how sorry I am, that his birthday has gone down as the worst in history.

But there are also no words to express how proud I am of him, and how grateful I am, to be such an integral part of his life.

I never expected him to choose me over his mom, because I was happy to play nice with her. I would have ignored the snide remarks and kept my mouth shut because I knew how much it meant to Jasper for us to get along. It's too bad Danielle couldn't do the same.

We pull into his driveway and he hurriedly exits without a word, slamming the car door behind him.

I quickly unsnap my seatbelt and follow, but I stay a few steps behind, not wanting to crowd him, as he has that damn, unreadable look that I hate.

As we ascend the stairs, his silence frightens me, but I quietly follow him into the house, hoping he'll speak to me.

"Jasper?" I ask softly when he tears off his jacket, throwing it onto the recliner. He begins pacing.

I wait for a response, or a glance, but he doesn't and I begin to think the worst.

Watching him pace the room is giving me sea legs, so I sit onto the edge of the sofa and curl my legs underneath me, silently begging him to talk to me.

After a few minutes he finally speaks. "I'm sorry, Ava."

"Sorry?" I question on a gulp as I look up at him timidly. I'm terrified to find out what he is apologizing for.

Jasper nods and his head dangles low, his posture is that of a defeated man.

"For forcing this on you. My mom hasn't changed. She's still the same selfish person she was when I was a kid. She never gave you a chance, and I just thought that maybe..." His voice falters, but he continues, "That maybe things in my life could go right for once, you know."

Even though he can't see me, I nod, because I completely understand.

"And I'm sorry I told her about our baby. I just—" He turns his back on me, and my stomach fills with knots.

"Sssh, you have nothing to be sorry for," I say with conviction, jumping up from the couch and rushing over to him.

But he won't turn to face me, and I won't force him.

"I just... I don't know what to do, Ava. She's my mom and you're—" he pauses. "You're my everything. I can't lose you, I just can't. But I can't expect you to stick around when she's treating you like shit."

I really don't like where he's going with this conversation. So I put as much passion and honesty into my response.

"Hey, I'm not going anywhere, you hear me? Yes, your mom is a total bitch, and yes, she hates me. But I love you, and she comes with you, so I just have to deal. I'd rather deal with her than not have you in my life, Jasper. I can't do that. Not ever again," I whisper sadly.

He turns to me quickly when he hears the catch in my voice.

"Hey, hey," he says, searching my eyes. "No talk about us being apart, okay?"

I nod, wiping my nose on the back of my hand.

"What did you mean about me not sticking around, then?"

I can see him choosing his words carefully as he replies, "I don't expect you to put up with my mom treating you like dirt."

"But—" I interrupt, but he doesn't let me finish.

"So, if she can't deal with us being together... then I'm done with her."

"What?" I ask, stunned. "Jasper, no, she's your mom. You can't just cut ties."

"Yes, I can. I've lived without her for most of my life, I can do so again. But you," he says, stepping closer until we're toe to toe.

"I cannot. I will not," he adds with conviction while giving his head a firm shake.

I don't know what to say, because this man in front of

me surprises me every day with his love and dedication. But giving up his mom for me, it's something I know he'll regret.

"But—" I refute, looking into his big blue eyes.

"No buts. The day I met you was the beginning of my life. Before I met you, my life was just a bleak existence of habit and routine. I was only surviving because I had to. But now, I'm surviving because I want to. I want to because of you," he says, his fingertips brushing over my cheeks.

Jasper has said some beautiful things to me in the past, but this, this is just too much. I can feel the tears approaching, and before they fall Jasper wraps me in his arms. I bury my head into his neck, crying.

He rubs my back, soothing me while I cry, thinking how fucked up this situation is. I also cry for him, while he remains my pillar of strength.

After I'm done slobbering everywhere, I pull back, wiping away my runaway tears with the back of my hand.

"I still haven't given you your birthday present." I sniff.

Jasper looks at his watch and smiles. "It's past midnight. Not my birthday anymore."

"Even so," I say, while I unwrap myself from his arms and search through my bag. As my fingers pass over it, I take a deep breath. I'm nervous he won't like it.

Holding it in my closed fist, I place my hand behind my back apprehensively.

"If you don't like it, or think its lame, I understand," I mumble.

Jasper holds out his palm, cocking his eyebrow with a smirk. "Hand it over."

Taking a deep breath, I drop the black velvet box into his outstretched palm.

He looks at it and studies it closely, while I'm about to hyperventilate.

I shuffle from foot to foot and Jasper chuckles, finally putting me out of my misery. The box hinges whine in protest when he opens the box. I close my eyes, afraid he's going to hate it.

After a few moments of stillness, I bravely crack open an eye to look at him.

He looks, well... he looks speechless.

"Don't you like it?" I ask when taking in his stunned expression.

Jasper's head snaps up like he's awoken from a dream.

He meets my eyes and swallows. "Ava, I... I love it. Thank you."

His long, elegant fingers pry the simple, silver ring out from its white pouch, and I swear I see him falter. He's holding the ring between his pointer finger and thumb, and is about to slip it onto his middle finger, but I stop him.

"It's engraved."

He halts, slowly drawing it closer so he can read it.

It is only one word, but that one word equates to a million words strung together.

His eyes flick to mine, and he reads out the inscription with pride. "Surrendered."

I give him a small nod, and my chest bursts in glee when I see how happy my gift has made him.

"I surrender to you, Jasper White. My heart, my soul, me... has surrendered to you."

Jasper bites his lip and exhales deeply before he replies, "You are my miracle."

"Ditto."

He slips the ring onto his right middle finger. It looks perfect. Jasper is not one for jewelry, as apart from his watch, he doesn't wear any. But this simple, yet elegant, handcrafted sterling silver ring sits stunningly on his long, slender finger.

"Happy birthday, Jasper." I smile, relieved he likes his gift.

"Thank you, baby. Best birthday ever," he replies, holding his hand out in front of him while examining the ring.

I raise my eyebrow at him and he lets out a small chuckle, meeting my eyes.

"Even the sucky parts were bearable because I was with you," he adds huskily as he hooks his thumb into my belt loop, pulling me towards him.

"Kiss me," I whisper when I am inches away from his wet, inviting mouth.

Jasper licks his upper lip quickly, and before smashing his lips to mine, he gasps, "With pleasure."

Waking to an empty bed isn't unusual, as Jasper is a night owl, and I often go to sleep before him. But it concerns me, as Jasper's side of the bed looks as if someone has had an epileptic fit in it. The sheet is creased and crinkled, and the woolen blanket has been kicked towards the end of the bed. I can tell by the disarray that Jasper has tossed and turned and not caught a wink of sleep.

Rubbing the sleep from my eyes, I peer over at the red numbers on the clock radio, which read, 3:35a.m. I can hear the light rain pitter-patter on the roof, and I wonder where Jasper is.

Quickly slipping out of bed and pulling on my Ugg boots, I grab Jasper's sweater off the back of the chair because it's freezing.

I search around the house, but come up empty. His truck keys are still on the kitchen counter, so I know he hasn't gone for a drive. Panic sets in and I grab his keys, ready to search the streets for him, just in case he's gone for a walk to clear his head.

Just as I'm about to charge through the front door, I see a red ember glowing through the front window.

Jasper.

Trying not to race through the living room, I attempt to act as casual as possible when I open the door quietly.

Jasper is sitting on the top porch step, topless and in black sweatpants, his feet bare. His head is bowed, hanging limply, with his long hair spilling over his brow and face. His hands are resting loosely between his legs, and he, without a thought, places the cigarette between his lips, drawing in a drag without really tasting it.

His whole stature is that of a man deep in thought. A broken man.

I wish I could sneak back inside so he's able to enjoy his stillness, but I know he's aware of me watching him.

"Come sit with me," he says, flicking his cigarette into the driveway, brushing the remaining smoke away with his hands.

Taking a seat near him on the top step, I lean my head onto his bare shoulder, which is freezing.

"You're going to catch pneumonia sitting out here in the cold," I say, rubbing his back quickly, attempting to generate heat and warm his chilly skin.

He shrugs but doesn't reply.

I don't know what to say to him, as I know the fight with his mom is preying on his mind. And I feel like I should say something to him. Anything.

"Come to bed. I can't sleep without you." Okay, lame, but true.

Jasper turns to me, the streetlight bouncing off the bottomless blue of his eyes.

"You go. I might stay out here. Watch the sun come up." He returns to peering out into the night sky.

I really don't want to leave him out here alone, especially half-dressed, but I'm exhausted. I try and stifle a yawn, but fail.

"Go to bed, baby. I'm really no company at the moment," he says in a low whisper.

Standing up after a few minutes of silence, I stretch my arms over my head, letting out yet another noisy yawn.

The sound snaps Jasper out of his thoughts, and he

looks up at me, surprised that I have moved. His usual bright, lively eyes now resemble that of a lost, innocent boy and my heart breaks. I go inside without a word, only to return a minute later with a big woolen throw, which I wrap around his hunched shoulders. No way am I leaving him outside to brood, especially when he's barely clothed.

He looks up at me, surprised that I returned, but gives me small appreciative smile as he nestles under the blanket.

"I can't sit out here and freeze to death while watching the sunrise," I joke while snuggling into him, reaching for the blanket to wrap around myself.

Jasper huddles close to me and pulls me into his side, shielding me against the cool night breeze. After a while, the warmth of his body and the steady shifting of his chest, rising and falling on inhalations and exhalations, lull me into a comfortable state.

I'm half awake, half asleep; my body sheltered into his when I hear him say, barely above a whisper, "We'll get through this. I promise."

I don't know if I'm dreaming or awake.

Either way, it sends a shiver down my spine, thinking of what's to come.

CHAPTER NINETEEN
Bottled Up

The next few days are painful, to say the least. Jasper's mom has called at least one hundred times.

An hour.

It's getting beyond ridiculous. And so is Jasper's foul mood.

Since the argument with his mom, he has been distant and often, very short tempered, which he's never been before.

I'm hoping his mood might improve, as P.O.E is playing a sold out show at Little Sisters tonight.

I know he's looking forward to the gig in Seattle, which is coming up really soon, so hopefully, being busy with P.O.E will keep his mind off his mom. But that's hard when she won't let up with the stalking.

"Ava, do you have any peanut butter?" I hear V yell from downstairs.

I give my reflection one last look in the mirror and mull over whether I should put my hair up. I twirl it up at the base of my neck and scrunch up my face, unhappy with how I look. Thanks to Jasper's moodiness, my frame of mind has also been shot, and I have been feeling unsettled and restless, which I don't like.

"Ava!" V shouts when I don't reply.

Groaning, I quickly grab a hair tie off my dresser, pulling up my hair messily, as I can't tolerate it being loose tonight. I grab my coat and quickly descend the stairs, in fear of V gnawing her arm off. As I round the corner, I see that her head is planted in my pantry, searching for God knows what.

"Ah ha! I found you," she mutters while reaching for the peanut butter and a loaf of white bread.

She tosses everything onto the counter as she turns to face me.

"You want one?" she asks, eagerly unscrewing the peanut butter lid.

Shaking my head, I take a seat at the kitchen table. "No, I just ate dinner."

V shrugs while opening the drawer, which rattles as she hunts for a knife. She searches through the cutlery, pulling out a huge butcher's knife when she's too impatient to look for a butter knife.

"You look nice," I say, totally loving her pretty black pinafore dress, with knee high white socks and mary-janes.

I laugh as she dips the inappropriate knife into the jar, and scoops out a huge clump of peanut butter.

"Gah, I feel fat. This is the only thing that doesn't make me feel like a heffa," she replies, not breaking concentration from spreading the peanut butter evenly onto her slice of bread.

"Well, maybe you should quit it with the carb overload then," I reply, giggling when she stacks up two sandwiches onto her plate.

She shrugs. "Whatever, I'm married. Isn't it socially acceptable to let yourself go after you say I Do?"

Shaking my head at her and laughing, the momentum loosens my messy bun, and tendrils of hair stick to my lip-gloss, which frustrates me. I regret not spending more time on my hair.

Here's hoping my mood improves, because the way I'm feeling at the moment, I'm ready to wage war with anyone who looks at me the wrong way.

"You're the one who's looking hot," she mutters around a mouthful of food.

I'm glad she thinks so, as I'm feeling anything but in my cute royal blue ruffled dress. I wore this dress because I usually feel like I want to frolic in fields of daisies, swishing my pleats in the wind. Sadly, today isn't one of those days.

"Thanks," I reply, half-heartedly.

V is well aware of my grumpiness, but has chosen to ignore it, as no matter what she says, my funk just won't dissipate.

"Pregnancy agrees with you."

I chuckle, grateful she has left my mood alone.

"Thanks. Married life agrees with you." I smirk as she spoons out a blob of peanut butter with her pointer finger.

V shrugs my comment off as she licks her finger clean. "Married life is going to turn me into Shamu, but whatev's. It's too late for Lucas now. He's already promised to love me for better or worse, in skinniness or heaviness."

"I think you mean in sickness or health," I correct while laughing.

V blows a raspberry at me.

"Same thing."

"**D**o I need to call A.A.?" I ask V, who is downing her third tequila shot.

She makes a pained face as she sucks on the lemon. "Nope, all good."

We're sitting at the bar with our backs pressed against the counter, waiting for P.O.E to commence their set. I'm so grateful we got these seats, as the place is packed.

I always get a bundle of nerves in the pit of my stomach when I watch Jasper perform. I don't know if I'm nervous or excited, but I do know if I were him, I would be shitting bricks backstage. My little stint the other night at karaoke gave me a small taste of what Jasper experiences every time he gets up in front of a crowd. He does it with such poise and confidence, and makes it look so easy. Just looking up at the stage and the microphone is giving me stage fright. This just confirms what I already know—Jasper was born to perform.

The lights dim and my stage fright turns into undeniable lust, as I know Jasper is about to rock the socks off of everyone.

Lucas strolls out to a massive round of applause and a

piercing wolf whistle from V. She elbows me in the ribs while bouncing in her seat.

"That's my husband, just in case you were wondering."

I can't help but smile, because I adore how head over heels in love she is with him.

The other two boys walk out, giving the crowd small waves as they adjust their guitar straps. They then begin their usual intro, a tease for the audience, giving them a taste of what they're in for. They are amazing, and I never tire of seeing them look like total Rock Gods up on stage.

Scooting forward on my stool, I await the arrival of Jasper, and I don't have to wait too long. The music stops, and after a few seconds, Lucas counts in, tapping his drumsticks, and out saunters Jasper.

The crowd goes wild, and the applause is deafening. People around me begin bopping to the music and clapping, and my heart swells. I'm so proud of him because he deserves this. He gives the crowd a small smile, but that smile is quickly replaced with a frown.

He usually works the crowd into a frenzy, saying a few words, but tonight—nothing. He skips the long intro and heads straight into the verse.

V looks at me with big eyes and I just shrug. I have no idea what's going on. I've never seen him so disinterested before.

The first song ends and I hold my breath, hoping that maybe he'll get a little more enthused, but I know better.

The whole set is painful to watch. Jasper doesn't interact with the crowd, and barely makes any eye contact with his band members. He misses cues and hits a few off notes, which has NEVER happened before.

At first the crowd believes the performance will get better, but sadly, it only gets worse. One by one, the sea of people begin to dissolve, preferring to play pool than watch the disaster occurring up on stage. I can hear patrons mumble amongst themselves that they are far from impressed with tonight's performance, and some have even requested a refund.

I want to tell them to shove it, but they're right. Still, I sit tall and watch my boyfriend proudly, because no matter what, he'll always be a star in my eyes.

Forty-five minutes later, they finish their set and Jasper walks off without a goodbye. The boys try and cover with a longer outro, but it's obvious he's not coming back. With no other choice, they finish off and are applauded lackadaisically.

I can tell Lucas is far from impressed, and he has every right, but I can't help but defend Jasper when V demands, "What the fuck?"

"It's because of his mom. I didn't realize how badly this has affected him," I admit shamefully.

V jumps up, slipping on her cardigan angrily. "Well, that's no excuse to ruin it for the rest of the boys."

"I know, V," I mumble.

She doesn't give me a chance to add anything further. "I'm going to find Lucas." She walks off in a huff.

What the hell was that? That uninspiring performance will have Jasper kicking himself. With Rip It Up just around the corner, tonight was their chance to really promote the hell out of it. But, they most certainly didn't do that. If anything, Jasper may have lost a few loyal fans, and that thought angers the crap out of me. Like I needed another reason to hate his mom with a passion!

Jasper needs to address this situation with his mom one way or the other, because ignoring her is obviously not working.

"Hey, beautiful, can I buy you a drink?"

Deep in thought, I fail to notice a patron standing way too close for comfort. He's a preppy looking guy, with way too much hair product in his blond, curly hair.

I pull away, leaning sideways.

"No, I'm good," I reply, giving him a dismissive smile, hoping he gets the hint. Sadly, he doesn't.

"Aw, c'mon, one drink won't hurt," he slurs, leaning into my face. His cheap aftershave, applied with a heavy hand, assaults my nostrils so I try to shuffle further away.

His brown beady eyes fall to my cleavage. I cross my arms over my chest, clearing my throat.

He flicks his eyes to meet mine and sneers, "What, you think you're too good to have a drink with me?"He's creeping closer, and because I'm sitting on a backless chair, I can't lean back any further without falling off.

"No, of course not, but I'm waiting for my boyfriend," I reply quickly, not liking the sleazy look in his eyes.

"I don't see a boyfriend," he taunts' and turns to his friend, who has randomly appeared.

Great, now I have to deal with two preppies!

I'm about to excuse myself when I feel someone come up behind me, wrapping his warm, familiar hand around my waist.

"You heard her. She said no."

Jasper.

I sigh into his grip, blessing his impeccable timing.

Preppy number one turns to look at his friend, and lets out a loud, inappropriate laugh.

"This wannabe rock star is your boyfriend? How tragic for you. You're all class, baby, and your *boyfriend* is just that, a boy. He can't support you and look after you the way you deserve to be looked after." He lets out yet another loud laugh while high fiving his friend.

He edges closer to me, while I lean further back into the shelter of Jasper's chest. "Well, today is your lucky day. I'll show you what a *real* man looks like," he says, leaning into my face. "And if you're real lucky, I'll show you how a real man fucks."

I'm about to smack him in his crude mouth, but in a lightning fast move, my barstool spins quickly, and I'm repositioned, facing the other direction.

I leap off the stool, as there's no mistaking the sound of someone's face getting punched, and hard.

I witness Jasper launch onto the jerk, them both tumbling to the ground. Jasper's fist connects with the guy's jaw and eye in quick succession. He's about to go for the trifecta, when thankfully security arrive, pulling Jasper off.

The fight lasts no longer than five seconds, but it's enough.

"Let me go! I'm going to kill that fucker!" Jasper says' squirming, trying to break free from Paul's death grip. Paul is the head of security, and also Jasper's friend.

"No, man. Just walk it off," Paul replies, trying to contain a struggling Jasper.

Jasper responds to Paul's suggestion of walking it off by lunging forward, eager to finish what he started.

"Jasper, enough!" Paul says firmly, escorting him towards the door when it's apparent he won't calm down.

I follow quickly, and as soon as we're outside, the cool air seems to snap Jasper out of his rampage.

He paces angrily with his hands by his sides, blowing out big breaths, which flick his messy hair out of his eyes.

I watch with my mouth agape. I'm shocked how livid he is. Yes, the guy was a rude jerk, but Jasper flew off the handle in naught to one hundred in point two seconds. His short fuse tonight scared me.

Thankfully, after a few minutes, Jasper seems to calm down.

"Sorry, man," Jasper says, turning to face Paul.

However, he still looks enraged as he's working his jaw heatedly, and his nostrils are still slightly flared.

"It's fine, J. Just do me a favor and go home, okay? The boys can finish packing up," Paul replies, his huge biceps twitching when he crosses his arms over his massive chest.

Jasper nods, his jaw clenching as he looks through the open door.

Paul looks at me and I nod, silently confirming I will take Jasper home.

Satisfied there will be no more trouble, Paul goes inside, leaving me alone with Jasper.

The whole time Jasper has been out here, he won't meet my eyes, which troubles me. I hate this distance between us.

"Jasper..." I attempt to talk to him, but he begins walking down the street, without hearing a single word.

I'm shocked he would turn his back on me, when we clearly need to discuss what just happened, but judging by his huge strides, talking is the last thing on his mind.

"Jasper, wait!" I cry, chasing after him.

Thankfully he slows down and I can catch up to him, slightly out of breath. "What was that back there?" I ask, hooking my thumb behind me.

Jasper runs his hands through his hair angrily, leaving them interlaced on the top of his head. After a few deep breaths, he finally speaks to me.

"You expect me to stand back while that asshole talks dirty to you?" he shouts, glaring at me.

I don't understand why he's mad at me. What have I done?

"Jasper, calm down," I plead. "What's the matter with you?"

Jasper snickers. "What's the matter with me? What's the matter with you? Why didn't you say anything to that motherfucker?"

I gasp. Is he accusing me of encouraging the guy's crude behavior?

"Are you serious? You didn't give me a chance!" I yell back.

I cross my arms over my chest, and when Jasper sees my defensive stance, he calms down. "I'm sorry, Ava."

He places his palm on my hand, attempting to uncross my arms, but I'm still mad at him, so I leave them crossed.

"I'm sorry, okay?" he says again, dipping his head to meet my downcast eyes.

My eyes flick to his, and I can see he means what he says.

"Fine," I mumble, dropping my arms by my side.

We're both silent, not knowing what to say to one another, which scares me. So I say the only thing I can, because there's no sugarcoating this situation.

"Has this got something to do with your mom?"

As soon as the words leave my mouth, I know I've hit the nail on the head.

He closes his eyes and shakes his head, but I know he's lying to me, and I don't like it.

"Jasper, please, talk to me," I beg, stepping towards him.

Jasper opens his eyes when he hears the desperation in my voice. We stare at one another, my eyes beseeching him to tell me what the hell is going on.

He clears his throat before he speaks. "I'm sorry, baby. I'm such a hothead when it comes to you. I just... this thing with my mom... is screwing with me. I'm sorry. It'll never happen again. Let's just go home, okay?"

He pulls me into his arms and tucks my head under his chin.

"No, it's not okay," I reply, shrugging out of his warm embrace, not wanting the comfort of his arms to distract me.

Jasper blows out an annoyed breath, and rubs his brow. "Ava, what? What do you want from me? I said I'm sorry. I know I overreacted, can't you just drop it?"

"No, I will not just 'drop it.' This is crazy, Jasper.

Something isn't right, and I'm afraid it's just going to get worse," I confess, proud that I have expressed my fears aloud.

Jasper is now the one with the defensive stance, crossing his arms over his broad chest. "Ava, look, I'm going home. You can either come with me, or you can stay here. I don't want to talk about this anymore."

I can't believe this!

I'm not happy, but with no other choice, because we're obviously done talking, I snap, "Fine, give me your keys. You're not driving in the state you're in."

"Fine," Jasper retorts, tossing his keys at me.

I catch them, but before I can say a word, he's turned his back on me and stormed off.

CHAPTER TWENTY

Kiss and Tell

"Jasper, answer the phone. Please," I plead.

I'm sprawled out, lying on his bedroom floor, surrounded by mounds of books, trying to study for final exams. But the constant ringing is doing my head in, and I'm getting absolutely no studying done.

Jasper lifts his head, which is buried in yet another newspaper.

"No."

He picks up his iPhone, ending the call, and goes back to scouring the paper, like his phone ringing off the hook for the past week isn't an issue.

"What are you looking for?" I ask, pointing at the paper.

He's been awfully secretive about what he's doing, even though I know damn well he's looking for work. Whenever I try to address the issues, he either avoids the question, or dances around it.

However, this time I won't let it lie. "Are you going to quit the shelter?"

Jasper rests the paper on his knee and spins in his chair to face me. "I dunno. Maybe. I can't work there forever," he replies honestly.

Even though I don't like his answer, I'm so happy he's finally opening up.

"Yeah, but you love it there."

Jasper shrugs. "It's time for a change," he replies, his eyes flicking down to the paper.

I know this has got to do with some macho pride thing of supporting me. And ever since that night at Little Sisters, when that jerkoff ran his mouth off, Jasper has been more adamant than ever.

"You don't have to support me. I can work before and after the baby. Once I graduate, I can get a job, earning good money. With all the experience I've had on my scholarship, I have an advantage over all the other people applying for the same jobs as me."

Jasper shakes his head, his eyes narrowing. "No offense, but I'm not living off my girlfriend."

"This isn't the 15th century where I need looking after. You don't have to support me. See it as me supporting us. Us three," I reply, because this isn't about him and his pride anymore, it's about what's best for our baby.

Jasper pinches the bridge of his nose. "Drop it, Ava."

"But..."

He gives me a stern look, raising his eyebrow, so I don't push.

"Okay, okay," I whisper. "Letting it go." But of course I can't. "What are you going to do?" I ask softly, trying not to come across as being rude.

"Anything," he sighs. "I don't care. Anything that will bring in a decent income. I'll work three jobs if I have to," he confesses.

"Three jobs?" I ask, sitting up. "But when will I see you?"

Jasper shrugs. "You said we have to make sacrifices... well, I'm making mine."

What the hell is he thinking? Sacrifices I get, but this isn't a sacrifice, this is suicide.

"But..."

"Ava, please. I'm doing this, okay? I may not have some fancy title under my belt, but I'm not afraid to get my hands dirty," he says, slightly annoyed. "I am supporting you and my child, no matter what the cost is."

I lower my eyes because although he means well, the cost is slowly chipping away at my sanity.

"I know, Jasper, I just don't want—"

"You don't want what?" he asks defiantly, folding up the paper and tossing it onto the desk.

Is he trying to pick a fight with me?

"I don't want to fight. I just want you to be happy," I admit, hoping to knock some sense into him.

His phone starts ringing for the ten thousandth time, and by the hard resolve of his jaw, I know who it is.

"I'll be happy when my mom gets the hint," he says, rubbing his eyes with the heels of his hands.

The phone thankfully stops and I don't pester him any longer, because he looks like he's about to snap.

I continue with my studying quietly, hating the tension in the room. I don't know what else to do. I've tried talking to him about this whole situation, but he won't open up to me, and that scares the living hell out of me.

After a few minutes of silence, his phone sounds again.

"God dammit!" he snaps. "I've gotta get out of here."

He stands up quickly, reaching for his black sweater lying on the bed.

I look up at him, and down at my pile of books. "Oh, okay. Give me a minute to finish up this chapter, and I'll come with."

"No, you stay. I know you're busy studying," he says, looking down at me.

I know he's just being polite and doesn't want me to come. The reality of the situation breaks my heart, but I try to play it off, as I don't want to crowd him. I think he's had enough crowding to last him a lifetime.

Giving him a quick nod, I highlight something in my book, pretending that I'm not about to scream in frustration.

He kneels down in front of me and searches my eyes. "I just need time to think. Away from that incessant thing," he says, pointing to his flashing phone. "I promise I won't be long. I just need some time to clear my head, okay?"

"Okay," I reply softly.

But it really isn't.

After another hour of Jasper's phone ringing constantly, I turn it off before I throw it out the window.

I know Jasper is frustrated with his mom and this fucked up situation. He's just lashing out, but I hate it. I can't stand to see him hurting this way. And I can't stand this friction between us.

Damn his mom. She's causing problems in and out of his life. How can someone be so toxic without even being a part of one's life?

My phone rings, interrupting my depressing thoughts.

Half hoping its Jasper, because he's been gone for a while, I answer it eagerly.

"Hello."

"Hello, ah, is that Ava Thompson?"

My heart sinks. Has something terrible happened?

"Yes, this is she. Who is this?" I ask breathlessly.

"Hi Ava, my name is Thomas Carey from the Board of Studies."

"Okay," I reply, waiting for him to continue.

"I'm just giving you a quick call to let you know your application has been reviewed, and I'm pleased to say you've been accepted. We've emailed you all the dates. See you at the interview."

Whoa, what the hell?

Before I have time to question what the fuck is going on, the line goes dead.

What the hell just happened? My over-tired, over-stressed brain can't process this situation fast enough. So

I quickly fire up my laptop and impatiently tap my fingers on the keyboard, waiting for Outlook to load.

Finally, the program opens up and I scan through a bunch of junk mail. My eyes then fall on the two emails I want. One is from Thomas Carey. The other is from Sally Spencer.

I decide to open Sally's, as I have a sneaking suspicion she's behind this confusion.

Ava,

I will keep this short, because I know right about now, you're calling me every name under the sun. LOL

I went ahead and handed in your application form because you deserve this, Ava. This is your future. You deserve this more than anyone else I know.

Please don't be mad.

Just go to the interview, and if you hate it, then I promise I won't pester you again about it. I don't know what's going on in your life at the moment, but I can't let you pass up this opportunity.

Just give it a go.

Btw. Thomas is an old buddy of mine. ;)

S

Well, that explains it then.

I have a read through the email from Thomas Carey and open the attachment with all the interview details.

I can't believe this. I made the cut. And I didn't even know I was in the running!

I should be overjoyed, exhilarated, all those adjectives, but I'm not.

All I can think about is Jasper.

This would solve any financial problems we might have in the future once the baby arrives. And of course, it would also stop Jasper from working a trillion jobs. But I know it would be a slap to Jasper's ego. I also know, the job being in New York, makes this dream impossible.

I have to let this go, because there are too many factors working against me.

If only those factors were working in my favor, then I'd be set.

I have been pacing Jasper's living room for the past thirty minutes, peeking out the front window in hopes of seeing him walk up the driveway.

So far, nothing.

It's now 1:20 a.m., and he's still not home.

I have tried calling everyone, but no one has seen him. Well, I've called everyone, bar one person.

His mom.

I'm holding onto his iPhone, slapping it against my palm, and have been debating whether to call her for the past hour.

There's nowhere else he could be. So I suck it up, switching on his phone to search through his contacts for her number.

As soon as the phone fires up, there is a constant beep, after beep, after beep. All are messages indicating he has voice message, after voice message. No guessing who from.

In the end, I give up and let the phone do its thing while I run to the bathroom. When I return, it indicates Jasper has fifty-six voice messages and thirty-nine text messages.

Gee whiz.

I scroll through the texts and most are from his mom and Indie.

I decide to listen to the voice messages, as I'm sure he won't mind, seeing as he has a million others to go through.

As soon as I hear her voice, my skin crawls.

"Jasper, please talk to me. I can't stand this. I've just gotten you back. Call me."

Next message.

"How could you turn your back on me? You're breaking my heart. Call me."

Next message.

"She is bad for you, son. Look what she's made you do. Call me."

Next message.

"Jasper, I love you. Call me."

I've had enough and hang up quickly before I gag.

Now I understand why Jasper has been so moody. If I had to listen to obscene messages, such as the ones I just heard, I would be border lining on homicidal.

I look at the clock, and with no other option, I scroll through his contacts to find his mom's number.

I'm trying to gather enough courage to call her, when

I hear keys jingling outside, attempting to unlock the front door.

Jasper.

His keys drop with a heavy thud onto the porch, and I then hear hushed voices and giggles.

I'm quite certain one voice belongs to Jasper, while the other belongs to a female.

My blood begins to boil.

Racing towards the front door, I stop with my hand braced on the handle, when I hear a musical laugh I know all too well.

Harmony.

I yank open the door, and Jasper, who's being held up by Harmony, stumbles forward.

She has her slender arm wrapped around Jasper's neck, and he's holding onto her, attempting to stay balanced, as he is obviously blind drunk.

When she meets my eyes, they instantly dart away guiltily. She is looking, as usual, like a catwalk model in her chic, modern bohemian dress, with her lush brown hair cascading down her back.

What. The. Fuck!

"Hey baby," Jasper slurs, straightening up and shrugging out of Harmony's grip.

But he ends up wobbling on his feet, and both Harmony and I reach to steady him.

I can't help myself as I hurl a death stare her way, and she instantly pulls her hands away.

Jasper, of course, is oblivious to it all and chuckles.

"I'm hungry. Who wants pizza?" he asks, finally steadying himself as he brushes past me, walking inside.

I'm furious at his carefree response at being out all night without a word. And to make matters worse, when he does turn up, he does so drunk, AND on the arm of Harmony!

"Where have you been?" I snap, catching up to him as he fumbles with the light switch in the kitchen.

Jasper finally finds the button and then, let there be light, although, I wish it had remained dark.

The bright lights amplify the disgusting lipstick stains smeared all over his cheeks. And if that isn't bad enough, he also has bright red lipstick lips on his forehead.

Storming over, I grasp his chin in a firm grip and turn his face from side to side, examining the proof of his infidelity.

"What the fuck, Jasper?" I ask, slightly stunned when I see there are about twenty different shades of lipstick kiss marks on his cheeks.

Before he has a chance to reply, Harmony butts in quickly. "He didn't do anything wrong, Ava."

I turn to her, Jasper's chin clasped between my fingers. "Oh, so you call this," I say, showing her his face, "nothing wrong?"

Harmony bites her lip and my stomach drops, not liking what she's about to tell me. My free hand twitches, as I'm about to take this bitch out.

"He was at Lights Out, and I was there with some girlfriends. He was drinking alone, and he looked really sad, so I invited him over to have a few drinks with us. He declined, but I couldn't stand to watch him drink alone, so we all joined him."

I drop my hand from his face, suddenly feeling dirty.

"That's a lovely story. But how does having a drink lead to him looking like he's been attacked by an entourage of hookers?"

Jasper has the audacity to laugh at my comment. I spin on my heels to glare at him. He stops laughing abruptly, placing his hands behind his back while lowering his head like a naughty little school boy.

Harmony continues. "Everyone was buying everyone drinks... and we were all having a good time."

"Spit it out," I interrupt.

I've had enough of her dancing around the truth. I want her to get down to the truth before I pull out her long, lush hair.

She wrings her hands nervously when she feels the tension bouncing off of me.

"I noticed Jasper was getting really, really drunk—"

"Yeah, I was," he pipes up like it's something to be proud of.

When I shoot him a death stare, he resumes his schoolboy position.

"Anyway," Harmony continues. "My friend Alice thought it would be fun to enter Jasper into a stupid competition the bar was running."

I cross my arms over my chest. "What competition?"

Harmony squirms, nervously brushing her hair behind her ear. "Um, well, the girl patrons voted for the five hottest guys in the bar. The guys were then brought up on stage, and the women who wanted to participate chose who the hottest guy was out of the five."

"How did they vote?" I ask, although I know the answer.

Harmony clears her throat, and hesitates before she answers. "By kissing the guy they liked the best on the cheek."

I gulp, feeling sick.

Judging by the lipstick marks all over his face, Jasper was one popular boy.

"What did he get for bringing home the title?" I ask, disgusted, not able to look at Jasper without wanting to slap his sleazy face.

"Free drinks for the rest of the night," she replies softly.

My face turns into an ugly scowl. Like he needed any encouragement! He seemed to be doing okay all on his own without the freebies!

"I stopped drinking and sobered up so I could drive him home," she confesses.

When I don't reply and rub my temples, trying to massage away my approaching migraine, she says, "He loves you, Ava. He only has eyes for you. Don't be mad at him."

Is she really pleading on his behalf? How wrapped around his little finger is she?

"Thanks, Harmony, for bringing him home. I appreciate it," I utter on a sigh.

I look at Jasper, who seems to be listening to us, but has an unreadable look on his face.

"I better get going. I'll see myself out."

She smiles at Jasper. "Goodnight, Jasper. I hope you feel okay in the morning."

Jasper drunkenly waves goodbye and looks to be falling asleep on his feet.

Harmony gives me a small, timid smile and walks towards the front door.

Suddenly, I realize that Harmony, out of all this, is the good guy. No one can help who they fall in love with. And sadly she's fallen for someone who doesn't feel the same way. No matter how beautiful she is, she realizes Jasper will never have those kinds of feelings for her. But still, she's kind enough to take him home. She's happy to settle for friendship and has respected the fact, unlike most of the other females in Jasper's life, that he has a girlfriend and is off limits.

Maybe in a different time and place, Jasper and Harmony would work, but now, now she has to admire him from afar. And for that, I feel sorry for her. Something I never thought was possible.

"Harmony?"

She turns around, a few steps away from the front door.

"Yes?"

"Thank you," I say, giving her a curt nod. "For everything."

She understands my double meaning and returns the gesture.

"You're welcome, Ava." She closes the door softly behind her.

Now, time to deal with the kissing magnet.

I turn to face him, but he won't meet my eyes. He's just standing motionless, looking at the floor guiltily.

"So, do you have anything to say for yourself?" I ask, my arms crossed.

Jasper shrugs, eyes still downcast.

He looks a mess. His hair is sticking up in disheveled peaks, and his demeanor is that of a man who feels sorry for himself.

And that pisses me off.

"Oh okay, so you have absolutely nothing to say? You don't think sorry is in order for leaving me without a word, for worrying me sick, and allowing me to envision every gory scenario possible?"

Jasper closes his eyes and clenches his jaw, but remains silent, which enrages me further.

"How about, 'Sorry, Ava, for getting kissed by every pair of lips in L.A.?' Or how about, I'm sorry for coming home drunk, and on the arm of a girl who's obviously in love with you!" I yell, storming towards him and poking him in the chest with my finger, probing him to answer me.

Jasper shakes his head and takes a step back because I'm invading his personal space.

He finally meets my eyes, and they look bloodshot and heavy.

"I'm sorry! I'm a fuck up! Is that what you want to hear?" he asks, his hands spread out wide, emphasizing his point.

"No! I want you to talk to me," I reply furiously. "Tell me what the hell is going on with you!"

When Jasper doesn't reply, I explode.

"Is this what you want?" I ask animatedly, pointing to his face.

He looks at me, obviously puzzled by my comment. So I make myself brutally clear.

"Being single, is that what you want? Do you like

receiving kisses off of strange women, without having to worry about a pregnant girlfriend at home? Who, I might add, was waiting up for you like a fucking idiot! Because if that's what you want, then tell me now. Because once this kid comes, things will change. We'll change."

Saying my fears out loud makes them all the more real.

"You don't think I know that?" he yells, fisting his hair. "You don't think I know that having this kid changes everything? I know that it will, and it scares the shit out of me. Every day I wake up and think to myself what a lowlife like me could possibly offer you and our child. I have no job, no money, no education. I've got nothing. I am nothing," he admits, defeated, throwing his hands out to the side.

"But I'm too selfish to give you up. You and our baby deserve better than a fucked up mess like me!"

Tears begin streaming out of his eyes and my heart breaks, looking at the wounded man in front of me.

I can't allow him to think something which holds no truth.

"You're everything, Jasper. You're our everything," I whisper, trying to be strong.

"No, I'm not. Everything I touch turns to shit, and the sooner you and me accept that, the better."

"That's not true," I rebuke, attempting to touch him, but he shrugs away from me.

"Yes, it is," he replies, wiping away his tears. "You're just blinded by all this," he says, flicking at his shirt.

I take a step back, utterly offended. Surely he isn't insinuating that I'm only with him because of his looks.

When he doesn't elaborate, I know he indeed is implying just that. Drunk or not, I won't allow him to speak to me like some groupie.

"You jerk! Unlike your Harem of Harpies, I actually love you for you. Not your looks, but for you, and for what's in here," I snap, whacking my hand against his heart. "I take the good and the bad. But sadly, the bad is totally running laps around the good at the moment!"

Jasper looks down at me, and his constant silence angers me. I know this has to do with one woman, and in this moment, I hate her.

"This pity party you're throwing is turning you into a cynical asshole, just like your mother!"

It's out before I can stop myself. But I don't apologize, because I mean every word if it.

Jasper blows out a breath and interlaces his hands atop his head.

"I can't deal with this, Ava. This thing with you and my mom, it's driving me crazy," he confesses honestly.

Finally! The truth! But I hate that he's implying that I'm the one who had any part in her petty games.

"There's only a thing between us because she's the Antichrist! If you're going to have a go at anyone, I suggest you call her!" I yell at him, choking on my deep breaths.

I know by the look on his face that Jasper is beat. He thought cutting his mom out of his life was going to be easy. He thought wrong.

"Ava, I just want to go to sleep. I want to be alone tonight, okay? We'll talk about this tomorrow," he says, rubbing his temples.

His comment hurts and stuns me. But for the first time in my life, I don't want to be anywhere near him, so I happily comply.

"Fine! See you when I see you. Sweet fucking dreams," I snarl as I grab my keys and bag off the sofa.

"No, I will see you tomorrow. We've still got to organize Seattle," he says, walking towards me as I head for the front door.

Slipping my strap over my shoulder, I spin to face him. "Yeah, about that, I'm busy. Have a nice trip."

"Ava, wait!" he says, latching onto my arm when he realizes I'm serious.

"No, Jasper," I answer, shrugging roughly out of his grip. "I want to be alone," I snap sarcastically, using his words. However, I fail to add tonight, because at the moment, I'm not sure how long I need time away to think.

Jasper can sense the gravity behind my words and steps back, hands raised in defeat.

"Okay, fine, have it your way." He sighs heavily and I storm out the front door without giving him a second glance.

For once, he doesn't follow me.

For once, I don't want him to.

CHAPTER TWENTY ONE
Silent Influences

How did my life go from being perfect, to semi-perfect, to fucking apocalyptic before my eyes? It's been about half a day since I've spoken to Jasper, and I already feel like I'm losing it.

I'm lying in the middle of my bedroom floor, staring at my iPhone, willing it to ring. But it doesn't, and it hasn't since I started staring at it like five hours ago.

This time I'm not going to give in and call, because I'm not at fault. I understand he's got a lot on his plate, with finding out he's going to be a dad, and this whole mess with his mom. But lashing out at me when all I've done is try and support him is not cool. I get we hurt the one we love, but Jasper acting this way is beyond being hurtful, it's border lining on him pushing me away.

That thought sends a tsunami of fear and panic through me, and I begin to re-evaluate if waiting for Jasper to call is the best decision after all.

I thump my head on the carpet and decide I need a distraction. My eyes fall on the pile of brochures I received from Doctor Reger, and I decide now is the time to begin my education.

So, who knew?

Unborn babies can feel, see and hear.

I place my hands on my belly, and a lone tear spills from the corner of my eye. If Jasper doesn't want to be a part of our baby's life, then I'll raise this child the best I can.

To hell with waiting for him to call. It's not just me I have to think about anymore.

I type out a short text because there's no sugarcoating what has to be done.

> We need to talk

Within a minute I receive a response.

> C u in ten

Looking up at Jasper's house usually gives me the warm and fuzzies. However, today is not one of those days.

On the drive over here, I couldn't stop thinking about

his unusual brief reply. No smiley faces or kisses, or any sign of affection like usual.

That thought almost has me reversing down the driveway like a bat outta hell. Instead, I take a deep breath and check my reflection in the rear view mirror, hoping I don't look as nervous as I feel.

Well, I don't look nervous.

I look more like shit.

My eyes have sunken into my face and are terribly blood-shot, thanks to my lack of sleep. My mouth had dipped into a permanent frown, and when I attempt a smile, I resemble a deranged circus clown, so I settle on the frowning. My hair has seen better days, and as I peer down at my torn jeans and my baggy sweater, which is three sizes too big, I stop with the observation because it's not helping my nerves.

With what little strength I have left, I exit my car and quickly ascend Jasper's porch steps before I chicken out.

As I'm about to knock, the door opens, and I look into the eyes of the one person who makes me feel alive, and my heart suddenly sinks.

"Come in," he says without a hello hug or kiss.

He steps aside so I can brush past him, and I enter the house, deflated.

Taking a seat on the sofa, I tuck myself into a small ball because suddenly, I feel chilled to the bone.

He takes a seat near me and turns to look at me, but I can't meet his eyes, because I know when I do, the hard resolve of me coming here will melt into nothingness.

The silence is killing me, and the ticking of the wall clock is in sync with my beating heart.

"Ava, I'm sorry," Jasper finally says, breaking the silence.

I nod, but still keep my eyes downcast.

"I..." Jasper hesitates. "I'm so ashamed of myself. I let you down. I let our baby down."

This gets my attention, and I lift my eyes to meet his worn, exhausted ones.

He looks how I feel, which is comforting, as I'm glad I'm not the only one who looks and feels like a big bag of shit.

"Jasper, what's going on with you? Please talk to me." I try not to beg, but he can hear the angst in my voice.

He reaches for my hand and squeezes it lightly. His usual warm hands are now freezing cold.

"I love you, Ava. My life is nothing..." he pauses, then continues. "I'm nothing without you."

"I feel the same," I whisper, relieved that he still loves me.

"I want to be the best man I can for you. And I feel like I'm fucking failing," he admits. I can hear the defeat in his voice.

Since the night at the bar, a switch has been flipped, and I can't flip it back.

"I have no qualifications. I can't go out there and get a fancy job, earning enough to support you. And the fact that I can't support you the way that I want is eating me up inside," he confesses sadly.

"Jasper, I don't need you to support me," I say with conviction.

"I know. But I want to provide for my family, and give you and our baby everything I never had."

I know this stems from his shitty childhood, and this is just another reason to hate his mom. Like I needed another reason.

Jasper's eyes search mine, and I know what he's about to tell me next is going to suck.

"I thought I could deal with my mom not being in my life, but I can't, Ava. I just... I don't know what it is. Call it some fucked up childhood need for acceptance, but I can't just cut her out."

I bite my lip as I knew this was coming, but hearing him come clean, it just blows.

"I know you and her don't see eye to eye, but I need you both in my life to be happy. And I know how much of a pussy that makes me, but it's the truth. I think about it every single minute of every single day. I'm thinking of ways that I can have you both in my life without losing either one of you."

I don't know what to say. I feel slightly betrayed, but I understand it's his mom, and at the end of the day, she'll always share a connection with him that I won't.

"I don't expect you to choose, Jasper. I never have." I sigh.

"I know, but she does," he says sheepishly, as if he knows how lame that sounds.

I bite my tongue from verbally bashing him.

After a calming breath, I ask, "What does that say about her then, Jasper?"

Jasper nods. "I know, Ava. I just—" He runs both hands down his face, overcome. "I don't know what to do. I feel like I'm losing it. Piece by piece."

I hate to be Captain Obvious, but I question him anyway.

"So, what happens now? She obviously hates my guts, and won't quit trying to hook you up with Indie. How do you propose we work this?"

Jasper meets my eyes, defeated. "I don't know."

He doesn't know.

Is he shitting me? Is he really going to let his mom rule his life?

Suddenly, I see red. I jump up like my pants are on fire. "I need to get out of here."

Jasper looks confused by my sudden movement. "What? Why? We haven't finished talking."

"I'm done talking," I spit.

Jasper rubs his brow, totally crushed. "You wanted me to be honest with you, and now you punish me for it."

I choose to ignore him before I say something I regret, and storm towards the front door.

"Ava!" Jasper says, latching onto my forearm.

I pull my arm away, furious at him. "Don't. I need to leave before I say something—" I don't finish the sentence.

"Before you what?" he presses. I see the conflict flickering behind his blue eyes.

Conflict or not, he can go to hell!

"Before I tell you what a spineless asshole you are!" I yell, my control slipping away.

Now that the flood gates have opened, I can't stop.

"Jasper, your mom is a horrible person. I just wish you could see her the way I do."

Jasper opens his mouth, ready to rebuke, but I won't let him.

"I refuse to stand here and listen to you defend her, or tell me you don't know what to do. Last I checked, she's the one with the problem. She's the one who can't accept who you've chosen to be with. She's not even in our lives, and she's still causing problems because you can't let it go!"

I take a step forward and poke him in the chest.

"But I'll make it real easy for you. She can have you." I snatch my hand away from his when he reaches for me.

"Don't you dare do this," he begs.

"Do what, Jasper? Be the man in the relationship? Well, someone has to be, because when it comes to your mom, you're a scared little boy."

Jasper takes a step back and I know I've struck a nerve.

"Have fun in Seattle."

"What? You're not coming?" he asks, stunned.

"No," I reply curtly as I yank open the front door, ready to make my escape.

But I stop in my tracks when I hear, "But I've organized a ticket for you."

I turn around, hand braced on the doorframe. "Give it to your mom." And I storm off, slamming the door behind me.

CHAPTER TWENTY TWO
Not Another Groupie!

I haven't spoken to Jasper for two whole days.

My phone has been switched off as I'm afraid it might ring. But more importantly, I'm afraid it might *not* ring. Afraid of being afraid, I instruct my mom not to tell me if Jasper calls.

And if by chance he does, she is to tell him that I'm not home, or I'm washing my hair, or I'm walking the dog—even though we don't have dog. All the usual excuses used when trying to evade someone.

I know I said some harsh things to Jasper, but do I regret them?

No.

The only thing I regret is not saying them sooner.

I rub my belly, and the gesture is something I've found myself doing subconsciously over the past couple of days. What if this is it for Jasper and I? After everything we've been through, could this really be the end for us? That thought is one I don't want to think about unless I have to.

But I know Jasper, and I know he would never abandon his child. Whether he and I work or not, he'll always be a constant presence in our child's life.

Throwing myself back against the sofa, I curl my legs

underneath me, trying to focus on the random movie flickering on the TV.

But I fail miserably.

My eyes dart to my phone, which is sitting on the coffee table in front of me. Should I?

With nothing left to lose, I reach for it, switching it on while holding my breath.

It takes a minute or so to fire up, and when it does, I get inundated with message after message after message. The beeping sounds, until the next message overtakes it, and in the end, it just becomes a constant sea of beeps. Finally it stops and I look at the screen, which tells me I have a zillion and one messages.

Scrolling through the text messages, each one breaks my heart as they are all from Jasper, expressing how sorry he is, and how he fucked up. The more I read, the more desperate he becomes.

At around the fifteenth message, I have to stop because my tears are clouding my vision.

But I decide to torture myself further, and listen to the voice messages he has left. Hearing his deep, husky voice after so long, begging for forgiveness, tears me into two.

Sobbing as I listen to message after message, I wish I had just left my phone on.

The last message, which he left this morning, was just before he left for Seattle.

"Baby, I'm—" Pause. "Fuck, Ava, please forgive me. Please, I—" and I can hear the catch in his voice. "I love you so much. Please just give me another chance. Please talk to me. I'm dying inside. Each unanswered call is etching away at my heart. I fucked up. I know that now, and I know I don't deserve your forgiveness, but I need it. I need *you*. Please just let me make it up to you."

The line goes dead and I drop my phone, covering my face with my shaking hands.

How could I have been so stupid? This is what I do in times of crisis. I hide and cry.

But no more.

I reach for my phone, which has slipped in between the sofa cushions, and scroll through my address book and dial.

She answers on the third ring. "Please tell me you're coming."

"You bet. Just tell me when."

"**A**va, I swear to Christ, your life sees more drama than a teenage girl's diary," V says, dumping her backpack onto the green carpet of the Edgewater Hotel.

Letting out a small laugh, I hunt through my overnight bag, searching for the perfect outfit to knock Jasper's socks off.

"So how long does this festival go for?" I ask, pushing garments aside, unhappy with my findings.

V plonks onto the bed beside me, spreading her arms out wide with her feet dangling off the edge.

"Three days. The boys are on at 8:15p.m."

Looking at the clock, which reads 3:47p.m., I blow out a relieved breath. "Good. I can see Jasper before the show."

V shoots up and wiggles her finger at me. "Oh no, you don't. I'm keeping you a secret."

"What? Why?" I ask, confused, still rifling through my bag.

"Let that jerk suffer a little while longer. Putting you through the shit he has, he's lucky you're even here. He really needs to cut the apron strings with Mommy Dearest, and what better way to show him you mean business than by making him sweat it out for a few more hours," V explains with a menacing look on her pretty face.

Shaking my head at her, I reply with a smile, "You are one devious woman, my friend."

She shrugs. "It's one of my many talents. Now, let's get you ready so you knock his socks off and he comes begging for forgiveness. Preferably on his hands and knees," she adds with a wink.

"That's not really necessary." I giggle.

"Oh yes, it is. Trust me. You'll thank you me when he has you pressed up against a wall, showing you just how much he missed you."

I don't argue with her because I'm hoping she's right.

"I'm nervous," I whisper to V as we stand backstage, watching roadies zip around the stage, setting up P.O.E's gear.

"Why?" she asks, sucking on a bright red lollypop.

"I dunno. What if Jasper doesn't wanna see me?" I confess.

I'm rethinking V's plan. Maybe turning up unannounced isn't such a good idea. It sounded like a good idea at the time, but now standing in the wings, in front of forty thousand people, I realize it's a freakin' horrible idea!

What if he sees me and asks security to escort me off stage? What if he sees me and chokes, and I'm the cause of him stuffing up the performance of his career?

"Stop fidgeting. You're making me dizzy," V says, pointing her lollypop in the direction of my foot, which is tapping nervously.

I stop with the tapping, but then begin tugging on the silver charm bracelet Jasper gave me for Christmas. I twirl the single charm, which is a bird, around and around. V slaps her hand over mine, stilling me.

"Seriously, stop. It'll be fine. He'll be falling all over himself when he sees you, because not only does he worship the ground you walk on, you look freakin' hot. He'll be putty in your hands."

Toying with the hem of my green baby doll dress, I'm glad I went with V's wardrobe suggestion. It's a tad short and I better not drop anything, as the person behind me will get VIP access to my ass, but it's comfy and also kinda sexy. I've added my black combat boots with chunky heels, as this is a rock festival, so I figure I better dress the part.

"Thanks, I don't know what I'd do without you." I give her a big smile because I mean every word of it.

"You'd be a crazy cat lady if it wasn't for me," V states seriously, popping her lollypop back into her mouth.

I shrug, because I tend to agree with her.

Looking at my iPhone, it reads 8:12p.m. and P.O.E. will be on at any moment. Although I'm nervous to see Jasper, as I look out into the crowd of forty thousand people, I can't wait to see him win over every single person.

The backstage area isn't awfully large, so when two girls push their way to the front and block my view, I'm about to give them an earful but I zip it when I hear one of them, with gorgeous wavy black hair and violet eyes, speak to her redhead friend animatedly.

"Wait till you get a look at the singer in this band. Holy fuck! There's no doubt that God is a woman, as no man could create such beauty."

My voice gets caught in my throat as they are talking about Jasper.

"Oh, is he the guy you were telling me about? The one who does that *thing* with his tongue?" the redhead asks, motioning a circular action with her finger.

Whoa, what now?

I look at V desperately, while she places her finger over her lips, allowing the girls to finish, before I show them what I can do with *my* tongue. And fist!

"Yup, the one and only. We were a thing a while

back, but I heard he's gotten all serious with some chick. How boring," she laughs, flicking her long mane over her shoulder and swatting me in the face with her luscious locks.

Redhead laughs. "Can't be too serious if she's not here."

Blackie nods, and much to my dismay, I can't help but notice how pretty she is. She's a typical rock chick. Black short skirt, studded belt, some obscure band t-shirt and boots. Her short nails are painted black and she has silver rings on most of her fingers. Her hair is straightened, and under the bright lights, it gleams because it's so vibrant and bouncy. I wonder if it'll look so vibrant if I light it on fire.

But her snide comment snaps me out of my pyromaniac dream.

"Hey, good point." She readjusts her ample bust, winking. "He could never resist these."

I feel sick. I literally just gagged on a bit of bile.

V punches her fist against her open palm, gesturing with her head that I should get physical with the black-haired Goddess. I think about her suggestion for about five seconds and shake my head.

V then points to herself and raises both eyebrows, indicating she would be more than happy to do it for me.

However, no one is punching anyone, as the lights dim and the crowd goes wild.

The two in front of me start hooting and hollering for Jasper, and I wish they were standing anywhere but here, as they're ruining the moment.

I focus my attention on Lucas, as the girls have moved a few feet forward and thankfully given me some breathing room. Lucas gives the cheering arena a big wave and sits behind his glowing blue drum kit, twirling his sticks.

V squeals, latching onto my arm. "I'm so proud of him, Ava."

I am, too.

And just when I thought the crowd couldn't get any louder, out stroll Andy and Shooter.

They give one another a silent confirmation that they're ready to start, and commence on the count of four.

My heart begins to race, because after this short intro, Jasper will walk out onto that stage and own it.

As I peer out into the crowd, it seems like the female patrons are preparing for the arrival of Jasper, as most are applying lip-gloss, fluffing up their hair, and staring up at the stage with dreamy eyes.

The music stops and the stage fades into blackness. The stage is outdoors, and the only light falls from the star-filled sky. The murmurs from the audience can be heard loudly, catching on the night's cool breeze. I'm about to ask V what's going on, as I've never seen them do this before.

However, before I get a chance to do so, the lights flash back on and the boys continue their rocky tempo. I blow out a relieved breath, as I know this was done to increase the anticipation, to prep the crowd for their Rock God, Jasper White.

As if on cue, out runs Jasper with his blazing red guitar strapped to him. He starts playing animatedly, joining in with the rocky beat.

The arena shakes because thousands of fans are screaming out their love for Jasper. I don't blame them, because he looks amazing.

He's dressed in black jeans and a black t-shirt, which he's cut the sleeves off of. I notice a lot of side flesh showing as he bends down, rocking out to the music. I then see he has cut down the side seams, so the only thing that's keeping the shirt from becoming a smock is the hem.

His lean torso ripples with each movement, and his arms look fierce as he begins strumming the guitar wildly. His tousled hair is styled into a total 'fuck me' look, and under these bright lights, his eyes appear penetratingly blue.

He runs his elegant fingers up the length of the microphone stand and all the girls swoon, imaging it's their body his hands are running over. He then leans down, lets out a growl, and begins singing.

My insides vibrate with how loud it is up here. I know my ears will be ringing for days after, but it's so worth it.

Thankfully Jasper's performance is much better than his last, and he seems to be in better spirits. I begin to think about my journey and how I got here. As I look around in awe, not once did I imagine that when I returned to Los Angeles, close to two years ago, would I be standing in the wings, pregnant, and watching my incredibly hot boyfriend win over a crowd of forty thousand.

Each song just gets better and better, and I almost forget the two skanks in front of me. I haven't been able to catch Jasper's eye as there are so many people up here. And it's virtually impossible to peer over them, seeing as I'm so short. The two groupies however, have made their presence quite clear, by pretty much standing on top of the band.

"If she touches any of them, watch me clothesline her ass!" V shouts into my ear.

I give her a thumbs up and she laughs.

They finish up the song and Jasper gives the crowd a big wave. The applause is deafening. He motions with his hands for them to quiet down, which they do.

"Thanks. You guys are amazing," Jasper says in awe, looking out into the sea of fans.

The crowd cheers again.

"So, what would you guys say if I brought out a special someone to help me sing the next song?" Jasper asks cheekily.

A who what when?

I turn to V, but she looks just as confused as I.

The crowd cheers crazily, so Jasper continues. "I'll warn you, she bites. And she's a little crazy, but some-times a little crazy is not necessarily a bad thing," he says with a crooked smile.

Who the hell is he talking about?!

Leaning forward, as I'm desperate to know who this 'special someone' is, I nearly fall flat on my face when the pretty black-haired skank walks out, sauntering towards Jasper.

I look around frantically. Where's security to haul her offstage?

However, when the crowd see her, they go crazy.

What am I missing here?

Jasper answers my question.

"Ah… here she is, ladies and gentleman, boys and girls. Brace yourself… it's Delilah Rose!"

I look at V and mouth, "Who?"

V shrugs, giving Delilah Rose a scowl which rivals mine.

As I take in her Rock Goddess stature and look at Jasper, my heart sinks because they look perfect together.

She stands too close for my liking, bumping him with her shoulder, giving him a sultry wink. The band takes that as their cue and begins playing. She waits for the chorus and joins in, singing along with Jasper and using his microphone, so their lips are inches apart.

Suddenly I want to look anywhere but the stage, but I can't pry my eyes away because I need to see what she's going to do next, as she's clearly flirting with him.

Jasper looks over at her, giving her a small dimpled smile when she begins prowling the stage, encouraging the crowd to let lose.

His dimple only makes an appearance when he's genuinely happy. I feel sick, and unexpectedly, I feel claustrophobic.

"V! I need to get out of here," I scream, feeling my stomach roll.

V gives me a sympathetic nod and turns to leave.

I place my hand on her shoulder, shaking my head.

"Stay!" I yell, because I don't want her to miss Lucas because of me.

She looks surprised. "You sure?"

"Yes," I reply quickly, and head down the stairs before I vomit all over my pretty green dress.

CHAPTER TWENTY THREE
Reality Bites

This VIP pass has permitted me backstage access, allowing me to visit whichever stage I want. Seeing as there are four stages in total, I have been visiting them all, except the one Jasper was playing at. I know his set is over, as I've been gone for roughly two hours, but I can't face him. What if what Delilah said was true and Jasper does want to revisit her bouncy assets?

After the rough patch we've been experiencing, I really don't want to think about that, as she and her gigantic boobs are a big temptation.

A big, easy, non-complicated, non-pregnant temptation.

No baby. No mom who hates her guts. No fighting over work.

It's easy.

But with me lately, it seems like an effort to even talk to me.

That thought sends me into a deeper funk, and luckily one of my favorite bands is playing the main stage in five minutes.

I flash my laminated pass and security escorts me to a wooden rafter above the stage. It's really cool up here and not something I've ever seen before. It's amazing having a bird's eye View. I settle off to the end, away from every-one, happy to get some space.

Muse hits the stage, and being up here, listening to their hypocritical music, sends me into a lull. The lighting is soft and actually quite romantic, and the area I'm standing in is shrouded in almost complete darkness.

"Take a Bow" commences, which is my favorite song, and my hips begin swaying to the music, my eyes drooping shut. I'm lost in the mesmerizing rhythm, when suddenly a pair of hands snake around my middle, setting low on my hips.

I yelp, startled by the contact, swatting the hands away. But as my back is pressed into a firm front, I freeze. His smell is all man, and so is the hard erection, pushing into my lower back.

Jasper leans forward, his light stubble tickling my neck as he whispers into my ear, "Sway your hips again."

I gulp.

I'm frozen solid, so he tightens the grip around my waist and begins swaying his hips, encouraging me to move mine in sync with his.

Feeling stupid and rigid in his arms if I don't follow, I slowly mimic his movements and begin rotating my hips.

Because Jasper has me in a tight grip, pressed up so closely against him, I can't help it as I rub my ass over his crotch. And with each shift of my body, I can feel how turned on he is.

His hand travels up my front and his wicked thumb rubs over my nipple. It instantly peaks in my thin cotton dress, awakened by his touch. He hisses in a breath and licks the outer shell of my ear. My eyes flicker and I can't keep them open as he trails hot, wet kisses down my neck, sucking on the tender flesh just below my ear.

My head falls to the side of its own accord, as I have no control over my body when Jasper is involved. His sucks turn into longer, harder draws, and I begin panting heavily as I want him, like yesterday.

I know I shouldn't be doing this, as I want to find out who Delilah is, but my body betrays me and wins out in the end. I've surrendered to his skillful mouth and hands, and it feels... fucktastically amazing.

The sounds coming out of me rise louder and louder, and every part of me feels like it's on fire. With my eyes still closed, I'm blinded, but I feel like I can see everything he's doing, as every part of my body is in tune to his.

His fingers stop rolling over my nipples, and I almost whimper when he removes his hand from my breast. But I'm quickly rewarded with more delicious friction, as his hands descend down my body, while he's still sucking and kissing my throat.

His right arm wraps around my middle, holding me securely to him, but his left begins sliding lower, and lower.

His large hand is splayed out across my tummy, and the tips of his fingers are inches away from the top of my panties.

This is crazy. I'm totally getting felt up in an arena full of people!

"Do you want me to stop?" Jasper asks into my ear as he pulls away from my neck.

I shake my head quickly, as I would rather jump off this railing than have him stop.

He chuckles hoarsely and the sound has my stomach flipping in cartwheels.

He kisses my temple and glides his left hand down my side, snaking it up under my skirt.

Electricity jolts through my body as his warm hand squeezes my bare thigh. But a current of 100,000 watts, zaps me into shock when he cups me between my legs, pressing the heel of his hand against my core.

"Holy fuck, baby, you're soaked. You know how much of a turn on that is? Knowing I'm doing that to your body, I want to be inside of you so bad," Jasper whispers, his lips grazing my ear as he speaks.

He occasionally likes to speak dirty to me and each time he has done so, it has turned me into a shameless, wanton sex fiend.

Now is no exception.

Because of the loud music, he's basically tonguing my ear, and his breath is caressing the outer shell with each word.

I shift my hips, attempting to give him a sign of what I want. But Jasper knows my body better than I. He's just playing me until I beg for more.

Thankfully I don't have to beg this time as he slips his hand into the front of my underwear. He glides two fingers up and down my entrance, and then slowly, he slides into me.We both groan at the contact and I grind myself against his skillful fingers, my body loving the intrusion.

The devilish rhythm of his fingers is steadily torturing me, and the way his hips are rocking into my back, his impressive length rubbing against my ass, is just adding to the torment.

As hard as it is, I still my hips and turn my head at an uncomfortable angle, wanting to see his face. It's so worth it because he looks fucking sex crazed. Pupils dilated, mouth slightly parted, and hair disheveled, has my insides quivering in desire.

"I want you inside me," I say, feeling like a total sexual deviant.

Jasper gifts me a dimpled smile. "Yes, ma'am."

He slides his fingers out of me, and with both hands, he discreetly pulls off my underwear, which I step out of as soon as they reach my feet.

The cool breeze brushes over my wetness and I shiver, anticipating his next move.

I don't have to wait long.

Jasper discreetly lifts up my dress, unnoticeably from behind and presses himself up against me.

"I'd give anything to bend you over this railing, but this will have to do... for now," he whispers, angling himself as he pushes into me from behind.

I cry out loudly and thankfully, "Invincible" drowns out my passionate cries. Jasper stills, allowing my muscles to accept him, and then he begins rocking into me, holding my waist prisoner in both hands, maneuvering my body to get the angle just right.

I feel so full, especially with him taking me from behind, but I like it and I want more, so I thrust back, taking him in deeper as I hold onto the rail for support.

"Holy shit!" Jasper cries as he pushes into me, my body

milking every stroke. "I'm so sorry," he says breathlessly, which surprises me. "I've missed you so much. Please don't run away from me again. You're my everything, Ava."

As he speaks, he increases the speed of his thrusts and tightens his grip around my waist, his fingers pinching into my skin.

I'm just holding on as his heartfelt words, combined with the feel of him imbedded so deeply within me is tipping me over the edge. I'm trying my damnedest not to explode, but it's virtually impossible because Jasper is engulfing me with his huge body, inside and out.

Jasper knows I'm close, so he begins pushing into me harder and faster, leaving no part of me unexplored. His labored breaths tickle my neck, and as he leans forward, biting me softly, I come undone with a loud scream. Aftershock after aftershock rocks my body, but Jasper is still not done.

His movements cease and he pulls out leisurely. I miss his warmth already. But then he pushes back into me, deliberately slow, allowing me to feel EVERY single, hot inch of him. My eyes roll into the back of my head, because the sensation is stimulating every nerve in my entire body.

The crowd erupts into a loud applause, reminding me of where we are, and I feel like a total exhibitionist, as there are thousands of people below, probably looking up my dress right now. That thought slows my frantic rocking.

"Don't worry, they can't see us. The glare of the stage lights is too bright," Jasper says on an exhalation.

But even if they could, I wouldn't stop.

He begins driving into me powerfully, and I have to brace my hands on the railing to stop myself from slumping into a legless mess.

"It wouldn't matter if they could," he breathes. "Because I want everyone to know you're mine. This is mine," he says, pushing into me so deeply, I gasp with the force of it.

I know he's close as he's quickening his strokes, and I thrust back, meeting him stroke for stroke.

He tightens his grip on me and the pressure is sure to leave a bruise, but I don't care. I want him to explode like never before, so I tighten my muscles and grind my ass against him.

It has the desired effect as he blows out a curse and a moan of pure pleasure. However, he surprises me, as he's about to pull out before he's done.

"What are you doing?" I ask, panting.

"It'll be messy if I don't pull out," he says on quickened breaths.

"I don't care. Life is messy," I reply, meaning every word of it as I slam my hips backwards, rocking into him.

Jasper groans and within one, two stokes, he comes undone with a frantic moan. He drops his chin onto my shoulder, totally spent.

His heart is beating wildly against my back, in sync with mine, as mine is about to leap out of my throat. But I wouldn't give this feeling up for anything.

After a few moments, he pulls out and I miss the connection. We arrange our clothes and I tastefully slip on my underwear, while trying not to blush.

"You're beautiful," Jasper says, looking at me

hungrily. "The hint of pink on your cheeks makes me want you all over again."

He runs his fingertips down my cheek, stopping at my lips and thumbing my bottom lip. As he fixates on my mouth, we hear the shuffling of feet and realize the band has finished.

Wow, when did that happen?

"Looks like we should go," Jasper says sadly, watching the dispersing crowd.

I nod, slightly depressed. Up here, high above everyone, just me and him, I could pretend it's our world. No bitchy moms, or catty exes, or new black-haired threats.

But reality comes crashing down and as Jasper grabs my hand, walking towards the exit, I am totally one with the saying, Reality Bites.

CHAPTER TWENTY FOUR
Births, Deaths and Marriages

After our very PDA, we go back to the hotel and have more of a *private* display of affection, all night long.

Both were amazing because they were with Jasper, but I know the conversation we're about to have is going to be anything but amazing.

I'm sitting up in bed, sipping my tea, when Jasper strolls out of the bathroom in jeans and a big white fluffy towel wrapped around his neck.

His wet hair is flicked everywhere, and as he runs a hand through it, droplets skim down his long neck and splash onto his chest. I can't help myself as I wet my lips longingly.

"You keep giving me those eyes, Ms. Thompson, and I'm going to do something about it."

I quickly drop my eyes, embarrassed I've been caught ogling him—again.

He lets out a deep laugh while pouring himself a cup of coffee.

One Mississippi.

Two Mississippi.

Surely enough time has passed and I can totally start checking him out again.

He takes a seat at the end of the bed and softly tugs on my big toe.

Damn, looks like no more eyeballing because now it's time to get serious.

"Jasper..." I start.

But Jasper holds up his hand. "Let me talk before you say anything," he says quickly.

I give him a small nod and he takes a deep breath before he speaks.

"Ava, I'm sorry. Again. There are no excuses for the way I've treated you. And I don't blame you if you hate me."

"I don't hate you, Jasper," I whisper.

If I hated him, I sure as hell wouldn't be riding around buck naked in public with him.

"And for that, I am so lucky. I fucked up. Putting my selfish needs before you. Before our baby. I'll never forgive myself for that," he says sincerely.

"Jasper..."

"No, Ava, please, let me finish," he says, taking a hold of my hand and rubbing his thumb over my knuckles.

I nod, biting my lip, a little afraid of what he's going to say next.

"You walking out on me, it was the best thing for me. I needed that as a wakeup call. I'm not going to lie to you, cutting my mom out is going to be hard, it has been hard. But I mean it, baby, I can't live without you. I'm an asshole for even giving my mom another chance. I'm done with her, I swear it. Just please tell me you forgive me," he says, begging me with every inch of his body.

I'm speechless. I love him more than words could ever express, but I have a feeling his mom won't let him go as easily as he hopes.

"Jasper... I understand how hard this has been on you. But you cutting your mom out, it's too much. You can't do that."

Jasper is about to retaliate, but I clarify my point.

"I mean, I don't think that you can."

Jasper nods when the realization of what I've said hits home.

He meets my eyes, pinning me with a serious, heartfelt stare. "You're right, Ava. But I'm going to try. If she wants to be in my life, then she has to accept you. If she doesn't, then that's her problem. Okay?"

I give him a small smile. "Okay."

But anything involving his mother will never be okay.

The day in Seattle has been wonderful.

Jasper and I visited the famous Space Needle and strolled down the streets of Seattle, taking in all of its beauty. We stopped at Pioneer Square and snuck in a few kisses on the stairs like a couple of teenagers.

It's been perfect.

Now we're standing in the wings watching Flames

perform. Flames are on the same record label as Jasper, and are great friends with all of the boys.

I'm nestled into Jasper's arms, my body enfolded into his chest. I always feel smaller when wrapped up this way, as his strong arms engulf me whole.

Everything between us seems to have settled. Here's hoping when we return home that continues, as I've had enough drama to last me two lifetimes.

And of course, I've just jinxed myself, as I see the minx that is Delilah Rose looking our way. She saunters over to us and narrows her eyes at me quickly before giving Jasper a sultry look.

"Hey, babe," she says, giving Jasper a kiss on the cheek.

I only just stop myself from head butting her smack bang between the eyes.

"Hey, Delilah," Jasper replies, tightening his hands around my waist.

"You coming to the after party? It's P.O.E vs. Roses in a drink off. Seeing as we're festival buddies and all, we totally need to fight it out in a messy, drunken fight, to determine who the better band is." She smirks at him innocently.

Nothing about this girl is innocent.

I keep my eyes on the band, not wanting to appear like I'm eavesdropping.

Jasper rests his chin on my head and replies, "I dunno, I'm probably going to turn in early. Got things I gotta *do*." He squeezes my waist lightly.

As he says the word *Do*, I know he's referring to me.

And judging by the deep scowl on Delilah's face, so does she.

I'm internally fist punching my way to happy town right now, and I only just resist the urge to poke my tongue out and give her the infamous, 'na na nana na' chant.

"Oh c'mon, don't be a pussy. I remember a time when you and I would be the last two men standing. Or lying," she adds with a wink.

Seriously? Did she really just say that?

I shuffle uncomfortably in Jasper's arms and he senses my discomfort.

"Yeah, well, that was a lifetime ago and I'm a different person now, thanks to this little lady," he says, kissing the top of my head.

Delilah isn't happy with his response but shrugs it off. "Okay, whatever. Your loss." She strolls off, making sure she wiggles her ass on her exit.

I exhale, thankful she's gone.

Jasper kisses my cheek reassuringly, but I feel anything but reassured when I know Delilah Rose has her sights on my man.

I hate parties.

I especially hate parties where most of the female attendees are trying to make out with my boyfriend.

I've watched Jasper play conversational ping pong with anyone who can get their acrylic nails into him.

But I haven't stormed off, or kicked up a stink, as I know he's only talking to them because he has to. And if this relationship is to last, then I have to trust Jasper, which I do.

It's them I don't.

"I'm mighty proud of you," V says, plonking onto the barstool near me.

"For what?" I reply, swizzling my swizzle stick.

"For not gouging out the eyeballs of every female, and the occasional male, who's looking at Jasper," she replies seriously.

I laugh, because as always, she's so eloquent.

"I'm trying, but it's hard. Especially when girls like her," I flick my head towards Delilah, "are throwing themselves, basically naked, at him."

V glares at Delilah as she's standing way too close, showing Jasper her new leg tattoo, which of course, is high up on her inner thigh.

"In times of crisis, the only thing to stop one from going postal is alcohol. But seeing as I feel like ass, and you, well, you're knocked up, we can only sit here and make fun of their rancid fashion sense."

She laughs, pointing at a girl's shoes which are made up of furry pom-poms and glitter, and are the shoe equivalent of a My Little Pony birthday cake.

"What's the matter?" I ask, looking at her pasty form rather than the hideous shoes.

Now that I take a closer look, I realize that she does look a little pale and has dark circles under her eyes.

"Are you okay, V? You look horrible," I say without thinking.

"Thanks," she laughs, sipping her flat lemonade.

"Do you wanna go back to the hotel? I'd be more than happy to go with you," I say, secretly hoping she says yes.

"No, it's okay. I've just been feeling flat and off color all week. I think I might go to the doc when we get back home."

"I'm seeing Dr. Hemming soon," I reply, as my results should be in by now. "You could come with me?"

V nods. "Thanks. I might just do that."

Hearing loud laughter, I turn to see Delilah whispering something into Jasper's ear. He's laughing, shaking his head, and seems totally oblivious to her blatant flirting.

I'm sure it's innocent on his behalf, but I still hate it.

"I'm going outside to get some fresh air," I sigh to V, standing up.

"Okay, babe. Want me to come with?" she asks, but looks to be in no shape to move.

"No, it's okay. You're not well. Stay here where it's warm. I won't be long."

Giving her forehead a quick kiss, I push my way through the crowd of partygoers.

As I walk out into the hallway, I have no idea where to go, so I decide to ride the elevator to the top floor and hope for the best.

The lift takes me to the twenty-sixth floor, and as I poke my head around the corner, hoping I don't get carted away by security, I see a big rooftop balcony.

I make a quick, silent beeline for it, and that's where I

end up, looking over the railing at the hustle and bustle of the ants below. Being this high up, I feel its okay to snoop in on the lives of those below me and remain undetected.

There is an immense, posh hotel across from me, and as I look into the glowing room, I see a young girl, about my age, sitting on her bed, head in hands, crying. I feel for her and I wonder if she too, has the weight of the world on her shoulders.

"There you are."

A voice says from behind me.

Jasper.

"Here I am," I reply half-heartedly. Gee, that sounded lame even to my ears.

"What's the matter?" he asks, stepping beside me and clasping my hand in his.

"Nothing," I lie, as my eyes are still glued on the crying girl across from me.

"You don't look like nothing is wrong. You've got a something face, not a nothing face."

I should have known there's no fooling him.

I watch the girl with interest as she turns and stares back at me, like she only just felt eyes watching her. I give her a reassuring smile and she returns it, wiping away her tears.

"Who is Delilah?" I ask.

Jasper hesitates, but answers with a sigh. "Okay, that's not what I was expecting, but um... she's just an old friend."

The girl is now the one to give me a reassuring smile, as I'm sure she can read my face for what it is.

Surrender and defeat.

"An old friend you've slept with?" I ask quickly.

I probably should have been a little nicer about it all, but I seriously don't have the energy to dance around in circles tonight.

"Yes," Jasper replies. He pauses. "You're not jealous of her, are you?"

I turn to face him and confess, "No. Yes. Maybe. I don't know."

Jasper's mouth twitches. "Okay, how about you choose one answer and we'll roll with that."

"This isn't funny. I overheard Delilah telling her friend some personal things, and I hate that these girls know you in that way."

He raises his eyebrow at me.

I clarify, "You know, intimately."

Jasper sighs, running a hand through his hair which is blowing in the breeze. "Ah."

He gets it.

But he doesn't really get how uncomfortable it makes me when girls of all shapes and sizes talk to their girl-friends about conquering my boyfriend.

I bite my lip and tell myself now is not the time to cry, and hope my tear ducts listen.

"Ava," Jasper says, dipping his face to meet my eyes. "If I could erase every girl I've ever slept with, I would, because they meant nothing to me. Every kiss, every touch, was in vain. To fill some fucked up, lonely hole, that was eating away at my soul. But with each faceless person I slept with, that hole just got bigger and bigger and before long, it was a gaping cliff edge. And then... then I met you, and everyone else became void. That hole started closing over with every smile, every kiss, and every touch you ever gave me. You are my miracle."

I don't know when I started crying, but now that I've started, I can't stop.

Jasper turns to face me and I replicate his movement.

We're standing, facing one another silently, with the full moon illuminating Jasper's beautiful cerulean eyes. I don't know what it is about a full moon. Its appearance never changes, but its beauty leaves me speechless, time and time again.

"Shit," Jasper mumbles, breaking the silence.

"What?" I ask, sniffing back my tears.

Jasper rubs the back of his neck uncomfortably and I begin to panic as I recognize this gesture as one of nervousness.

What does he have to be nervous about?

"What, Jasper?" I ask a little more forcibly when he doesn't reply.

"I wanted to do this a little differently, with flowers and candles. Stuff that you deserve," he says softly.

"Do what?" I ask, confused.

His Adam's apple bobs and he swallows quickly. "Ava, I love you. You've given me a reason to get up in the morning, and you've given me reason to fight for what I want." He places his hand on my tummy as he refers to our child.

"You're my forever and a day, baby."

Is he?

He answers my question within seconds as he pulls a blue velvet box from his leather jacket's inner pocket.

"Marry me."

He opens the box, and inside lies the most beautiful ring I have ever seen. Simple, but elegant, this ring is timeless. A white gold plain band catches the moonlight, and it shines brightly. But the centerpiece is an impressive solitaire cut diamond, and I can't help but contrast its sparkling appearance to the stars twinkling above.

My eyes are glued to the ring before me, and I am so goldfishing it right now.

I can't speak.

He wants me to marry him? Seriously? I don't know what to say. We've never discussed marriage. Or kids.

And now, here I am, thinking about both!

"Ava?" Jasper asks softly.

My eyes meet his worried ones.

"Will you marry me?" he asks again, and my heart begins thumping uncontrollably.

"I... I... I," I stutter.

"I know it's a shock, but with the baby coming, I want to give him or her a stable upbringing."

That snaps me out my stupor.

"What do you mean?"

Jasper scrunches up his brow, confused.

So I clarify. "Is that the only reason why you want to marry me? Because I'm pregnant?"

"What? No, Ava, of course not," he says, his voice rising to emphasize his point.

But it's too late.

"If I weren't pregnant, would you propose to me?" I ask, searching his eyes to find out the truth.

Jasper answers without delay. "I would marry you in a heartbeat."

"That's not what I'm asking, Jasper," I reply softly.

I know what his answer is going to be, even before he replies.

"Ava, I love you. Whether we get married today, tomorrow, or in the next five years, I want to be your husband. I just think now would be better timing."

That's all the answer I need.

"Then my answer is no," I whisper, my heart breaking as the words leave my lips.

"No?" Jasper gasps, taking a small step back. "But why? Don't you love me enough to marry me?" he asks.

"That's the problem," I sigh. "I love you too much, and marrying you when neither of us are ready will taint that love. Marrying me just because you think it's the noble thing to do isn't how I envisioned you proposing to me."

Once or twice, I may have gotten lost in the whole fantasy of if we were to get married, how would he do it. And this most definitely is not a scenario my romantic mind conjured up.

"That's not why I asked you to marry me," Jasper says, but I can tell by the guilty look on his face its part of the reason why.

"Would you have asked me to marry you if I wasn't pregnant? If we came here to Seattle, and did all the things that we have, and experienced everything that we have, would you still be standing here, proposing to me?"

I put it to him as simply as I can.

Jasper lowers his chin, his hair dipping into his eyes as he tucks the ring safely into his pocket. He doesn't reply and that's okay, because I know what his answer would be. And so does he.

The sight of the beautiful ring being tucked away is heartbreaking, and I wish I could accept it.

But I just can't.

Jasper's eyes look plagued and he opens his mouth, ready to defend his case, but the ringing of his phone interrupts him.

Jasper reaches into his jacket pocket and retrieves it. "Hmm," he mumbles, looking at me, asking if it would be okay to answer it, seeing as we're kinda in the middle of something important.

I nod and feel a migraine approaching after what just happened.

"I don't recognize the number," he says, scrunching up his brow.

His face contorts in rage within a second of answering the phone.

"I don't want to talk to you!"

I can hear a loud, panicked voice yell at him through the phone, and then I witness all the color drain out of his face.

"What? When?" he gasps.

Jasper listens as he yanks at his messy hair, his eyes closed tight.

"Where is she?" he asks, opening his overwhelmed eyes.

I hear more yelling and make out a female voice.

"Just answer the fucking question, Indie! Where is she?"

Indie?

"Fuck!" Jasper roars.

He ends the call and looks at me, eyes frantic.

"Jasper, what is it? What's happened?" I ask in a quiet, scared voice.

Jasper fists both hands through his hair and shuts his eyes tight.

As he reopens them, I can see the pain flashing behind them. "It's my mom."

"What about her?" I ask apprehensively.

Jasper draws in a deep breath before he replies, "She's in the hospital."

"Oh my God," I gasp, covering my mouth with my hands. "Is she okay?"

Jasper shakes his head and his eyes begin to fill with tears.

I stalk over to him, latching onto his arm. "Jasper, what happened?"

Jasper's blue eyes search mine and a single tear rolls down his cheek.

"She tried to kill herself."

CHAPTER
TWENTY FIVE

No

"Jasper, please let me come with you!" I plead, following behind him as he charges down the long hallway to his hotel room.

He barges through the door, heading straight for the bedroom.

I watch as he stuffs his belongings into a black backpack and zips it up quickly.

"Ava, no, please just stay here," he says, throwing his backpack onto one shoulder.

"But I want to be there for you," I answer, standing in the bedroom doorway so he'll stop and listen to me.

"I know, and I love you so much for that. But no," he replies, walking towards me, and shifting me out of the way gently.

"Why not?" I plead, chasing after him as he rushes through the hotel, looking for anything he may have left behind.

"How are you going to get back home? There will be no flights available at this time of the night," I yell, trying to appeal to his rational side.

He spins around to face me and he looks a mess. "I don't know. I'll drive, hitchhike, whatever, but I just need you to stay here, okay? Can you do that for me?"

I nod, knowing this is a discussion not up for negotiation.

I lower my eyes and can't help the sinking feeling that he's leaving me here because he knows I'm not welcome anywhere near his mom.

"Hey, look at me," he pleads, closing the gap between us in two steps.

I raise my eyes to his and can't help but frown.

"I need you to be safe, Ava. In your condition, you can't be gallivanting the streets with me, trying to find a way home."

I look away from him as tears are forming, because I know he's right.

He grabs my upper arms and squeezes lightly to get my attention. "I promise I'll call you as soon as I get home and know what's going on. Just promise you'll wait for me to call," he says desperately, searching my eyes.

"Of course I will," I reply, slightly confused.

Why do I feel like there's an ominous message behind his words?

"I love you, Ava."

He bends down, kissing my forehead quickly. I watch his retreating form as he charges through the door, leaving me alone with my fears.

The plane ride home was horrible. V tried to cheer me up, but all I could think of was Jasper.

It's been close to a day since I've heard from him. We left Seattle this morning and now that I'm back home, the urge to go see Jasper is overwhelming.

But I don't know what hospital his mom is at, and I made a promise to wait until he contacted me.

So, here I sit, in my favorite armchair, which overlooks the neighborhood. The moon lights up the quiet street, but it may as well be black outside, as there is no light in my world until I speak to Jasper.

"Are you okay, V?" I ask from outside her bathroom door.

I hear her throw up yet again.

Well, that answers my question.

My phone chirps and I reach for it in my back pocket, thinking it's Jasper, as I have yet to hear from him.

But it's not him.

"Hello?"

"Hi, Ava, this is Shelley from Doctor Hemming's clinic. We have your results here. Did you want to make an appointment to see Doctor Hemming?"

I breathe a sigh of relief. "Yes, please. Do you have anything available today?"

I can hear keys clicking. "Sure. Does 3p.m. suit you?"

"Yes, that's fine. Thank you."

I hung up, thankful I'm able to finally talk to Doctor Hemming, but also a little jaded since Jasper won't be with me.

"V," I whisper from outside the door, knocking softly.

She groans as she trudges over to the door, opening it, and leaning onto the frame for support.

I recoil when I see her.

"Oh V, you look like shit," I say without thinking, taking in her pasty appearance and crazed hair.

"Gee thanks," she replies in a hoarse voice.

"Sorry," I reply, making a pained face.

"Hey, good news. I'm seeing Doctor Hemming today at three. You still wanna come?" I ask, hopeful.

"You bet your ass I do. I need some killer drugs. And pronto."

We arrive at the doctor's office early, and I'm sitting in the world's most uncomfortable chair reading a two year old copy of *Cosmo.*

But I'm only half reading it, as I'm using the magazine as a veil, peeping over the top of it, trying to figure out who the receptionist is.

I've seen her before and by the way she's staring at me, she also recognizes me.

"V. Who is that?" I whisper, using the magazine as a shield to cover my mouth.

"Who's who?" V yells, looking around the waiting room.

"Sssh," I hiss. "Her," I whisper, indicating with my head to the receptionist sitting behind the glass screen.

V looks over and shrugs. "Oh, who cares? Brad Pitt could be sitting near me and I couldn't care less! What's taking so long?" she groans, clutching her stomach.

Thankfully the nurse comes out, announcing it's my turn.

Both V and I spring up and as I walk past the reception desk, I give the blonde pixie behind the screen one last look, but still nothing.

The nurse takes us to an exam room and gets my vitals.

Doctor Hemming has been my doctor since I was five years old, and even though it's time for retirement, he still won't hang up his white coat.

"Hello, girls," Doctor Hemming says, entering the room.

He takes one look at V and frown lines furrow his brow.

"Are you okay, Veronica? You look unwell," he says, taking a seat behind his computer.

"No, I'm pretty sure I'm dying. Please give me drugs to make me better," V replies, slouching into her seat.

Doctor Hemming's mouth twitches. "Oh, well, let me go over Ava's results first, and then we'll get to you."

He opens my file and looks over the results with a big smile.

"Everything looks great, Ava. No problems whatsoever. Maybe a little low in iron. I can prescribe you some iron tablets, or you can just eat a little more red meat, legumes, et cetera."

"Oh, that's great news," I say happily, clasping my hands in a thankful prayer. "Will it be okay to take iron tablets?" I ask.

Doctor Hemming's pen pauses, as he writes something in my file. He meets my eyes and raises an eyebrow, appearing utterly confused.

So I explain. "You know, will it hurt the baby?"

Doctor Hemming scrunches his brow. "I don't mean to be rude, Ava, but what baby?"

"My baby," I answer, beginning to panic.

V sits up in her chair and looks at me.

Doctor Hemming shakes his head. "I'm not following, Ava."

My throat has gone dry and trying to swallow, feels close to impossible.

"Doctor Hemming... I'm pregnant," I say slowly.

"You are?" he questions.

The room begins closing in on me.

"Yes. That's what I'm here for. For you to tell me how the baby is going. How far along I am? That's why I got the blood work," I explain, on the verge of tears.

Doctor Hemming clears his throat and quickly flicks through my file, adjusting his glasses. After a minute or so, he shakes his head.

"Ava... I'm so sorry, but no, you're not. When your blood was taken... you were not pregnant."

His words sound foreign, like he's speaking to me in a different language. A horrible, deceitful language.

I can't speak.

I can't move.

I can't think.

All I can hear on repeat are the words, "You were not pregnant."

Only when V stands up, do I snap out of my catatonic state.

"There has to be some mistake. She did the test! It was positive, wasn't it, Ava?" V demands, looking at me, beseeching me to make sense of what's going on.

I nod, thinking back to V's words when we were both taking the tests.

"Here, I'll do one with you. I can be your pee buddy."

Holy shit.

Oh...

Fuck.

"What's the matter, Ava?" V asks, her voice quivering.

"It was positive," I whisper, looking up into my best friend's face. "But it wasn't my test."

"Whose test was it then?" she asks quickly.

She knows the answer, but she needs me to confirm it, to make this all real.

"Yours, V. The test was yours. You're pregnant, not me," I whisper sadly.

"That's impossible! Isn't it?" V asks, looking at a confused Doctor Hemming.

"How have you been feeling lately, Veronica?" he

asks, pulling out a new piece of paper and writing something down.

"Hungry, all the time. And just lately, I've been feeling sick to my stomach and I can't keep anything down."

As soon as the words pass her lips, she slumps into the chair.

"Fuck me dead. I'm pregnant! I'm motherfucking pregnant."

Doctor Hemming clears his throat, and both V and I snap back into reality.

"I'm a little confused as to what's going on, but I'm guessing, Ava, you believed you were pregnant, but Veronica is actually the pregnant one?"

I nod, as I'm incapable of speech.

"Well, Veronica, congratulations!"

V scowls.

"Or not," he adds quickly.

"How could this happen? This makes no sense. I haven't had my period for weeks, months," I state, my voice becoming hysterical. "How is that even possible? There has to be some mistake!" I cry, not wanting to believe him.

Doctor Hemming steeples his fingers in front of him and speaks to me in a gentle voice. "I've gone over your file. It said you were in the hospital, beat up quite badly, and you banged your head?"

I nod, cringing when reliving the memory of being beaten to a pulp by Harper.

"Well, stress does amazing things to the body. Also,

were you on medication to help manage the pain, and to help you sleep?"

I nod again.

"Your body has been through a lot of stress Ava, physically and emotionally. The body heals in its own way. You're low in iron and a little underweight, sometimes these things just happen," he explains sympathetically.

This didn't just happen.

Did it?

I feel hollow inside as I unconsciously rub my tummy, which is now only filled with Captain Crunch.

V leaps up from her chair with her hand covering her mouth, rushing out the door. "I'm going to be sick!"

I quickly stand to follow, but Doctor Hemming stops me. "Ava."

I turn to face him. "I'm very sorry. Judging by your reaction, you really wanted this baby."

I give him a small smile and excuse myself quickly, because only now do I realize how much I really did.

"**D**o you want me to pee with you?" I ask V, as I unwrap the pregnancy test in her bathroom.

I don't fail to see the irony in this whole situation.

V looks at me as she's sitting on the toilet, cradling her brow.

"I do not, seeing as the last time this happened, you got the results mixed up. Sheesh, lucky you didn't become a midwife. Otherwise, there would be a lot of parents with God knows whose babies," she says, only half joking.

"I don't know how many times I can say I'm sorry without it becoming annoying," I reply, feeling like the world's worst friend.

"Not enough," she replies, extending out her palm. "Give me the damn test already."

I do, but only because she asked so nicely.

I decide to wait outside as I need the fresh air to clear my head.

Sitting on the top step, I rest my elbows on my knees and support my chin with my steepled fingers, deep in thought.

How am I going to tell Jasper? This is going to break his heart, and I'm not sure if it'll ever heal. He wanted this baby so much, and now, now I have to break the news that there is no baby. That I was mistaken.

How could I have been so stupid? I shouldn't have had those glasses of wine. My whole thinking was off course, and when I saw the test was positive, I didn't stop to look whose test it actually was, because not once did I think V was pregnant.

I fucked up.

I have really fucked up this time.

"So, I'm pregnant," V says, taking a seat near me.

Looking over at her, I give her a strained smile.

"I'm sorry, V. I should have made sure the test was mine." I hide behind my hair as I lower my head, ashamed of myself.

"Ava, stop apologizing. I know you didn't do this on purpose. You're not one of those pseudocyesis women."

I nod, so grateful she isn't chewing my ass out right now, as she has every right to.

"Well, on the bright side, at least I know I don't have worms. I was getting worried there for a while, seeing as I was eating and drinking anything within a five mile radius."

She's about to continue when her mouth pops open.

"What is it?" I ask, concerned.

"OhMyGod, Ava, my baby is going to be a fat alcoholic!"

"What?" I ask, scrunching up my face.

"All I've wanted to do is eat and drink. I've craved it. But now I know it's the baby whose been craving it. My baby is a total lush, with a serious addiction to peanut butter!"

I can't help the laugh that cackles out of me. I try to stop it by clamping my mouth shut, but it breaks free and I just go with it.

Soon after my outburst, V is cackling along with me.

V's neighbor strolls past, walking her poodle, Marcia, and she quickens her step when she sees us rolling around in fits of laughter, with tears spilling down our cheeks for no apparent reason.

The more we try to stop ourselves, the more we laugh.

But V and I both know these laughs are really tears in disguise.

"Ava, honey, do you want dinner?" my mother asks as I try to creep up the stairs without detection.

I fail.

"Um, no, Mom, I'm fine. I'm just going to take a shower and go to bed," I reply, looking at her as she pokes her head around the corner.

"Oh okay. You not feeling well?" she asks, stepping out of the kitchen.

She wipes her hands on her strawberry print apron and feels my forehead.

"I'm just tired," I reply lamely, trying to avoid her knowledgeable eyes.

"Okay, sweetheart." She nods, but can see the tension around my eyes.

I ascend the first step and halt when my mom says, "Jasper called."

I close my eyes, biting my lip. "He did?" I ask, with my back turned to her.

"Yes. He said he's tried your cell, but it's been switched off."

I turned it off before I went into the doctor's office, and haven't switched it back on.

"He said he's at the hospital with his mom, and that he'll call you later on tonight."

I nod. "Thanks, Mom." I turn to finish climbing the rest of the stairs.

"Are you sure everything is okay, honey?" my mom asks, as I must resemble someone walking in a death march.

No, I internally reply. It most certainly is not okay.

But instead I reply, "Sure, Mom. Everything is fine."

Who would have thought a phone could be your worst enemy. I know what I should do, but I just can't.

Not tonight.

My brain feels fried and my emotions are running haywire. All I want to do is shower and sleep, and deal with the mess that is my life tomorrow.

God knows it'll be there when I wake up.

I eye the phone, which is sitting harmlessly on the end of the bed. But it may as well be a snake. I toe it off, hearing it fall with a loud thud onto the carpet.

Out of sight, out of mind.

Hunting through the bag I have hanging off the back of my chair, my hands pass over what I'm searching for.

I turn the shower onto hot, and as I wait for the water to warm up, I unwrap the spare pregnancy test I swiped from V's and do my thing.

Again, I don't fail to see the irony in the first time I took the test, as opposed to this time around. The first time I was scared, scared that the results would read positive. But now, now I'm scared the results are going to be negative.

I decide some music might cheer me up, so I crank on the stereo and hop into the warm spray of water after I strip. The feeling is bliss, and getting out is not going to be happening any time soon.

As I lather up the soap and begin washing myself, my hands fall to my belly and suddenly, I feel that empty feeling wash over me again.

How could this be? This morning I thought there was a living being inside of me. But now, I just feel barren. How can it be that something I was so uncertain I wanted is something I so desperately crave? Looks like life's old saying, 'you want what you can't have,' is true.

I left the pregnancy test on the edge of the basin. I wipe down the steam that has collected on the frosted shower glass. I don't need to see it to know the results, but this will make what I already know to be true all the more real.

The test reveals that I am not pregnant, but I just had to be sure.

If my mood isn't depressing enough, "My Immortal" by Evanescence comes on, and the tears I have been bravely holding onto, not wanting to crumble in front of V, come cascading down my cheeks. Before long, I don't know what is water spray from the showerhead, and what are my own tears, as they both mingle together in a wet, slippery mess.

Once the floodgates open, I can't stop.

I cry for my nonexistent baby.

I cry for V.

I cry for Jasper.

But most importantly, I cry for me.

I don't know how I'm going to get through this without drowning in my fears.

I slide down the shower wall and crumble into a heap, sobbing on the shower floor.

It's not until my teeth are chattering and my body is shivering do I realize the water has run cold.

But regardless of the temperature, I feel dead inside.

CHAPTER TWENTY SIX
The Last Kiss

I can't put it off any longer.

I switch on my phone and wait.

Taking a deep breath as it finishes doing its thing, I look at the screen and see I have a few texts from Jasper, asking me to call him and asking where I am.

I can't do it.

I quickly switch it off and hide back under the covers, waiting for sleep to drag me into oblivion.

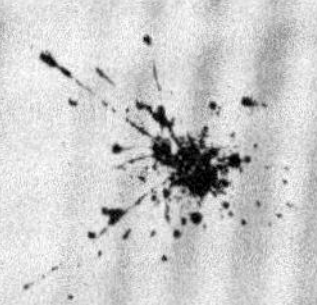

I wake and know I'm not alone.

"Hey, sleepyhead."

Opening my eyes, I take in Jasper White lying beside me.

He looks beat, but he still takes my breath away.

"Hi," I croak. "What time is it?"

I feel the bed shift as Jasper props up on an elbow to look over at the bedside table.

"A little past four," he replies, shuffling closer to me.

"How'd you get in?" I whisper, staring into his beautiful eyes.

Jasper smirks and it's the best thing I've seen all day.

"I have my ways," he replies, tapping the end of my nose playfully.

I don't even question him as I'm just so happy he's here.

"How's your mom?" I ask quickly, not wanting to discuss anything else.

Jasper sighs. "Well, she's alive."

"That's a start," I reply, hoping I sound encouraging.

Jasper nods.

There is a long pause as I wait for him to speak.

"She tried to kill herself by OD'ing," he admits, closing his eyes tight.

I gasp, as this must bring up some painful memories for Jasper. His mom is no stranger to making prescription drugs her best friend, and it looks like old habits die hard.

"Oh my God. That's horrible," I whisper, placing my palm on Jasper's stubbled cheek.

Jasper nods, reopening his eyes and leans into my palm.

"Sure is. You'd think she'd stay away from that shit after everything. You know," he says, referring to her addiction to drugs when he was younger. "They pumped her stomach and she's now in for observation."

"What do you mean observation?" I ask, confused.

Jasper rolls onto his back, interlacing his hands behind his head while staring up at the ceiling.

"Suicide watch," he clarifies, spitting out the words.

"What?" I gasp. "She's still suicidal?" I ask, nearly choking on the words.

Jasper nods, still staring up at the ceiling.

"Jasper, I'm so sorry," I whisper, snuggling into him.

"It's okay," he answers half-heartedly, kissing the top of my head.

"How long is she staying in the hospital?" I ask apprehensively, not sure how comfortable he is talking about this.

"I dunno." Jasper shrugs and sighs. "Her doc said it all depends on her. She's not eating, and well, she looks like she wants to raid the medicine cabinet the first minute she's left alone, so I'm guessing a while."

"Oh Jasper, this is horrible. I wish I could do something to make you feel better," I confess, feeling hopeless as I pull back to look at him.

Jasper blames himself for her attempted suicide. I can see it weighing heavily in his guilt-ridden eyes. I know he's just putting on a brave face for my sake, because deep down, he knows Danielle did this to punish him because he chose me over her.

"Just being here makes me feel better," he whispers, his fingers grazing my bare shoulder.

I shiver with the contact, wanting to do anything I can to take away his pain.

"Well, in that case, you can stay as long as you like," I reply, wanting to be his rock.

Jasper half smiles, his left dimple making a welcome appearance.

"Yeah?"

"You bet that hot ass, yes," I smirk, trying to cheer him up.

Jasper pulls me into his chest and I climb on top of him happily, as I've missed him desperately.

We're laying chest to chest, my heart thumping against his, and deep down, I know I should tell him. But looking into his intense blue eyes, I open my mouth and choke.

Jasper looks up at me, waiting for me to speak, but I just can't.

How do I tell him this now?

I can't tell him when his mom is in the hospital under suicide watch, just waiting for the moment to be alone so she can finish what she started. I just can't tell him this. Not now. He's got enough on his plate.

For one more day he can sleep with one less worry.

"Everything okay?" he asks, his warm breath caressing my cheeks.

I nod.

"It is now." I close the gap between us as I crash my lips to his.

The action takes him by surprise, but surprise is quickly replaced with desire as he stakes his claim on my mouth. I need his clothes off, like now.

I claw at his t-shirt, pulling it up until it bunches underneath me and I can't go any further. So I sit up quickly and try to pull it off. He half sits, so I'm able to yank it off over his head in lightning fast speed, and then I push him back down, resuming my straddling position.

As I look down into his perfect face, my heart swells. And my love turns to desperation at the thought of losing him. That thought turns me into a reckless woman, and I can't get close enough to him fast enough.

Before I know it, we're tearing at each other's clothes, frantic to be skin to skin.

I'm in my panties, lying beneath Jasper, waiting for his next move.

"I want you so fucking bad," he whispers, his hand resting on the curve of my hip.

He licks his lips, gazing down at my near naked body. His look of need awakens every part of my soul.

"Then take what you want," I reply breathlessly.

I'll give him whatever he needs, because in this moment, we're both desperate, lost people, clinging to each other for some glimmer of hope, that everything will be okay.

"Don't say that," he says, working his way down my body.

He leans up on his knees while hooking his thumbs into the waistband of my panties, eagerly sliding them down my legs, his hand following in hot pursuit.

His eyes devour every single inch of my flesh, and as I shift my legs, needing to do something as I feel vulnerable under his penetrating stare, a soft sigh slips past his lips.

"Beautiful," he murmurs under his breath, his eyes never leaving my body.

With his heated gaze, I feel like he could burn a hole straight through me, and I love that I can inflame these feelings in him.

"Tell me what you want me to do," Jasper whispers, his eyes flicking to mine.

His question catches me off guard.

"Um… whatever you want," I reply breathlessly.

Jasper smirks, covering my body with his. "That's not what I asked. I want you to tell me."

Really? He wants to be all kinky, now? Looking into his heated eyes, I know the answer is yes.

"I want you to kiss me," I say lamely.

"Where?" Jasper asks.

"Here," I reply, pointing to my neck.

Seriously, he could kiss my eyebrow and I would be squirming for release.

Jasper kisses the tip of my nose before working his way down to my neck. His heavier stubble tickles and I squirm underneath him, as the feel of his wet mouth and tongue, plus rough stubble, is incredible.

As he trails his tongue alongside the length of my neck, I tilt my head backwards so he can get better access. After a few minutes of his mouth finding spots on my neck I never thought could feel erotic, he pulls away.

"Where now?" he asks breathlessly, inches away from my face.

Really? How does he expect me to think after that?

Biting my lip, Jasper's eyes follow the movement, but he doesn't budge. He's waiting for me to give him direction.

I point to my mouth and he swoops down, kissing me until I am panting. His kisses alone are enough of a trigger for me to be embarrassingly winded. But when he explores my mouth with his sinful tongue, I explode.

And that's when he pulls away.

"Now where?"

Oh my God, he is nothing if not persistent!

Damn my bashfulness.

I point down.

"Where?" he smirks. "Can you be a little more specific?"

He is so going to make me say it!

I quickly point between my legs, and then move my hand away just as quickly.

Jasper chuckles, but thankfully complies as he works his way down my body, kissing me along his journey.

He stops as he reaches my bellybutton, and I am all but pushing down his head, begging him to continue. He gives me a heart-stopping dimpled smile and exhales as he looks up, meeting my eyes. His breath fans out across my stomach, sending goosebumps down my entire body.

"Watch me," he says deeply, skimming his hands up and down my legs.

"Watch what?" I reply bashfully.

"Watch how much I want you," he simply replies.

I don't know what to say as I feel like a total pervert, thrilled at the idea of watching him go down on me.

Jasper gives me a heated look as he lowers himself between my legs. As I raise myself up on my elbows so I can watch him, Jasper smirks, happy that I've complied.

"That's it, baby."

Giving him a shy smile, he pushes my thighs further apart so I'm spread out wide before him.

"Beautiful," he whispers once again, before he lowers his mouth onto me.

It takes all my willpower not to throw my head back, or collapse onto the bed, because the feel of him is mind blowing.

Clenching my core muscles, I raise myself higher, watching Jasper's clever tongue worship my body. The sight of his hands splayed on my thighs, clenching lightly as he increases the speed with his mouth is beyond erotic. Watching his dark hair leisurely bob up and down between my legs, combined with the sight of his broad back muscles, shifting with each movement of his body, is nearly the death of me. But it's his eyes. When he raises his cerulean eyes, meeting mine, that's when I come undone.

His pink, wet tongue slips out, caressing me between my aching flesh, and I bite down on my lip with such force, I taste blood.

"Oh fuck," I groan when he adds a finger to the mix.

But still, my eyes never waver, as the sight before me is the most wicked thing I've ever seen.

Jasper knows my body better than I and as he does that *thing* with his tongue, the feeling shoots through my body and I explode.

After riding my post orgasmic bubble, I watch as Jasper kisses my sensitive flesh one last time. He then shifts and I fall onto my back as he crawls slowly up my body. Leaning down to kiss me, I turn away, embarrassed to taste myself on his lips, but he grips my chin in his fingers and pulls my face to his, kissing me passionately.

He smirks as he pulls away.

"See how good you taste?" he whispers.

I pull a face, as that's kinda gross, and he chuckles.

"I want in." He smiles, running his hand between us.

I gasp. "Me too."

He kisses me, sucking on my bottom lip, while I reach around and slide off his CK boxers.

We are now pressed up against one another, skin to skin, and this act of becoming one is the one singular act you can do with another person which connects you in a way like no other.

"I love you," I whisper.

"And I you," he replies, nuzzling my entrance.

"Promise me that whatever happens," I gasp as he pushes into me softly. "Promise me that you'll never leave me," I say on a sigh as he sheathes himself fully into me.

The look he gives while moving slowly into me is picturesque.

"I promise," he breathes heavily, claiming my body like only he can.

"I promise."

CHAPTER TWENTY SEVEN
And Just Like That ...

It's been about three days since I've seen Doctor Hemming. And it's been about three days since I've lied to Jasper.

I can't find the right time to tell him, as I'm pretty certain there is no right time to tell someone what I have to say.

But with his mom still being under suicide watch and showing no sign of improvement, Jasper has been going through hell. I know this is just a lame ass excuse, but it's the truth.

This is going to break Jasper's heart, and I will prolong that from happening for as long as I can, because his heart is already broken, thanks to his mom.

"What's the matter?" Jasper asks, looking over at me while waiting for the light to turn green.

Oh nothing. Just not looking forward to seeing your mother, I internally say.

But I settle for, "I'm just nervous to see your mom. Last time I saw her, we weren't really on friendly terms."

Jasper nods. "I know. But the doctors think it'll help her recovery, dealing with me and you, and she's all for the idea," Jasper replies encouragingly.

Now that I find hard to believe. Danielle is up to something.

I just don't know what.

"You go in first, tell her I'm here and make sure she's okay with it," I say to Jasper, while waiting outside Danielle's room.

Jasper nods, kissing my lips quickly. "Okay, I'll see you in a bit."

Standing out here, looking at my sterile surroundings, I realize that maybe I have been a little hard on Danielle. The nurses are speaking in gentle whispers, coaxing a patient in the next room, whose mouth is shut tighter than a clam, to eat.

Placing a spoon of food in front of his lips, the patient suddenly commences screaming loudly, blocking his ears while rocking backwards and forwards.

Wow.

Jasper ducks his head around the corner. "You're good to come in," he says with a small smile.

I take a deep breath, giving the guy in the next room a quick look, hoping that's not what I'm walking into when I see Danielle.

I follow behind Jasper, who extends his hand. I latch onto it quickly, grateful for the support.

As I enter, I hear the TV sounding softly, almost on

mute, obviously just background noise to lull out the beeping machines.

I peer around Jasper and see Danielle propped up against a pillow, remote in hand, staring at the TV with vacant eyes. She looks a little frazzled with crazy hair and a white hospital gown which is two sizes too big, but other than that, she has color in her cheeks and doesn't look half as bad as the guy next door.

When her eyes meet mine, I prepare for a scowl, but it never comes. Instead, I get sweet, innocent eyes and a small smile.

WTF?

"Hello, Ava," she says softly. "Thank you for coming."

"It's okay," I reply, totally stunned she's talking to me without it involving the words, 'get out of my room, you dirty whore!'

Jasper lets go of my hand and takes a seat on the bed, leaning forward and kissing his mom's forehead.

"How you feeling today?" he asks kindly.

Danielle shrugs. "Okay. Better once they let me out of here."

Jasper nods. "I know, Mom. The doc said you're making progress and should be out real soon," he says positively.

Danielle nods, and peers back at the TV lucidly.

Looking at the way he's taking care of his mom is simply beautiful. Jasper would be a wonderful father and that thought kills me.

Feeling stupid just standing there, I quietly take a seat on the green plastic chair by her bedside. The movement snaps her out of her daze and she turns to looks at me.

Her hair spills lose from her lopsided ponytail, but she doesn't attempt to tie it back. She just stares at me for a long while with dilated pupils and a creepy serial killer grin.

"Ava, I was horrible to you. Downright mean. I hope you can find it in your heart to forgive me."

I fight the urge to wiggle my finger in my ear, because surely I haven't heard her correctly.

Jasper looks at me with a big, beaming smile.

My mouth is agape and I try desperately for the right words, but all I can manage to squeak out is, "Okay."

I've never seen Jasper this happy before and therefore, I'm happy.

I think.

"Thank you, Ava, your forgiveness means a lot to me," she says, smiling creepily.

I nod with a stiff upper lip. "Sure."

I don't think the grin will ever be wiped off Jasper's face and he leans down, embracing his mom into a big hug.

As Danielle looks over his shoulder, still in his arms, she looks at me and if I blinked, I would have missed it. But there's no missing the split second where her face turned from sweet to sinister, all in the span of a nanosecond.

Before I know it, it's gone.

Jasper pulls away and holds out his hand, encouraging me to come sit near him. I gingerly take it, and as Jasper and Danielle chat about random topics, I tune out.

I revisit that look and have a sinking feeling I'm being played.

What is Danielle up to now?

How the hell can I burst Jasper's bubble?

That's right, I can't.

I can't just say, 'Jasper, your mom is up to something.' I mean, what proof do I have? A misconstrued look, that's all.

What if the meds are throwing her nerves off and she just had a nervous tick?

I bet that's what it was.

Lame, Ava, lame.

"Ava, what's the matter with you?" V asks while tattooing a love heart on a young girl's foot.

"Huh? Sorry, what? I spaced," I admit, turning to look at her.

"Duh!" she replies, the tattoo gun buzzing to life.

"What did you say?" I ask, fidgeting on the sofa.

"Don't worry about it, it's not important. What you were thinking about obviously is, so spill."

I shrug. "I was thinking about my visit with Jasper's mom," I confess, scrunching up my face.

"What about it?" V asks, shading in her tattoo.

I watch her handiwork, mesmerized by the needle and space... again.

Only when V clears her throat do I reply, "V, she

looked at me, and I swear, it wasn't good. She's hiding something. I don't buy her whole 'let bygones be bygones' speech."

"What do you think it is?" she asks.

"I don't know, but I know when I do find out, I'm not going to like it."

"Are you sure you're not just reading into things? You know how much you like to overanalyze. I mean, the way you were talking, it sounded like she could be an extra for *One Flew over The Cuckoo's Nest*. I doubt she's in any shape to be planning your demise," V says, dipping her needle into an ink pot.

"I don't know. I just don't trust her," I admit, shivering when I think about the look she gave me.

V shrugs. "I don't blame you, but give her a go. Seeing as you haven't told Jasper about the pregnancy, the least you can do is cut him some slack with his mom."

She's right again. I feel absolutely awful for not telling him—I owe him this.

"I know, you're right."

She grins and tells the pale looking client that she's done.

As V cleans up, my phone rings. I glance at the screen. It's a number I don't recognize.

"Hello?"

"Ava! Why aren't you at school?"

I instantly recognize the voice.

"Because I don't have class today, Sally."

V looks at me, puzzled, and I shrug, just as confused as her.

"No, silly. Today is the interview for the job at Metropolis," she clarifies.

"Oh. That's today?" I ask, surprised.

"Yes, didn't you read the info?" she asks, a little concerned.

"I did. I just lost track of time."

And date, I silently add.

"Well, you've got thirty minutes. Get your butt down here."

"Sally," I say in heavy tone.

"Ava," she mimics.

There is dead silence, and I know she's probably pacing the classroom, waiting for my answer.

I instantly feel horrible.

Sally has been there for me whenever I've needed her, and she's bailed me out of some sticky situations.

I know me not turning up will look bad on her, so with no other choice, I sigh. "Okay fine, I'll be there in twenty," and I hang up.

"What was that about?" V asks, prepping for her next client.

"It was Sally, reminding me about the interview for that job at Metropolis," I reply, standing up.

"How could you forget something like that?" V asks, staring at me like I've sprouted wings.

"Because I wasn't going to go. What's the point? It's not like I'm going to accept it if I get selected. But I'll go to the stupid interview, just to humor Sally. I'll engage in some idle chit chat and then come home to my real life," I reply sullenly.

V shakes her head, tearing off her gloves. She stalks

over to her bag, which is stowed behind the counter, and pulls out her keys.

Grabbing my hand, she all but drags me out the front door.

"Hey, wait. Stop!" I screech. "Where are we going?"

"I'm taking you to that interview. Kicking and screaming if I have to, but you're going."

"**A**va, don't make me carry you in there," V threatens from the front seat of her V.W.

My foot taps restlessly on the floor. "I can't do this. I'm in a Guns 'n Roses t-shirt for God's sake! They'll take one look at me and be like, 'next!'"

"But why should that matter? I mean you're not interested in making an impression, right?" V throws at me.

I can't help myself and blow a raspberry at her.

"Ava!" V reprimands. "Go!" she says, pointing to the building in front of me.

My school has never looked so big and daunting before.

With no other choice, I take deep breath. "Fine, I'll go. Sheesh."

V throws her hands up to the heavens. "Finally!"

Pulling down the visor, I'm hoping to make myself a little more presentable. I yank out my hair and fluff it up, but it's still bushy, and no matter how many times I try and tame my stubborn flyaways, they just keep on flying!

Thankfully, V lends me her pink lip-gloss and some eyeliner, so I don't look too pasty.

"Lose the tee. You look like you belong at Ozzfest."

"I'm not wearing anything underneath." I gasp at her suggestion.

V shrugs and laughs when she sees my mortified expression.

She unbuckles her seatbelt and removes her black v-neck top.

"Here, don't say I never do anything for you," she says, tossing it into my lap. "I am literally giving you the shirt off my back. I expect some kind of reimbursement, in the shape of Hershey's Kisses, thank you very much."

I love her so much. Seriously, where would I be without her? If it's Hershey's Kisses she wants, then Hershey's Kisses she will get.

By the boatload.

I slip on her tee and admit, it looks better than my previous garment.

"Okay, go," V says, leaning over me and opening my door. She's about to boot me out the car when I jump out.

"Okay, okay. You do realize how bossy you are, right?" I smile, leaning into the car.

V pokes her tongue out and I playfully flip her off. "Good luck," she yells, hanging out my door when I'm a few feet away.

Thanks, I need it.

CHAPTER TWENTY EIGHT
Surprises

"Ava, I'm not going to lie to you, you're our first pick for this job offer."

I hear Thomas Carey talking, but his words don't sink in.

First pick?

Really?

I'm fiddling with my silver charm bracelet, not able to meet Thomas' eyes.

This can't be happening. This is my dream come true. So why does it feel like a damn nightmare?

"Ava?" he asks, as I'm all but mute.

Taking a small breath, I look up at him.

He's a handsome man, with sincere hazel eyes and a dimpled smile. I have remained transfixed on that dimple throughout the entire interview, as I can't help but think about another dimple.

Because that dimple is the reason why I have to say no.

"Thomas, thank you so much for this opportunity, I just... I just can't accept."

Ugh, man, that sucked.

Thomas looks surprised by my response as he slouches in his leather chair.

"You can't accept?" he asks, ensuring he has heard me correctly.

I nod, as I'm scared word vomit might rear its ugly head if I have to elaborate why.

There's a lengthy silence and I look out the window, watching the dark rain clouds wrap around the clear sky. And that's how I feel. I feel as if a darkness has overtaken my light. If only I was so lucky and once the storm cleared for me, everything would become brighter once more.

Sadly, it just seems to get darker and darker with each corner I turn.

"I'm extremely disappointed, Ava," Thomas says in a low voice.

Yeah, join the club.

"But this is your decision, and if it's something you don't wish to pursue, then so be it."

He closes my file and folds his hands over it.

"Off the record, may I ask why?"

"Gee, how long do you have?"

It's out before I can stop myself.

Surprisingly, Thomas lets out a loud laugh and leans back, interlacing his fingers behind his neck.

"Sally told me I would like you, and she wasn't wrong."

With big kind eyes and that damn dimpled smile, I can't stop myself as I confide in a complete stranger.

I blame the dimple.

Forty-five minutes later, I leave Thomas' office, feeling like I have just left a therapy session. Wow, talk about embarrassing with a capital E.

I don't know what possessed me to speak in confidence to Thomas, and spill every single detail of the mess my life is currently in.

And I mean EVERY single detail.

"So, how'd it go?" V asks excitedly, pen in hand, completing a Sudoku puzzle.

Slumping into the car, I snap on my seatbelt.

"Horrible," I curtly reply. "Since when are you a mathlete?" I ask, nodding toward the puzzle.

V throws the book in the backseat. "Ugh, it's Lucas', not mine. You took your damn sweet time, I needed something to occupy myself." She huffs, starting the engine, which splutters to life.

We pull out of the parking lot and hit peak hour traffic.

Great! No escaping V and her twenty questions.

"So," she asks, tapping her fingers on the steering wheel. "What happened?"

Oh God, I feel ill. I have bad heartburn and severe stomach cramps. If I didn't know better, I would say my period has decided now is a good time to pay me a visit.

Freakin' wonderful!

"Ava!" V says, throwing a brown M&M at me.

The M&M bounces off my forehead and I turn to glare at V, who is biting back a laugh.

My mouth twitches as the situation is truly ridiculous.

I give in and laugh hysterically, snatching the bag of M&M's out of V's lap, grabbing a handful and throwing them at her.

"Hey!" she laughs, her hand flying up to her eye. "That one hit me in the eye!" she says, referring to the airborne blue missile I just threw at her.

"Serves you right!" I laugh. "You deserve that for making me go to the interview, and FYI, I just divulged all my deepest darkest secrets to a complete stranger."

V looks at me, shocked. "You didn't?"

"Yup, I did," I reply, popping M&Ms into my mouth. "And you know what, it felt good."

"You didn't tell him everything, did you?"

"I sure did. Right down to the sneaking suspicion that Danielle is plotting some evil scheme to take me down."

I pale as the words leave my lips.

Holy shit, what the fuck did I just do?

I just couldn't stop. Once I started, it was like I was possessed by some truth demon.

V indicates to make a right turn, and finally the traffic begins thinning out.

"Well, he might give you points for being honest," she says, trying to make me feel better.

"Yeah, brutally honest, and borderlining on being clinically insane!" I cover my hands over my face and groan. "Well, I guess I don't have to worry about being top pick anymore," I reply, shoving handful after handful of candy into my mouth.

V snatches the bag from me before I drown in M&Ms.

"You're top pick?" she asks, giving me a sympathetic look.

"I was," I mumble. "Now I'll be lucky to get a job within a fifty mile radius of Metropolis."

Why does that thought depress me? I don't care.

Right?

V drops me home after being stuck in traffic for over an hour. Luckily we had a gallon of M&Ms to keep us entertained.

I slump onto my bed, exhausted and totally drained. Even after V's encouraging words, I still feel like shit.

And to make matters worse, I got my period.

Not only am I depressed, now I'm depressed *and* bloated.

Changing into my torn jeans and a sweater, which looks more like a moo-moo, I decide I need to spend some quality time with a block of chocolate and Zac Efron.

Just as I'm popping in a DVD, the doorbell chimes.

I contemplate ignoring it because I have the house to myself, as my parents are out for the evening and I really don't want company, but as the door chimes again, I fold and answer it.

I'm greeted by a pair of cerulean eyes and a whole lotta sexiness.

"What are you doing here?" I ask without thinking.

"Nice to see you, too." Jasper smirks, pulling me by my belt loops into his arms.

"I missed you," he says, his chin resting on my head as I cuddle into his chest. "That's as good as an excuse as any."

Under normal circumstances, I would be all over that excuse, but not right now. Right now I feel like a bloated balloon, not to mention, I don't want Jasper to know what I did today.

"Get dressed," he says, stepping out of our embrace.

Gee, I know a look a little casual, but I don't look *that* bad, do I?

Jasper reads me instantly and laughs. "We're going out."

"We are?" I ask.

"Yup," Jasper replies, giving nothing away as he swats me on the butt, while turning me in the direction of the stairs.

I ascend the first step and spin around. "Where are we going?"

"It's a surprise," he answers ambiguously.

"Can you give me a hint?" I ask.

Jasper shakes his head, his messy hair slipping into his eyes. "The longer you take, the longer..." and he leaves the sentence hanging.

"The longer what?" I press, starting to get a little excited.

"Go," he smirks, pointing upstairs, his eyes full of promise.

I race up the stairs, two at a time, suddenly excited at the possibility that maybe just for tonight, I can pretend that everything is okay.

CHAPTER TWENTY NINE

The Last Supper

"Jasper, where are we going?" I ask, feeling my way around. I am currently blindfolded.

Thankfully, Jasper's hands are around my middle, directing me wherever we're going. About ten minutes ago, Jasper stopped his truck and placed a black bandana over my eyes, telling me that I wasn't allowed to peek.

It takes all of my willpower not to rip off the wretched thing and find out where I am.

"It's not too far now," Jasper whispers into my ear.

I would be a big fat liar if I didn't admit I liked being blindfolded and having Jasper as my guide. I trust him completely, and all my other senses are on high alert, seeing as my eyes are covered.

I can feel soft grass squishing under my navy Converse, and I'm pleased I didn't wear heels. I can also hear wildlife; birds chirping, bugs rustling, mosquitoes buzzing by my face, which I swat away.

It's only when we stop do I smell something absolutely mouth-watering, and I'm not talking about Jasper.

I can smell food.

I launch forward excitedly, only to remember I can't see where I'm going. Fortunately, Jasper still has his hands around my waist; otherwise God knows where I would have face planted.

Jasper laughs, tightening his hold on me. "You're so impatient, Miss Thompson."

"Well, that's because you're killing me, Mr. White," I reply quickly.

We stop walking and I'm practically dancing on the spot, waiting for this damn blindfold to come off.

"Surprise," Jasper whispers, removing the bandana.

It takes a few moments for my eyes to adjust to the light, but luckily it's not bright, it's simply perfect.

"Do you like it?" Jasper says into my ear, still standing behind me.

I can't speak as my eyes scan over everything before me.

There are twinkling fairy lights dangling from a large oak tree, and underneath the tree sits an elegant, candlelit table set for two. My eyes dart to the center of the table, and I find out the source of that delicious smell. There are takeaway containers with the words, 'Fork You' printed on the side, waiting for us to dig into.

Sally.

Does she know about my disaster of a day?

"What is all this?" I ask in awe of the beautiful setting.

"It's all for you," Jasper replies, kissing my cheek.

I turn to face him.

"But why? I don't understand."

Jasper reaches forward, tucking a loose strand of hair behind my ear.

"Sometimes life is about not understanding and just going with it."

I feel my eyes well with tears, but I brush them away, as they will have no part in tonight's proceedings.

"Thank you," I whisper. "It's beautiful."

"No, that would be you," Jasper says, reaching for both of my palms, pulling me toward him so we're standing inches apart.

He searches my face and I search back, and this moment is one I will remember forever. The silence is not uncomfortable, like it has been of late, it's tranquil and reflective.

The slight breeze whips Jasper's long locks over his brow, but he doesn't brush it out of his eyes. He stands completely still, staring at me, like he has only just seen me for the first time.

"Ava..." Jasper says, rubbing my cheek with his thumb. "I know our life has been crazy, but I wanted to give you this. One night where it's just Jasper and Ava, and the rest of the world can just disappear, and so can our worries. Just for one night."

Jasper feels it, too. The weight of our situation falls on both of our shoulders heavily. But I can do this. I can forget for one night.

"Sounds good to me," I whisper. "Just as long as you're by my side, I can do anything."

After three courses, I am about to pop.

It's so worth it though, as I never could say no to Sally's Mushroom Risotto.

Jasper is sitting across the table from me, his lips twitching as I'm all but licking my plate clean.

"What?" I ask innocently, while scraping any remaining sauce from my plate.

"Nothing," he replies, sipping his beer with a smirk.

This is so... nice.

We haven't done something like this in, well... I can't remember when. The night is simply perfect, and I can almost forget the drama that is my life.

Well, almost.

Jasper's phone rings and he exhales in annoyance. "Sorry, baby."

Giving him a small smile, I sip on my sparkling mineral water while he takes the call.

"Hello. Oh hey, Mom, how are you?"

As soon as I hear it's Danielle on the other end, my troubles seem to creep back in.

"That's great, Mom. Uh-ha... no, not yet. I haven't had a chance to sign the paperwork."

Paperwork?

"Okay, no worries, I'll do it tonight. See you tomorrow, Mom. Love you."

He hangs up, putting his phone on mute before slipping it back into his jacket pocket.

"How's your mom?" I ask, genuinely concerned.

"She's good. The doctors said she'll be able to go home in a couple of days," he replies, stretching his hands above his head and yawning.

Jasper has been at the hospital every day, pretty much day and night, keeping his mom company. He looks beat.

"That's great news," I reply, as this means he's finally able to stop running himself into the ground.

"Sure is. Once she's back home, life can go back to normal. I am so over the drama," Jasper confesses.

I bite my lip guiltily. How can I tell him that the drama is far from over?

"Hey, what's the matter?" he asks, when I avert my gaze from his wise eyes.

Oh, you know, just the usual. You know the baby we are meant to be having, well about that, there's actually no baby. Surprise!

Ugh, even thinking the words sends me into a cold sweat.

I know I have to tell him. But here? Now?

I just can't.

Not yet. Not when tonight we're meant to be, 'just going with it.'

Tomorrow I will.

"Nothing," I reply, hoping he believes me.

To change the subject I ask, "What paperwork does your mom want you to sign?"

Jasper takes a long sip of beer and looks uncomfortable, gauging how to answer me. "Mom asked me to sign some paperwork from the insurance companies. In relation to my dad's death."

I scrunch up my brow, as this is the first time he's ever mentioned any paperwork. I'm not sure if I should pursue the subject, as I know Jasper's dad is a touchy topic. I decide to leave it, as tonight is meant to be drama free. It's funny how every time his mom is involved, drama just seems to follow in hot pursuit.

"So, where's dessert?" I ask, trying to change the subject.

I look around as if my dessert is hiding under a shrub to my left.

Jasper chuckles and it's nice seeing him so carefree and relaxed.

"Well, about that..." he replies, peeling the label off his beer.

I am about ready to leap over the table and demand he tell me. No one messes with my dessert!

"I thought we could be each other's dessert," he replies, and the look in his eyes reveals he is dead serious.

Usually, I would be jumping up and down at the idea of being Jasper's meal, but now, thanks to my little friend, that's impossible.

Jasper senses my apprehension and reaches for my hand, which I have unintentionally turned into a tight fist. His warm palm comforts me and I know I should tell him.

I have to tell him. I can't lie to him. Not again. I know we're meant to be having a drama free night, but not telling him this is eating me up inside.

He squeezes my hand lightly and gives me a crooked smile, his eyes shimmering under the fairy lights and a slither of the moon.

"Ava, whatever you have to tell me, it can wait."

"No, it really can't," I mumble to myself.

I shake my head, taking a deep breath before I confess my sins. "Jasper... I..."

But as I meet his peaceful stare, I don't want to be the cause of that tranquility turning into pain.

He shakes his head. "Tell me tomorrow."

I bite my lip and nod, feeling like a total asshole for not telling him what he needs to know.

"I..." he says softly, but doesn't finish.

"You what?" I ask curiously when he runs a hand through his hair.

He reaches into his jacket pocket and pulls out a familiar box, and just like when I first saw it, my heart begins beating wildly.

He places it onto the white tablecloth and slides it towards me with two fingers.

As I stare at it, my throat closes over. What does he want me to do with it?

Shuffling in my seat, I clear my throat.

"I know you said no to me, and I agree with you. How I proposed to you, it fucking sucked. But the offer still stands. It always will. I want you to be my wife, Ava, and not just because you are carrying my child. I love you regardless. I want to marry you, regardless. I just wanted you to know that," he says with conviction. "That's what my answer should have been in Seattle," he adds softly.

I continue staring at the box, not able to meet Jasper's eyes because once I do, he'll know that I'm carrying nothing of his.

All I'm carrying is this feeling of guilt.

I nod, and being the chicken I am, I give him a small smile.

"I know, and I love you so much. But let's talk about it tomorrow, because now, now I feel like dessert," I whisper, reaching over the table, yanking on his shirt and smashing his lips to mine.

So for tonight, I will just pretend, pretend like everything is okay, because I know when tomorrow comes, there will be no more pretending.

CHAPTER THIRTY

Who's Your Daddy?

I am going to spend the day with Jasper.

And his mom.

The doctors are quite confident that Danielle will be released in two days' time, believing that she's on the mend.

Here's hoping they're right, as this past week has been a nightmare.

Parking my car in the underground car park, I ride the elevator to Danielle's floor.

I've decided that I'll tell Jasper my news once she's home. Focusing on his mom is the most important thing at the moment, and my news can wait another day.

I head straight for Danielle's room, trying to bypass the nurses and doctors who are attempting to contain a screaming girl, writhing on the floor.

I don't know how Jasper spends every day cooped up behind these sterile, white walls.

As I reach Danielle's room, I see Jasper standing down the hallway, pointing animatedly to a middle-aged doctor in a white lab coat. He-s holding a clipboard towards his chest, using it as a barrier against an irate Jasper.

I can tell by Jasper's clenched jaw and slanted eyes that something's wrong.

My sneakers squeak on the floor with each frantic step I take, as I sprint towards him, anxious to discover what's going on. I reach Jasper's side within seconds and hear the doctor talking to him in a hushed tone.

"I'm sorry, Mr. White, but this is hospital policy. We really need that information," he says, looking mighty uncomfortable when Jasper pinches the bridge of his nose, looking as if he's about to explode.

"What's going on?" I ask, hooking my arm through Jasper's and kissing him on the cheek.

Jasper turns to me and gives me a small smile. "Hey, baby."

"Hey yourself. What's up?"

Jasper turns to stare at the doctor, and I feel sorry for the poor guy.

"Doctor Fitzgerald is giving me a hard time, that's what's up," he replies while glaring at the man.

Doctor Fitzgerald clears his throat. "I'm sorry, but this is out of my hands. We need your mother's paperwork to be able to dismiss her. We didn't obtain these documents right away, as we knew what a trying time it was for your family. But we have asked for this paperwork for a couple of days now."

"What paperwork?" I ask, looking up at Jasper.

"Her I.D., Social Security, Medicare, fucking high school diploma, I don't know," he replies, raising his voice.

Both the doctor and I squirm because Jasper is really pissed.

"Jasper, calm down," I whisper, tugging lightly on his arm to get his attention, and to stop him from glaring daggers at the doctor.

Thankfully, he does.

He takes a deep breath and closes his eyes. When he reopens them, he looks a little less murderous.

"Sorry, Doc, I just want to get her out of here."

The doctor nods, pushing his glasses up his nose. "That's okay, Mr. White, I understand, and she will be, once we get her documentation sorted. We need to ensure all medical expenses are covered by her health insurance before we can release her, and we need her admission letter. We don't usually accept patients without it, but your mother needed our help, so we made an exception," he says kindly.

Jasper looks down at me with tired, weary eyes and sighs. "I'll get the paperwork to you this afternoon."

"Thank you, I really appreciate it."

With that, Doctor Fitzgerald scurries off down the hall, away from the incensed crazy person that is my boyfriend.

"Hey, why so agro?" I ask, turning to face him, searching his face.

Jasper blows out a loud breath. "I'm just tired, Ava," he admits, scrubbing his hands down his face.

"Tell me what I can do," I reply quickly, latching onto his hands that are interlaced over his mouth.

"I need to get this paperwork organized, but in about half an hour, Mom is having her psych assessments and meeting with the social worker. I really want to be there for that. I'm going to have to blow off band practice so I can sneak in five minutes of sleep before I leave for work. I'm just so exhausted, and all this running around is killing me."

"Then I'll go," I say.

Jasper shakes his head. "No, it's okay, this isn't your problem. I'm just being a little bitch," he says with a smirk, but I can tell he's running on empty.

"Your problems are mine. Let me go. Just tell me what you need, and I'll be back within an hour with everything. This way you can stay with your mom. I'm sure she would like that."

I give him a small smile, as I know how Danielle loves spending time with Jasper, especially when I'm not around.

"You sure?" he asks.

"Yeah, of course." I nod happily.

"Thank you, baby. Fuck, I love you." And he pulls me into a tight embrace, resting his cheek atop the crest of my head.

I nestle into his arms, surrounded by everything that I love.

"It's okay," I mumble against his chest. "It's no trouble at all."

In hindsight, I wish I knew how wrong I was.

Danielle is a slob or a damn hoarder!

I've watched those shows where people's houses are filled to the brim with shit. Well, Danielle's home could definitely be the star of one of those shows.

Jasper said all of Danielle's paperwork is in a white filing cabinet in her study.

Check.

He also told me it is listed alphabetically.

Not check.

It looks as if she's filed her paperwork with her eyes shut.

There is crap everywhere!

There's no way I'm finding anything in this mess. Her desk looks as if an explosion of stationary has detonated, and the flying debris is lining every corner of it. There are papers upon papers strewn everywhere and anywhere.

I look at the clock, which tells me I've been gone for forty-five minutes, and I'm still no closer in finding what I'm looking for.

Where would I be if I was her paperwork?

I tap my foot, hands on hips, looking around her study, hoping that something, anything will lead me to the documents I seek.

Sadly, it's going to take more than hope to find the floor in this chaos.

After ransacking the filing cabinet, which looks no different than when I first started, I slump into her study chair and roll forward, determined to fight this mess and win.

I push aside junk mail, catalogues and a used tissue—gross.

Still nothing.

Just as I'm about to give up, my eyes drop to the desk drawer.

Bingo.

I pull on the handle, but it's locked. Why would someone, who has every document she owns thrown around the room, need a locked drawer?

I look at it and suddenly I need that drawer open, like pronto.

Hmm, key. I need a key.

My eyes scan the desk and I see a letter opener.

Surely it can't be *that* hard, can it? I mean, they do it in the movies all the time.

I reach for it instantly.

As I jam the blade into the drawer, jiggling it around, I tell myself this is technically not breaking into Danielle's personal information, as I have permission to be here.

Who am I kidding? Even if I didn't, I would still be all over this drawer like a rash.

After fruitless attempts to jar it open, I give up.

I throw the letter opener onto the desk, frustrated, and it slides off onto the carpet, the momentum pushing most of the documents off the desk and onto the floor.

Great.

Pushing back from the leather chair, I drop to my knees to gather all the paperwork, which looks like confetti scattered all over the floor.

I am blindly collecting the papers, but for some reason, one document catches my eye.

I hold it out and scan over the contents quickly. The paper drops from my hand, as I have thrown it to the ground like it has just bitten me, and its venom has begun spreading through my veins.

My hands fly to my mouth as I go into shock.

This can't be. This can't be.

I tell myself to breathe and snap out of it, because I need to ensure what I just read is really true. After I have collected myself, I eye the paper like it's a landmine, and it will ignite if I go anywhere near it.

But I need to.

I have no choice.

I gingerly reach for the piece of paper, my hand shaking uncontrollably. As I slide it towards me and reread it, my stomach flips. I'm afraid I'm going to be sick. I shove that feeling aside and jump up at lightning speed, pushing the leather chair out of my way as I slam to my knees and frantically begin jamming the letter opener into the locked drawer.

I need what's inside to make sense of what I have just read.

I'm like a madwoman, stabbing viciously at the drawer, attempting to jar it open. Only when it clicks, do I take a breath.

I stare at the drawer and begin breathing hysterically. Please be wrong. Please be wrong.

With shaky fingers, I yank open the drawer and throw everything out, tossing lie after lie over my shoulder.

When I find what I am looking for, my heart stops.

A tear rolls down my cheek and more follow as I look at an aged photo, a photo taken twenty-six years ago.

It's a photo of Jasper when he was just a baby.

A photo of Jasper in the arms of a man holding him lovingly.

As I flip the snapshot over, it reads, 'Jasper and Jeremy.'

There's no mistake that the cerulean eyes staring down at Jasper belong to his father.

But the problem is, Jasper's dad... the man he knew to be his father, the man who abused him every day of his young life... is not the man in the picture.

CHAPTER THIRTY ONE

It's All About the Money, Money, Money

I am so going to end up on *COPS*, as I zip in and out of traffic, desperate to get to Jasper.

I'm mulling over everything, over and over again, and no matter how many times I chew over it, it all leads to one conclusion.

Jasper's dad, the one who died in a house fire, is not his real father.

I think back to last night, when I overheard Jasper talking to his mom about signing some paperwork. Surely the paperwork I found is different than that his mom has given him, because there's no way Jasper knows his dad is not actually his biological father.

And that's exactly what the document I found reveals.

Now that I'm not a hysterical mess, I can piece together Danielle's devious plot. She's one messed up, evil bitch, and she would have gotten away with it, if not for the evidence I have stowed away in my bag.

I didn't think it was possible to hate a person as much as I hate Danielle, but the rage I feel inside of me, because of her, because of her lies, stems into homicidal territory.

How could she do this to him?

I blindly reach for my bag, ensuring the document and photo is safe inside. With no other choice, I have to show Jasper that his mom has been lying to him all this time. Her intentions were not to rekindle her relationship with her son, like she claimed. No. Her motivation to reconcile with Jasper has got to do with money.

Jasper's money.

Money he's unaware he's inherited.

Money his biological father, Jeremy Blackwood, left for his son in a trust fund, which Jasper was entitled to when he turned twenty-five.

Jasper is the sole recipient to the staggering amount of one million dollars.

His father set up the trust fund the day Jasper was born, and continued adding funds up until his twenty-fifth birthday.

Now that Jasper is twenty-six and he hasn't claimed the money, his mother is next in line for receiving the unclaimed funds.

It was a clause Jeremy Blackwood ensured was written into the contract. If, by chance, the money wasn't claimed by Jasper's twenty-sixth birthday, then Danielle is entitled to it.

All of it.

He must have really loved her.

The thing is, Jasper doesn't even know this money exists. Nor does he know that Jeremy exists.

Of course, Danielle knows everything. She signed the

original document, stating she would inform Jasper of the fund when he was old enough to understand.

She didn't.

Screeching into the lot, I zip into a parking spot and charge out of the car, racing up the stairs, two at a time.

The lift stops at every floor, and I impatiently shuffle from foot to foot, waiting to get to my floor. Finally it stops and I shove past two people, apologizing over my shoulder. I skid down the hallway and come to a dead stop, millimeters from Danielle's door.

How am I supposed to tell him this? After I discovered what Danielle is up to, I charged out of her house with the devil on my heels, without really thinking of the impact this will have on Jasper.

How do I sugarcoat, 'Jasper, your mom never wanted to reconcile with you. She's just using you to inherit money that is rightfully yours. She needs you to sign on the dotted line for her to get a single penny of that money.'

That's the catch.

For Danielle to receive any money, she needs Jasper's signature, to confirm that he wants nothing to do with the inheritance, and therefore signing it all over to her.

That's why she's back in his life. It's got nothing to do with turning over a new leaf. This is all about greed and deceit, as I know Danielle would have tricked Jasper into signing another document, and somehow using it to appear he signed everything over to her.

I have no doubt that this whole suicide attempt was staged. It was done so Jasper would feel guilty for pushing his mom away, and she hoped his guilt would compel him to do anything she said. And believe anything she said.

She knew she couldn't tear us apart, and in the end Jasper would choose me. So with no other choice, she attempted to take her own life, trying to win Jasper over by playing with his heartstrings.

I. Hate. Her.

I decide I'm just going to wing it, as there's no way to cushion the blow for Jasper. This isn't something I can sugarcoat, as this is just a cruel, calculated betrayal to the worst degree.

I charge into Danielle's room, only to be greeted by her empty, made-up bed.

They must have gone to her therapy sessions. I decide to look for Jasper because I can't sit here waiting, I'm a tight ball of nerves.

Running out of the room' not looking where I'm going, I bump into Doctor Fitzgerald out in the hallway, spilling all of his paperwork onto the floor.

"Oh, sorry!" I mumble, embarrassed, as I drop to my knees and attempt to pick up his documents.

"That's okay, Miss," he says, joining me on his knees, collecting his paperwork.

When I pass him the documents, his eyes meet mine, and recognition instantly flashes behind his brown eyes.

"Oh, you were here this morning with Mr. White, weren't you?" he asks.

"Yes, I was," I confirm, reaching for a folder and passing it to him, which he thankfully accepts.

"Is everything okay with him? He charged off in an awful hurry."

"He did? When?" I question, my hand stilling from retrieving any more paperwork.

Doctor Fitzgerald shrugs, his brow furrowing. "About half an hour ago. He stormed out of here in a rage. We thought it had something to do with his mom, and him still being in a huff about the paperwork we needed. But her daughter brought in the documents after I spoke to him this morning."

I begin breathing heavily and my heart commences slamming against my ribcage, threatening to explode out of my chest.

"What daughter?" I ask in breathless anticipation.

"Danielle's daughter. What did she say her name was again? She was blonde, about yea tall," he says, gesturing with his hand about eye level on him.

"Indiana?" I ask, but I know the answer.

"Yes, that was it. She spoke to Mr. White just after she handed in Ms. White's paperwork, and that's when he charged out of here. Off the record, I think something she said angered him, to the point of him doing that."

Looking at the direction he's pointing, I'm confronted by a large hole in the plaster. No points for guessing whose fist fits into the hole like a jigsaw piece.

Rising to my feet, I pass the doctor the last of the paperwork and sprint towards the elevators.

What the hell is going on?

CHAPTER THIRTY TWO

Let it Be

I throw my cell onto the passenger seat, enraged. Where is he?

I've tried Jasper's cell a gazillion times, and every time I get through, it goes straight to voicemail.

A sense of dread is beginning to form in the pit of my stomach, as I know whatever I'm about to find out isn't going to be good.

I don't know what Indie and Danielle are up to. Indie calling herself Danielle's daughter doesn't make a lick of sense. And how did Danielle get discharged from hospital when I was the one sent looking for the paperwork?

Unless the reason why I couldn't find the documents, was because Indie beat me to Danielle's, grabbing the paperwork before I could. That makes perfect sense, as Danielle wouldn't want Jasper snooping in her study, for fear of him finding what I did. That must mean, holy shit... Indie knows the truth.

I'm seriously just holding on, and if I saw either Indie or Danielle, I wouldn't think twice about running them over.

As I pull up into Jasper's driveway, I breathe a sigh of relief when I see his truck sitting on the grass. Jumping out without locking my car, I barge through the front door, not bothering to knock, afraid he would shut the door in my face if I did.

As soon as I enter the living room, all my fears are confirmed.

Something bad has happened. Something life changing.

Jasper is a broken man.

He's standing with his back facing me, but by the hunch of his shoulders and the droop of his head, I know that whatever is about to happen will mark the end of an era.

It will mark the end of us.

"Jasper?" I whisper, my voice wavering.

He doesn't turn around. He doesn't move.

The only thing that changes is his breathing, which becomes severe and harsh.

"Jasper?" I ask again, taking a quiet step towards him.

As I get within a few steps of him, he turns slowly and faces me, and I look into the eyes of a damaged, shattered man.

The walls start closing in on me and I struggle to breathe.

He knows.

Jasper's beautiful lips dip into a melancholy frown, and the sight breaks my heart. And I doubt it'll ever heal.

"Are you pregnant?" he asks simply, his voice hoarse.

I lower my eyes, because I can't bear to face him when I break his heart.

"No," I whisper, shaking my head slowly.

The second the words leave my lips, my world will forever be changed.

Jasper blows out a deep breath, but remains silent.

I courageously raise my eyes to meet his, and feel empty when he returns my gaze.

"How could you lie to me? About something so important. How?" he screams, leaping forward.

I flinch and try to steady myself before I answer him.

"I didn't... I couldn't... It was..."

But I can't construct a sentence because I'm on the verge of hysteria.

"You what, Ava? Forgot to tell me that our baby is actually nonexistent?"

"No, of course not," I choke. "I was only thinking of you."

"Oh, I seriously doubt that," he replies sarcastically.

"It's the truth!" I plead, reaching for him, but he steps away from me like my touch will set him alight.

"I couldn't tell you. With everything going on with your mom, I didn't want to make things worse for you. You had enough on your plate. I was going tell you once she was released," I say, beseeching him to believe me.

"Oh, that's rich." He snickers, interlacing his hands behind his neck and staring up at the ceiling.

"What are you talking about?" I ask, wishing he would stop being so angry and talk to me.

"Quit with the act, I know everything," he replies, meeting my eyes.

What the hell is he talking about?

"What act? I have no idea what you're talking about," I insist.

"I know you found out you weren't pregnant way before my mom. Way before Seattle. And you made me feel like such an asshole when I proposed to you. Using our bogus baby as an excuse not to marry me, when really you just didn't want to be my wife!" he yells, throwing his hands out to the side.

He's livid as he runs a hand through his hair and tugs on it roughly.

"That's not true!" I shout.

What is he talking about? Why does he think I've been lying about the pregnancy for weeks?

Then it all clicks into place.

"Who told you?" I ask, stepping towards him and latching onto his arm.

"It doesn't matter who," he barks, shrugging out of my grip.

"Like hell it doesn't. Tell me who!" I scream, but I know who.

"Indie," he replies, and the word sounds like nails raking down a blackboard.

How did she know I wasn't pregnant? And more importantly, why does he believe her?

"How can you believe her over me? I'm telling you, I've only known for a few of days," I say on a whisper, not meeting his eyes.

Jasper reaches into his back pocket and tosses a piece of paper at me. I catch it and open it cautiously.

As my eyes scour over the words, my heart stops.

How does Indie have my medical file from Doctor Hemming's office? And why does the date read weeks before my actual appointment?

Think, Ava.

OH MY GOD.

The receptionist. I now remember who she is.

She was at Jasper's party, the one with stars in her eyes for him. The blonde pixie Danielle all but threw into Jasper's lap.

She's the one who stole my file and gave it to Indie. And of course Indie changed the date so it appeared I've been lying to Jasper this whole time. If matters weren't bad enough, she has gone and made it so much worse.

Looks like I was right about Danielle all along. I have no doubt Indie came to her with this information and as the saying goes, 'Keep your friends close, but your enemies closer.'

Danielle's whole ruse was to convince Jasper that I'm the bad one, leading him astray with my lies, while she was the good, perfect mother, only wanting what's best for her son. I was right. Danielle's suicide attempt was all part of her ploy to side Jasper with her, against me.

I scrunch up the piece of paper in my fist and throw it onto the floor.

"How could you believe her?" I ask sadly, holding onto my tears.

My whole world is tumbling around me and I can't do anything to stop it.

"Because the proof is there, Ava!" he says, pointing to the piece of paper.

"But I'm telling you that it's not true. I found out I wasn't pregnant a day after I returned from Seattle. The night you came to my house, I was going to tell you. But then you told me your mom was under suicide watch.

How could I tell you? You had so much going on. I didn't want to make matters worse. I saw how stressed out you were with everything and I just couldn't tell you, I was afraid you'd break. It was wrong, and I'm so sorry. Please, believe me." I know I sound pathetic, as I'm all but begging him to believe me.

But I know he doesn't.

By trying to save Jasper the heartache of knowing the truth, I have just made things a lot worse.

"I would never lie to you, especially about this. I wanted to tell you at dinner, but we both needed one night, just one night where we could pretend that everything was going to be all right. Please believe me, Jasper," I plead, looking into his face, memorizing every feature, as I know he's about to break my heart into a million pieces.

I haven't lied to Jasper. All I've tried to do is save him from a cascade of tears and pain. He's had enough lately to last him ten lifetimes. But it's all backfired, and now, now things will never be the same.

Jasper snickers, meeting my eyes. "How can I trust you ever again? I hate that you've given me reason *not* to believe you. I can forget all the misunderstandings in the past, but this," he says, sighing. "I just can't. I can't forgive you, Ava, this is just too much."

His voice breaks when he confesses my fears out loud.

The tears I've been holding onto break free and stream down my face uncontrollably.

"But I'm telling you the truth!" I cry.

Jasper only shrugs, shaking his head, lost.

"So now what?" I sniff, wiping away my tears, but it's useless as more fall to take their place.

Jasper sighs, his hands dug deep into his jeans.

"Ava... I wanted our baby so much. You'll never know how much I wanted to be a dad. To be a father to our child. But now, when I look at you, all I can see is..." and he leaves the sentence hanging.

"What? What can you see?" I ask, close to being hysterical.

"I see my past."

He lowers his head, his hair dipping over his face, blanketing his beautiful eyes as he tears my heart into two.

"We're done, Ava... I'm sorry. I can't... do this anymore. I don't want to hear anymore."

I can actually feel my heart break. The pain rips through my chest, and I feel like a tsunami has just pulled me under, and I'm struggling to breathe.

I have to fight for him. I have to show him what's sitting in my handbag, the proof that Danielle and Indie are the liars, not me.

But I can't.

I can't move.

He doesn't believe.

How can he not believe me?

"Let me explain. I'll show you," I beg, reaching inside my bag.

He shakes his head, meeting my eyes.

"No."

I gasp, my hands ceasing on their search for the truth.

By the look in his eyes, I know he wouldn't believe

me anyway, because he's done with me. And this time, he really means it. How many times can he forgive me before he's had enough?

Obviously, he's all out of forgiveness, because he has finally given up on me, when he promised he never would.

How am I to survive this?

I can't.

But I also can't force him to love me because I too, have had enough. I can't do this anymore. This constant tug of war with his mom, I know now, that I will never win. And that just fucking hurts. I'll always be second best, and the only reason to put me first has just been taken away from him.

But it's been taken away from me, too.

I wanted our baby as much as he did.

"Ava," Jasper whispers, and I can hear the finality in his voice.

My bottom lip trembles as I meet his eyes and the distant, unreadable stare I'm greeted with is the end of me.

I sob so hard the noise rattles inside my chest and echoes off the walls.

He's leaving me.

He's really leaving me.

If this is the end, then I need to tell him how I feel. How he's made me feel. I need him to know that no matter what, I will always be his.

Even though he doesn't want me to be.

Sniffing back my tears, I stand tall because when I tell him this, I don't want him remembering me as a weeping mess. I want him to remember me as the girl he fell in love with.

Before all of this.

"Every single day, I will regret not telling you about our baby." Jasper closes his eyes, pained when he hears the word baby. But I continue, as I need to get it all out before I crumple into a heap. "But I will never regret a single day I spent with you. Thank you for showing me that it's okay to love again, to follow my heart and never let go. And I won't let go, I will never love anyone as much as I do you. You're imprinted on my heart, Jasper White. I just hope I'm imprinted on yours."

Jasper opens his eyes and tears fall down his stubbled cheeks, slipping into trembling lips.

"Ava—" he says, his voice rough.

But I stop him, planting a soft kiss on his wet lips. He returns the kiss, but for the first time ever, there is no love behind that kiss. I only feel regret and broken promises.

I pull away, turning my back on the man I will love with my last breath.

My hand is braced on the doorknob, and I'm ready to face the unknown without Jasper.

"Ava... I'm sorry. I—" Jasper chokes, sniffing back his tears.

I don't turn to face him because if I see him weeping, I will never leave.

I commit to memory everything about Jasper, and smile at all the happy times we've shared.

And that, that is something I will never forget.

With a deep, final breath I smile. "Don't," I whisper, my tears now spilling free. "Let it be. Just let it be."

CHAPTER THIRTY THREE

It's War

I drive home in a haze.

I don't remember signaling or stopping at red lights. I'm on autopilot. And that's because I know once I let the reality of what has just happened sink in, I won't resurface. Jasper and I have fought, and we have broken up, but not once did I feel this hollow, this broken inside. I know this is it. This is really the end.

Slipping into my bed, I shut out the world. I close my heart on all things Jasper because it just hurts to feel.

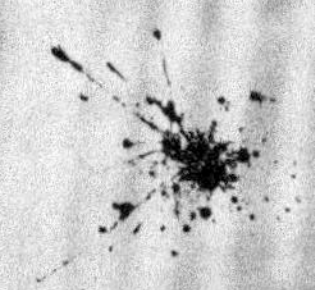

Sleep is normally the best cure for a heartache. But what happens when you can't sleep? What happens when you get hit with the insomnia bat, and all you crave is to slip into a thoughtless slumber, but can't?

I tell you what happens. You go crazy.

You think about every single word you have ever spoken. Every single kiss you have ever received. Every single moment of your life comes crashing down, and is amplified by ten thousand because you can't shut it out with sleep.

I haven't slept for three days, but I'm not tired. I'm just numb.

I have taken up permanent residency in my favorite armchair, staring out at the world before me, watching people living life like it is worth the trouble.

I look like shit.

I smell like shit.

I feel like shit.

I don't deserve Jasper in my life. I don't deserve someone as good as him, because all I seem to do is fuck it up. Is it in my DNA for me to fuck up with the best thing that has ever happened to me time and time again?

I should have told him. I should have shown him. But I know it wouldn't have made a difference. In hindsight, I would have done so many things differently. I would have said things I should have said. But that's the fucked up thing about hindsight, you can't change it.

Wrapping the woolen blanket around myself, I curl up into a ball, willing sleep to numb the pain.

It never does.

Day five of my life without Jasper—yup, still sucks.

I have showered but not eaten, as the

thought of putting anything into my stomach actually makes me feel nauseous.

Thankfully, the world has let me switch off, and when I say world, I mean V. Knowing Lucas, he probably has her under lock and key, but I'm certain any moment now she will come charging through my door, telling me to snap the hell out of it.

I'm attempting to study, as I have finals just around the corner, but all the words may as well be in Hungarian because they read in a different language.

Thumping my head on the desk, I eye my iPod longingly; I'm not going to listen to my depressing playlist... again.

As Igaze out the window in a daze, my bedroom door swings open and hits the wall with a loud thud. I don't have to turn around to know who it is.

"I don't want to talk, V."

V storms over to me, spinning my chair around to face her. "I don't care what you want. This isn't about you."

I scrunch up my brow. "Then who is it about?"

"Me!" she says, like I'm daft for not knowing the answer.

"What about you?" I ask, humoring her.

She slumps onto the bed and grabs the edge of my chair, rolling me towards her.

"I want my best friend back," she says seriously.

I instantly feel bad. I have totally ignored my best friend. My pregnant best friend.

"I'm sorry, V," I mumble, trying to push away from

her but am unsuccessful, as she still has a tight hold on my chair.

"Tell me in ten words or less what happened." She huffs, holding up ten fingers.

Looking at her and her fingers, I sigh, as I don't need ten words. Three will suffice.

"We broke up."

V pushes my chair away from her and stands, hands on hips. "I figured as much. What happened?"

Oh God, I don't even know where to begin, as so much has happened there isn't one singular event to summarize why it went to shit.

I decide to show her as I hand her the photo, whose edge I have been fingering over and over, deep in thought.

The confusion on V's face is clear when she sees it. But before I get bombarded with questions, I hand her the piece of paper that confirms Danielle is Lucifer.

V reads over it quickly and her mouth drops so far open, I can see the back of her throat.

"Hey, when did you get your tongue pierced?" I ask, which is totally irrelevant and random.

V ignores me and instead yells, "MOTH-ERFUCKER!"

"V! My parents are home," I whisper, not wanting them to know something is up.

So far I have been able to evade them, but with V hollering the way she is, my ruse will soon be busted.

"Sorry," she says, thankfully a lot quieter. "I don't get it. Why did he break up with you? Shouldn't he be breaking up with his mom, or at least breaking her face?" she adds, sitting back down.

I shrug and explain the whole situation, not leaving out a single detail.

"MOTHERFUCKER!" she yells once I have finished telling her my depressing tale.

This time however, I don't reprimand her, as my feelings echo her choice of words.

"Why didn't you tell him about all this?" she asks, holding up the photo. "He has a right to know," she adds.

"I know, V, but he won't believe me. He chose to believe his mom and Indie." Saying their names feels like I have tar in my mouth.

"Why didn't you fight him? Make him believe you," V asks, biting her nail nervously.

I shrug. "Because I'm tired of fighting, V. He wouldn't believe me anyway, and I've got no one to blame but myself. I just should have told him I wasn't pregnant the day I found out."

I know I'm to blame for the mess I'm in, but it still doesn't make me feel any better admitting fault.

"Well, he's a jackass. I know you two will work it out, you always do."

Biting my lip, I pull my sleeves over my fingers as I suddenly have a chill. I give V a ghost of smile, because this time around, I don't agree with her.

I don't know how, or why, I agreed to come to the mall with V, because whichever way you look at it, it's just a horrible idea.

V has dragged me to store after store, adamant I need a graduation outfit. I bite my tongue and decide not to tell her that I haven't even passed yet. And also, this 'outfit' won't be seen, as I will be wearing a gown over it.

But, whatever. It's better than sitting at home and staring at the walls like I belong in a straightjacket.

V finally decides on an outfit (which I don't even recall trying on). I pay for it, without even looking at the garment or price. I just want to get out of the store, because the sympathetic eyes of the sales clerk begins tugging at my heartstrings, and my eyes instantly begin to water.

"I need a coffee," I sigh, walking through the crowded mall, dragging my feet.

"You need more than a coffee," V adds. "Hairbrush, Ava. You and it should become reacquainted, and soon."

I run my fingers through my hair and it catches on the knots.

Yikes, I'm glad I don't know what I look like.

Oblivious to my surroundings, V yanks my upper arm and drags me into an Adult Superstore, stocked with the latest 'toys' from God knows where.

"What the hell?" I question, cringing when I see a sign, announcing they have the Thumper Three in stock.

I don't even want to know what Thumper Three, Two or One can do.

V puts her finger to her lips and gestures with her head to the front window. I humor her and look, not seeing anyone or anything of interest. That is, until I see three people, who look too painstakingly happy for my liking. Well, two look happy, the other looks... well, he looks kinda like how I look and feel.

Like shit.

And those three people are, Danielle, Jasper, and Indie. And in that order, as Jasper is wedged between the two wicked witches of the west.

Spinning around, I lose my footing, but thankfully V is there to lend me her shoulder.

"What. The. Fuck?" I sneer silently.

V shrugs, subtly looking over my shoulder.

"What are they doing?" I ask, about to burst.

V shrugs. "Not much. Jasper looks like you, good to know," she comments.

"I'm following them," I declare, storming off in hot pursuit.

"Wait, Ava, slow down," V says, chasing after me.

I stop and face her. "I'm doing this."

V nods, smiling cheekily. "Oh babe, I wasn't going to stop you. I was going to say wait for me."

I give my best friend a big smile, and we start our hunt.

After forty-five minutes of trailing Jasper and the Whores of Babylon, they thankfully sit down at the food court. My feet are killing me.

V has gone to get us some nachos, and I'm slouching low in my chair, snooping the hell outta the situation in front of me.

Jasper has nodded and half smiled his way through conversations, but I know him, and I know he's not happy. And as morbid as this sounds, it actually makes me feel remotely better that he isn't out celebrating our separation.

I cringe when I witness Indie reach for Jasper's hand and he doesn't push her away. He doesn't look happy about it, but he also doesn't tell her to keep her claws to herself.

Surprisingly, it isn't Indie who makes me break out into a cold sweat. It's Danielle. With every laugh, smile, and breath she takes, she's driving me deeper and deeper into a raging fury.

She looks… happy, elated actually. And I know the reason for that happiness is because I'm out of the picture.

Well, she has another thing coming!

Kicking back my chair, I storm off, so tempted am I to slam her face into the curry she's eating.

V chases after me, and I only stop when I've placed enough distance between me and Danielle.

"What's the matter? Well, apart from the obvious," V asks breathlessly.

"I fucking hate her!" I yell.

A mother walking past us ushers her child away from the crazy, swearing person that would be me.

"Okay, calm down, what happened?" V asks kindly, putting her hand on my arm.

The sentiment is enough to tip me over the edge, and I begin crying angry, gut wrenching tears.

"Ava?" V asks, looking at me with a worried gleam in her eyes.

"Why does she get to have him? She doesn't deserve to be happy. I will not... let... her... win," I say, gasping for air.

"That's my girl," V smirks. "What do you have in mind?" she asks, clapping her hands sinisterly.

"Something I should have done five days ago."

CHAPTER THIRTY FOUR

I'm Ready

Have I done the right thing?

It's too late now, my conscience pipes up. What's done is done.

I just hope I won't regret my decision in the morning.

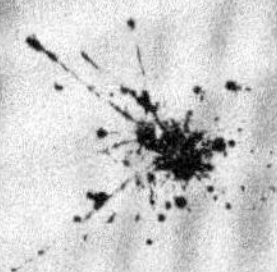

It has now been nine days since I've spoken to Jasper. He hasn't tried to contact me, nor I him, and I feel fucking empty inside.

But now that my plan has been set into motion, I have hope that maybe, just maybe, things will be okay.

I'm dressed in jeans and my favorite Little Sisters t-shirt, and am ready for 'Operation Danielle is Going Down' to commence.

I chew my fingernail anxiously, looking at my phone, waiting for it to ring.

Thankfully, I don't have to wait too long.

"Hello," I answer, a little too desperately.

"Ava?"

Okay, not who I was expecting.

"Yes, this is she."

"Oh hello, Ava, this is Thomas."

Oh shit.

Silence.

"Are you there?" Thomas asks.

"Yes, sorry, um, I'm here," I reply, flustered.

"Ava, I'll keep this short... we would like to offer you the job at Metropolis in New York."

Silence.

"Ava?" Thomas asks once again.

I can't speak so I let out a croak, hoping Thomas will know I'm still on the line.

"I know this comes as a bit of shock—"

A bit of shock? Try freakin' rendered speechless!

"You have three days to think about the offer, and come back to me with an answer," Thomas says happily.

Has he forgotten what a disaster my interview was? Like a rambling, incoherent, spilling my guts kinda disaster.

"Talk to you soon, Ava," Thomas says and hangs up.

Well, I'll be damned. I never thought I had a chance, but now, now this changes everything.

The phone vibrates in my hand, indicating I have a new text message.

My heart begins beating wildly when I see who it's from. After a minute of centering myself, I read the text aloud:

I'm ready.

CHAPTER THIRTY SIX
Once Upon a Time ...

I have to pee.

But as I stare up at Danielle's house, I know using her toilet is not an option.

Taking one last look at myself in the visor, I chant my mantra: I can do this, I can do this.

I pin back a tendril of hair, which is annoyingly slipping into my eyes, because when I do this, I want nothing inhibiting my vision.

I wait for the text message, which I receive right on the hour.

It's time.

With one last brave breath, I look at my reflection and nod—it's time.

I slam my car door shut, as I'm not trying to be quiet or sneaky. I want them to know I'm here.

As I pass Jasper's truck, which is parked on the front lawn, I fondly extend my hand and stroke the panels as I walk past. Here's hoping once this is over with, I get to see the inside of it once again. But I know, once this is over, things will change. Life as we know it will never be the same.

As I ascend the porch steps, all my fears disappear as I see Danielle and Indie, cackling together through the front window. They don't have a care in the world. Well, that's about to change.

I approach the front door and knock loudly to be heard over the shrieking that is Danielle, laughing like a hyena at something Indie has just said. Thankfully it stops, and the door opens seconds later.

"What are you doing here?" sneers a seething Danielle, her eyes narrowing when she sees me standing voluntarily on her porch.

I shrug, not fazed by her death stares. "To give you your birthday present," I smile sweetly, attempting to walk inside.

She slaps her hand against the door frame, prohibiting me from entering. She looks a little startled that I'm aware of the fact that today is her birthday, but she doesn't address it. She, however, addresses me in another way.

"Oh no, you don't!" she snarls. "You're not welcome in my home. Leave."

I don't budge however, and stand my ground, making it clear that I'm not moving an inch.

This angers her further, her cheeks flushing a scarlet red. Her voice raises an octave as she leans forward sinisterly. "You have some nerve showing your face here, after everything you've done to my son."

I clench my fists behind my back as I'm tempted to slap her lying face. I take a deep breath to calm down, closing my eyes to center myself.

As I reopen them, I reply calmly, "This won't take a minute."

"No," she sneers. "Get off my property and stay away from my son!" She yells so loudly, I swear birds have taken flight.

"Mom... let her in."

I hear him before I see his cerulean eyes looking at me longingly, and we start doing our stare off where no one else exists. My pulse begins galloping violently, like a wild horse has taken over my body and is currently running circles around my heart. I have to remind myself that I need air to breathe. But looking into Jasper's hungry gaze, I know I only need him to survive.

"Jasper, no," Danielle says, never taking her eyes off me.

Jasper never breaks eye contact with me as he sighs. "Mom... move."

When Danielle shows no sign of budging, he clenches his jaw and says, "Now."

"What the fuck is she doing here?" Indie screeches as she makes her way to Jasper's side. "Haven't you done enough?" she says, latching her arm through his and staring at me all smug.

Thankfully, Jasper shrugs out of her claws, and I try not to gloat at her surprised reaction.

So, I have a barricade of two women, determined to keep me away from the man I love.

But no more.

Pushing past Danielle, I bump straight into Jasper's solid chest, and he takes a step back to steady me. The feelings of familiarity overwhelm me, and I need to take a collected breath before I lose my nerve. I slowly meet his heated eyes, and he returns my gaze of reckless need.

But I shake those thoughts aside, because I'm on a mission to destroy the two people who destroyed me.

After it's done, I'll deal with Jasper and the repercussions of my actions, because what I'm about to do is going to change his life forever.

Jasper steadies me by my waist, his hands circling my middle.

"What are you doing here?" he asks, softly sliding his thumb under the hem of my t-shirt, stroking my skin unintentionally.

Old habits die hard.

Staring into his eyes, I know now is the time to shatter his world.

"I'm here to tell you the truth," I say cautiously.

Jasper's fingers are still on my skin, but he doesn't remove them.

"Ha! As if you know what the truth is!" scoffs Danielle, storming over to where we're standing and crossing her arms, glaring at me.

I ignore her and only focus on Jasper when I speak.

"I understand you're mad at me, and you have every right to be. But I need you to listen to me. Whatever I say, please just let me finish. Can you do that for me?" I ask, searching his eyes.

Jasper cocks an eyebrow, looking totally confused, but he thankfully nods.

"Jasper, this is ridiculous! Everything that comes out of her mouth is a lie. You have no sense when it comes to her!" Danielle says, her tone beginning to rise in hysteria.

Jasper ignores her and so do I as I continue. "Jasper, did you read the paperwork your mom asked you to sign?"

Jasper's brow furrows and he looks totally puzzled, but he answers, shaking his head. "No."

"Have you signed them?" I ask, my voice never wavering.

Out of the corner of my eye, I see Danielle begin to shuffle uncomfortably. I know she's just waiting to see where I'm going with this.

"No," Jasper replies. "What's going on, Ava?" he asks, his grip on my waist tightening.

I breathe out a sigh of relief.

"What's going on is that SHE is a bitch!" screams Indie, pointing at me and turning red.

She is the ugliest person I have ever met, inside and out.

Still in Jasper's arms, I shift to the left so I'm able to make eye contact with her. "Don't worry, Indie. Yours is coming," I say ambiguously, and that shuts her yapping.

"Ava?" Jasper asks, adjusting his fingers so he has a firmer grip on my middle.

I return my attention back to his confused eyes.

"Jasper, your mom... Your mom is using you. The document she wants you to sign has nothing to do with your dad's death. It's got to do with money. Your money," I add softly.

Jasper's eyes search mine, not understanding what I've just told him. And why would he? I can't even get my head around it, and I've been plotting this for days.

It would be easy for me to show him the proof that

lies in my bag, but not yet. I want him to believe me without any proof. I want him to believe me because I told him. If we are to get through this, then I need to regain his trust, and I'm hoping this is the answer.

"What?" Jasper asks, stunned. His hands drop to his sides.

I hate that we're no longer touching, and I'm afraid I've already blown it by not taking it slow.

"Jasper, she's a liar!" Danielle screams, her blue eyes livid.

Crossing my arms over my chest coolly, I shake my head. "No, Danielle, *you* are the liar. You are the one who would use your own son, you sick, evil bitch. I thought I knew what evil was when I nearly got beaten to death, but you, you bring a whole new meaning to the word evil."

"Jasper, don't listen to her," Danielle says in a panic, grabbing his arm, willing him to believe her.

He looks at his mom, his eyes narrowing, confused by her desperation. This is really too easy.

He turns to look at me and I meet his eyes, making it clear I'm not lying. After a pregnant pause, Jasper asks, "What money?"

Danielle yells hysterically and shoves her way between us, clasping Jasper's cheeks in both of her trembling palms.

"Jasper, son. Don't listen to a word that comes out of her deceitful mouth. She lied to you about your baby. You saw the proof, Indiana showed you. She is the liar, son, not me. I've only wanted what's best for you. But she,"

she sneers, turning over one shoulder to glare at me. "She lied to you about the baby you wanted so much."

I see Jasper flinch at the mention of our baby. What a low blow. But she doesn't stop, not even when the pain is clearly reflected on Jasper's face.

"She did it to entrap you, to make you hate me. Don't let her poison you again, Jasper. There is no money, I promise you."

Danielle grabs him by the shoulders, shaking him lightly. Her actions are that of a desperate woman. I can't help myself as I begin clapping loudly.

Danielle turns to me, baffled by my reaction. I spare a look at Indie, and somehow, she knows. She knows what I'm about to say. Well, who would have thought, she isn't as dumb as she looks.

When I have Danielle's full attention, I stop clapping.

"Nice performance," I faux yawn. "A few tears would have made it a little more believable," I sarcastically add.

She begins shaking in rage. "Leave my home, now!" she screams, pointing to her front door.

I shake my head stubbornly, my hair swishing with the momentum. "Not until I give you your birthday present. They have waited a long time to see you," I reply, making it clear her present is in the shape of a *who*, not a what.

Danielle's eyes widen as she takes three steps backwards, and I can see it all click into place.

"No," she gasps, her hands flying to her gaping mouth. "You wouldn't dare."

"Baby, tell me what's going on," Jasper pleads, willing me to explain everything.

He called me baby and my heart expands at the term of endearment. He believes me, he really believes me.

I take a deep breath, and no matter how many times I prepared myself for this, it still doesn't make what I'm about to tell him any easier.

"Jasper... your dad—"

Danielle lunges for me like a bat outta hell and I stumble, bumping into the edge of the sofa, trapped.

"Shut your mouth! You shut your mouth!" she yells, storming over to me with her fists clenched.

I drop onto the sofa because I have nowhere to go and no time to move.

Jasper is following in hot pursuit. "Mom, stop!" he screams, as Danielle is about to slap me, but I don't cower.

I face her and dare her to touch me.

"Enough!"

Danielle pauses, her face turning a deathly white when she hears a voice from her past. She spins in slow motion, and is confronted by a pair of cerulean eyes. But those eyes don't belong to her son. No, they belong to someone who has impeccable timing.

"Hello, Danielle," Jeremy Blackmore says, his arms crossed over his broad chest.

Danielle gasps and her eyes are about ready to roll out of her head.

She slowly turns to me, mouth wide, and the biggest grin I have ever smiled in my entire life paints my cheeks as I say, "Happy birthday... bitch."

CHAPTER THIRTY SIX
Once Upon a Time ...

"Wh... who are you?" Jasper stutters, while looking at a spitting image of himself.

There's dead silence, and I can't stand to see him looking so plagued, so I whisper, "Jasper... he's your father."

Jasper spins to face me so quickly I'm surprised he hasn't fallen over.

"My who?" Jasper gasps, begging me with frantic eyes to explain.

But I don't have to.

Jeremy Blackmore takes a step inside and softly closes the door. I stay seated on the sofa arm, grateful I'm sitting as my legs feel like jelly.

"Jasper, my name is Jeremy Blackwood, and Ava is right, I am your father."

Jasper turns to face the man who is about to change his life.

Jeremy clears his throat, taking a visible breath before he begins his tale. "Will you let me explain?" he asks, his eyes never leaving Jasper's.

Jasper slowly nods, while I hear Danielle sniffle, but surprisingly, she remains quiet.

"Your mother worked for my family as a housemaid, and I fell in love with her the moment I laid eyes on her. But your mother was engaged to William, and your brother Stephen, he was only a baby, so I knew I could only love her from afar. Your mother," Jeremy pauses, looking off into the distance with a faraway look in his eyes. "Your mother, Jasper, she was beautiful. Full of life and spirit. She could light up a room with just a smile."

Looking at the horrible woman Jeremy is speaking so fondly of, I find it hard to believe she had any redeemable qualities. But I stay silent and allow him to continue.

"She came into work one day with a black eye, and when I asked her what had happened, she broke down and told me how unhappy she was. William had a heavy hand with her when he was drunk, which was most of the time, and she was afraid for her safety, and that of your brother. I told her I would do whatever I could to help her, and if she needed any assistance moving out, I was more than happy to lend a hand. But she declined, saying William would kill her if he found out she had spoken to me about their situation. I think in her own way, she really loved him and never wanted to leave."

Jeremy takes a deep breath, and I see Jasper watching the man before him closely.

"What happened next, son, I'm not proud of. Your mother and I, we grew closer, and we began having an affair, and she got pregnant... with you. The day she told me she was carrying my child was the happiest day of my life."

Even though I have heard this story before, I can't

help the tears that fall down my cheeks, as it reminds me so much of when I told Jasper he was to be a father.

"She wanted an abortion, but I begged her not to kill my boy, because I knew," he says, looking at his son proudly. "That we had created an amazing baby boy."

Jasper clears his throat but he doesn't move, his eyes are glued on Jeremy.

"She promised to keep the baby, only if I married her, and of course I agreed, as I wanted nothing more than to have Danielle as my wife, and raise you as my son. Danielle told me she had left William, but didn't want to get married until after you were born, and I believed her. I mean, why wouldn't I? I insisted she come live with me, but she declined, saying she wanted us to be married before we lived together. I told her I would marry her in an instant, but she wanted a white wedding, and she couldn't really have that while pregnant. Looking back now, I realize how stupid I was to believe her."

Jeremy takes a big breath and continues. "I paid for all her medical expenses, baby supplies—anything she wanted, it was hers. And everything was perfect, up until the day you were born. I was the proudest dad the day I got to hold my son," he says, tears pricking his eyes. He wipes them away so he can finish his story.

"But I only got to hold you long enough for the midwife to take a photo, and then you were gone. William arrived, demanding security escort me outside as I was bothering Danielle. I pleaded with her to explain what was going on, and she looked at me with such cold eyes, like she didn't know me. She had told William he was your father, not I. Security didn't have to throw me out. I left a broken man, not understanding what was happening. I refused to believe Danielle was using me this whole time," he whispers.

"I tried weeks after you were born to contact Danielle, but she wouldn't speak to me. Little did she know, the day you were born, I opened a trust fund in your name, hoping that one day I could give it to you." Jeremy sniffs.

Jasper wipes his tears away with the back of his hand, and my heart breaks. But I don't console him, he needs to know the rest.

"I tried everything, Jasper. I tried pleading with your mother, I begged her to marry me so I could take care of you and Stephen, but she would hang up on me, never giving me a chance. I became incessant, calling almost every day, and when she finally understood I wasn't giving up, she begged me not to call because William was home, and she would call me instead. She never did. When she finally got around to contacting me days later, it was because she wanted money. She promised she would use it to look after you, as William wanted nothing to do with you, because she had told him you were my son. But he wouldn't let her leave, threatening to make her life a living hell if she left him. She promised me, Jasper, that she was leaving him, but she was just waiting for the right time. And I believed her because I wanted so badly for it to be true. This went on for three years. Your mother played me all those years, keeping me sated by allowing me to see you for the first year or so in secret. When she claimed it was too dangerous, she kept me sated by giving me pictures of you. But occasionally,"

Jeremy pauses, looking ashamed. "Occasionally she kept me sated in other ways."

No guessing how so.

"I was a fool," Jeremy concludes.

"Three years?" Jasper gasps.

"I know it's a long time, Jasper, but I knew what kind of man your father was, and your mother was that good—I fell for her empty lies."

I have to bite my lip to stop a string of profanities flying her way.

Jeremy continues. "The whole time, your mother had no intention of leaving William. She was using the money I sent her to feed her and William's gluttony. It took me three long years to realize this, but when I did, I had no other option but to hire the best lawyers in the country to work my case, and try to gain full custody of you. It took months, but finally, the day came when they told me I had a good case, as they discovered that William was not only an alcoholic, but also a drug user. Your mother had told me William had stopped drinking, and that he was clean. I am so sorry, Jasper. Only now do I know he was hurting you, and I'm so very sorry I wasn't there for you."

Jasper nods, his face contorting in pain.

"When you were three and a half, your mother came to see me, begging me to call off the lawyers as they were building a strong case against her. I told her no, absolutely not. I would fight for you until my last breath. She begged me, offered to sleep with me, she tried everything. But when none of her pleas worked anymore, she used something I could never say no to."

Closing my eyes, I bite my lip because my heart is breaking.

"What?" Jasper asks, barely above a whisper.

"You."

I can hear Danielle sob, and I know the only reason behind her tears is because Jasper is finally seeing her for what she really is. A heartless bitch.

"She went out to the car and came back with you. I couldn't take my eyes off you. I hadn't seen you in so long. You were perfect. But then Danielle... she asked you if you wanted to live with me. The look in your innocent eyes, that look will never leave me and will haunt me to my grave. You said no. You began crying when Danielle said you were going to live with me, and you would never see Stephen again. She was using you as collateral and it broke my heart. I couldn't stand to see you in pain, so I agreed to grant her full custody, on the proviso that I could see you. She agreed, but she lied. I never saw you ever again after that.

"But I saw Danielle. She returned a few months later, begging me once again for money to help support you. I knew the money was to support her habit, as she no longer resembled the woman I fell in love with. I told her no, but your mother, Jasper," he says, looking over at a sniveling Danielle. "She is a master manipulator and turned on the charm, and I fell for it—again. I'm so ashamed of myself for making the same mistake with her, time and time again. I mentioned the trust fund in a moment of weakness, and she wanted access to the money to buy you all the things she couldn't afford. But there was no way I was giving her that money. I may have been in love with her, but I wasn't blind."

"I came to an agreement with her. You were to inherit the money on your twenty-fifth birthday. But if by chance you were to deny the funds, then your mother was entitled to all of it. If you hadn't claimed the funds by your twenty-sixth birthday, then your mother was to become heir to one million dollars."

Jasper's mouth opens in disbelief, and I bet he never guessed the amount of money left to him was of such an astronomical figure.

Jeremy rubs his crinkled brow. "But there was a catch. She was only permitted the money if she told you about me. That's why my lawyers stipulated that she needed your signature to release the funds over to her. If you wanted nothing to do with me or the money, then you were the one to sign it over to her."

Jeremy meets my tear-stained eyes, giving me a gentle smile. "And she would have gotten away with it if it wasn't for Ava. She's a smart young lady, Jasper. And she never lied to you. Your mother, however..." he says, giving her a pitiful look.

Danielle crumples onto the sofa near me, burying her head into her hands and sobbing loudly. Indie runs to her aid, wrapping her in a tight embrace, allowing her to cry her crocodile tears.

I don't know what to do, so I get up, as I don't feel an inch of pity for her.

Leaning up against the wall, I wrap my arms around myself, as I feel nauseous. Jeremy's story the second time around, is just as painful as the first. I look at Jasper, who's staring at the wall in front of him, blankly. I want more than anything to comfort him, but I know he needs time to process everything.

I watch Jeremy gaze at his son lovingly. The adoration he feels for Jasper is clear as day, and I can't help the steady flow of tears that spill over my lashes, hitting my cheeks, as Jasper deserves at least one good parent in his life.

After a few minutes of silence, Jasper clears his throat.

"How could you leave her that money? After everything she did to you…… how?" Jasper asks, trying to make sense of it all.

Funny, I asked the exact same thing.

Jeremy lowers his head in shame. "Because I loved her, Jasper. Deep down, I secretly hoped the young girl I fell in love with would do right by you and tell you about me. But I was wrong. I was a naïve fool. She never breathed a word to you about me, and pretended that pathetic excuse of a man was your father."

Jasper runs a hand through his hair, his eyes searching his father's. "How could you stop trying to see me? Fighting for me? When I was older, I could have made up my own mind," he says, his voice breaking.

Jeremy nods and looks ashamed to admit his error. "I did try, Jasper. I tried and tried. But whenever the lawyers and I took a step forward, we then took three steps back, as taking a child away from his biological mother is not as easy as it sounds. The father doesn't have a lot of rights, especially when he abandoned his child for the majority of his young life. I fought for you for so long, and then the day came when your mother told me you wanted nothing to do with me. She came to me with tears in her eyes, promising me that she had explained every-thing. But it didn't matter; you didn't want to know me. I wasn't your father, and I never would be."

Jeremy looks at Danielle, disgusted. "All I could see was that three year old little boy, crying in front of me, begging me not to take you away from your family. That's why I believed her, because your mother, she broke everything inside of me, she broke my will to survive. I gave up and I hated myself for it, but I didn't want to hurt you any longer. You didn't know who I was, I wasn't your father. I was a stranger who wanted to take you away from the only family you knew. I couldn't blame you for wanting nothing to do with the man who abandoned you, because that's what I did. I left you when you needed me the most. I didn't deserve you in my life, and I gave up."

Jeremy looks grief-stricken. "I continued giving your mother child support, not knowing if you ever saw a penny of it. But I couldn't stay in America, it hurt too much. So I went to live in Europe, and not a day went by that I didn't think of you, Jasper, or regret my decision. I was a coward and I don't expect you to forgive me, because I will never forgive myself."

Jeremy looks my way, smiling. "But then something remarkable happened. Three days ago, a young woman named Ava tracked me down after, no doubt, an exhausting search, and told me all about my son, Jasper White. She told me everything, Jasper, who you were, what you liked, what you did, and what a good man you turned out to be. And I listened to every single word, because it was information I was craving to hear for twenty-six years. It was the truth about my boy."

Jasper turns to look at me, his eyes wide, and I give him a shy smile, my tears slipping into my lips.

"She told me you weren't even aware of my existence, and that your mother had lied to me. She had lied to you. She was after the money. After all this time, that's all she ever cared about. And that's why I'm here. I'm here to do what I should have done twenty-six years ago. I'm here to take back, my son."

Jeremy takes a step towards Jasper, his eyes filled with fear.

Jasper takes a small step back, and I know this is too much for him to process all at once.

Jeremy looks at me and I give him a small, encouraging smile.

However, my smile fades as Danielle jumps up, running hysterically towards Jasper.

"It's all lies!" she cries, trying to latch onto him, but he sidesteps her. "Jasper, don't believe them!" she sobs. "Please, son!" she begs, and it's her final plea.

"I'm not your son," he sneers, taking a step closer to his dad. "How could you?" he says, between clenched teeth. "You let that *man* beat me every day of my life. And you never stopped it. You had a choice, you had someone who loved you, but you chose *him*. That spineless asshole who wasn't even my father!"

Danielle begins sobbing uncontrollably but I feel nothing for her.

Jasper is shaking in rage and I look to Jeremy for help. But Jeremy shakes his head, and he's right. Jasper needs to let it all out, because I know once he says his peace, it'll be the last thing he ever says to his mom.

"I could probably overlook the fact that you tried to steal my money, money that I don't even want. But I will *never* forgive you for lying to me. You had the chance to make our lives better, mine and Stephen's, but you didn't. What kind of person does that?"

"Jasper, no. I loved your father, he was a good man," Danielle sobs, snot running down her face. "He loved us. He never meant to hurt you."

She drops to her knees, reaching out for him, but Jasper turns away, disgusted. In her own twisted way, Danielle actually loved William, that's why she lied to Jeremy about telling Jasper the truth. As I have no doubt, William would have threatened Danielle, demanding Jeremy get out of their lives, or he would. When William realized Jeremy wasn't falling for Danielle's lies any longer, and the extra money stopped rolling in, Jeremy was no use to William. He would have wanted Jeremy out of their lives, as he was nothing but a reminder of the son he hated. The money, in the end, wasn't more impor-tant to Danielle than William, and she cut Jeremy out. Too bad she doesn't feel the same way about her son's money.

Danielle could have had a happy life with Jeremy, but she didn't love him. Love makes people do crazy things, and I feel a smidge sorry for her, but as I look at her, peering up at Jasper, that pity fades.

"Good man?" Jasper snarls. "He wasn't a good man

when he beat me senseless when I was six years old for spilling juice onto the carpet. Nor was he a good man when he knocked me out, laughing when I came to, calling me a pussy for not fighting back! I was eight fucking years old! You could have stopped that, all of it, but you didn't. You let him demoralize me and Stephen every day of our lives, and for that, I will hate you with every inch of my beaten body and soul till the day I die!" Jasper yells, and Danielle recoils when she hears the bitterness behind his words.

She sobs hysterically, screams tear from her throat, knowing Jasper means every word.

"Get up! No amount of begging will make this right. You're dead to me," Jasper spits.

"Jasper," she chokes, but Jasper shakes his head and turns away.

Danielle sobs and punches the floor repeatedly.

She turns her bloodshot eyes to me and curls her lips in rage. "This is your fault. All of it!" She points her finger at me, glaring. "You are going to pay!"

I meet her glare with one of my own.

"I dare you," I snarl.

Danielle is up in a heartbeat and before I have a chance to react, she comes charging towards me like she's possessed. I brace my hands on the wall and close my eyes, expecting some kind of impact. But nothing comes.

I bravely sneak open an eye, and all I can see is Jasper's broad back, his shoulders rising and falling in quick succession.

"You've got to go through me," he sneers, taking a step backward, so I'm nearly flush against his back.

"And me," Jeremy says, stepping in front of Jasper protectively.

I'm surrounded by two protective men and my heart swells.

I can't see much, as Jasper's body towers over mine, but I don't need to see her. I can feel the rage pouring off of Danielle.

"Jeremy," she gasps, stunned.

"Danielle, I should have done this a long time ago. You will not hurt my son a moment longer," Jeremy says with conviction.

Jasper's shoulders depress, the tension easing out of him when he hears Jeremy's comment. I can't help myself as I slide my hand around his waist, and am relieved when he wraps his fingers through mine.

Danielle lets out one last final sob, and I hear her barge out the front door, her feet pounding on the porch steps as she makes her escape. Even though this is her house, she knows she's outnumbered.

One down, one to go.

I turn to look at Indie, who is sitting on the couch, drawn into herself, trying to hide.

No such luck.

Jeremy steps aside and Jasper follows, but he turns to face me. He looks beaten and worn, but he looks relieved. And I know I have made the right choice, reuniting him with his dad.

Now, there's one more thing I need to make right.

I give Jasper a small smile before I turn my attention to Indie. As soon as my eyes lock with hers, she cowers.

"You're awfully quiet," I say sarcastically.

Indie lowers her eyes. This is almost too easy.

Pushing off from the wall, I slip past Jasper to confront a guilty looking Indie.

"So, what did she promise you?" I simply ask.

Indie looks mortified that I would insinuate she had any part in Danielle's evil plan.

But I call her bluff. "We can do this the easy way, or my way." I smirk, crossing my arms over my chest.

Indie's frantic eyes flick to Jasper when he moves to stand beside me. "I swear I didn't know, Jasper!" she pleads, tears pooling in her deceitful eyes.

"We all know that's a lie." I scold. I'm standing my ground and not backing down. "What were you getting out of hurting the man you supposedly love?" I choose my words intentionally.

Jasper looks at Indie, his eyes narrowing, waiting for her to answer.

She places her hands over her face and confesses, "She was going to give me a cut of the money."

My insides actually turn in disgust.

"And you were okay with that?" I ask, mortified she would actually use Jasper.

Indie lowers her hands, her mascara running down her tear-stained cheeks.

"It was all for you, Jasper," she sobs, looking at him pleadingly. "I was going to share it with you, I promise."

I take it back; she is as dumb as she looks.

"Did you know about Jeremy?" I ask, even though I know the answer.

Indie nods and I can hear Jasper grinding down on his jaw.

"For how long?" I persist, glaring at her.

She returns my stare and snaps, "Since we were kids. I overheard Danielle talking to my mom about it and Danielle caught me. She said she would give me money, like a weekly allowance, if I never told Jasper the truth. Happy?"

She has been using Jasper this whole time—they both have been. Even when they were 'together' in high school, and Jasper thought Indie genuinely wanted to be friends with him, it all came down to money. That's why Indie hung around with him. I have no doubt she was receiving a large sum of money, money that Jeremy was giving Danielle to give to Jasper. I'd like to believe that once she got older, Danielle stopped with the bribes, as in her own warped way, I believe Indie loves Jasper.

Closing my eyes, I count to ten before I reopen them.

"I am anything *but* happy. How could you?" I sneer, shaking my head at her.

She guiltily turns her eyes up to Jasper, flinching when she sees his reaction to her confession. His jaw is clenched and his nostrils are flaring; I know he's barely holding on.

"Get. Out," he snarls, closing his eyes tightly so he no longer has to see her deceitful face.

Indie jumps up, running over to where he stands. "Believe me! It was all for you, all of it. So we could live comfortably together. At first it was for the money, but it's not now," she cries, attempting to justify her deception.

Jasper scoffs, narrowing his eyes at her. "Are you listening to yourself? You are trying to justify lying to me this whole time, betraying me in the worst possible way, by saying you were only thinking of me. You make me sick," he spits, turning away from her, disgusted.

Indie latches onto Jasper's arm, sobbing. "Please forgive me!"

Jasper pulls out of her grip. "Get away from me, you're pathetic. If I never see you again it'll be too soon."

"Jasper, I love you!" Indie cries hysterically, pleading with him to believe her.

Jasper chuckles low, unmoved by her pleas. "Love? You wouldn't know the first thing about love. The only person you love is yourself. And that's a good thing, because no one could ever love a lying, manipulative bitch like you. You'll be forever alone, Indie, and you'll have no one to blame but yourself," Jasper sneers. I flinch at the harshness of his words, but she deserves it.

Indie sobs, choking on her tears.

But this isn't over. She has one more lie to confess up to.

I stand near Jasper, crossing my arms over my chest.

"Seeing as you're in a sharing mood, how about you tell Jasper the truth about my test results."

Indie sniffs back her tears and narrows her eyes at me. "There's nothing to tell."

"I beg to differ," I sinisterly chuckle, incredulous that she's still lying.

Jasper turns to me, his eyes softening.

"I believe you, baby."

His words are like music to my ears and I bite back my tears, but I'm like a dog at a bone.

"I'm giving you one last chance to redeem yourself."

I need to hear her confession so I can bitch slap her into next week.

But no such luck as Indie scoffs, "Dream on. I'm not going to cover for you. Jasper has a right to know you lied to him, and made him believe you were pregnant when you weren't."

Still with the lies.

It takes all my restraint not to punch her in the mouth. But I play it cool as I shrug, looking at my nails. "Okay, have it your way. I mean, I'm sure Doctor Hemming will be interested to know that one of his employees is a thief."

That gets her attention as her head snaps my way. Her eyes narrow and her lips curl in fury as she snarls, "You cun—"

Jasper cuts her off before she reveals just how classy she really is.

"Get out. Before I throw you out." His jaw hardens as he adds, "And I mean that literally."

Indie's gasp can be heard three doors down, and I can't wipe the smile off my face.

"This isn't over!" she sneers, collecting her bag, wiping away her tears.

Jasper puts his arm on mine to stop me from launching at her, but I push him off, getting into her face.

"Oh yeah?" I taunt. "Bring it. I'll be waiting for you, you low-life tramp."

Indie looks completely stunned by my bravery, and I think I've seen the last of her. But she surprises me as she quickly raises her hand to slap me. But I'm quicker, as I duck out of the way and punch her straight in the face.

She staggers backward, her hand flying to her nose.

Indie-nil.

Ava-two.

"You bitch! You broke my nose!" Indie muffles, blood pouring down her face.

"You're lucky that's all I broke," I reply furiously.

Indie stares at Jasper, her eyes begging him to help her, but he shakes his head, making it clear she is dead to him.

"Get out," he growls.

She gives me one last glare, and I'll never forget the image of Indie storming out of Jasper's life for good.

As soon as she's out the door, I cradle my right fist into my left hand and bite my lip.

Jasper is over in an instant. "Are you okay?" he asks, reaching for my hand.

I hiss in pain as soon as he makes contact, recoiling.

"It might be broken," he says, his blue eyes searching my body for any other cuts or bruises.

Raising my shoulders in a carefree shrug, I smile. "So worth it."

Jasper smirks, but he looks like death. His hair is sticking out riotously, and his eyes are bloodshot and worn.

I touch his arm with my non-injured hand, still cradling my right to my chest.

"Are you okay?" I ask stupidly, because of course he's not.

He looks down at my hand and then back up at me, his hair slipping into his tired eyes. "I am now. Ava, I'm—"

I place my finger over his lips to stop him. "Sssh."

He kisses my finger lightly and the simple gesture warms my heart.

I look over at Jeremy, who's quietly waiting off to the side, his hands clasped behind his back. I know he's waited his whole life for this moment.

To see his son.

Jasper turns to follow my line of sight and meets his father's eyes. As I look at the similarities between them, with their matching cerulean eyes, strong angled jaws, tipped up noses and dark hair, there is no doubt that they are father and son.

Jeremy clears his throat and takes a hesitating step towards Jasper. "Jasper, I..." Jeremy says, but stops as his voice catches in his throat.

His eyes are scanning Jasper from head to toe, in total disbelief that he's really standing before his son.

I take a small step to the side, as this is Jeremy's time with Jasper.

Jasper however, doesn't move; he stands still, his chest rising and falling slowly. And he too, is examining his father with careful scrutiny.

Jeremy runs a hand through his groomed hair, so different to his son's, but the nervous habit is the same.

"Son, I'm so sorry. I thought I was doing the right thing by you, I swear it."

Jasper still stares at Jeremy, unblinking.

"I want to get to know you. I know we can never make up for lost time, but I really hope you can find it in your heart to forgive me. Please give me a chance to be the father I should have been all those years ago," Jeremy says, his eyes revealing nothing but the truth.

I can't stop the tears that begin streaming down my face.

Jasper, his whole life, has been surrounded by darkness, but now, now he has his chance at being surrounded by nothing but light.

Jasper swallows deeply and takes a small step towards his dad, and Jeremy's eyes begin to moisten, pools of happiness and sorrow forming in his blue eyes.

Jasper takes yet another step, and then another, until he's standing in front of his father.

The sight before me is a beautiful one, and I silently sob for the Blackwood family.

Jeremy shakily extends his hand out in the form of a handshake, and Jasper stares at his hand for the longest time, unsure of what to do. After a moment, he places his hand into his father's, and tears cascade down his cheeks.

Jeremy's eyes also fill with tears, and he takes a visible breath before pulling Jasper into his arms, embracing him lovingly. Jasper, at first, stands rigid and unsure. But as Jeremy wraps his arms around his son's back tightly, Jasper mimics the movement and slowly raises his arms, holding onto his dad like he is his savior.

And in a way, he is. Jeremy saved Jasper. And he saved me.

I meet Jeremy's eyes over Jasper's shoulder and he mouths, "Thank you."

I wipe away my tears with the back of my hand and give him a small nod.

Little does he know, I'm the one who should be thanking him.

Watching their reunion has shifted my priorities, and I feel like I've had an epiphany.

When I wake tomorrow, everything will be different.

For the both of us.

CHAPTER THIRTY SEVEN
I'm Already Gone

I don't want to get up, but I know I have to, otherwise I never will.

Opening my weary eyes, I take in my bedroom. Everything looks the same from when I saw it last. The dresser is still strewn with random items—my favorite perfumes, lip boosting lip glosses, and an empty packet of Hot Tamales.

But I'm different. Something happened last night and I will never be the same.

After Jeremy and Jasper's reunion, we decided it best to leave Danielle's house, as we felt we were in the lion's den. We ended up at Jasper's house.

At first, it was nothing short of awkward, with uncomfortable silences and strained conversations. But as Jeremy spilled his heart out, Jasper's wall broke down, and with each confession and apology, they were catching up just how father and son should. I left them mid-conversation, not wanting to interrupt their reunion, and as soon as I got home, I collapsed into a heap and slept like the dead.

Both Jasper and Jeremy know they have a lot to work on, as this is real life, and not some happy fairytale, but they will get there, because that's what families do.

So, there's a reason why I've woken, and that's because today is the first day of a new era.

Reaching for my iPhone on my bedside table, I dial a number I never thought I would.

He picks up on the third ring.

"Hello."

I get the formalities out of the way and get down to business.

"After much consideration... I've decided to accept your offer."

The recipient expresses his delight at my decision, and for once, so do I.

I'm plodding around in my PJ's and sweater, but no matter how high I crank the heater, I just can't seem to get warm. I'm quite certain the stress from the past few weeks has finally caught up with me, and my body is going to remind me of it for the next week.

I haven't spoken to Jasper since yesterday's drama, as I have wanted to give him time alone with his dad, and also some space.

What happened between us has changed everything, and will forever be a turning point in our relationship.

Whether that's a positive or negative thing, I have yet to decide.

With my head buried in the pantry, I fail to notice I have company until I turn around and am caught shoving a handful of Skittles into my mouth. I nearly choke, and thump my chest with my fist to help swallow the sugary goodness.

Jasper is sitting in my kitchen, looking like a total sex god, while I have to look twice to make sure I have pants on.

"Hi," I squeak, swallowing the last of my Skittles.

Jasper is straddling a chair casually, resting his chin on his interlaced arms, which are crossed over the top of the seat. After everything he's been through, he still looks freakin' amazing.

"Hi," he simply replies, his hungry eyes burning a hole straight through me.

I begin tugging nervously at the frayed hem of my sweater, unsure of what to say.

"Come here," he says, crooking his finger my way.

Meeting his eyes, I take a small step towards him.

As I stand in front of him, the realization of my decision hits home and my knees begin to give out. I sink into the seat next to him and he turns his chair, facing me.

We stare at each other for minutes, surrendering to silence, as we both know everything is about to change.

Jasper breaks the silence.

"Thank you."

Okay, not what I was expecting.

I give him a small smile, but don't speak.

"What you did for me, I didn't deserve any of it. You could have let it be, and I would have been none the wiser to what my mom had planned. But you didn't," he whispers, his eyes softening.

"I couldn't," I reply gently. "No matter what happens

between us, Jasper, I will always try and do my best by you."

And I mean that.

And that's why I had to make the hardest decision of my life.

Jasper nods and the air is charged with an electrical static I can't explain.

"I didn't deserve it, though," he says, his head drooping sadly.

Reaching out, I cover my hand over his.

"Yes, you do. You deserve everything and much, much more."

I take a deep breath, because the next thing I'm about to say is going to kill me.

"And that's why...that's why we can't keep doing this," I whisper.

Jasper's eyes snap to mine, and I know he knew it would end this way for us.

I don't need to clarify what 'this' is, as he knows it, too.

"Too much has happened between us, and my heart... can't take it anymore. I need to take a break from life, and the drama. I need a break...because each day, I'm struggling to breathe. We both need to find where we belong, and I think the best way to do that...is on our own. It's not just the thing with your mom, or Indie, or the... baby. It's everything. Love shouldn't be this hard. I know love isn't perfect, but ours...ours is just destructive," I confess, wishing what I said was a lie.

I love Jasper, and that's the problem. I love him *too* much, and that's taking over who I am. I know Jasper would never move to New York, but I want to. And this time, I can't say no. If I were, it would be lying to myself, and in the end, I would resent him for standing in the way of my dreams.

Now that Jasper has Jeremy, I know he'll be okay. I can do this and we'll both survive it, because we both need to do this. Not only for each other, but for ourselves. The man I fell in love with, and am still in love with, is a man who has been reborn. Jasper needs to find his path, just how I need to find mine.

Jasper swallows deeply before he answers me. "Where will you go?" he asks.

We both know living in the same state and attempting to stay away from each other will be impossible.

"New York," I reply. "I got the job at Metropolis."

Jasper nods, giving me a small smirk. "I knew that you would. How could they say no to you?"

I return his smile. "What about you?" I ask, needing to know he will be okay.

Jasper's shoulders rise up in a shrug. "I might go stay with Jeremy for a bit. He said I have grandparents and cousins...can you believe that shit?" he says in disbelief.

I give him a small smile, but am on the verge of tears.

"So...when are you leaving?" he asks softly.

"After graduation," I reply, biting my lip.

Jasper nods, his hair veiling his eyes, but I can still see how hard this is for him.

"So, how do we do this?" he asks, reaching out and stroking the inside of my wrist.

I shiver under his touch.

"I dunno," I reply, because I really don't know what the right protocol is when dealing with a situation such as this.

"I'd still like to see you until you leave," he says, his voice quaking.

I nod, but gnaw my bottom lip miserably. "Me too," I reply on the verge of tears as I lower my eyes.

"But?" Jasper asks, sensing my lingering doubts.

"But I know how hard it'll be when we have to say goodbye," I softly reply, still looking at the floor.

"You want to say goodbye now?" he asks sadly.

Nodding miserably, my heart crumbles.

I know I'm doing the right thing, but it still fucking hurts.

"I wish—" Jasper says, sniffing. "I wish things turned out differently for you and me." And the tears begin to fall.

"Me too," I sniff. "But too much has happened, Jasper...I never meant to hurt you, but I just can't seem to stop. I want you...to move on, okay? I want you to be happy, and I don't think I'm the person to make that happen for you. Not now, anyway. I need to follow my heart, and right now, it's telling me to follow this road."

I can't control my tears and I doubt they'll stop anytime soon.

Jasper wipes the tears from my cheeks with the back of his knuckles. "For what it's worth, knowing you, and being loved by you, has been fucking epic. I'm a better man because of you, Ava. And one day, I hope I'm good enough for you, because you're it for me. But...you're right. We need to surrender to ourselves, before we can surrender to each other."

I barely manage to speak because he's right. In the end, we *have* surrendered to one another, but the most important person to surrender to is ourselves. And that's where the problem lies. In life and love, you have to put yourself first. But me staying in L.A., and Jasper not pursuing who he really is, is not.

"You are good enough, Jasper, you always have been," I whisper.

Jasper places his palm on my cheek and I lean into it, memorizing his final touch.

"I need to believe that, though, Ava. And that's why I'm letting you go. Maybe if we met at a different time, different place, different life, we'd work, but now... we just don't. But you'll always be in here." He sadly smiles, placing his hand over his heart. "No one can ever remove you from here."

I sob so hard I find it hard to breathe. Why am I doing this? Why am I leaving the best thing that has ever happened to me?

The answer is simple: We both need to find who we are.

Sometimes love makes sense, but most times, it doesn't. And this is one of those times. It may not make sense for me to leave Jasper, but it feels right.

Jasper is out of his seat, hugging me into his warm chest. A chest I have cried into endless times. A chest I don't know if I'll cry into ever again.

The next few days pass in a daze.

I tell my parents of my decision to move to New York, and they're incredibly supportive, even though they'll miss me horribly.

V's reaction was surprisingly not as scary as I thought it would be. She was happy, but burst into tears when I told her I would be leaving after graduation, which is about a month away.

I ghost around for the next month, and am functioning on auto-pilot. I finish up all my classes and lose myself in studying for exams, which have helped me stop thinking about my decision. Even though I have accepted my decision, it doesn't make it any easier to breathe.

I have cried myself to sleep every night, and somehow, I don't think that'll stop this century.

Jasper has respected my decision and not contacted me, as it would be too hard hearing his voice, or seeing those cerulean eyes I long to look into. But I've made my decision and I have to live with it, because funnily enough, as much as it hurts to be without Jasper, it hurts more to not put myself first. And that's what I have done, even if all I feel is this cruel wanting, I have to do this.

Like I promised myself months and months ago, the next person I am going to be in a relationship with is me.

And this time, I mean it.

CHAPTER THIRTY EIGHT

When I Was Your Man

"I can't believe you're leaving tomorrow!" V sniffs, wiping her eyes as we hit the pavement.

"Can you stop with the crying already?" I try and joke, but it just sounds lame, as I'm about to join her in five seconds.

Today I graduated, and at the moment, so many feelings and sensations are running through my body. I don't know how to make sense of them all.

So, the only thing that makes a lick of sense is getting wasted. Short term, but it'll do for now.

We're walking down the familiar streets, and a hint of nostalgia hits me. I'm really going to miss L.A. She has been a bitch to deal with at times, but was it all worth it?

Fuck yes!

I can see the flashing neon sign, announcing we have arrived at Little Sisters, and my heart slightly plummets. I'm really going to miss this place. This place holds so many wonderful memories, and those memories consist of a man I will miss most of all.

As we are about to enter, I hesitate, as I'm afraid those wonderful memories will turn into big, fat, ugly tears.

V senses my apprehension and tugs on my arm. "It's

okay, P.O.E aren't playing tonight. Scout's honor," she says, holding up her fingers.

I know they aren't because today is Tuesday, and Jasper works at the shelter most weeknights.

Stalker much?

We enter and my eyes scan the area that has been my second home. I wonder if I'll find something as homely as this in New York.

As I take in the scuffed dance floor, the thirsty patrons bopping away, waiting in line for their drinks, and the scantily-dressed waitresses, zipping around in clothes that still make me blush, I know the answer is no. Los Angeles will always be my home, but I'm leaving because my home has caused me nothing but grief.

"Okay, enough with the moping," V says, tugging me towards the bar. "Time to get you nice and drunk."

I couldn't agree more.

After way too many cocktails, I'm beginning to see double.

"V," I slur. "I really need to go home. My plane leaves early and I need to get at least one hour of sleep."

V chuckles and waves me off. "Don't be such a party pooper. You can sleep all you want when you move a zillion miles away from your best friend."

I give her a sheepish look and suddenly, I feel tears spring to my eyes. "I'm really going to miss you," I say. "After everything we've been through. I just... I really love you, V."

V bites her lip and tears begin falling down her rosy cheeks.

"Am I doing the right thing?" I ask.

V wipes away her tears and smiles. "Who knows, Ava? But if you aren't, you can always come back. This will always be your home. And I'll always be here, welcoming you back with open arms."

Her words are exactly what I needed to hear, as I know I just have cold feet.

"I must admit, it'll be good to not have to deal with your drama," she jokes, bumping me with her shoulder.

I let out a sniff mixed with a laugh, because it's true. V has been with me every step of the way, and it saddens me that she won't be with me to share the highs and lows of my new life.

But I brush those thoughts aside as a piano is being pushed out on stage by security. I sit up from my barstool, looking at the beautiful black piano which is sitting center stage, gleaming under the dim lights.

"I didn't realize anyone was playing tonight," I say, sipping on my drink.

V doesn't answer me, and when I look at her, she's doing everything *not* to look at me. Oh no, I know that look.

"What?" I ask, raising my eyebrows.

V sips her mocktail and begins whistling, looking over her shoulder guiltily.

"Veronica!" I say, trying to catch her gaze, but she is avoiding me like the plague.

"What are you up to now?" I ask, knowing that she indeed has one final scam up her sleeve.

"This better be good," I mumble, downing my drink in one hit, as I have a feeling I'll need it.

V turns her attention back to me and half smiles.

Oh, great.

The lights dim and I sit up higher, craning my neck to see over the heads of the patrons in front of me.

Nothing happens for a while, and I feel I may have overreacted.

But as I see a familiar form stroll out onto the stage, a whirlwind of longing hits me so hard, I have to hold onto the seat for support.

Jasper.

V whispers in my ear, "I said P.O.E weren't playing, and *technically*, they aren't."

Under normal circumstances, I would be scolding her for being a meddlesome pain in my ass. But now, now I can't seem to move. And that's because, staring at the man I love with every fiber of my being is all that matters.

He takes a seat at the piano and rests his long, elegant fingers on the keys. But he doesn't play. He just sits there, his head bowed, deep in thought.

He remains this way for minutes, and the world around me doesn't exist, but he breaks my stupor when he finally begins playing.

And when he does, I know nothing will ever be the same.

The song he has chosen is "When I Was Your Man"

by Bruno Mars. And as soon as the first word leaves his beautiful lips, the floodgates open.

He looks so beautiful up on stage. It's so simple—just him and a piano. But there's nothing simple about this situation.

As my tears begin clouding my vision, I can no longer see him. But I don't need to see him, because his words are telling me he feels it, too. He feels this desperate longing to be together, but he knows why we need to do this. And that's because this is the right thing to do.

As he sings about me dancing with another man, I know my other man is New York. He wants me to be happy, to move on, and do this for myself. It may be too late for us, but the happy memories of our journey together is what will get us through. We have both made mistakes in our relationship, and this is his way to let me know it's okay to let go.

I can't stop crying and V pulls me into her familiar arms, crying with me.

I sob and sob, my heart breaking with each word he sings, because this is our real goodbye. This is it for us.

His voice quivers when he sings his apology, but he composes himself quickly. A small smile tugs at his lips when he sings about how much I love to dance. No doubt, he's remembering all the times he caught me shuffling around clumsily.

The last verse of the song breaks my heart, because once it's over, then this is it.

This is really it.

But I don't want to say goodbye, I never will.

So I jump up, shouldering past people, and I thankfully reach the exit before I hyperventilate. Once outside, I take a deep breath but it doesn't help.

Nothing will.

So much has happened during the course of our relationship, when will it stop? Our desperate love for one another has unintentionally destroyed the purity of it, and now there's nothing left but pain.

And this is why I have to leave.

"Hey," a voice softly says behind me.

I close my eyes, but that doesn't stop the tears.

I can hear his heavy footsteps echo on the footpath behind me, but I don't have the nerve to turn around to face him. I know if I do, I won't leave him.

He's flush against my back, his fingertips brushing my hair to one side. I shiver as the cool wind passes over my bare shoulder, but that shiver turns to desire when I feel his warm breath on my neck.

"Just listen," he whispers.

I couldn't speak, even if I wanted to.

"You believed in me, in our love...but I am broken. I promise you, I will come back to you when I heal. Whether it's in this lifetime, or the next, I promise you, it'll never be the end for us. One day we won't feel this pain anymore, and when that day comes... it'll be our day. Go be happy. Go live your life, and go find someone who will give you everything I can't. You be free, baby, like you told me, you fly away and never land until you want to. And I swear to you, if you still want me when you've done everything you've wanted to do, you come and find me, because I promise...I'll be waiting. Like I said to you once before, if you love something, set it free. If it comes back, it's yours. If it doesn't, it was never meant to be... you go and be free, Ava."

I hold back my sob, biting down on my lip so brutally I know it's beginning to bleed.

"So, let's leave it to fate," he whispers. "Because fate brought you to me, and I believe it will do so again. I love you, Ava... I always will."

With one final kiss to my shoulder, Jasper leaves me.

He leaves me standing, silently sobbing for the man I want, but can't have.

And now, I'm lost.

Alone.

Scared.

I reopen my eyes, wiping away my tears, and a bitter-sweet smile sweeps across my lips.

I may be lost, alone and scared.

But...I will never surrender.

And with that, the final chapter closes on Jasper White and Ava Thompson.

CHAPTER THIRTY NINE
Surrendered

One Year Later

"C'mon, guys, let's get this food out A-sap." I clap, looking around the kitchen, which is filled with my brilliantly talented chefs.

"Yes, Chef!" they say in unison, totally making fun of me.

Giving them all a pointed look, I laugh lightly when they rush to their stations, prepping for the mad dinner rush.

It's 7:00p.m., and I know the night has only just begun.

I have been living in New York for one year, and what a year.

After getting over the hustle and bustle that is New York City, I actually fell in love.

New York is truly the city that never sleeps. And that's one thing that New York and I have in common. But that's okay, because when I sleep, I only dream of one thing—a pair of cerulean eyes. And that's something I've been trying to forget, but no matter how many miles are between us, I don't think I ever will.

My life without Jasper has sucked, but I've made it work.

The night Jasper and I said goodbye was the last time I ever saw him. Not that I actually saw him, as my eyes were shut tight, afraid to meet his because I couldn't deal with the pain.

Jasper White—even till this day, my heart belongs to him, and I have a small confession to make. I have been keeping track of him because P.O.E broke it big. Like *real* big.

Jasper's face has been on more than one cover of Rolling Stone, just like I knew it would. I never doubted he would succeed in something he was born to do. I have read each article more times than I care to admit, but I'm just so proud of him, and it comforts me to know that our journey together was all worth it.

For the both of us.

As I look around my baby, Metropolis, my heart swells in pride. I built this up from the ground, and all the blood, sweat, and tears were so worth it.

Every night has been insanely busy, with most Friday and Saturday nights booked out weeks in advance. And that's all because people want to try my food. My creations that may be a little different, but somehow, they work.

I have redecorated and given the place more of a romantic feel. Soft lighting adds to the atmosphere, as do the pillar candles, which burn brightly in the middle of the square tables. I know, I know. I'm a hopeless romantic, but hey, it works. And besides, I need a little romance, seeing as I've been off the romance chart since I moved here.

Not that I'm complaining.

I have accepted that I'll become the crazy old cat lady, screaming out gibberish to anyone who will listen—and I'm okay with that.

But in all seriousness, I just can't. The thought of being involved with anyone other than Jasper just isn't worth it. I know who I want, I found my Mr. Right.

He just wasn't my Mr. Right at the right time in my life.

Not that there is ever a right time for love.

I give myself a mental slap and snap out of my funk, as these thoughts are not welcome here in my workplace. I can think about them when I slip into bed, alone at night, because God knows, that's all I ever think about.

"Gee, the service here really blows," I hear to my left.

Now that snaps me out of my mood.

I spin around quickly and see a familiar face, smiling at me cheekily.

"V!" I exclaim, running around the counter to tackle my best friend into a bear hug.

She lets out a huffed laugh as I squeeze the air out of her. "Ava... can't... breathe," she says, slapping me on the back.

"Oh shit, sorry," I quickly let her go, apologizing for nearly crushing her lungs.

But I can't help it, I'm just so happy to see her, as I haven't seen her in months.

"Where is she?" I ask, looking around eagerly, hoping Lucas will be carrying in his little bundle of joy.

V brushes back her long pink bangs, which I think complement her black hair beautifully. But V will always be beautiful in my eyes.

"I left her in the car with the window down, she'll be fine," she says, waving me off playfully.

My eyes bug out of my head and she laughs hysterically. "Oh, Ava, what kind of parent do you think I am? I left her with that hot guy you have working up front," she says, waggling her eyebrows up and down, elbowing me.

"Oh my God, you're so bad," I laugh, knowing that Cara is with Lucas.

"What are you doing here?" I ask, untying my apron and escorting my best friend to a table.

She latches onto my arm before I have a chance to sit.

"It's a surprise," she says vaguely.

"Okay," I reply apprehensively, as I never know what I'm in for with V's surprises.

I look around, waiting for the surprise to magically appear, but then I bounce up and down, jumping to conclusions.

"You're pregnant!" I shout, and receive a few disapproving stares from a couple off to the right.

"Sssh, you'll jinx me," V says, looking totally disgusted I would even suggest such a thing.

"Watermelon and lemon, Ava, that's all I'm saying."

I laugh, as I've heard her analogy about birth a billion times.

"What is it then?" I ask curiously.

"Come with me," she says, tugging on my arm.

Giving my regulars a small smile, I try to play off the

fact I'm being dragged through my restaurant by a crazy, tattooed woman.

"Where are we going?" I whisper out of the side of my mouth, attempting not to draw any more attention to myself.

"What part of surprise don't you understand?" V states as she pushes through the double glass doors.

I try to shrug out of her firm grip, but she continues dragging me down the street like I'm a naughty child.

Thankfully, she doesn't manhandle me for too long and we hit a local bar, a few doors down.

"What are we doing here?" I ask, shooing her hands away as she pulls out my ponytail and begins fluffing up my hair.

"V, stop," I yelp, as she unbuttons two of the buttons on my fitted white shirt.

But of course, this falls on deaf ears.

"Take your top off," she says seriously.

I look at her like she's lost her mind. "What? No," I reply, crossing my arms over my chest protectively.

"Ava, don't make me undress you here on the side-walk, because you know I will," V sighs in boredom, and I know she'll make good on her threat.

She begins rummaging through her bag, and pulls out handfuls of baby paraphernalia, something I never thought I'd see my friend ever doing.

As I stare at her, my arms still crossed, she looks up, giving me a sharp look.

"Okay, okay, sheesh," I say, taking off my shirt, thankful I have a blue silk camisole on underneath.

V pulls a tight sapphire one shoulder top out of her

bag. "Put this on," she says, and I don't even argue with her as I slip it over my head.

She stands back and taps her chin, deep in thought.

"That'll have to do." She shrugs and starts yanking on my arm.

"V!" I say, but she's ignoring me, as she's all but dragging me into the venue, people watching our unusual exchange.

Mercifully, she lets go and sits me onto a seat, rotating me so I'm staring at the stage. She sits near me, looking around the packed venue, impressed.

There are red leather couches and tables casually placed around the venue, and it works really well. The bar is off to my right and I turn to see patrons waiting patiently to be served. The place has a calm, laid back feel, and I wonder why I haven't been here for a few drinks after work.

Oh that's right—my hermit status might be the cause.

There's an old, rickety stage in front of me, and I have no idea what she's up to.

"V?" I ask, as she applies lip gloss, ignoring me.

"V, what is—" Before I have a chance to finish, she grabs my cheeks in one hand, pursing my lips to stop me from talking.

She cocks her head to the side, examining my face, and decides I need a coat of lip-gloss as she applies a thick layer.

Pulling out of her grip, I shake my head. "What is the matter with you?" I ask, afraid for her sanity.

The lights dim and V cocks an eyebrow, gesturing with her head for me to look up at the stage.

A microphone stand and a lone stool are sitting center stage. A single spotlight is beaming down, highlighting its simplicity. My heart begins pounding against my chest because this is a scene I've seen before. It may be with a different instrument, but the effect is still the same.

This is a memory I revisit often.

But *she* wouldn't.

He wouldn't.

Would *he?*

Could it be?

All my questions are answered when out strolls a man who has taken my breath away from the first moment I saw him.

He doesn't look as I remember him.

He looks better.

He looks happy and he looks healed.

I can't take my eyes off him.

It has been one whole year since I've seen the man I dream about. The man I have dreamt about every single night since I left him. The man I will want for the rest of my life.

He coolly sits on the stool, adjusting his left-handed acoustic guitar, so it rests snugly across his lap. It takes all my willpower not to jump up and wrestle him to the floor. He is yards away from me, not miles, but mere yards. How am I going to control myself?

But I wait, because I know Jasper, and what he has to say, he'll do through song.

I sneak a quick peek at V, who has a big smile on her

face, and pokes her tongue out at me when I give her a 'you're so dead' look.

I will deal with her later, as the man in front of me has my full attention.

He is breathtaking.

His hair is still tousled, giving him that rebelliously carefree look, and his full lips are pulled in tight, deep in concentration.

But it's those eyes. Oh, those eyes.

Those cerulean jewels that render me speechless.

Jasper won't meet my eyes, but I know he's aware of my presence.

He always is.

His elegant fingers correct the positioning of the microphone, and he angles it perfectly, so it rests inches away for his cherub lips.

"This is called "Surrendered,"" he simply says, still not meeting my eyes as his windswept hair slips over his brow.

Oh God—I just died.

He takes a visible breath which expands his broad chest, and his grey t-shirt stretches over his taut torso, showing me a slice of heaven I want to snuggle into and never let go.

His fingers flutter over the strings, and he deeply exhales before he starts playing the most beautiful song I have ever heard. The intro is melodious and heartfelt, and I know he's written this song for me.

I am mesmerized by his graceful fingers working over the strings, and as he parts his beautiful lips and begins singing, my heart kicks against my ribcage, demanding to break free. I haven't heard him sing in so long, and up until now, I didn't realize how much I needed it to breathe.

My eyes take in the beautiful scene before me as Jasper sings the verse of how we met, and how I made him feel. All the ache, and all the turbulent highs and lows, he expresses so beautifully, and I almost forget how much they near broke me into two.

He makes this song his and totally owns it, showing off his incredible talent by hitting all the high notes flawlessly.

I can't tear my eyes away from the miracle in front of me, and as he opens his lungs to the heavens, starting on the chorus, he finally meets my eyes.

Our eyes stay locked when he sings, 'I have surrendered to you,' and I know he means that literally.

He's come back to me.

The audience hums along with him, some locking arms with strangers and swaying to his angelic voice.

The entire song my eyes stay glued to his, and his only waver when he lowers his head to look at the strings, which isn't often, as he is a musical genius.

As he sings about our journey together, and what it took to get to the here and now, there are no tears in my eyes because I'm not sad. No, I'm thankful. Thankful he still feels the same way about me as I do about him.

He ends the song with the heartfelt and emotional phrase, 'I have surrendered to you,' and the crowd erupts into a loud applause. But the deafening sound doesn't interrupt our stare off. And that's because in this moment, no one else exists.

It's only me and Jasper.

Just how it should be.

I can't stop my feet as I jump up and run towards him. He rises with a dimpled smile, knowing me all too well.

Charging up the stairs, I throw myself into his arms and feel my feet leave the ground as he wraps me into his tight embrace, not letting go.

I vaguely hear a wolf whistle, which I know belongs to V, but the building could be crumbling around me and I wouldn't care.

I am in the arms of Jasper White—my miracle.

Burying my nose into the crook of his neck, I inhale the only fragrance in the world that smells like home.

I'm not sure how long we stay intertwined, and only when my feet touch the ground do I come back down to earth. Well, only just.

I'm afraid to pull out of his embrace and I hold on tighter, just in case this is all a dream. But as I feel his familiar fingers rub circles on my lower back, I know this is real, and then...the tears start.

Once they begin, they don't stop, and I don't expect them to, as I'm crying a year's worth of tears.

Jasper takes my hand and leads me someplace, and only when light raindrops tickle my skin, do I realize we are outside.

I feel like an idiot. I know I need to stop crying, so I bite the inside of my cheek and tell myself to breathe.

It thankfully works, and after a few calming breaths, I stop sobbing.

I look at Jasper, and my God, he is beautiful.

My memory has done a poor job at remembering him.

I stare at him, just like I was when we first met, and it's funny, because that's how I feel. I feel like I'm meeting him for the first time.

And then I realize, this isn't Jasper White.

No, this is Jasper White Blackwood. A confident, brave survivor who has finally grown into the man he was determined to become. But I know Jasper, and he will always remain Jasper White. No matter how horrible his past, his name is a reminder of what he endured to survive.

"Ava..." he says in a soft whisper.

Oh dear Lord, his voice is music to my ears, and I wonder how I survived without it.

I close my eyes, afraid if I take in another inch of him, I'm going to collapse.

I feel his warm hands snake around my middle, and my breath catches in my throat.

"I love you."

It's amazing that three simple words can change a person's life.

I reopen my eyes, watching raindrops race down Jasper's chiseled jaw, slipping into his parted, lush lips. It's only then do I realize it is pouring. But I'm not moving an inch, as this moment is everything it should be.

"Ava, I—"

I peer at him curiously, what is he going to say?

The rain is matting my hair to my forehead, and it's

getting into my eyes, but I'm frozen. I need to hear what he came a billion miles to tell me.

"I surrender," he simply says, a dimple hugging his left cheek.

"Surrender?" I softly question.

Jasper nods, his hair sticking to his brow. "I have surrendered to you."

I don't fail to notice the significance in that one tiny phrase.

Jasper and I have surrendered to each other—completely.

No more fears, or apprehension, this is it this time. The time apart, no matter how hard and painful, and at times unbearable, was worth it. And that's because it has led us to this. We have both grown and accomplished our dreams. And now, our dreams can be shared together.

Jasper reaches into his back pocket, producing something that regardless of the rain, catches the shine off the full moon. The rain begins pounding heavier, and my teeth start chattering because I'm sopping wet. But this, *this* is how I envisioned being proposed to.

This... this is simply perfect.

Jasper drops to both knees, yielding before me, clasping my trembling left hand in his. He peers up at me, and the sight before me is ethereal.

"Marry me."

This time around, when he says it, there is no doubt in my mind what my answer will be. I don't care where we go. New York, L.A., Australia—it doesn't matter as long as I'm with him, everything else will fall into place around us.

"Yes," I whisper.

Jasper closes his eyes, a dimpled smile spreading from cheek to cheek.

As he reopens them, his eyes shine, rivaling the bright moonlight. But his shine won't fade by dawn. No, his will last for an eternity.

He slips the ring onto my finger, and I notice he's wearing the ring I gave him on his left hand. In his eyes, we are already one.

He places his left hand under mine, angling it perfectly, so our fingers are entwined. Looking at the rings on our fingers, he smiles, his tears mixed in with the pouring rain.

"Forever," he whispers.

"Forever," I confirm, choking back a sob.

He pulls me towards him, resting his head against my belly, still on his knees.

"I thought you wanted to leave it to fate," I whisper, remembering his words.

Jasper takes a moment, finally replying as he raises those hypnotic eyes to meet mine. "Fuck fate. You're my destiny," he says with sincerity. "You always have been, and always will be. You're my forever and a day."

I nod because he's right.

Life.

We are all just bystanders in its path.

What we make of it, well...that's entirely up to us.

And me...I choose Jasper White.

Forever and a day.

ABOUT THE AUTHOR

Monica James spent her youth devouring the works of Anne Rice, William Shakespeare, and Emily Dickinson. When she is not writing, Monica runs her own business, but she always finds a balance between the two. She enjoys writing twisted AF stories, hoping to terrify her readers...just a little.

She is a bestselling author in the U.S.A., Australia, Canada, France, Germany, Israel, and the U.K. Monica James resides in Melbourne, Australia, with her Unicorn, and her three crazy cats. She is slightly obsessed with red lipstick, heels, and crime documentaries, and is that person who always runs late.

CONNECT WITH MONICA JAMES

Facebook: facebook.com/authormonicajames
Goodreads: goodreads.com/MonicaJames
Instagram: @authormonicajames
TikTok: @authormonicajames
BookBub: http://bit.ly/2E3eCIw
Amazon: https://amzn.to/2EWZSyS
Reader Group: http://bit.ly/2nUaRyi
Newsletter: https://tinyurl.com/mvjjk6k2
Patreon: https://www.patreon.com/c/
AuthorMonicaJames
Shopify: https://authormonicajames.store/